THE SUN-NYMPH BRIDE

CALATINI TALES BOOK 5

KATHERINE DOTTERER

KatSpell Press

The Sun-Nymph Bride

Cover by 100 Covers

Edited by Susan Bischoff, Lauralynn Elliott

A KatSpell Press Book

- ISBN 978-1-955614-17-7 (ebook)
- ISBN 978-1-955614-18-4 (trade paperback)

 Formatted with Vellum

CONTENTS

ABOUT THE SUN-NYMPH BRIDE

*I*n the Regency-inspired kingdom of Calatini, magic can complicate anything... even true love.

When Pippa Hawke sees Edouard, Lord Blaine, at a family wedding, it's love at first sight. Sunny, cheerful Pippa charms Edouard unlike any lady has before, and she's just as enthralled. But Pippa has yet to be introduced to society, with her reclusive father intending to keep it that way. And Edouard is too conscientious to court a lady as young as Pippa before her debut, no matter how much he loves her.

Yet Pippa knows that Edouard is the gentleman she'll marry, regardless of the many others attempting to court her. She sends heartfelt letters and arranges intimate outings that deepen their love, until serious, careful Edouard is taking delicious risks that cause her father to denounce him as a rakehell and forbid their betrothal.

But Pippa's father isn't the only threat to their courtship. In Calatini, magic is real... and sometimes, it's a curse that destroys even the strongest love.

. . .

THE SUN-NYMPH BRIDE IS A COZY, fairytale-inspired low spice historical fantasy romance, perfect for romance lovers looking for a little extra magic. Fans of Robin McKinley's fairy tale retellings will fall in love with the Calatini Tales.

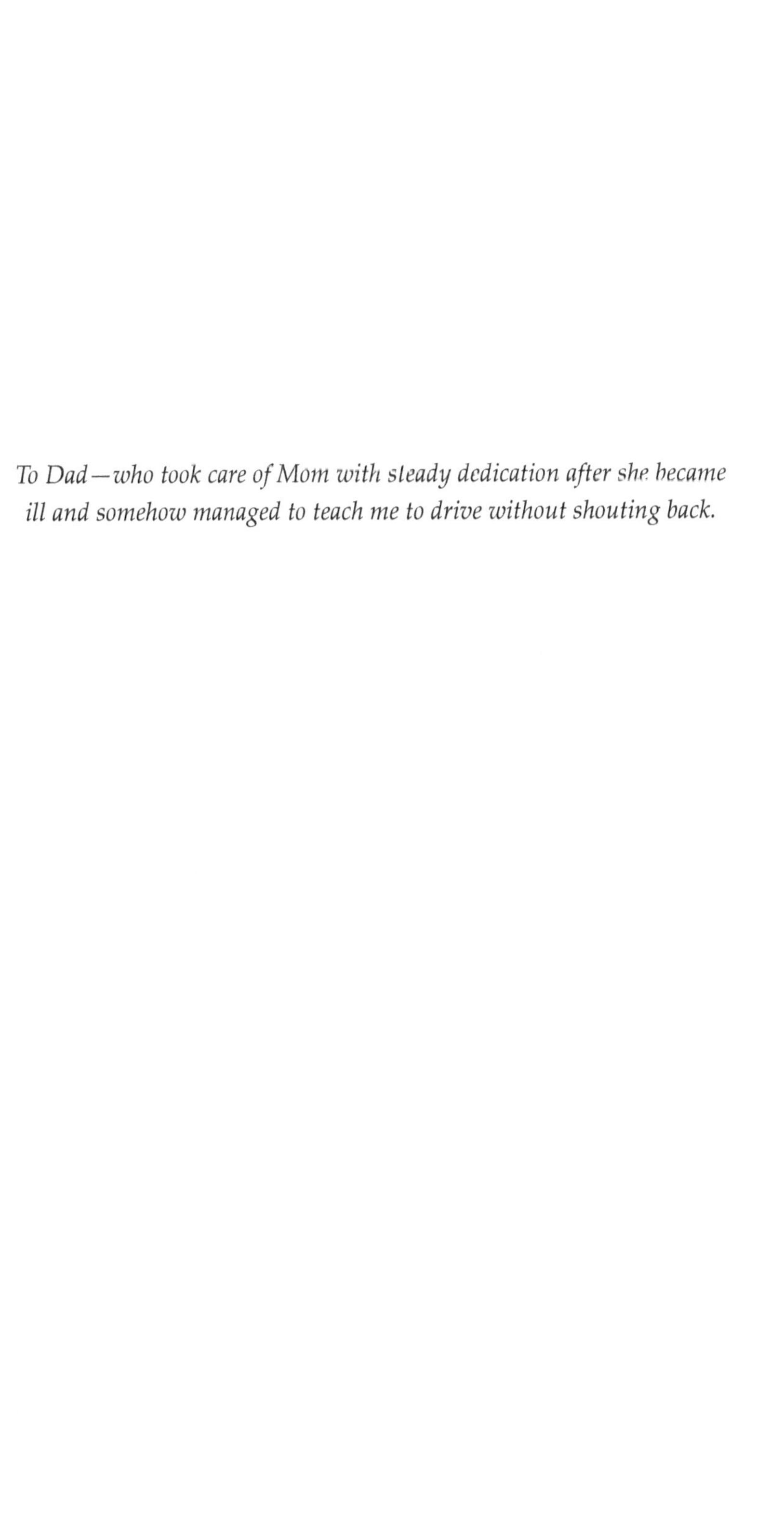

To Dad—who took care of Mom with steady dedication after she became ill and somehow managed to teach me to drive without shouting back.

CHAPTER 1

While Edouard processed down the aisle as his cousin Aragon's third groom witness, a beaming young lady near the front on the groom's side caught his eye, and he nearly stilled. The morning sun streaming through the many stained-glass windows of the Great Temple illuminated the young lady, making her creamy skin glow, kindling the warm shimmer in her upswept chestnut hair, and brightening her peach gown. He couldn't help smiling at the young lady's sweet and radiant joy—the opposite of his sober nature.

Their gazes met when he passed, and her warm-brown eyes widened before she beamed straight at him. He inhaled, his heart fluttering for the first time in his life. He *must* meet her at the reception after Aragon and Selena's wedding ceremony hosted by Aragon's wealthy and influential parents, the Duke and Duchess of Childes.

As Aragon's priest brother Mel performed the ceremony, Edouard kept darting glances at the bubbly young lady. On her right was a rumpled older gentleman with similar chestnut hair, and on her left were Dane and Xavier Hawke, distant paternal cousins of Aragon and his brothers, who were a year or two younger than Edouard. Dane and Xavier had mentioned a little sister, doubtless the young lady, although he'd never met Miss Philippa Hawke since she wasn't out yet. The older gentleman must be their father Sir Julian, an eccentric recluse who never attended court events.

Soon, Aragon and Selena's grand yet brief ceremony ended, and Edouard followed them from the nave with the other witnesses and Mel. He resisted the urge to fidget as he waited to sign the matrimony certificate, which seemed to take forever. After Aragon and Selena signed, King Devon, Aragon's third cousin and best friend, signed before passing the pen to Madeleine, the new Lady Frederic Cassell. Aragon's youngest brother, who went by the Childes's family surname Hawke since he despised his given name, signed next, followed by Lady Cecilia Cassell. Then Edouard swiftly signed and thrust the pen at Miss Blakeley, who signed as well before handing everything to Mel. While Mel signed as the officiating priest, Edouard exhaled to settle his unusual impatience. Surely Miss Hawke wouldn't vanish before he arrived at the reception.

Intent on meeting her, Edouard said little on the carriage ride to Childes House after congratulating Aragon and Selena, and as soon as he arrived, he drifted toward Miss Hawke without finding his twin Elise like he normally would. He should wait to feign disinterest and prevent gossip, but somehow he couldn't be his typical prudent self today. He *had* to talk to Miss Hawke at once.

Flanked by her brothers and sipping sparkling wine, Miss Hawke quieted when he halted beside them, her eyes widening. Their father was nowhere to be seen. For a moment, he and Miss Hawke simply stared at each other. She appeared just as enthralled by him as he was by her.

When her brothers began to frown, Edouard shook himself and forced a polite smile. "Dane, Xavier, could you perform the official introductions?"

Dane nodded and waved toward him. "This is Lord Edouard

Gernand, son of the Count of Blaine." Dane waved toward Miss Hawke. "Our sister, Miss Philippa Hawke."

Still staring up at him, Miss Hawke beamed. "But everyone calls me Pippa."

Xavier sighed. "You aren't supposed to tell gentlemen that, you know."

Leaning toward Pippa, Edouard swallowed and gripped his sparkling wine to avoid capturing her hand and pressing a kiss against her palm. Such an impulse wasn't at all appropriate. "A pleasure, Miss Hawke. Did you enjoy the wedding ceremony?"

Pippa exhaled, her lips curving in a dreamy smile. "'Twas so romantic. Aragon and Selena clearly adore each other. I'm glad Father decided we couldn't miss attending the future duke's wedding ceremony even though he hates visiting Ormas."

Edouard eyed Pippa's lips. What would kissing them be like? He sipped his sparkling wine to distract himself. He shouldn't be thinking about kissing a girl who wasn't even out yet. "Does Sir Julian prefer life in the country?"

As her brothers snorted, Pippa grinned and replied, "Not exactly. He hates leaving behind his magical experiments."

Edouard's brows rose. He'd not realized his cousins' cousins were witches. People who could sense and wield magic, witches made up less than a quarter of all humans, although more were witches in Magehaven and Wildewall, the two duchies closest to the Walle that separated Calatini and other human kingdoms from the kingdoms of magical creatures. He himself didn't possess the slightest magical powers, even though he used small spells and charms purchased from those who did. "How interesting. What's it like being witches?"

Pippa giggled into her sparkling wine. "Oh, we're not witches. Even Father is barely one."

Her brothers traded a wry glance, then Xavier drawled, "Father still can't understand how he married into one of the few magicless families in Magehaven."

Dane added, "Yes, he'd hoped at least one of his children

would make an adequate assistant for his magical experiments. But none of us inherited any magical powers."

Edouard blinked. Dane and Xavier made it sound as if Sir Julian cared more for his magical experiments than his children. Perhaps 'twas why the baronet wasn't here watching over his unfledged daughter like he should.

Pippa frowned at her brothers. "Father eloped with Mother when they were seventeen because they were madly in love, not because she was from Magehaven." She turned to Edouard with a glowing smile. "Tell me what enjoying the season in Ormas is like. I can't wait until my first season next spring once I turn eighteen, although Father is already grumbling and attempting to persuade me to wait another two years until I'm twenty since I'll no longer be underage."

Dazzled by Pippa's smile, Edouard swallowed. So she was five and a half years younger than him—much too young. "Busy with balls and other court events. Although I much prefer family events like this one, visiting art galleries, or quiet evenings at home."

Pippa hummed. "That all sounds lovely. I've never attended a ball, but they sound so romantic. Do you enjoy dancing?"

Edouard studied the bubbles in his sparkling wine. With Pippa's cheerful vivacity, he'd definitely enjoy dancing with her. Not that he should, given how young she was. "Yes. 'Tis excellent exercise and allows stimulating conversation."

Pippa beamed and leaned toward him. "I agree, although I've only ever danced with my brothers and my dancing instructor. I hope *we* can enjoy a dance together at my presentation ball next spring."

Edouard inhaled, burning to request her first dance. But to ask almost a year in advance was mad, and he couldn't restrict her choice so. She was too young to court anyone, and she might prefer another gentleman by then.

Both Dane and Xavier frowning, Dane muttered, "Pippa,

you're not supposed to talk to gentlemen like that, even if they are almost family."

A blush darkening her cheeks, Pippa lowered her gaze. Then she glanced at Edouard through her lashes. "I never have before, but... 'tis different with you somehow."

Edouard couldn't help smiling at Pippa. She was adorably candid and sweet. Perhaps if she was still interested after her come out next year, he could risk courting her, although he must take care not to rush her. "Yes, it *is* different with you."

Inhaling, Pippa fully met his gaze and flashed a radiant grin even brighter than the one she'd worn during the wedding ceremony. 'Twas like a clear sunrise after a fortnight of rain.

Breathless, Edouard stared at Pippa again. Goddess, resisting their attraction would be arduous. But he must for her sake.

Pippa leaned toward him. "Do you reside in Ormas all year?"

Her brothers' narrow-eyed scrutiny heavy on him, Edouard managed to smile and shake his head as he replied, "Just the season. I spend the rest of the year in Landcastle tending the Blaine estate. Father had me assume his duties as count two years ago when I attained my majority."

Pippa twirled her flute of sparkling wine before her lips. "How unusual."

Edouard shrugged. "Not entirely. The Duke of Childes did the same when Aragon turned twenty-five last year." Perhaps inspired by Father's example. "'Tis prudent for heirs to learn their duties while their parents are still around to provide advice."

Her eyes flickering, Pippa sighed. "True." She tilted her head. "Do you prefer residing on your estate or in Ormas?"

Studying the rich gleam of Pippa's hair, Edouard finished his sparkling wine to give himself time to consider her question. "I enjoy both. At the Blaine estate, I'm kept occupied with my duties, yet the pace of life is slower, and I can spend more time at home. In Ormas, my twin Elise and I can see each other often. She always attends the season since her husband Lord Farson is one of the king's councilors, but they return to Golddell afterward."

Pippa sighed again and touched his arm. "You must miss your twin terribly being apart so much."

Warmed by Pippa's sympathy yet stiffening at her brothers' frowns, Edouard briefly squeezed her hand on his arm. "Yes, but we've our communication mirrors when we're apart, so 'tisn't too bad."

Father strode over with Kit, Father's sultry second wife who'd beguiled Father into marriage five years ago despite being months younger than him and Elise. Their gazes on Pippa's hand on his arm, Kit smirked while Father smiled and said, "Although Edouard and Elise use their communication mirrors so frequently that the spells enchanting them must be renewed twice a year rather than once like usual."

His neck hot, Edouard shifted back until he and Pippa no longer touched. His familiarity with a young lady he'd just met who wasn't even out yet would concern his always careful father.

After Dane and Xavier performed the introductions, Father grinned at Pippa and asked, "How do you like your first visit to Ormas?" When she blinked at him, he chuckled and added, "Caro—the Duchess of Childes—mentioned it when we saw you and my son talking together."

Edouard sighed. Of course Father's cousin had. Not only did the duchess know everything about everyone, Hawke often accused his mother of meddling, although Aragon and Mel were more tactful and simply said she liked managing others.

Pippa returned Father's grin. "I've liked visiting Ormas so far, although we only arrived the day before yesterday, and we're leaving in two days."

Her gorgeous face nonplussed, Kit stared at Pippa. "You're not staying to enjoy the season?"

Edouard nearly snorted. Not surprising that his fashionable and frivolous stepmother was astonished. She was forever attending social events to enhance her influence at court, so she couldn't fathom not attending the season.

Pippa shrugged and shook her head. "Father insists I must wait until next year."

Still smiling, Father nodded. "Most sensible, although 'tis unfortunate you're not staying longer. We could have had you and your family join us for dinner."

Edouard almost gaped at Father. He must like Pippa a great deal to offer that. Father disliked entertaining and insisted Kit hold the court events she hosted away from Blaine House. The few people Father invited were either close family or art enthusiasts who wanted to view his renowned art collection, and he'd not asked Pippa about art.

Pippa blew a sigh. "We'd enjoy joining you for dinner." Then she smiled. "But perhaps another time."

Smiling back, Father allowed Kit to draw him away to speak with King Devon, who was laughing with the newlyweds nearby.

Alone with Pippa and her brothers again, Edouard swallowed and shifted his weight. He should circulate too, but somehow he couldn't. He arched his brows at Pippa. "So what of Ormas's diversions shall you enjoy during your too brief visit?"

Pippa bounced like a cheery sun nymph at dawn. "Dane and Xavier showed me all of Ormas yesterday, including the palace —so many exquisite buildings. And tomorrow we're going riding then attending a sirenic play, which I've heard are spectacular."

Disregarding her brothers' near frowns, Edouard leaned toward Pippa. If only he could join them tomorrow, but 'twould be too much like courting. "Quite a whirlwind. Which diversion shall you enjoy most?"

Pippa hummed as she finished her sparkling wine. "I'm not certain. Riding is always delightful, and I've never seen a sirenic play before. But I *adore* seeing different types of architecture. The aesthetics are often lovely and reveal a lot about the time the buildings were created. 'Tis fascinating."

He grinned, his chest warming. "I feel the same about art. But architecture is really just the art of buildings." When Pippa beamed back, he blurted, "Father has a fine art collection of masters from the previous century. Perhaps you'd care to see it when you visit us for dinner next season."

Beaming brighter, Pippa bounced again and began to reply until Elise drawled from behind him, "You're inviting *another* lady to see the art collection? How interesting."

Edouard tensed and nearly flushed. When he'd discovered Selena was a fellow art enthusiast last year, he'd invited her to see Father's collection hoping to court her, although he'd withdrawn as soon as he'd realized Aragon loved her. But his mild interest in Selena had been nothing compared to his overwhelming attraction to Pippa, as his impetuous and premature invitation had proved. And his twin who knew him better than anyone could surely tell that. Please let Elise not reveal her insight to Pippa—'twas much too soon.

CHAPTER 2

$\mathcal{P}$ippa stiffened at the warm feminine voice teasing Edouard. The lady was definitely intimate with him. Was she the *other* lady he'd invited to see his father's art collection? Her chest tight, Pippa turned to face the lady behind Edouard and relaxed. From the lady's pale coloring that matched his, she could only be his twin. Thank the Goddess.

On the arm of a bearded gentleman who was doubtless her husband, Lady Farson grinned at Pippa and said, "Since you're new to Ormas, I must tell you that invitations to visit Father's art collection are rare and coveted by every art enthusiast at court. And Edouard respects Father's preference for privacy too much to often invite anyone himself."

Pippa gripped her flute, now regrettably empty of sparkling wine to soothe her constricted throat. The other lady Edouard had invited must have been special to him. Was he in love with her? Since he appeared around Dane's age, he must have been in society several years, so a previous attachment was entirely possible. Although she shouldn't, she couldn't help asking, "But what about the other lady you mentioned?"

As both Dane and Xavier frowned at her, Edouard coughed and nodded at the newlyweds, his blond hair glimmering like fresh sand in the sun. "When I discovered Selena loved art, I asked Father to invite her, and he was happy to invite the art enthusiast his cousin's son was courting."

Exhaling, Pippa smiled at Edouard. So the other lady had been a mere family connection. Good. His obvious attraction to her was genuine then, just as hers for him was. If only she was already out and free to remain in Ormas, so he could court her. She leaned toward Edouard. "I'd love to see your father's art collection sometime. Tenth-century art is so vibrant and vivacious yet still natural and bucolic."

Edouard grinned at her. "That perfect balance of reality and exuberance is why Father and I adore tenth-century art. It reminds people of the joy and wonder found in the world around us."

She nodded, her heart fluttering. Precisely. And no doubt their opinion on tenth-century art wasn't the only one they shared. Too bad she couldn't invite Edouard to join her and her brothers on their ride and to the sirenic play tomorrow to discover what else they had in common. But 'twould be much too brazen, especially since they'd just met.

Instead, she made herself turn to Lady Farson and her husband. "Your brother mentioned you live in Golddell. Have you ever met any nightmara?" The Nightmara Plains, where the magical, horse-like nightmara lived with the human mara clans, dominated the duchy of Golddell.

Lady Farson chuckled. "Of course. As the councilor representing Golddell, Seanian must visit with various nightmara herds whenever we're home. And I always accompany him, along with our ward Arvan, the Duke of Golddell."

While Pippa smiled at those surely extraordinary visits, Dane and Xavier swiftly traded a wide glance, then Dane asked, "Have you ever ridden a nightmara? I've heard riding them is exhilarating."

Lord Farson grinned at her brothers. "No, nightmara rarely carry anyone other than a mara. Besides, I'm usually speaking with the dominant mares who lead the herds, and they often don't allow *anyone* to ride them."

Pippa hummed. Not surprising. A dominant mare carrying anyone would be like a duke cooking and serving dinner.

Lady Farson chuckled again. "Although we've never ridden any, visiting the nightmara is still fascinating. Arvan especially adores visiting them, much more than he enjoys attending wedding receptions. He's a fourteen-year-old boy, after all." She smiled at Dane and Xavier. "You two are the gentlemen closest to his age. Could you join him for a while? He's lurking near the refreshments table."

Dane and Xavier nodded, then Xavier chuckled and replied, "We could do with more refreshments, anyway."

When her brothers beckoned her, Pippa smiled and shook her head. She couldn't separate from Edouard so soon. "You should go without me. The young duke shan't appreciate a girl intruding."

Dane and Xavier almost frowned at Edouard before returning their gazes to her. But they could doubtless tell from her brilliant smile that she'd no intention of leaving Edouard because they sighed and strode across the drawing room without another word.

Her eyes gleaming, Lady Farson smiled. "Thanks for considering Arvan's feelings, Miss Hawke."

Not daring to glance at Edouard, Pippa nodded as a blush warmed her cheeks. "'Twas nothing. And call me Pippa, please. We're practically family." And hopefully more than practically one day.

Lady Farson grinned while her husband's lips twitched. "As long as you call me Elise." Once Pippa repeated her nod, Elise tugged on Lord Farson's arm. "We should go talk with Mel before he returns to the Great Temple."

Pippa blushed harder when Elise winked before leaving her alone with Edouard. His twin evidently approved of their mutual attraction. She let herself face Edouard again, and her pulse surged. She'd never been alone with an eligible gentleman before; not that she'd ever wanted to. But with Edouard, she wanted that and more. 'Twas almost painful not to reach out and touch him.

She licked her lips, warming as Edouard's gaze fixed there. What was it about him that drew her like a sailor to a singing siren? Although he was handsome with pale coloring unlike the gentlemen in her family, that hadn't been what had drawn her interest in the Great Temple. No, it had been his palpable air of calm certainty and thoughtful steadiness.

She exhaled. And speaking with Edouard had only deepened her fascination. He was clearly a gentleman a lady could always rely upon, and he'd never forget those he loved. Plus, whenever a smile lit his serious face, her heart quickened, and she burned to keep him bright with joy. He needed that. She licked her lips again.

His pale-blue eyes darkening, Edouard swallowed and rasped, "Shall we circulate rather than staring at each other?"

Tingling flooded Pippa at the hunger resonating in Edouard's deep voice. "I enjoy staring at you."

Edouard shuddered. "Me too, but 'tisn't appropriate. You're not even out yet."

She lifted her chin. She was more mature than her age would suggest. Unlike most young ladies, she'd been managing a household for years because Mother had died giving birth to her. Father was too engrossed with his magical experiments, and her brothers managed the estate instead. She leaned toward Edouard. "I'm not a child."

Edouard stepped back. "But you are young—five and a half years too young."

Before she could retort that most ladies were years younger than their husbands, Father shuffled over and mumbled, "There you are, Pippa. Xavier fetched me from the duke's excellent library to stand with you. Not sure why when 'tis a family event."

Pippa blinked. How had Xavier managed to pry Father from his studies? Doing that was always difficult, so her brothers normally didn't bother. Then she blushed. Xavier had no doubt bothered because he and Dane were concerned by the obvious attraction between her and Edouard.

Edouard nodded at Father. "Perhaps your younger son fetched you because not everyone is your family. I'm a maternal cousin to the groom."

Father tilted his head. "You do have the look of the duchess about you." He frowned. "If you're not related, why are you alone with my daughter?"

Still blushing, she interjected before Edouard could reply, "We're in the middle of the drawing room, hardly alone."

Father humphed. "Still engaged in a private conversation with an unrelated gentleman. You're much too young for that." He grasped her arm. "Let's head to the library."

Pippa stiffened, her chest squeezing at leaving Edouard. "But—"

Father continued, "I want to finish my book. The duke's library is the only good thing about visiting Ormas."

Edouard nodded with a polite smile, nothing like the heart-warming ones he'd given her earlier. "I must circulate before I leave. 'Twas a pleasure to meet you, Miss Hawke. Until next spring."

She stared after Edouard as he joined Aragon and Selena. He was definitely determined to wait because he thought her too young. But at least he was planning to approach her next year. She allowed Father to pull her to the library then selected a novel to amuse herself rather than brood about Edouard.

She was several chapters in when Dane and Xavier strode into the library. Dane said, "The other guests have left. Shall we take a turn about the garden?"

Sighing, Pippa marked her place and stood. Her brothers must want to talk about Edouard without Father overhearing. Not that he would, since he was absorbed in the magical tome he was reading. Yet walking outside would be enjoyable, even with the upcoming lecture from Dane and Xavier.

In the sunny garden, her brothers flanked her as they began strolling beside the trellises of climbing roses. Ignoring them, she smiled at Childes House's ornate turrets, chimneys, and battlements of white brick as well as its numerous windows. The ducal townhouse was a beautiful eighth-century mansion, one of the finest in Ormas, and she was fortunate enough to be staying in it during their visit. She'd spent happy hours studying the townhouse from various perspectives since she'd arrived.

After a moment, Dane coughed then asked, "*What* were you doing with Edouard, Pippa?"

Xavier smoothed his mustache. "You kept staring at him and acted almost brazen. Not your usual behavior."

She dragged her gaze from Childes House and bent to sniff a rose to disguise her blush. "I know, but I couldn't help myself."

Dane exhaled. "You can't treat gentlemen like that. You'll gain a reputation as a flirt who's no better than she should be."

Pippa glared at her oldest brother. Must he be so insulting? "I don't intend to treat *gentlemen* like that. Edouard is different."

Xavier gripped her elbow, halting her. "*Edouard*? You can't call a gentleman you just met by his first name."

Blushing again, she pulled her elbow free. True, but somehow she couldn't think of Edouard by his title. "I don't feel as if we just met." When her brothers frowned, she added, "And he felt the same too. I doubt he's ever treated a lady like he did me."

Dane and Xavier exchanged a narrow glance, then Dane rumbled, "No, Edouard is much too serious and deliberate to flirt."

Xavier snorted. "He's certainly not the gentleman we worried about flirting with you—Hawke was. We're merely distant cousins, and he's a rakehell."

Pippa blinked and tilted her head. "Really? But Hawke is

plainly in love with Wren." And Hawke's shy best friend appeared equally in love with him, so why was he a rakehell?

Dane grimaced then shrugged. "Yes, but Hawke hasn't realized that yet. I'm simply relieved he considers you family and hasn't flirted."

She swallowed. "Me too." The only gentleman she wanted flirting with her was Edouard. She turned and faced her brothers with a brilliant smile. "As for Edouard, don't fret about him. He's determined to wait until my come out to approach me again, and he's not the type to take advantage when courting a lady."

Xavier's mouth quirked. "We were more concerned about you taking advantage of *him*."

Pippa raised her eyes skyward. "As if I could. Or would." She arched her brows at her brothers. "And I swear not to call E— *Lord* Edouard Gernand by his first name aloud again—at least until we've been courting for three months."

Dane and Xavier sighed but nodded. Then Dane said, "I suppose 'tis enough. Shall we finish touring the garden?"

She and her brothers spent another hour in the fragrant garden before returning inside for dinner. The following day, none of them mentioned Edouard as they enjoyed their ride and the sirenic play, but her mind kept returning to him. How often would he have smiled if he'd joined them?

When she and Father began the journey back to Hawke Manor the following morning, she sighed as they traveled past Blaine House, mentally bidding Edouard farewell. And once home, she continued thinking about him, especially when she received letters from the Duchess of Childes, which now contained news about him in addition to the rest of the family.

Two months after leaving Ormas, Pippa gasped at the duchess's latest letter, her chest aching. Edouard's father had unexpectedly died. He, Elise, and Lady Blaine must be devastated. Particularly Edouard since he and his father had clearly been close and very much alike.

She leapt upright then grasped a pen and some paper.

Although 'twasn't appropriate for a young lady to write an unrelated gentleman, she must write Edouard to express her condolences and cheer him however she could. As soon as she'd finished, she sent her heartfelt letter to Ormas. Please let it help. Perhaps it might even make him smile briefly even though she'd not be there to see it.

CHAPTER 3

The morning after Father's tasteful funeral in the Moon Chapel at the Great Temple, Edouard scowled into his kahve as he endured an uncomfortable and silent breakfast with Kit. Not because he disliked mornings and talking to anyone before his first bracing cup of kahve, which he did, but because he and Kit eating breakfast without Father was so damned wrong. Yet he forced himself to devour his usual hearty breakfast of eggs, beefsteak, and tubers even though his tight throat almost choked him.

As soon as he finished, he leapt upright with a polite nod at Kit, who appeared surprisingly subdued in her somber black dress. He'd not expected his fashionable stepmother to grieve for Father at all, but instead to grumble about all the court events she'd miss during their year of mourning. He grimaced as he strode from the breakfast room. Although Goddess knew how long Kit's genuine grief would last.

He retreated to Father's—no, his—study then flung himself into the chair behind the desk. His eyes burning, he glowered at the gray urn painted with asymmetrical scrolling curves favored in tenth-century art that contained Father's ashes. How could Father be dead? He'd only been sixty and seemed as hale and hearty as ever this season. They'd even made plans to ride to Blacke Woods just over a week ago. Yet the morning of their ride, Father's valet had roused Edouard with the news that Father had died in his sleep. The healer said it had been a seizure and very quick. At least Father hadn't suffered and was with Mother again.

Edouard let his gaze fall to the pair of gold, tenth-century garden rings on a gold chain sitting in a clear bowl on the desk—his parents' wedding tokens and Father's necklace for them. Father was doubtless happy to be at peace with Mother. He'd adored his sweet Genevieve and had missed her since a wasting disease had taken her eight years ago. Even after marrying Kit, Father had continued to wear his and Mother's wedding tokens beneath his clothes. And he'd visited the art room every day to listen to the dancing music-box sculpture's melody that they'd danced to until she became ill.

Swallowing, Edouard exhaled a lengthy breath. Although finally with Mother again, Father would miss a lot by dying so suddenly. Father would never see him marry or meet any grand-children. So much for Father's promise to Mother on her deathbed that he'd tell her all about their children's happy lives and offspring after he also returned to the Goddess. But at least Father could tell Mother about them growing up and Elise's marriage.

Edouard rubbed his aching chest. He and Elise were the last of their immediate family now, although she'd Farson and Arvan still. They'd their cousins, but 'twasn't the same. And he was stuck with Kit until she married again, which was sure to be an ordeal. He sighed. He'd not feel so hollow and alone if he'd a loving wife at his side. Pippa's radiant grin flickered before him, and the ache in his chest swelled.

He buried that and straightened when his butler Rooke entered with a thick stack of correspondence. Doubtless more letters of condolence. They'd been pouring in since the morning after Father died. He rifled through the stack, pausing at a middle one from Hawke Manor written in a rounded hand, surely from Pippa. His heart quickening, he tore open her letter.

Dear Edouard Gernand, Lord Blaine—

My deepest condolences on the loss of your beloved father. Although we only met briefly, he seemed a wonderful gentleman—warm, steady, and kind. I liked him a great deal, and I'm sad I'll never get to accept his invitation to dinner and get to know him better.

My thoughts and prayers are with you and Elise during this difficult time. Your father clearly loved you both very much, so he'd want you to remember all the joyful times you shared rather than dwell on your grief. Please know I'm here for you, and write to me how you fare. I just wish I was in Ormas to console you in person.

Yours,

Pippa Hawke

Tears burning his eyes again, Edouard smiled at Pippa's sweetly candid letter. Father had liked her a great deal too. He'd made that clear when they'd relaxed at Blaine House the evening of Aragon and Selena's wedding.

After Kit had left to attend the Landrys' ball, Father had smiled at him over his spiritwine. "That bubbly lady you spent most of the reception with seems lovely. Her sensible sweetness reminds me of your mother. An excellent choice for a wife."

Edouard had shifted in his chair. "She's just seventeen—five and a half years younger than me. Much too young to court."

Father had chuckled. "Seventeen is old enough for a sensible lady like Miss Hawke. And five and a half years isn't too large of an age difference. Your mother was fifteen years younger than me, and we were fiercely in love throughout our marriage, and I miss my sweet Genevieve still."

Having forgotten his parents' age difference, Edouard had blinked but nodded.

Father had leaned forward. "Miss Hawke shall be in Ormas tomorrow. You should join her on the ride that Caro said she and her brothers have planned."

Edouard had sighed as he sipped his spiritwine. "I can't. She's not met other gentlemen yet, and I don't wish to rush her choice. If she's still interested, I'll court her after her come out next spring." He'd coughed. "Although I already invited her to view your art collection next season. I hope you don't mind."

Father had grinned. "I don't mind, and I'm certain Miss Hawke shall still be interested. We can invite her and her family to dinner during the week of her presentation ball. I'll ensure you've time alone to show her the collection."

Forcing himself back to the present, Edouard caressed Pippa's signature. She'd asked him to write, and although 'twasn't truly appropriate for gentlemen to write ladies not their family, betrothed, or wife, he couldn't resist her offer. He grabbed a pen and some paper.

Dear Pippa Hawke—

Thank you so much for your letter and asking me to write despite our brief acquaintance. Your kind offer means a lot since I've only Elise left to confide in, and she's grieving too. And thanks for reminding me to remember the many joyful times with Father. With my grief so raw, 'tis easier to remember everything I've lost.

I enjoyed meeting you two months ago, and I'm eager to see you again after my year of mourning ends. We'll arrange your visit to see the art collection then. Did you enjoy the rest of your visit to Ormas, and are you settled back in at Hawke Manor? Please share everything, as hearing about your days would brighten mine.

Yours,

Edouard Gernand, Lord Blaine

Before he could reconsider writing Pippa, he sealed his letter and gave it to Rooke to post. Thanks to the magical transport system for letters and small parcels run by the Ministry of Health and Community, Pippa should have it within a few days.

ALTHOUGH IN MOURNING and not attending court events, Edouard stayed in Ormas throughout the season since Elise needed to remain because of her husband's duties as one of the king's councilors. After just losing Father, he and his twin couldn't separate, and they met often, usually with Farson, Arvan, and Kit, but also just the two of them at least once a week.

He and Pippa also continued exchanging letters even though they probably shouldn't, and her letters were soon the brightest part of his days. They never failed to make him smile, and his attraction grew into something deeper as they shared their lives in their letters. He grew increasingly eager to see her again and court her properly.

The day before Harvestfete, he and Elise celebrated their natalday together with a ride to the royal bay and a picnic there with Farson and Arvan. When he returned, he grinned at Pippa's letter waiting for him. In it, she wished him happy natalday and teased him for turning the ancient age of twenty-three. She also enclosed a pocketcloth she'd embroidered with his initials in an ornate tenth-century style, and he immediately tucked his new favorite pocketcloth into the pocket above his heart.

Two days later, Edouard said farewell to Elise then left for Blaine Castle. Although he'd be spreading their parents' ashes once he returned, he still traveled alone this year. Kit had decided to remain in Ormas because she preferred it to the country, while Elise had to return to Golddell with Farson and Arvan. With the nightmara delegation's visit to renew the essential Nightmara-Calatini Treaty set for the following summer, they needed to meet the nightmara queen-heir Lady Moonbud who'd be negotiating for the nightmara. Who'd be negotiating for Calatini was still unknown because King Devon had yet to find a queen.

The morning after returning home, Edouard fetched Father's urn before collecting Mother's ivory urn painted with peonies from the family crypt. Then like Father had requested long ago, he rode to Father and Mother's favorite spot, a massive oak not far from the garden. He activated his communication mirror so Elise could watch then spoke a few words and spread their parent's ashes around the oak.

Although alone at Blaine Castle for the first time, he kept himself occupied handling duties about the estate, and he'd his letters from Pippa and his mirror calls with Elise to keep him company. Yet his evenings were too quiet, and celebrating Longnight with just servants was lonely. Perhaps next year he'd be married and celebrating with Pippa. If not, he could spend the winter with Elise in Golddell.

Despite still being in mourning, Edouard returned to Ormas for the start of the season at Plantfete. Even though he couldn't attend court events for several months, he and Elise could at least meet in person again. And Pippa was much closer too since her family had rented a townhouse for her first season. However, he couldn't risk seeing Pippa until he was free to court her, although they continued exchanging letters.

For Pippa's natalday a month later, he sent her a bouquet of white daffodyls with his letter wishing her happy natalday. Sadly, sending a true gift would have been inappropriate since they weren't even courting yet. She replied with an invitation to her presentation ball the following week, writing that she knew he couldn't attend but that she needed to invite him anyway.

He sighed as he caressed the edge of Pippa's vellum invitation. She was right that he shouldn't attend since he was still in mourning, yet Father would have been the first to encourage him to do so because he'd wanted both his children to find the joy he'd had with Mother. And he'd definitely wanted Pippa as a future daughter-in-law.

So on the evening of Pippa's presentation ball, Edouard dressed and headed to her family's townhouse. He'd attend, although he'd not dance out of respect for Father.

When Pippa, so lovely in her shimmering cream ballgown, spotted him in the receiving line, her welcoming smile brightened to a radiant grin as glowing as a sun nymph's, and she kept glancing at him despite the other guests she was greeting.

Warmth filled his chest. Pippa was clearly elated to meet again too. Hopefully, her interest would last after she danced with other eligible gentlemen tonight. Her sweet and bubbly nature would draw them to her like nectar drew the bee-like melissae, so they'd all seek to court her.

As he halted to greet her, Pippa beamed and leaned forward, despite Sir Julian almost frowning beside her. "E—Lord Blaine, I didn't think you'd attend tonight."

Gazing into Pippa's warm-brown eyes, Edouard bowed with his hands laced behind his back to not take her hand and kiss her palm. From how she'd said his title, she thought of him by his first name like he did her. "Father would have wanted me to attend."

Pippa held his gaze and nodded, her rich chestnut hair gleaming in the witchlights. "Are you dancing?"

He swallowed a sigh. If only he was. "No, I can't disregard my mourning that much, and I doubt I'll stay long." Watching Pippa dance with everyone else would be painful.

Her beam flickering, Pippa nodded again. "Before you leave, we should enjoy a flute of sparkling wine together. 'Twould be a welcome respite from dancing."

Edouard smiled at Pippa as his heart warmed further. "I'd like that."

Scowling now, Sir Julian humphed. Clearly, he didn't approve of the warmth between his young daughter and a gentleman she'd only spoken to twice. Or was he scowling because he knew about their letters over the past nine months? An unbetrothed lady and gentleman exchanging letters *was* near scandalous and could damage her reputation if they were discovered. A pang darted through Edouard. Now that Pippa was out, they must quit their letters, no matter how much they both enjoyed them.

Sir Julian shifted closer to Pippa. "Lord Blaine has lingered long enough. You've other guests to greet."

Edouard and Pippa traded a final warm smile before he strode across the ballroom. He fetched a flute of sparkling wine then stood along the far wall where he could feign that he was watching the other guests even though he was mostly watching Pippa.

He'd only taken two sips of sparkling wine when his cousin Hawke joined him. Flashing his usual crooked grin, Hawke drawled, "What are you doing here, Edouard? You're still in mourning."

Edouard forced a shrug. "Father liked Miss Hawke and would have wanted me to attend tonight to wish her well."

Hawke's brows rose. "Don't let Mother hear that. She'll make you take Pippa's first dance instead of Aragon. Then she'll have the two of you betrothed by Summerday. It takes prodigious stubbornness to resist Mother's meddling."

Edouard swallowed. Too bad he couldn't allow the Duchess of Childes to matchmake him and Pippa. But his mourning didn't end until nearly a month after Summerday, and Pippa was much too young to be rushed into a betrothal just two months into her first season. He sipped his sparkling wine before asking in a purposely light voice, "Why isn't King Devon opening the dancing with your cousin? She's his distant cousin too, and 'twould impress court more."

Hawke shrugged, his gaze on Pippa greeting his best friend Wren Keyes and her parents Sir Alaric and Lady Keyes, who were also his parents' best friends. Hawke replied, "Mother wanted to ask Devon, but Pippa insisted on Aragon for some reason. Excuse me, I should go rescue Wren. You know how she despises court events."

As his cousin hurried away, Edouard snorted into his sparkling wine. When was Hawke going to admit he loved Wren and marry her? The shy lady had always returned his love, so she'd not refuse him. And unlike Pippa, Wren was their age and old enough to know her own mind.

After Edouard finished another sip of sparkling wine, the opening strains of the first waltz began, and Aragon escorted Pippa to the center of the ballroom. Gripping his flute, Edouard clung to his smile as his gaze followed the couple twirling about the floor. Although Pippa was grinning at his happily married cousin, her grin held none of the radiant joy she'd shown when first spotting him. So why had she insisted on opening the dancing with Aragon? And how many dances would he need to wait until she required a respite and they could enjoy a flute of sparkling wine together?

CHAPTER 4

*A*s she twirled with Aragon about the ballroom, Pippa kept glancing over his shoulder at Edouard standing by the far wall. Barely smiling with his blond hair a beacon, he was watching her as intently as a golden gargoyle. Did he regret that another had taken her first dance at court? If only Edouard wasn't still in mourning. She'd have insisted he take her first dance instead of their happily married cousin.

Aragon smiled at her after a deft twirl that turned her away from Edouard. "What has you so riveted?"

Her cheeks warming, she made herself grin back. She'd been rude thanks to her preoccupation with Edouard. "All the guests. I didn't expect so many influential members of court to attend tonight."

Aragon chuckled. "You *are* a distant cousin of Devon and my family. Plus, Mother has been persuading everyone to attend even though you refused to let her present you."

Pippa blushed harder. She'd refused because the Duchess of Childes would have ensured all of her dances were claimed by eligible gentlemen interested in courting her, and she already preferred Edouard. "Your mother has been very kind. 'Tis simply that all these influential guests are somewhat overwhelming to a country miss."

Aragon smiled at his wife dancing with King Devon, his face soft. "Selena felt the same at her presentation ball."

Squeezing Aragon's shoulder, Pippa sighed. The deep love Aragon and Selena shared was so beautiful. Hopefully, one day she and Edouard would enjoy the same. "Thanks for relinquishing your wife's first dance tonight to open my presentation ball with me."

As the first waltz faded, Aragon inclined his head. "Of course, you're family. What gentleman shall I escort you to next?"

She glanced at Edouard across the ballroom. Too bad she couldn't request a respite from dancing yet. "Mel, I think." Not only was he family, but as a priest for the Goddess, he'd not be interested in her.

Aragon left her with his middle brother, and Mel was as kind as ever during their waltz and danced with surprising panache. At her request, Mel handed her to their youngest brother for the third dance. Hawke was safe enough since he never flirted with her despite his rakehell reputation.

When Xavier led her out for the next waltz, he grinned down at her. "Enjoying being the focus of every eye tonight?"

Pippa shrugged as they romped across the floor. The only eye she wanted was Edouard's. She glanced at him again. Surely a respite after the fourth waltz wouldn't be too soon. She smiled at Xavier. "'Tis fine. All the attention doesn't bother me."

Xavier chuckled. "But you don't crave it either. Yet you were *so* excited for your first season."

She pursed her lips, not letting herself look at Edouard. She didn't want to spark a brotherly lecture like after Aragon and Selena's wedding ceremony or when Dane and Xavier had discovered she and Edouard had been exchanging letters since his father died. "Not for the additional attention."

Snorting another laugh, Xavier narrowly eyed Edouard, who was still watching her dance. "Except from one gentleman in particular. Which you seem to have found, considering he's disregarding his mourning to glower at you from across the ballroom."

Pippa huffed at Xavier's teasing and stepped on his foot. "He's not glowering."

Xavier arched a brow as their waltz faded. "If you say so."

Before she could ask Xavier to escort her to Edouard, Dane strode over and captured her arm. "I'll take Pippa's next dance."

She sighed. From their elder brother's near frown, he was about to lecture. So she flashed a brilliant smile while they began dancing.

Dane shook his head. "You are aware that the point of a presentation ball is for you to dance with eligible gentlemen?"

Not glancing at Edouard, Pippa brightened her smile. Except she couldn't dance with the eligible gentleman she wanted. "I know."

Outright frowning now, Dane spun her in a complicated turn. "Then why have you only danced with family tonight?"

She shrugged instead of answering. Her reason would only make Dane lecture more.

Dane shook his head. "You shan't get to know eligible gentlemen if you don't dance with them."

Pippa kept her gaze on Dane's face as they twirled past Edouard. "There *are* other ways to get to know eligible gentlemen besides dancing."

Dane snorted and slanted Edouard a narrow glance. "Like letters, perhaps?"

She beamed. "Yes, exactly." When Dane opened his mouth to lecture again, she added, "But I'll dance with eligible gentlemen tonight to please you."

Dane exhaled as their waltz ended. "Good. You can't settle on the first eligible gentleman you met, no matter how much you liked him. Now whom shall I escort you to for the next dance?"

Her lips tightening, Pippa looked about the ballroom. She

wasn't *settling*. Why couldn't Dane and Xavier understand the depth of her attraction to Edouard? Her gaze fell on Lord Alexander Greysnowe. He was eligible, but he was her age and doubtless not ready to marry. "Lord Alexander Greysnowe."

Dane hummed but escorted her to Lord Alexander. "Although a future count, be careful with him. He's young and mightn't be sensible given how obsessed the Greysnowes are with their ridiculous feud with the Ravenstones."

She squeezed Dane's arm. He was always so protective of her —probably because Father often forgot to be. She glanced around the ballroom. Was Father even still here? Her brows rose when she spotted him frowning alone beneath the musicians' balcony. The Duchess of Childes's admonishment during dinner about Father remaining the entire evening had actually succeeded.

Turning away from Father, she smiled at Dane and replied to his earlier comment, "Yes, the Greysnowe-Ravenstone feud is why I didn't invite Lord Ravenstone tonight as well." Plus, inviting the Greysnowes meant Lady Annalise Greysnowe, the most beautiful lady in Calatini, could distract the eligible gentlemen.

Once Dane left her with him, Lord Alexander led her onto the floor with an irrepressible grin. Despite her brother's warning, the young lord was observant but playful, so their dance was great fun. Yet even though Lord Alexander was handsome with similar coloring, he didn't attract her like Edouard.

Pippa glanced at Edouard across the ballroom. He was gripping his half-empty flute of sparkling wine tighter now. She risked giving Edouard a warm smile to reassure him.

She was about to ask Lord Alexander to escort her to Edouard when the suave Duke of Oakmoor swept over and claimed her next waltz. She swallowed a sigh but managed to smile as they began to dance. Although the rakehell duke was older than Father, he was also an influential and wealthy councilor for the king, so she mustn't be rude. Thankfully, the duke was charming during their dance, although his habitual flirting was a bit much.

Before she could ask the duke to leave her with Edouard, who *was* glowering now, King Devon strode over and captured her arm, saying, "I'll take my cousin's next dance."

The Duke of Oakmoor relinquished her with a smooth nod. "Of course, your majesty."

As the duke left, Pippa darted a curtsy but smiled. Although she and King Devon were distant cousins, she'd only met him a few times and had never spoken privately with him. "Your majesty."

King Devon flashed an avuncular grin. "No need to be so formal, Pippa. We *are* cousins." While they began waltzing, he murmured, "Be cautious about encouraging the Duke of Oakmoor. Although he's not known for seducing innocents, he's still a rakehell."

She chuckled and smiled brighter. "I know, but rakehells don't interest me. Not that the duke attempted anything other than flirting."

King Devon hummed as he twirled her. "Good."

At the end of their dance, Pippa asked the king before another gentleman could approach, "Could you escort me to Lord Blaine? He promised to fetch me sparkling wine when I required a respite from dancing."

His mouth quirking, King Devon nodded but silently left her with Edouard. Her brothers would have grumbled.

She beamed and leaned toward Edouard, her pulse quickening. Finally, they could talk alone. 'Twas almost as good as dancing.

While the next waltz began, Edouard smiled back and gestured toward the refreshments table. "Shall we?" At her nod, they glided that way. "How are you enjoying your presentation ball?"

Pippa glanced at Edouard beneath her lashes. "'Tis fine, except I'm sad we couldn't dance together." She chuckled.

"Although that *does* mean I've something to look forward to later in my season."

Edouard blinked then grinned as he handed her a flute of sparkling wine. "I'd not thought of it that way." They began drifting along the edge of the twirling couples. "But I'll look forward to it too. When you dance, you appear like a sun nymph romping about a sunlit meadow."

A blush warming her cheeks, Pippa sipped her sparkling wine. The serious Edouard was inspired to near poetry for her. "My hair is much too dark for me to resemble a sun nymph. You might though."

Edouard chuckled. "No, my nature is too sober to ever look so cheery. Unlike you." His jaw tightened. "After tonight, I expect you'll receive many invitations from gentlemen seeking to court you."

She tilted her head. Perhaps, but such invitations would dwindle once she showed her lack of interest. She smiled at Edouard. "Only invitations from the right gentleman matter."

Edouard studied her over his flute of sparkling wine. "You know I can't openly court you until after my year of mourning—almost three more months. And now that you're out, we must quit exchanging letters. Gossip about them would damage your reputation."

Pippa kept smiling and held Edouard's gaze. If only she could reach out and squeeze his arm without everyone noticing. "I'll miss our letters, but three months isn't long."

Edouard exhaled then finally returned her smile. "Despite my mourning, I could meet for small family events or private outings."

Her heart surging, she couldn't help a tiny bounce. Edouard was too eager to delay courting her. She grinned up at him. "I'd enjoy that. Very much."

Edouard leaned toward her. "How about you and your family join us for dinner two weeks from now, and I can show you the art collection?"

Pippa beamed and swayed closer still. "Sounds perfect. Invite your sister and her family too." Like before, Elise would distract Dane and Xavier.

His pale-blue eyes flaring, Edouard studied her lips then swallowed. "Of course." They stared at each other as the final strains of the waltz played. Then he straightened and plucked her half-full flute of sparkling wine from her fingers. "Time for you to dance again."

She sighed and made herself turn toward the floor. She'd rather remain with Edouard, but 'twould cause talk.

Edouard coughed. "Before another gentleman whisks you away, I must ask—why did you insist Aragon open the dancing with you instead of King Devon? The king would have been more advantageous."

Pippa lifted a shoulder. "Because Aragon is happily married." As Edouard blinked, she smiled at the approaching Lord Morwynne, an affable count her age and son of a councilor to the king. Like Lord Alexander, he was surely too young to want marriage, so dancing with him should be fine.

While she and Lord Morwynne danced, she sighed at Edouard slipping from the ballroom. The rest of her presentation ball would be dull without him. But at least they'd talked before he left.

She spent the remainder of the evening dancing every dance, but she never danced with the same gentleman twice and avoided any gentlemen seriously pursuing marriage. Yet she still received multiple invitations over the following two weeks from gentlemen seeking to court her. Although she wasn't interested, she accepted a few invitations from the more indifferent gentlemen to prevent another lecture from her brothers. However, none of those dutiful outings made her bounce down the stairs like dinner at Edouard's townhouse did.

Before she left, Pippa swept into Father's workroom to encourage him to accompany them even though he rarely attended social events. Him getting to know Edouard was important. She smiled at Father. "You should join us for dinner at Blaine House tonight."

Father sprinkled faedust into various vials without glancing at her. "I can't leave my experiments at this critical stage. I'll have a tray of bread and cheese here."

Her chest squeezing, she sighed at Father's frequent excuse. But forcing him would only upset him, and he'd have plenty of time to get to know Edouard later. She straightened. "Very well. Make sure to eat when your tray arrives."

After arranging Father's dinner tray with their butler Hodges, she bounded into the entrance hall and grinned at Dane and Xavier. "Shall we leave?"

Her brothers traded a lengthy glance, then Dane murmured, "You appear excited."

Xavier smoothed his mustache. "More than you've appeared since your presentation ball."

Pippa blushed and studied her lymon-yellow silk gown. Hopefully, 'twould remind Edouard he'd compared her to a sun nymph. "Anyone who enjoys art would be excited to view Lord Blaine's collection."

Dane and Xavier exchanged another glance, but they didn't lecture as they climbed into the carriage and headed to Blaine House.

When they arrived, she smiled at the mansion's sophisticated facade of white limestone with evenly spaced pillars and nature carvings, interspersed with many tall windows. A lovely representation of ninth-century architecture—the first of its style built in Ormas. And the vivid painted ceilings inside representing events from Edouard's family's past were stunning. He was fortunate to live in such a grand townhouse so rich in family history.

Once the impassive butler ushered them into Edouard's drawing room, she settled on the chair beside the sofa where Edouard and Elise were talking while the gangly Duke of Golddell hurried over to Dane and Xavier before they could follow. She beamed at Edouard and Elise. "Lovely to see you again."

As Edouard grinned back, Elise smiled then replied, "Yes, it is. How have you been enjoying your come out?"

Pippa shrugged, studying Edouard through her lashes. "'Tis fine, although tonight is the most interesting event I've attended so far."

Elise tilted her head. "You must be eager to see the art collection." She turned to her twin. "You should show Pippa before dinner. I'll keep everyone occupied until you return." She rose and joined Lady Blaine, who'd just sashayed into the drawing room.

Still grinning, Edouard stood and waved toward the door. "Come, the collection isn't far."

Breathless and tingling, Pippa followed Edouard into the hall. They'd be truly alone for the first time. Perhaps in addition to showing her his art collection, he'd pull her into his arms and kiss her.

CHAPTER 5

His pulse swift, Edouard waved Pippa into the art room without touching her. He'd doubtless kiss her if he did, and 'twas much too soon for that. Her come out had only been two weeks ago, and tonight was their first courtship event. Besides, he was still in mourning and shouldn't be courting Pippa at all. Yet he liked her too much not to, *and* Father would have encouraged his quiet courtship. He really must speak to Sir Julian about courting Pippa as soon as he saw the baronet again. Which unfortunately wasn't tonight since Sir Julian hadn't accompanied his children. Hopefully Pippa's father wasn't too ill.

Her face radiant, Pippa halted just inside the threshold and gaped at the paintings lining the walls and the sculptures in the middle of the open room. She breathed, "Your collection is exquisite."

As Pippa swirled over to the closest painting, he swallowed and followed her. Her glowing delight made her more tempting than ever. Not kissing her 'twould take painful fortitude. He never should have shown her the collection alone. He fisted his hands behind his back. "This is the painting that started Father's collection. He purchased it to impress Mother during their courtship."

Pippa read aloud the plaque beneath the vibrant painting of a fae queen gifting a young lady enchanted gold thread at the heart of a forest grove, "*Sylviana's Faegift*." She glanced at him. "Was your mother passionate about tenth-century art too?"

Edouard smiled at Mother's fond forbearance whenever Father waxed eloquent about his art collection. "No, but she enjoyed songs by Lantos, and this painting depicts the climax of Lantos's best-known ballad, *Sylviana and the Fae Queen*. Lantos-themed artwork is quite rare since the troubled bard was only fashionable for the first decade of the tenth century."

Pippa arched her brows with a laughing smile. "And did this extraordinary painting impress your mother?"

He chuckled. "Mother said not, but Father would tease her that it did since she accepted his proposal the following week. Mother always tsked at him and replied she'd accepted because they loved each other."

Her lips dreamy, Pippa sighed. "How romantic." She drifted to the next painting, a lady swinging in the woods with dryads, gold deer, and melissae peering at her from the trees. "So what made your father continue collecting?"

Edouard studied *The Swing's Allure*, which Father had purchased from the Duchess of Wildewall's grandfather. "Father fell in love with the vivacious yet natural style of tenth-century art, and he enjoyed the hunt for his next piece and learning everything about it. We spent many happy afternoons here with Father telling us the tales of the pieces in his collection." Edouard glanced at Pippa, his voice deepening, "I hope to do the same with my wife and children one day."

Pippa smiled and leaned toward him. "Tell me your favorite tale."

He grinned as he led Pippa to the middle of the room to a pedestal with an apparently ordinary marble sculpture of a couple dancing. Their adoring gazes locked, the gentleman was spinning the lady in a complicated turn, making her flower-adorned skirt twirl. "Father purchased *Fantasia Dance* for Mother for their tenth anniversary. 'Tis the only other Lantos-themed piece in his collection, featuring *Fantasia in Minor for Keyharp*. He found it at an estate sale of the son of two famous dancers who'd become known for dancing that song at The Nightingale. After seeing one of their performances, Lascelle—an equally famous sculptor—immortalized them dancing together and gifted it to them on the birth of their son."

Pippa exhaled as she bent to study the piece. "What a sweet tale. And the sculpture is lovely too. So dynamic that I can almost see her skirt swirl and his next step."

Edouard hummed, warmth filling him. "Yes, but 'tis more than an ordinary sculpture." He clapped then said, "Sonareh," and a delicate, haunting melody played as the marble couple began dancing. "Lascelle had his bard witch cousin enchant it. 'Tis one of the first dancing music boxes created in Calatini."

Pippa beamed and clasped her hands together. "Amazing."

His chest squeezed while they watched the dancing music-box sculpture. "Until she became ill, Father and Mother used to dance to its melody whenever they visited the art room. Elise and I would groan when they did, but now 'tis one of my favorite memories of them. They loved each other so very much."

Pippa offered him her hand, her face aglow. "Dance with me like they used to as a tribute to their love."

Edouard inhaled and eyed Pippa. He really shouldn't. He might kiss her if he did. And dancing couldn't count as a tribute to his parents. Yet dancing with Pippa would be delightful and would have pleased both Father and Mother. Plus, no one was here to see him disregard his mourning by dancing.

He took Pippa's outstretched hand and drew her into his arms. Tingling warmth flooded him as they twirled about the art room to the enchanted sculpture's lyrical melody. Her sweet peach scent weaved about him, making him ache to pull her closer, yet he forced himself to hold her at the proper distance.

Then the melody faded, and they stilled. Although he should release her, he simply couldn't, so they gazed into each other's eyes, their chests moving in unison. After several heartbeats, he began lowering his head while she lifted hers.

"What's going on here?" Dane's voice echoed through the quiet art room.

His stomach tightening, Edouard jerked away from Pippa. How could he have been about to kiss her after telling himself he couldn't yet? He swallowed then faced Dane and Xavier standing in the door with stern frowns. Heat crept up his neck. "We were dancing to the melody of Father's dancing music-box sculpture like my parents once did."

Pippa flashed a brilliant smile. "As a tribute to them."

Still frowning, Dane and Xavier glanced at each other, and the heat suffusing Edouard flared. Pippa's brothers clearly didn't believe their excuse for dancing. Perceptive of them.

Xavier strode to Pippa and captured her arm. "We're here to fetch you for dinner. Arvan said he's perishing of hunger."

Edouard sighed as they left the art room with Pippa between her brothers on the other side of the hall. Dane and Xavier mustn't trust him near their sister. He managed to quirk a wry grin. "Arvan is always perishing of hunger. He's a fifteen-year-old boy. I required constant feeding at his age too."

Their frowns vanishing, Dane and Xavier chuckled. Then Dane murmured, "So did we."

Pippa grinned and laughed. "Yes, back then I quickly learned to set aside food for me and Father before you two began eating."

Edouard eyed Pippa then asked lightly to avoid upsetting her, "And how is Sir Julian? Not too ill, I trust."

Her brothers stilling beside her, Pippa sighed and replied, "Father's never ill."

Edouard tensed. Then why wasn't Sir Julian here tonight to

inspect his daughter's suitor during their first courtship event? Especially when his misgivings had been obvious at her presentation ball. He made himself shrug. "'Tis unfortunate your father couldn't attend tonight. I instructed Cook to prepare her best dishes to impress you, so he'll miss a superb dinner."

Pippa quirked an almost smile. "Father shall be just as happy with a tray of bread and cheese in his workroom. He rarely attends social events if he can avoid it." Her eyes flickered. "Him attending my presentation ball and remaining the entire evening was unusual."

His jaw clenching, Edouard glanced at Dane and Xavier, who were frowning worse than before. No wonder they were so protective of Pippa. Sir Julian was too engrossed in his magical experiments to bother. Somehow he must reassure them that he'd never hurt or take advantage of her. Burying his anger at her father, he warmly smiled at Pippa. "Once I can attend court events again, I'll escort you to any you wish and remain as long as you like. Elise shall be glad to join us." He turned to her brothers. "Then you two needn't escort your little sister everywhere."

Her beam incandescent once more, Pippa bounced and touched his arm. "I'd like that. Thank you, E—Lord Blaine."

Their frowns fading again, Dane and Xavier exchanged another glance then nodded while they entered the drawing room.

The others following, Edouard escorted Pippa to the family dining room without touching her. During the delectable dinner —Cook had truly outdone herself—he remained attentive but didn't flirt. Their courtship was too new for that, and 'twould make her brothers nervous. The meal passed swiftly amid lively conversation and laughter, both of which had been scarce at Blaine House since Father's death. But too soon he was escorting Pippa to his front door with her brothers behind them.

Pippa smiled up at him as Arvan distracted her brothers. "I'd a marvelous time tonight, even though I didn't get to see your entire art collection."

He grinned back, his pulse quickening as he eyed Pippa's sweetly curved lips. Too bad 'twas too soon to kiss her. "You'll simply have to return for another family dinner. But before then, would you and your brothers care to join me, Elise, and her family for a morning ride? I must warn you they ride obscenely early."

Pippa giggled. "I'd ride with you before dawn if you asked."

Once Pippa and her brothers left, Edouard couldn't help his broad grin while rejoining his family in the drawing room. He sank into the chair closest to Elise, who was talking with Kit on the sofa. He said once they quieted, "I hope you don't mind, but I invited Miss Hawke and her brothers to join us on one of your family's morning rides."

Kit smirking beside her, Elise chuckled then replied, "You must truly like Pippa to rise early for her." She squeezed his hand. "We'll be happy to help further your courtship. Just let us know when."

A blush warming his ears, he freed his hand. "In a few weeks. I'll write to King Devon about riding to the royal bay." Since visiting there required royal permission, they'd not likely encounter anyone, so gossip about him courting Pippa before his mourning ended wouldn't spread.

Kit tsked and shook her head. "At least your destination shows your usual prudence."

Edouard stiffened at his too-young stepmother's gibe. What would the grasping lady who'd beguiled his father into marriage understand about the genuine attraction that drove him? He arched a brow and drawled, "I'm so pleased you approve. I know Father would have."

Kit's smoky eyes glinted, but she nodded. "Undoubtably."

Before he could reply, Elise smiled at Kit. "You should join us on our ride."

Kit tossed her head. "Thanks, but no. Riding reminds me of country life too much. I'll peruse some fashion magazines instead to prepare for the new wardrobe I can purchase once our mourning ends."

He suppressed a snort. Preparing for a wardrobe she couldn't purchase for over two months was ridiculous. And doubtless the longer Kit prepared, the more money his frivolous stepmother would spend. Great. As she and Elise began discussing this season's fashions, he headed to his study to write a note to King Devon.

WITHIN THE WEEK, King Devon wrote back approving their ride to the royal bay, so Edouard asked Elise to send Pippa an invitation because an outing arranged by his sister rather than himself would reassure her family. Pippa replied to Elise accepting the invitation on the same afternoon she received it. She must be as eager for their ride as he was.

The morning of their ride, Edouard rose early with a smile, and his valet Abbot chuckled at his atypical cheer while helping him don his riding clothes but said nothing.

Kit, however, smirked when he joined her in the breakfast room and drawled, "Smiling before your first cup of kahve? Today *must* be your ride with Pippa. But is it prudent to show your feelings so early into your courtship?"

He snorted as he served himself kahve, eggs, beefsteak, and tubers. Even if he could manage to hide his feelings, how would Pippa know them if he did? He slanted Kit a flat glance. "Unlike *some*, I don't consider courtship a game to be won. Excuse me, I must hurry to avoid being late."

Ignoring Kit, he devoured his hearty breakfast even faster than usual. Then he strode to the stables, leapt atop his yellow-dun gelding Dune, and rode to Golddell House to meet Pippa and the others. He blinked when he arrived. Only Pippa was with his family, radiant in her warm-brown riding habit trimmed with yellow ribbon. Where were her brothers?

Elise grinned at him. "Edouard, finally. I thought we might

have to throw stones at your window to wake you." When he grimaced, she chuckled then turned to Pippa. "My brother *hates* mornings."

Pippa patted her honey-roan mare, glancing at him beneath her lashes. "I wouldn't have minded riding later."

Edouard flashed a wry smile at Farson and Arvan beside Elise. "But Farson would have. Their daily rides are typically closer to dawn than this." Plus, a morning ride meant less of court would be awake to see him and Pippa together.

Farson laughed. "Early firebird gets the gold apple." He waved toward the street. "Shall we head out? We shan't arrive at the royal bay until mid-morning as it is."

Edouard and the others nodded, then they trotted through Ormas and out the northern gate, with Farson and Arvan in front and Pippa riding between Edouard and Elise. Yet once Ormas was out of sight, Elise urged her mare to join her husband and ward. Edouard smiled. His twin was a lenient chaperone.

Her face glowing, Pippa turned to him. "I'm so excited to see the royal bay. I've never visited before."

He swallowed as his heart fluttered at her radiant joy. If only he could lean closer and sneak a kiss. "You'll like it. The royal bay is lovely, but not many ride there since visiting royal lands requires permission from King Devon."

Pippa eyed the heavy clouds then grinned at him. "Even the rain shan't spoil our ride there. Thanks for inviting me."

Edouard smiled back. Like a true sun nymph, Pippa would likely still beam and laugh even if sodden from a tempest. His pulse surged. Inhaling to settle himself, he said, "I'm surprised Dane and Xavier didn't accept the invitation to visit the royal bay as well."

Pippa looked away and shrugged. "They decided they needn't accompany me on a ride with Elise."

He frowned. But this ride wasn't just with Elise, and his attempt to reassure Pippa's protective brothers couldn't have succeeded already. "They were fine with you seeing a fairly new suitor without them?"

Her gaze still averted, Pippa shrugged again as she steered her mare around a rock. "I didn't mention you were joining us."

Edouard gripped his reins and stared at Pippa. How could she have deceived her brothers like a thoughtless child? Once they found out he'd been on the ride too, they'd assume he and Pippa had lied about him attending, making them believe they couldn't trust him with her. They might mention their concerns to Sir Julian, who despite being a neglectful father still wouldn't approve of an untrustworthy gentleman courting his daughter and would likely forbid it. And Pippa would have no choice but to obey since she was underage for another two years.

Pippa sighed then turned to him with a pleading smile. "I wanted a chance to see you without enduring Dane's and Xavier's frowns."

His chest tightened. Not enduring that was nice, but at what cost? Holding Pippa's gaze, he leaned toward her. "I can understand that, but you shouldn't have deceived your brothers. They'll be more suspicious of me when they find out the truth, so we'll endure their frowns for longer, and they might tell your father I can't be trusted to court you."

CHAPTER 6

Pippa winced at Edouard's stern stare. Dane and Xavier *might* assume the worst if they found out she'd concealed that Edouard would join her ride with Elise, although they'd not bother to tell Father about it. And even if they did, Father would understand since he'd met and courted Mother young himself. But still. She blew a sigh. "You're right. I shan't deceive them again about our courtship events. But surely they'll not find out about today."

Edouard grimaced and eased his grip on his reins. "You're too optimistic. Such secrets have a way of getting discovered."

She opened her mouth to protest Edouard's pessimism when Elise turned in her saddle and called, "Why are you two dawdling? We're almost at the royal bay." She tsked. "And quit frowning at Pippa, Edouard. You'll spoil her first view of the bay."

Pippa and Edouard traded a wry glance before they urged their mounts forward to join Elise, Lord Farson, and the young Duke of Golddell.

When they halted at the edge of the grassy cliffs above the royal bay, Pippa gasped at the stunning view before them. 'Twas nothing like the ocean near Ormas. No docks or ships cluttered the natural beauty of the bay. Beneath the darkening clouds, gulls darted in the salty wind, and the white-capped waves from the steel-blue ocean crashed against the golden sand below the cliffs. Completely unspoiled by humans—except for the black-haired gentleman on a black-bay stallion galloping before the surf at the far end of the bay.

She gestured toward the interloper. "I thought not many rode here."

Edouard squinted at the galloping gentleman. "They don't. Is that Lord Ravenstone?"

Lord Farson rubbed his tawny beard. "Looks to be. Few other gentlemen at court have beards."

Pippa peered closer. She should have recognized the rugged count she'd met a few times since her come out, but she'd been focused on him spoiling the natural view.

The Duke of Golddell said in a hushed voice, "Lord Ravenstone rides almost as well as a mara on a nightmara."

Lord Farson chuckled. "High praise coming from you, Arvan. The count *is* renowned at court for being a fearless rider, keen hunter, and skilled swordsman along with his dislike of town life and not supporting his family's feud with the Greysnowes. Shall we introduce you?"

When the gangly duke vigorously nodded, Pippa almost laughed. He appeared as eager as a giddy girl about to meet the most eligible gentleman at a ball.

Elise smiled and shooed her husband and their ward toward the winding path down the cliffs. "Go on then."

As they rode down to the royal bay, Pippa purposely reined in Honey so she and Edouard trailed the others. She'd little interest in greeting Lord Ravenstone. She glanced at Edouard. "Shall we ride along the surf while the others are occupied with the count?"

Edouard studied her, his eyes intent. "You don't wish to greet Lord Ravenstone?"

She held Edouard's gaze then smiled and shook her head.

"I've met him before, and although he seems pleasant, I much prefer calm and steady gentlemen with hair matching the sand here."

A faint blush darkening his cheeks, Edouard leaned toward her. "And I much prefer sweet and bubbly ladies whose smiles are brighter than the sun that's hidden by today's clouds."

Pippa blushed too, her heart quickening. More near poetry from Edouard. "We seem ideally suited then. Shall we ride along the surf now?"

Edouard urged his yellow-dun gelding forward. "As long as we don't ride too far from the others."

She nodded but swallowed a sigh as she kneed Honey until she and Edouard rode side by side. If only they were completely alone. Then Edouard might risk kissing her like he almost had in his art room after their dance. Tingling filled her. She must arrange more such chances.

The waves crashing beside them a soothing melody, she beamed at Edouard. "Thanks again for inviting me. The royal bay is as lovely as you promised." A heavy raindrop splattered on her glove. Then another on her bonnet. And several on her riding habit. She laughed and raised her face to the wet sky. "Even with the rain."

His deep voice rough, Edouard rumbled, "I knew the rain couldn't dampen your beams and laughter."

Pippa lowered her face to meet his gaze then rode closer until they almost touched. "Why would it when I'm with you?"

Edouard shuddered and shut his eyes. "Must you make it impossible to resist you?"

Warmth surged through her despite the cool rain, and she leaned toward Edouard. Would he kiss her now? "Yes."

His eyes flying open, Edouard stared at her, as still as a gorgon's victim turned to stone. Why wasn't he kissing her?

Before she could kiss Edouard herself, Elise called, "Hurry up, you two. We must return to Ormas to escape the rain."

Pippa exhaled as she and Edouard jerked apart. Darn his

sister for interrupting them—again. While they rejoined Edouard's family, who were alone now, then galloped back to Ormas, she mulled over possible courtship events that would inspire Edouard to kiss her.

Once they rode through the northern gate, they slowed to a walk, so she turned to Edouard and asked, "Shall we arrange another family dinner to allow me to see the rest of your art collection?"

Edouard swallowed, his fingers gripping his reins. "Not yet. And we should probably avoid meeting for several weeks to let your brothers' suspicions cool after they find out about today."

She pursed her lips. Even *if* her brothers did find out, several weeks was much too long to remain apart. She hummed. But Summerday was around then, and that festival of the Goddess was full of romantic revelry celebrating fertility and courtship. No doubt Edouard wouldn't be able to resist kissing her if they attended. She smiled at him. "How about we meet for Summerday festivities?"

Edouard frowned. "I'm not certain 'tis a good idea. Most Summerday festivities are in public and meant for betrothed or handfasted couples. We're not that yet, and I'm still in mourning. We can't risk alarming your brothers and father by being too presumptuous."

Pippa urged Honey closer and touched Edouard's arm to persuade him. "Please. I can't imagine attending Summerday without you."

Edouard stared at her for a moment then sighed. "Very well— as long as your brothers agree to join us and we simply watch rather than participate in the festivities."

Pippa beamed, her pulse leaping. Edouard would *definitely* kiss her on Summerday. "Of course."

Edouard sighed again. "Let's get you home. I hope your family is as forgiving as you seem to believe. But write to me once you know if Dane and Xavier agree to Summerday."

She shifted in her saddle as Edouard escorted her back to her family's townhouse with the others close behind. His continued pessimism about her family was worrying. Yet once she arrived home, she relaxed. Dane and Xavier were still out, and Father remained in his workroom like usual, so they'd likely not find out that Edouard had joined her and Elise.

However, at dinner, she almost winced when Dane smiled at her over his creamy spinach soup and asked, "How was your ride with Elise this morning?"

Her fingers tightening on her spoon, Pippa managed a bright smile. "Lovely, although rainy."

Xavier chuckled and smoothed his mustache. "Somehow I doubt the rain bothered *you* at all."

She clung to her smile. "It didn't." Then she asked Father about his magical experiments, which he'd discuss for the rest of dinner. She couldn't have Dane and Xavier finding out the truth about today's ride. That might make persuading them to agree to Summerday with Edouard difficult.

Once Father had returned to his workroom after dinner, Pippa scrutinized Dane and Xavier over her embroidery of a grand castle. Her brothers both appeared cheerful while they talked and sipped their spiritwine. She should ask them now. She coughed to draw their attention. "I know 'tis several weeks away, but I was thinking about Summerday. I'd like Lord Blaine to join us."

Dane and Xavier exchanged frowns. Then Dane sighed and replied, "That doesn't surprise me, but I doubt 'tis wise."

She glowered at her brothers and quit embroidering to avoid stabbing her fingers. "Why not? Lord Blaine is honorable and shan't take advantage." Any more than she wished, at least.

Xavier shook his head. "True, but Summerday in Ormas can get rather... rowdy. Much more than in Childes because of the crowds that attend here."

Pippa tsked. Must her brothers always be so overprotective? "I'm not a child. I can handle rowdy, especially with three stalwart gentlemen to protect me."

Dane sighed again. "Fine." He narrowed his eyes at her. "As long as you swear to quit avoiding *interested* gentlemen at court events until then. No more settling."

She lifted her chin. When would her brothers forget that ridiculous notion? But enduring other gentlemen at court events would be worth it if Edouard kissed her on Summerday. She flashed a brilliant smile. "Very well."

OVER THE FOLLOWING WEEKS, Pippa no longer avoided eligible gentlemen possibly interested in courting her, yet she made sure not to encourage them. She never danced with them more than once in an evening or accepted any invitations to see them later. Socializing with interested gentlemen wasn't as dreadful as she'd expected, but she didn't particularly enjoy it either, and she missed Edouard. The one dance she truly enjoyed was with Lord Ravenstone at the Duchess of Wildewall's ball, but only because he asked after Edouard as soon as they began dancing, so he mustn't be interested in her himself. The genial count had obviously just used her to escape his confrontation with Lord Alexander Greysnowe. Everyone in the ballroom had been watching the two ancestral enemies, wondering if a duel would erupt.

On Summerday, she bounced from bed, her heart lighter than it had been in weeks. Tonight she'd *finally* see Edouard again. She could barely settle during the day, which even Father noticed at breakfast before disappearing into his workroom.

Pippa hummed a cheery melody as her maid Betty helped her into her gauzy peach silk and braided wildflowers into her hair that afternoon. Then she bounded downstairs to wait for Edouard in the morning room.

When he joined her, Edouard stilled and stared at her. He rasped, "You look lovely, P—Miss Hawke."

She grinned then swept toward Edouard until they were

close enough to kiss. Given his hungry stare, she mightn't need the Summerday festivities to inspire his kisses. "So do you."

Edouard swallowed and stepped back. "Where are your brothers?"

Dane and Xavier strode into the morning room, and Dane said, "Here. You're earlier than we expected, Edouard."

Edouard flashed a tight smile. "I knew your sister wouldn't want to miss any of the festivities. Shall we go?"

She and her brothers nodded, and everyone headed to the carriage. Although she willed Edouard to sit beside her, somehow he sat in the backward seat beside Xavier, and she had to settle for Dane instead.

As the carriage rumbled forward, Edouard said, "Summerday festivities are held across Ormas, but I thought we could attend those at Jade Garden. 'Tis one of the largest gardens in Ormas outside of the palace gardens, and 'tis just outside the fashionable area, so its festivities should be less wild than most."

Xavier arched a brow. "Those are also the most popular Summerday festivities with court. Someone might recognize you, and your year of mourning doesn't end for another month."

Edouard set his jaw. "That hardly matters compared to your sister's safety."

Pippa's chest warmed. If they were alone, she'd kiss Edouard for his solicitude. And once her brothers were distracted by the Summerday festivities, she would.

They arrived at Jade Garden just before the start of the Summerday festivities when the Summer Lord and Lady were crowned with garlands of summer flowers and gifted Goddess plantings from Plantfete. Then she beamed as they watched the three traditional pageants about the Sea God's courtship of the Goddess. So romantic. She glanced at Edouard beside her. Too bad she couldn't hold his hand without upsetting her brothers.

After the pageants, they enjoyed the customary honey feast of honey-roast chicken, honey-glazed salmon, honey-grilled vegetables, oatmeal cakes, and berry shortcakes. She and

Edouard drank elderflower tea sweetened with honey, while Dane and Xavier drank mead brewed in Wildewall. She didn't care much for mead, and she must keep her wits about her to kiss Edouard without her brothers noticing.

While multiple bonfires were lit across the sprawling garden, priests began marrying handfasted couples or handfasting new couples, and the children and elders at the festivities drifted from the garden, leaving behind only those interested in courtship. Edouard turned to Pippa and her brothers. "Perhaps we should leave as well. Festivities get wilder now."

She inhaled and lifted her chin. But Edouard hadn't kissed her yet. "I've never attended the Summerday bonfires before. I'm not leaving."

As Dane and Xavier frowned at her, Edouard sighed and replied, "As you like, but we shouldn't stay more than another hour. The longer couples dance around the bonfire, the bawdier they become."

Dane and Xavier glanced at each other, then Xavier asked Edouard, "Mind if Dane and I go fetch spiritmead before it gets too wild? Want us to bring you one?"

Pippa bit the inside of her cheek to restrain her grin. Her brothers were leaving her and Edouard alone? Perfect.

Edouard blinked at Dane and Xavier. "Thanks, but no. Your sister and I shall wait for you in an alcove along the far wall."

Once she and Edouard were alone in the alcove, she eased closer and laid a hand on his arm. "All this is so romantic, don't you think?"

His gaze on the marrying and handfasting couples, Edouard shrugged and stepped away. "I suppose. Although making a life long commitment while influenced by the romance of Summerday doesn't seem sensible."

Her heart softening, Pippa chuckled. She should have known her serious Edouard would say that. "So no impractically romantic gestures from you then?"

Edouard stiffened and eyed her. "Yes, likely not. Does that disappoint you?"

She threaded her arm through his and squeezed it to reassure him. "No." She tilted her head as she studied the amorous couples. "Although they do look so happy kissing."

Edouard shuddered but didn't step away again. "But to kiss in public like that. Some things should remain private."

Pippa sighed. He *had* only almost kissed her when they'd been alone. Even at the royal bay with his family he'd frozen. Attempting to inspire him to kiss her at the Summerday festivities had been a mistake. She must arrange time alone instead.

Dane and Xavier returned with their spiritmead just as couples began dancing around the Summerday bonfires. Her brothers glanced at her and Edouard's entwined arms but didn't frown or comment. And Edouard still didn't step away. So tonight hadn't been completely worthless.

She smiled as the couples danced faster and faster around the Summerday bonfires then began leaping through the flames to enhance their fertility. 'Twas an interesting sight, but not something she'd want to attempt. How did the ladies manage not to set their gowns aflame?

When couples began slipping away, doubtless to make love beneath the stars, Edouard coughed then said, "We should go."

Pippa squeezed Edouard's arm. "Yes, please." Once they settled in the carriage, with Edouard beside her this time, she beamed but didn't nestle against him like she wanted to avoid alarming him or her brothers. "Thanks for joining us."

Edouard returned her smile. "Of course." He paused then asked, "Would you care to go on a tour of the Great Temple in a week or two? Mel can arrange for a priest who knows all the architectural details to show us."

She grinned, her pulse quickening at another of Edouard's thoughtfully chosen courtship events. "I'd love that."

Edouard smiled and turned to her brothers across from them. "You two are welcome to join us."

Dane and Xavier traded a glance, then Dane replied, "No, thanks."

Pippa blinked. That didn't sound like her overprotective brothers. So once Edouard had left, she said, "I'm surprised you two are fine with Lord Blaine escorting me alone."

Dane shrugged. "Edouard's restrained behavior tonight proved we can trust him not to take things too far."

She hummed but nodded. Just like she'd always said.

Xavier waggled his brows. "And not even you can get into too much mischief at a temple surrounded by priests."

Lowering her gaze, Pippa concealed a smile. Fortunately, Dane and Xavier had forgotten the carriage ride there and back. She and Edouard would be completely alone then. A perfect chance for kisses.

CHAPTER 7

Two weeks after Summerday, Edouard grinned as he leapt from his carriage to collect Pippa for their tour of the Great Temple. Not seeing her for so long had been hard, but until his mourning ended and he could publicly court her, he couldn't risk meeting her too often. Besides, he still hadn't spoken to her father about courting her yet, and Mel hadn't been able to arrange their tour until this morning anyway.

His pulse surging when he met Pippa in the morning room, he swallowed and stared at her. Beaming in a light-yellow dress, she once again appeared as radiant and lovely as a cheery sun nymph. But he still couldn't kiss her yet—even if their destination had been appropriate for that, which it wasn't. "Good morning. Ready?"

Pippa bounced across the room and threaded her arm through his. "Oh, yes."

He inhaled but didn't free his arm even though he probably should since touching Pippa only tempted him to kiss her. Yet she seemed to need to touch him as much as he ached to touch her, so how could he deny them both that? As long as he controlled his hunger, they'd be fine. Perhaps reminding himself that they'd the rest of their lives to kiss would help. He smiled at

Pippa as he escorted her from the morning room. "You appear excited for our tour."

Glancing at him beneath her lashes, Pippa grinned back while they swept outside. "Not just for our tour."

Edouard swallowed again as heat flooded him at Pippa's flirting. Yes, touching her definitely wasn't prudent. So when they settled in the carriage, he sat across from her despite her faint frown. "I'm surprised Dane and Xavier didn't change their minds about attending."

Pippa hummed as the carriage rumbled forward, her tempting lips sweetly curved. "They trust you."

He gripped his hands at his sides to remain still. And he'd not betray Pippa's brothers' trust, and by extension their father's, by kissing her senseless on their first courtship event alone. 'Twas too soon for that regardless of how both he and Pippa wanted it. Especially since Sir Julian didn't even know they were courting.

Fortunately, they soon arrived at the Great Temple, and he helped Pippa alight then escorted her inside. Since they couldn't kiss in a temple with priests everywhere, he allowed himself to keep her arm. They met Mel in the back of the nave, and their priest cousin introduced them to Elder Priest Archibald, who led all of the Great Temple's temple priests yet had still agreed to show them around the Great Temple.

As Mel strode away, the rotund elder priest grinned at them. Such smiles were his usual expression from the faint lines creasing his round face. "My fellow priests run away when I begin discussing the Great Temple's architecture, so when Mel mentioned you wanted a tour about that, I seized the chance for a willing audience."

Pippa returned Elder Priest Archibald's grin. "Thanks for taking time from your duties to show us, and I promise we shan't run away until you tell me *everything*."

Remaining silent, Edouard smiled at Pippa during the lengthy tour. She beamed while the elder temple priest detailed the construction of the Great Temple. Then she and the priest chattered like excited sprites about how the founders of Calatini sourced the white limestone for the temple and the palace, how the master masons built the pillars, buttresses, and rib vaultings that supported the temple, and how long it took artisans to create the temple's stunning ornamentation. Pippa was enjoying the tour as much as he'd hoped.

When priests began entering the nave for Sext, Elder Priest Archibald reluctantly said farewell after inviting Pippa to visit again. The elder temple priest had clearly enjoyed the tour too.

Edouard and Pippa attended Sext with Mel then ate luncheon with him in the Great Temple's dining hall before Edouard escorted Pippa back to his carriage. As she settled on the forward seat, she gripped his arm and tugged until he sat beside her with a sigh. Hopefully, he could control himself.

Pippa nestled against him. "The tour of the Great Temple was wonderful. Thanks so much for arranging another thoughtfully chosen courtship event."

His body tightening at Pippa's curves pressing against him, he gulped a bracing breath, and her sweet peach scent filled his lungs, making him ache even more. But he mustn't kiss her—not yet. "Of course."

Pippa rubbed her cheek against his shoulder before lifting her head to smile at him. "When shall we meet for another? Soon, I hope."

Edouard held himself rigidly still to not capture her mouth in a hungry kiss. "I'm not certain."

Pippa grinned, her chuckle reverberating through him. "You've not planned our next meeting yet? How surprising."

He shrugged. He would have, except meeting privately made kissing Pippa too easy. Although perhaps... "Elise and her family are visiting for dinner on the anniversary of Father's death to celebrate his memory. Would you and your family care to join us?"

Pippa stared up at him and pressed a hand against his face.

"Are you sure you want us intruding on such an intimate family event?"

Holding Pippa's gaze, Edouard managed not to turn and kiss her palm. "I'd like you there."

Her eyes soft, Pippa smiled and lowered her hand. "Then I'll gladly attend."

He arched his brows at Pippa. "Perhaps you can encourage your father to attend this family dinner so I can finally get to know him." And speak to him about courting her.

Pippa's smile tightened. "I'll try." She laid her head on his shoulder again. "Your dinner shall be three evenings before the king's summer masquerade, right?"

Edouard let himself rest his chin on Pippa's head even though he should really withdraw. "Yes."

Pippa hummed. "Are you attending the king's summer masquerade?"

He blew a sigh. Although he didn't particularly care for masquerades, 'twould be the first important court event after his mourning ended, so he should attend. Plus, if he didn't, Pippa would be beset by gentlemen seeking to kiss her. Masquerades were known for frivolous dalliances that weren't permissible at ordinary court events. "I am, although I've no idea what costume to wear. I'm hopeless at deciding such things."

Pippa smiled against him and murmured, "How about a gargoyle? They're steady and strong like you."

A blush flared beneath his skin at Pippa's praise. "Very well. What are you dressing as?"

Pippa shrugged as the carriage slowed before her family's townhouse. "I've not chosen yet."

Edouard couldn't resist kissing Pippa's hair before separating. "You should dress as a sun nymph to match your dancing and radiant smiles."

Flashing one of those smiles, Pippa let him assist her from the carriage. "Only if you promise not to turn to stone like a gargoyle in sunlight. I expect two dances from you."

He released Pippa inside her entrance hall with a small bow. "Of course." The problem would be stopping at two dances. But he would since more was only appropriate for married or betrothed couples.

OVER THE TWO weeks before the family dinner to celebrate Father, Edouard purchased a gargoyle costume at one of the fashionable shops near Broad Street, but otherwise remained home. However, he did sort through invitations for after the king's summer masquerade and accepted those Pippa and her brothers would likely attend, including Kit's water party for the evening after the masquerade. He must attend that regardless, although Kit hosting an event so soon after their year of mourning ended was almost disrespectful to Father. All of court would attend his fashionable stepmother's first event since last season, and him not attending would cause talk.

When Elise and her family arrived for the dinner celebrating Father, Edouard smiled at his twin. "I hope you don't mind, but I invited Miss Hawke and her family to join us."

Kit snorting on the sofa beside her, Elise smiled and said, "Of course I don't mind."

He blushed at Elise's and Kit's knowing smiles, but before he could reply, Pippa entered flanked by her brothers. Sir Julian had clearly chosen not to accompany them again. He sighed. So much for his plan to speak to her father tonight about courting her. How could the baronet neglect his daughter so? Father *never* would have done likewise, and neither would he once he had children.

Yet when Pippa swept straight toward him with a glowing grin, he couldn't help returning it. She was so adorable. After everyone exchanged greetings, he escorted her into the family dining room for a dinner of Father's preferred foods.

As they began their creamy redkrab bisque, Pippa beamed at

him and Elise. "Tell us some of your favorite memories of your father besides your family afternoons in the art room."

Edouard hummed. They'd so many, especially from before Mother had died. Did Pippa and her brothers possess similar memories of their neglectful father? He studied Pippa. No shadows dimmed her bright grin. So even if they didn't, she still was eager to hear about his. He returned her grin. "I loved the rides Father would take us on about the estate, answering our questions about anything from the color of the sky to crop yields in thorough detail."

Elise chuckled while sipping her bisque. "Father taught us so much about estate management without us even realizing during those rides." Her smile turned wistful. "One of my favorite memories of Father is how he read to Mother every afternoon once she became ill."

Drinking some wine to ease his tight throat, Edouard nodded. "He always chose stories that made all of us smile, especially Mother, and he remained calm no matter how upset the rest of us were, even though watching Mother fade away must have devastated him."

Kit sighed into her scalloped tubers with bacon. "Lord Blaine was such a dear, thoughtful gentleman who was devoted to caring for those he considered family. Our first Longnight together, he gave me every cinnaspice gift he could find because he'd noticed how I enjoyed spiced cider."

Edouard blinked at Kit. Such a sincere sentiment was surprising coming from his brazen and grasping stepmother.

Farson chuckled as he waved his fork. "But Lord Blaine's devotion to his family could be daunting. I still remember how grave his face grew as I stumbled through asking for Elise's hand by describing what I could provide. Once I quit rambling, he simply asked if I loved her, and when I replied I did, he *finally* smiled and advised me to forget everything but the love when proposing to Elise."

Elise laughed and slanted her husband a warm glance. "Which, fortunately for you, you did."

Edouard swallowed, his chest tight as he served Pippa pastry-wrapped beefsteak. "Father invariably provided sensible advice." Like when Father had encouraged him about Pippa. "I miss that."

Her bright gaze tender, Pippa squeezed his free hand beneath the table. Their favorite memories of Father clearly hadn't upset her even though she might not possess the same herself. Definitely as full of sweet and radiant joy as any sun nymph. She leaned toward him. "I wish I could have gotten to know your father better. He sounds wonderful."

After returning her squeeze, Edouard reluctantly freed his hand then began describing the time Father had disturbed a nesting swan on one of their rides. He and his family continued exchanging anecdotes about Father throughout dinner amid laughter and tears. Over their blueberry crisp with vahnila sweetice, he raised his flute of sparkling wine and said, "To Father. Although tonight is our final evening of mourning, we'll never forget you—and Mother. But we'll endeavor to live our lives the way you taught us—with love, devotion, and wisdom."

The others echoed his toast before they all finished their dessert and the ladies withdrew. After a sip or two of spiritwine, he and the other gentlemen joined the ladies in the drawing room, where Kit was regaling Pippa and Elise about her plans to visit Celeste's tomorrow to purchase her new wardrobe.

Soon Pippa rose and joined him with a soft smile. "My brothers and I should return home. Escort me to the door?"

His heart quickening, he nodded and took her arm.

Once they were alone with her brothers several steps behind, Pippa murmured, "Thanks for inviting us. I enjoyed hearing about your father. You two seem very much alike." Squeezing his arm, she smiled at him through her lashes. "Tonight showed the type of husband and father you'll be."

Edouard blushed. "Thanks. I'm glad you were here." Her support and smiles had made everything easier.

Pippa grinned up at him. "Do you have your costume for the king's summer masquerade?" At his nod, she continued, "Me too. I can't wait for you to see it. Did you want to join us for dinner before you escort me to the masquerade?"

He sighed and released Pippa in the entrance hall. If only he could. "I think I'd better meet you at the masquerade. Otherwise, everyone might realize we've been courting before my mourning ended, and that shall cause talk." If her father heard such talk before he'd spoken to him, her father might decide to forbid their courtship. He *must* speak with Sir Julian at the masquerade, which even the reclusive and neglectful baronet would attend to protect his daughter from gentlemen emboldened by its bawdy ambience.

At his refusal to escort her, Pippa's smiled dimmed. Then she tilted her head and replied, "Shall it? Court has better gossip to talk about. The king's summer masquerade is the first event that Lord Ravenstone and Lord Alexander Greysnowe shall both attend since their nearly fatal duel on Summerday. And our courtship is nothing compared to their families' centuries-long feud."

Edouard rubbed his jaw. True, but still. "Their duel was a month ago, so court shall be eager for fresh scandals to talk about, and I don't want to risk it being us."

Pippa echoed his earlier sigh. "Very well. Yet we'll dance the first waltz together, right?"

He straightened. After missing that at her presentation ball, he couldn't miss it at their first public courtship event. "Definitely. And we'll dance the final one together too."

Pippa beamed, her eyes bright. "Until then."

Before the king's summer masquerade three evenings later, Edouard devoured dinner with Kit, who kept smirking about him openly courting Pippa at last. Unable to endure more of that, he requested his carriage prepared rather than riding with

Kit like he'd intended. Although 'twould make him later, he should arrive well before the first waltz. He donned his gargoyle costume then leapt into his carriage as soon as it arrived.

But midway to the palace, two drunken youths racing sport carriages through Ormas clipped his carriage before crashing on the street ahead. Thankfully, his excellent driver Frank managed to halt his carriage without hitting them or injuring his horses. Yet clearing the accident and tending to the injured drivers and their horses took almost an hour.

Edouard scowled as he continued to the palace. Damnation, he'd surely missed the first waltz. Not only had he been aching for that for days, but Pippa would be upset with him for breaking his promise. Please let her forgive him once he explained.

CHAPTER 8

$\mathcal{W}$hile she and her brothers rode to the palace for the king's summer masquerade, Pippa beamed out the carriage window at the sprawling castle of white limestone adorned with elaborate turrets and countless windows. Goddess, 'twas stunning. Built in the first century like the Great Temple, the palace glowed in the evening sun and was surrounded by extensive and verdant grounds filled with many beautiful gardens. Dane and Xavier had brought her to see the palace last year, but tonight was the first time she'd see the inside, despite them being distant cousins to King Devon.

Closely flanked by her brothers, she alighted from the carriage, and they joined the other elaborately costumed guests entering the palace. As they walked to the ballroom, she gaped at the palace's dazzling white walls, vivid painted ceilings, intricate nature carvings, exquisite art, and gorgeous tapestries. The inside definitely fulfilled the outside's promise.

Pippa inhaled when they reached the palace's elegant ballroom. As richly appointed as the rest of the palace, the ballroom was enormous with an impressive musicians' balcony and many massive witchlight chandeliers. Perfect for hosting events that the entire court attended, like the king's summer masquerade tonight. Once she regained her breath, she smoothed the golden skirt of her sun nymph costume and began glancing about the teeming ballroom for Edouard. But she didn't spot him anywhere, although his stepmother Lady Blaine was already here amid her fashionable friends. As were Elise and Lord Farson, although the young Duke of Golddell was absent tonight, so they were nestled together in an alcove practically kissing. Such intimacy would have been considered scandalous at any court event other than a masquerade, even between a happily married couple.

While Dane and Xavier narrowly eyed the nearby gentlemen, Pippa almost frowned as she and her brothers settled along the garden wall. Why hadn't Edouard arrived yet? Facing the front, she peered at every new guest, but none were Edouard. Where was he? She swallowed and laced her hands together. Could he have decided not to attend after all? Masquerades likely didn't appeal to his serious temperament. She gripped her hands. But he'd promised they'd dance the first waltz together.

As she scrutinized the guests for Edouard, several gentlemen braved Dane and Xavier's glares to request dances, but she dismissed them all with smooth refusals and polite smiles. She intended to remain beside Edouard for the entire masquerade. Neither of her brothers protested her refusing to dance for once because tonight being a masquerade had made them even more overprotective than usual. Not that she'd have listened if they had protested.

Suddenly, Xavier snickered, his grin as feline as his tygris costume. "Dane, you've a twin tonight."

She followed Xavier's gaze to where Mr. Winston, dressed as a griffin like Dane, leered at the ladies entering the ballroom.

Dane grimaced. "Of course it had to be that cad Winston." He turned to her. "Remember to avoid him."

Pippa inclined her head, a prickle skittering across her skin. Her brothers had kept the despicable fortune hunter away from her since her come out, but formalities were much less stringent at a masquerade. Thank the Goddess she knew Mr. Winston was dressed similarly to Dane. Otherwise, she might have been fooled into letting Mr. Winston near her, and her dowry was enough to tempt the destitute future baron.

Then the opening strains of the first waltz began, and she swallowed as her chest twisted. How could Edouard have forgotten their first waltz?

Dane and Xavier traded frowns, then Xavier grasped her wrist. "Let's dance."

She glowered at Xavier and tugged on her captured wrist. "No, E—Lord Blaine was supposed to dance the first waltz with me."

Xavier tsked while pulling her onto the floor. "Then he should have arrived on time. Now smile. You can't appear morose when he arrives."

Pippa sighed but gritted a brilliant smile and forced herself to romp through the waltz with Xavier, although she kept glancing at the entrance for Edouard. Yet he still hadn't arrived by the end of the first waltz, so Dane whisked her into another dance before she could protest. After that, she insisted they remain by the refreshments table and refused any offers to dance.

Clinging to her mendacious smile, she watched the entrance until King Devon swept a mysterious mermaid onto the floor directly before them even though he was practically betrothed to Lady Annalise Greysnowe. From his intense stare at his mermaid, the king was enthralled. She swallowed. She'd imagined she and Edouard would be dancing like that tonight. Why hadn't he arrived?

Midway through that dance, Edouard strode into the ballroom and halted as their gazes locked. Then he strode through the dancers and straight to her side, the wings of his gargoyle costume flaring behind him. He held her gaze and murmured, "I apologize for being late."

Pippa tightened her lips to keep them from trembling. "Where were you? You promised me the first waltz." Until tonight, she'd believed him too reliable to ever forget a promise —unlike Father.

Xavier glowering beside him, Dane glared at Edouard and said, "Pippa was upset you weren't here."

Edouard winced. "Two drunken idiots crashed their sport carriages ahead of me, so I spent almost an hour resolving that." He leaned toward her then rasped, "I'm sorry for missing our waltz. I've been aching for it for days."

As her brothers quit frowning, she exhaled and studied his tight face. Of course her steady Edouard hadn't forgotten, but he couldn't have abandoned an accident. She smiled at him. "I've been aching for our waltz too. Any serious injuries?"

Edouard snorted and shook his head. "Less than those idiots deserved. One driver broke a leg, while the other has a concussion. Thankfully, their horses escaped with nothing more than sprains, although their carriages were wrecked." He extended his hand as the next waltz began. "I know I missed the first waltz, but would you dance with me now?"

Pippa nodded and placed her hand in his. Her heart quickened when Edouard led her onto the floor and pulled her into his arms. If only he'd pull her closer. Yet he remained at the proper distance as they silently twirled, although his intense gaze never left hers. Exactly like King Devon had stared at his mermaid.

While they strolled beside the dancers after their waltz, she sipped the flute of sparkling wine Edouard had handed her and eyed him beneath her lashes. She must persuade him to slip away and kiss her at last. "I like your gargoyle costume. The mask, armor, and wings appear genuine granite."

Edouard chuckled. "They aren't. I'd never manage to dance if covered in granite. They're mere cloth enchanted by the witches at Bewitching Raiments." He toasted her. "But my costume is nothing compared to yours. You outshine the sun in all that gold, although I'm glad you didn't hide your rich chestnut hair beneath a blonde wig."

Pippa grinned at Edouard and slid her arm through his, her pulse surging. "Wigs are too hot. Besides, I didn't want to risk you not recognizing me. My golden ballgown, gold sun mask, and enchanted gold glitter from Charms and Nonsense were enough to make me appear a sun nymph."

Edouard's brows rose. "The glitter on your hair and skin is enchanted? Why?"

She giggled. Because ordinary glitter would betray their kisses by covering Edouard where they touched. "Ordinary glitter gets everywhere. But this glitter doesn't." She tossed her head to show the glitter remained in her upswept hair. "See? Plus, it has another feature, although we must slip into the palace gardens to see it."

His fingers gripping his flute of sparkling wine, Edouard swallowed. "Us slipping into the palace gardens isn't prudent. Just tell me instead."

Pippa squeezed Edouard's arm and beamed at him. "Showing you is more dramatic." And he'd never resist kissing her once they were alone.

Edouard stiffened. "We can't disappear into the palace gardens alone without causing talk, especially since tonight is our first public courtship event. Everyone shall suspect our prior courtship or call you a flirt."

She pursed her lips. True, but if they were never alone, when could Edouard kiss her? "You're right. We'll remain in the ballroom. You can see the glitter's other feature when you escort me home after the unmasking at midnight." Surely she could ensure her brothers didn't join them.

Edouard swallowed. "Shall I take you back to your brothers or father now?"

Pippa stared at Edouard. He wanted to end their time alone together so soon? Why? Then she exhaled. Doubtless to avoid causing talk. She smiled at him and replied, "Father isn't here."

Edouard frowned and eyed her. "He's not? But 'tis a masquerade, and he should be here to protect you from gentlemen emboldened by its bawdy ambience."

She shrugged. "Father couldn't leave his magical experiments. They're at a critical stage." A pang darted through her. Not that Father realized she was attending the king's summer masquerade tonight. When she'd visited his workroom earlier, he hadn't even noticed her sun nymph costume. He'd barely glanced up from his vials.

Edouard's mouth flattened. "I see. Well, your brothers and I shall protect you." As his solicitude banished her fleeting melancholy about Father, he glanced toward the dancers. He murmured, "You must want to waltz more, and the final one tonight that we'll share isn't for hours. I'll watch from the outskirts to ensure your partners don't take advantage. Who should I escort you to first?"

Pippa halted. Edouard wanted her to dance with other gentlemen? She turned him to face her and relaxed. From his tight jaw beneath his gargoyle mask, he didn't want that any more than she did. He was just attempting to not cause talk again. She smiled up at him again. "No one. I've endured the attentions of gentlemen I'm not interested in for nearly three months. I refuse to continue doing so now that you're free to publicly court me."

Edouard briefly shut his eyes then stared at her like a captured kelpie stared at the ocean. "We shouldn't."

She leaned toward Edouard and brightened her smile to convince him. "We are. If we remain near my brothers or your sister for much of the evening, we shan't cause too much talk."

Shuddering a sigh, Edouard nodded. "Very well."

So she and Edouard spent the rest of the king's summer masquerade together, talking and laughing as they either strolled beside the dancers or stood with Dane and Xavier or Elise and Lord Farson. 'Twas the happiest she'd been at court since their short time together at her presentation ball—and kissing him on the carriage ride home would make it perfect.

Just before the final waltz began, Pippa said to Dane and Xavier, "Lord Blaine shall escort me home directly after the unmasking. I'll see you later."

Dane and Xavier sighed, but they didn't protest because they could likely tell from her smile that she was intent on being alone with Edouard and they trusted him.

She beamed as Edouard twirled her about the floor until the bells tolled midnight. How she adored dancing with him. And she'd adore kissing him even more. During the final ring, she reached to remove her sun mask but stilled as the king's mermaid raced past them with King Devon close behind. She blinked up at Edouard. "Is such drama usual at the king's summer masquerade?"

Edouard chuckled while removing his gargoyle mask. "Never from King Devon at least."

Pippa finished removing her mask as well. King Devon becoming enthralled by a mysterious mermaid despite being practically betrothed didn't concern her and Edouard, and she'd a first kiss to arrange. She grinned at him. "Shall we leave while everyone is gossiping about King Devon's peculiar behavior?"

Edouard nodded then swept her from the palace's ballroom. When they strode outside, he stilled and scrutinized her. "Is it a trick of the lanterns, or is your enchanted glitter glowing?"

She giggled and leaned toward Edouard, tingling warmth flooding her at his thorough stare. "I thought glowing glitter was appropriate for a sun nymph, although the ballroom's witch-lights overpowered its glow."

Edouard shook his head as he handed her into his carriage. "Very appropriate. Not that you need enchanted glitter to glow."

When Edouard began settling in the opposite seat, Pippa bounced across the carriage and nestled against him. They couldn't kiss so far apart. "You say the sweetest things."

Edouard jerked away then returned her to the forward seat. "'Tis dangerous for us to sit so close. I doubt I can resist kissing you."

Her heart stuttering, she hunched her shoulders while the carriage rumbled forward. "Don't you want to kiss me?"

Looking away, Edouard croaked a laugh. "I do. Very much. But 'tis too soon for kisses."

Pippa straightened and frowned at Edouard. Too soon? "We've been courting for nearly three months."

Edouard sighed then faced her again. "Yes, but in private, and I haven't spoken to your father about courting you yet, so we've only met every few weeks. We must get to know each other better and obtain your father's blessing. After all, you *are* just eighteen and barely out."

She blinked. Edouard was worried about Father approving their courtship? She leaned forward. "Father shan't withhold his blessing. He met and courted Mother young himself, remember."

Edouard rubbed his jaw. "Even so, you still need time to know your own mind."

Pippa stiffened and lifted her chin. Edouard sounded like Dane and Xavier. "Are you implying I'm *settling* by courting you?"

Edouard winced. "No, but kisses are serious. You must be certain first, and I can't rush your choice."

She exhaled and leaned back in her seat. She *was* certain, but Edouard couldn't see that because of her age, so he was determined to be noble. Protective idiot. Her chest squeezing, she eyed Edouard. Continuing to push for kisses might make him avoid her, and she'd rather see him without kisses than not see him at all. Yet waiting for him to decide she was ready for kisses would be hard.

As the carriage slowed before her family's townhouse, Edouard cleared his throat then asked, "Are you attending Kit's water party tomorrow?" When she nodded, he smiled and took her arm. "Then I'll see you there."

Pippa smiled and squeezed Edouard's arm as he helped her alight. "I'll look forward to it."

• • •

THE FOLLOWING evening at the royal bay, Pippa grinned as she bounced onto the first barge at Lady Blaine's water party with Dane and Xavier behind her. She'd never been on the water before, and Edouard was already here and striding through the crowd toward her. While she and her brothers greeted Lady Blaine, the barge swayed beneath them, making her slightly dizzy. So different from solid ground.

When Edouard joined them, Lady Blaine smirked and drawled, "Here to whisk Pippa away again? How gallant."

As Edouard frowned at his young stepmother, Pippa beamed and took his outstretched arm, her stomach swirling as the barge swayed again. She replied to Lady Blaine, "I think so." She turned to Edouard. "Shall we?"

After nodding farewell to Lady Blaine, Edouard escorted Pippa along the railing with her brothers close behind. He smiled at them. "Shall we greet Elise?"

Pippa nodded, and Edouard led her across the bridge that connected the first barge to the next, which swayed even more than the barges themselves. The swirling in her stomach grew as her head whirled and knees wobbled.

Edouard slanted her a narrow glance and murmured too quietly for her brothers to overhear, "Are you all right? You appear somewhat pale."

She managed to grin despite her nausea. She couldn't spoil her and Edouard's evening together. She murmured back, "I'm fine. The swaying of the bridge just startled me. I've never been on a barge or boat before, let alone connected ones."

Humming, Edouard nodded but said nothing further as the four of them joined Elise and Lord Farson.

Elise grinned. "Evening, Pippa. Isn't Kit's water party as stunning as I said 'twould be?"

Pippa glanced about the barges bright with color-changing witchlights and teeming with excited guests. "Definitely. The setting is unique and decorations dazzling."

Lord Farson lifted his wine glass. "The refreshments are delicious too. Strawberry wine, krab turnovers, and shokolat truffles, among other delicacies."

As her stomach lurched at those rich refreshments, Dane whistled then said, "Such extravagance must have cost a fortune."

Edouard grimaced with a snorted laugh. "Oh, it did. I possess the bills to prove it."

Pippa couldn't help smiling. Her serious Edouard *would* find such frivolous extravagance irritating.

Elise tsked. "You know Kit never spends more than the estate can afford, and her stunning events are always worth the cost."

Edouard shrugged then murmured, "I suppose." He glanced at Pippa. "Shall we fetch some of those refreshments Farson mentioned?"

Her stomach lurching again, she nevertheless nodded. She wanted time alone with Edouard, and perhaps walking would ease her nausea. As he drew her away, she gestured for Dane and Xavier to remain behind, which they did with resigned sighs.

Edouard accepted two glasses of strawberry wine from a servant then handed her one. "Are you certain you're fine? You appear even paler than before."

She sniffed the strawberry wine, its sweetness making her nausea surge. She shuddered and lowered her wine glass. "My stomach has felt uneasy since I boarded."

Taking her wine glass, Edouard steered her into a seat beside the railing. "You must be one of the unfortunate people who become ill on boats. Kit should have some nausea-healing charms; I'll fetch you one. While I'm gone, stare at the horizon and breathe deeply. That might help." He squeezed her shoulder then strode through the crowd.

Pippa faced the ocean and gulped the salty air as Edouard had instructed, but each sway of the barge made her nausea deepen. Please let him return soon.

Then an unfamiliar gentleman behind her drawled, "The

lovely Miss Hawke, without her gargoyle brothers for once. How fortuitous."

She turned, and her nauseous stomach tightened. Mr. Winston. Of course the fortune hunting cad had found her when she was alone and ill. She opened her mouth to reply, but the barge swayed, and she heaved. Dear Goddess, she was about to vomit all over Mr. Winston before most of court. So embarrassing.

Suddenly, a cool necklace slid about her neck from behind, and her nausea vanished as if it had never been. She inhaled a bracing breath as gentle hands settled on her shoulders. Edouard. Smiling, she laid her hands atop his. Thank the Goddess.

CHAPTER 9

s Pippa rested her hands on his, Edouard glared at Winston and rasped, "Quit pestering the ladies at my stepmother's event before someone throws you overboard." Too bad he couldn't punch the damned fortune hunter without all of court noticing.

Winston stiffened. "You wouldn't."

Edouard leaned forward, still glaring. He would to protect Pippa. "Am I known for my jests?"

His face darkening, Winston spun and thrust through the crowd. Not that anyone paid any notice. Winston's reputation as a cad was so established that few at court bothered to gossip about it.

Edouard exhaled and sat beside Pippa, who was no longer white like before he'd fetched the nausea-healing charm. He smiled at her and risked taking her hand. "How are you feeling?"

Pippa beamed back and squeezed his hand. "Perfectly well again. Thanks for rescuing me from both my queasy stomach and the odious Mr. Winston."

Warmth filled his chest as he returned her squeeze. "Of course."

Her warm-brown eyes glowing, Pippa studied him. "Such a gallant rescue deserves a reward."

Edouard blushed and shook his head. "The only reward I need is enjoying tonight with you."

Pippa hummed. "But you'd have that in any event. How about a picnic and a ride five days from now? I promise to invite my brothers."

He arched his brows. Five days was specific. "Why five days from now?"

Leaning toward him, Pippa chuckled. "We'll have been courting for three months then. An occasion to celebrate."

Edouard nodded. He should bring Pippa a flower to mark the occasion. And he could speak with her father before they left to obtain proper permission to court her. "I'd like that." He rose and drew her upright. "Since you're feeling better, how about some refreshments?"

Pippa grinned and squeezed his arm. "Yes, please. Strawberry wine, krab turnovers, and shokolat truffles sound delicious now that I'm no longer nauseous."

OVER THE DAYS before their picnic and ride, Edouard joined Pippa at court events most evenings, and they spent them together, either with Dane and Xavier or Elise and Farson. Yet he still continued only dancing with Pippa twice during an event to avoid causing talk.

Despite all their time together, he couldn't help his grin as he left to meet Pippa at her family's townhouse for their picnic and ride. Seeing her in public was nice, but a private courtship event was more satisfying. His heart quickened when he strode into the morning room and she swirled toward him with a glowing smile. He handed her the thornless peach rose he'd brought. "To celebrate our three months courting."

Beaming brighter, Pippa accepted the rose and sniffed it. "'Tis lovely."

He warmed at her delight, but he couldn't help explaining, "I'd have brought peach blossoms instead of a peach rose, but they're four months out of season."

Pippa studied him over her rose. "How did you know peach blossoms are my favorite flower?"

Edouard shrugged, tingling as holding her close echoed through him. "I guessed from the peach scent you wear."

Pippa caressed her rose against her cheek and grinned at him. "Observant."

He fisted his hands behind his back to avoid pulling Pippa into his arms and kissing her. Dear Goddess, her sweet and radiant joy was more tempting than a voluptuous venus during a seductive dream. He cleared his throat. "Where's your father? I'd like to speak with him before we leave."

Pippa tucked her rose into the breast pocket of her dark-olive riding habit. "About courting me, I suppose." At his nod, her grin grew. Then she sobered and sighed. "Unfortunately, Father isn't here. His magical experiments exploded last night, destroying half his vials. He's out purchasing new ones."

Edouard grimaced. Wonderful. When would he ever get to speak with Sir Julian about Pippa? Given his success so far, he and Pippa would be done courting before he could. Then he'd need to ask for her hand instead of just permission to court her. And being so presumptuous would surely nettle her father. Burying his concern, he made himself smile as he asked, "Are your brothers joining us?"

Pippa tilted her head. "They should be."

He was about to suggest they find her brothers when Xavier strolled into the morning room and asked, "You two ready? Dane is waiting in the stables." His gaze lingered on Pippa's rose. "Nice rose."

Pippa beamed. "Edouard gave it to me."

Hunger flaring in his veins, Edouard inhaled and stared at Pippa. "You've not called me by my first name before." Although she almost had several times.

Still smiling, Pippa shrugged and slid her arm through his. "The day we met, I swore to Dane and Xavier I wouldn't call you by your first name aloud again until we'd been courting three months." She narrowed her eyes at Xavier. "Which we have now."

Xavier snorted and smoothed his mustache as they headed outside. "'Tis amazing you managed to keep your promise. Edouard's name has been burning on your tongue the past year."

Her mouth tightening, Pippa snapped, "*I* don't forget my promises."

Edouard eyed Pippa and Xavier. From what he knew of her brothers, neither did they, but from her unusually sharp tone, someone close to them did—their neglectful father, no doubt. He stiffened momentarily then forced himself to relax and squeeze her arm with a soft smile while they entered the stables. "Remembering promises is always important."

As Pippa's earlier glow returned, Dane handed her the reins to her mare and rumbled, "Well said, Edouard. But what brought up promises?"

Xavier flashed a wry smile. "Pippa and Edouard have been courting three months now."

While they led their horses into the stable yard, Dane hummed and arched his brows at Edouard. "Called you by your first name, did she?"

Pippa pursed her lips and began to retort, but Edouard smiled and replied before she could, "Yes, and I'm glad she did. Not calling Pippa by her first name was wearing on me as well." His chest warmed as he and Pippa grinned at each other.

Dane and Xavier traded a glance, then Dane asked, "Shall we go ride, or did you two want to stare at one another all afternoon?"

Xavier chuckled. "I say we ride. We'll never get to eat our picnic if we don't, and I'm almost as ravenous as Arvan always is."

Edouard and Pippa broke apart, then he helped her into her

saddle, not because she needed the help, but because it allowed him to touch her for a moment. She beamed at him as he mounted beside her afterward and murmured, "Thanks, Edouard."

He swallowed and nodded. 'Twould be so easy to lean over and kiss Pippa. She'd not protest and would doubtless eagerly return his hungry kiss. Thankfully, her brothers nearby strengthened his resistance to her allure. "My pleasure, Pippa."

They rode through the busy streets of Ormas then out the southern gate and picnicked on the rocky shore where kelpie races were held throughout the season. Edouard and Pippa's brothers spent most of their picnic telling her about some of the unpredictable and exciting kelpie races they'd seen here, which made her grin.

As they repacked their picnic, Edouard smiled at Pippa. "I'll escort you to kelpie races one evening if you like."

Pippa beamed. "Yes, please. They sound riveting. When are the next ones?"

Edouard helped her mount, almost kissing her upturned lips as he did. He should really quit finding excuses to touch her. "Next week, although I can't attend because Arvan is hosting his first court event with Elise's guidance. As the Duke of Golddell, Arvan must celebrate the arrival of the nightmara delegation that day."

While he climbed atop Dune, Pippa said, "Another time then. But the soiree should be delightful too."

He winked at Pippa. Always so adorably cheery. "It shall be if you're there." When she blushed, he asked, "Could I escort you to the Blackhams' ball tomorrow evening?" He and Pippa had been courting long enough that he could escort her to events, and he could speak with Sir Julian before they left so their courtship would be official at last.

Her beam turning radiant, Pippa bounced in her saddle. "Yes, please."

. . .

AFTER THEIR PICNIC AND RIDE, Edouard escorted Pippa to events every evening, always attempting to speak with her father about courting her beforehand, but with no success. Not that the baronet was avoiding him. He'd spoken with Sir Julian in his workroom several times, but the baronet invariably shooed him out before he could ask to court Pippa.

Despite his lack of success with her father, he and Pippa began spending less time with their families and more time alone but in sight at the events they attended together. Everyone started linking their names like they did longtime or betrothed couples—hopefully 'twouldn't nettle Sir Julian when he was finally able to ask about courting her. Once he and Pippa were considered a couple, fewer gentlemen asked Pippa to dance, and he never encouraged her to join other gentlemen even though he really should. He needed to be with her too much. And every day it became harder and harder not to yank her into his arms and kiss her senseless.

When he arrived to collect Pippa for Arvan's soiree, he smiled at her family's butler and immediately asked, as had become his wont, "Is Sir Julian in?"

Hodges gravely shook his head. "The baronet has requested not to be disturbed tonight, my lord."

Edouard sighed as he stepped inside. Of course Sir Julian had. The baronet somehow contrived to be reclusive in his own home. So frustrating. Then he turned to face Pippa, and his heart thumped in his chest at her glowing smile while she took his arm. He could taste that smile if he simply tugged her closer and bent his head. Shoving his hunger aside, he asked, "Are Dane and Xavier joining us?"

Pippa laughed. "No, they decided the kelpie races were too exciting to miss."

Edouard swallowed as he escorted Pippa out to his carriage. How was he ever to manage not kissing her without her brothers nearby? Yet he must since 'twas too soon and her father hadn't approved their courtship yet. He exhaled. "I'm surprised your brothers trust me alone with you."

While he settled across from her, Pippa folded her hands in her lap and quirked a wry smile. "Of course they do. They've witnessed your chivalrous restraint every time we're together."

He gripped his seat to remain still. Please let that restraint last until they were in public again. "Perhaps I was lulling Dane and Xavier into relaxing their vigilance."

Her face soft, Pippa shook her head. "You're much too serious and steady for such a trick." She sighed. "Not that I'd mind if your chivalrous restraint shattered—at least enough for a few kisses."

Those kisses flashing before him, Edouard shut his eyes and shuddered as heat flooded him. Pippa clearly shared his eagerness too. "We can't. Not yet."

Pippa sighed again. "I know I'm just eighteen and barely out, but have I ever hinted that I don't know my own mind?"

He hungrily eyed Pippa. True, she'd never wavered in her interest. She'd only accompanied other gentlemen since her come out because her brothers had demanded it, and as soon as he could publicly court her, she'd begun refusing everyone else. Perhaps 'twasn't too soon for kisses after all. However, her father still hadn't given his blessing for their courtship, so they must be particularly discreet to avoid causing talk. But kisses should be private anyway. Yet if he kissed her, would he be able to stop?

Thankfully, before he could crumble to temptation, the carriage halted at Golddell House, and he escorted Pippa to the drawing room, which was nearly empty. Not surprising since the kelpie races and one of the Westons' superb musical evenings were scheduled tonight as well. Besides, only those interested in politics cared about the arrival of the nightmara delegation that Arvan's soiree was celebrating, and although Arvan was a duke, he was much too young to marry, so even the matchmaking mothers at court didn't care to attend. Yet the sparse attendance probably delighted Arvan as well as Elise and Farson because that simplified Arvan's first court event.

Elise and Farson standing nearby to observe him greeting the guests, Arvan brightened when Edouard and Pippa joined him.

Once they'd exchanged greetings, Pippa beamed at the young duke. "Golddell House is charming. All the horse and nightmara decorations make it so different from Childes House even though both were built three centuries ago."

Arvan smiled. "My ancestors have always been horse mad." As Edouard suppressed a chuckle because Arvan was no less horse mad than his ancestors, the gangly duke glanced past him and Pippa then asked, "Are Dane and Xavier joining us?"

Pippa shook her head. "They're at the kelpie races this evening."

Arvan blew a sigh. "I wish I was too. I'm certain kelpie races are much more exciting than any soiree. Not that I've seen any, although Farson has promised to take me next time."

Edouard grinned. Definitely horse mad. "Once you see them, you must let us know if you prefer kelpie or nightmara races."

His eyes gleaming, Arvan chuckled. "As the Duke of Gold-dell, I can hardly prefer the kelpie races, can I? The nightmara would insist on a new duke."

Edouard winked at Arvan. "Not if you recant and plead the bad sense of youth." Then he escorted Pippa to the refreshments table so Arvan could greet the approaching Greysnowes under Elise and Farson's watchful gaze.

As Arvan wilted at greeting the forceful couple and their beautiful daughter, Edouard handed Pippa a flute of sparkling wine and sighed. "Poor Arvan is too young for all this. Not that it could be avoided since the nightmara delegation only visits Ormas every twenty-five years."

Pippa smiled and sipped her sparkling wine while they strolled about the drawing room. "I'm sure the duke shall do fine, and Elise and Lord Farson shall rescue him if he doesn't."

Edouard hummed when a blushing Arvan escorted Lady Annalise Greysnowe to the refreshments table. "I hope so. Arvan appears dazed by Lady Annalise's beauty."

Pippa slanted him a sidelong glance. "Have you ever attempted to court the beauteous Lady Annalise? She's near your age, I believe."

He blinked. Was Pippa jealous? She'd no need to be. Although not an extraordinary beauty like Lady Annalise, she possessed a glowing warmth that made her more than simply beautiful. He smiled at Pippa to reassure her. "No, I've never bothered to court Lady Annalise, although we've danced on occasion. She's impossible to get to know; 'tis why many at court call her Lady Snow." He toasted Pippa with his flute of sparkling wine. "Besides, despite her ice-perfect beauty, Lady Annalise lacks the power to brighten an entire room with her radiant smile, unlike a certain bubbly sun nymph I know."

Pippa blushed. "You truly do say the sweetest things, Edouard."

He leaned toward Pippa, and tingling filled him as he held her gaze. "Just to you, Pippa."

Her blush deepening, Pippa swayed closer. If only they were alone, so he could demonstrate his interest with more than words. Perhaps he could risk kissing her when escorting her home. If he waited until at her door, surely he could stop at one kiss. Although he'd have to ensure Hodges didn't see them since the butler would tell Sir Julian.

Yet he and Pippa weren't alone, so he made himself straighten and ask, "Did Hawke visit yesterday to invite you and your brothers to Wren's play at Waterstreet Orphanage tomorrow? He invited me and Elise, so I assume he invited everyone else performing in Wren's next play at the duchess's fete celebrating Aragon and Selena's first child."

No longer blushing, Pippa nodded. "Yes, Hawke invited us. I'm looking forward to it. Are you?"

Edouard grimaced and sipped his sparkling wine. "Yes and

no. Wren's plays are always entertaining, but we're attending to prepare for performing before all of court. And I'm *not* looking forward to that." In fact, he was dreading it. Yet when Hawke had requested he perform, he'd been unable to refuse because Hawke had asked on his mother's behalf, and saying no to the Duchess of Childes was nearly impossible.

Pippa squeezed his arm with a warm smile. "Performing shall be enjoyable, you'll see."

He sighed as he laid his hand atop Pippa's. Likely not, but since she was performing too, at least they'd be rehearsing together and would see each other more than before.

Pippa tilted her head. "Would you like to escort me to the orphanage play tomorrow?"

He sighed again. He would, except her brothers would be with her, and five people in one carriage would be too many. "I can't since I'm escorting Elise. Farson is meeting the nightmara delegation with King Devon and Aragon tomorrow, and Arvan refused to attend a '*children's* play.'"

Her eyes crinkling, Pippa chuckled. "Somehow I'm not surprised. Youth his age are so sensitive about appearing mature." She grinned. "Even though we can't ride together, we'll see each other there regardless." She glanced at Elise and Farson, who'd been talking with Arvan and Lady Annalise since they'd fetched refreshments. "Should we go greet your sister?"

Edouard shook his head. "Elise is busy watching over Arvan and handling the guests." Plus, he'd rather remain alone with Pippa. He could talk to Elise later.

Pippa nodded, so they spent the rest of the soiree alone engrossed in conversation, until Dane and Xavier arrived as the soiree was ending. Although Arvan was thrilled they'd attended to see how his first court event had gone, Edouard merely swallowed a sigh. So much for escorting Pippa home and kissing her at her door.

Wren's orphanage play the next day was as entertaining as he'd expected, although it didn't reassure him about performing in the fete play. Yet despite his reluctance, he almost smiled when Wren announced at the first fete play rehearsal two afternoons later that he and Pippa were playing the king and queen. With paired parts, they'd rehearse together even more than he'd thought, and when Pippa offered to practice extra together to help him memorize his lines, he eagerly agreed. As they left, they arranged to meet at her family's townhouse the following morning because the group rehearsals were in the afternoon.

When Pippa ushered him into the library the next morning, he arched his brows. "Where are Dane and Xavier?" He'd assumed one or both would be chaperoning them.

Pippa shrugged as she settled into the chair beside him. "Out riding, I think. Their approach to the fete play is to avoid it as much as possible."

Edouard inhaled, his pulse quickening. Then this morning would be perfect for their first kiss. When he'd asked after her father like usual, Hodges had said Sir Julian was ensconced in his workroom and too busy for visitors, so the baronet wouldn't disturb them. He exhaled. But he'd best wait to kiss Pippa until he was about to leave—otherwise, he mightn't stop at one kiss, and they'd never rehearse anything, which he needed. He hoisted his script. "Shall we get started?"

They began, and their rehearsal went smoothly until he stumbled over their melodramatic plea to distract the demon and allow their daughter to escape with her soldier suitor. He attempted his lines a second and third time, but his tongue kept tangling. He lowered his script with a groan. "This is impossible."

Pippa laid a hand on his knee. "You'll master it soon enough."

Heat suffusing him at her touch, he forced himself to remain still. "Goddess, I hope so. But this flood of words makes my tongue as clumsy as a cold wyvern."

Pippa squeezed his knee. "You're nothing like a cold wyvern." She beamed and leaned closer. "Besides, the longer we take to master our lines, the longer we can rehearse alone together. I may forget how to speak entirely."

Unable to resist any longer, Edouard pulled Pippa into his lap, and his body tightened at her soft curves and her sweet peach scent. "Then I should teach your mouth how to do something else." He lowered his head and captured her mouth in a hungry kiss.

CHAPTER 10

$\mathcal{A}$s Edouard kissed her—finally, thank the Goddess—Pippa threaded her arms about his neck and eagerly returned his kiss. Tingling warmth swept through her as their mouths fused in the ancient dance of love and passion. So much better than she'd ever dreamt.

Then Edouard wrested his head back and rasped, "Enough, Pippa."

Breathless and flushed, she attempted to pull Edouard down for another kiss. Not nearly enough.

Edouard dropped her back into her chair. "No. We must resume practicing for the fete play."

She licked her lips and eyed Edouard. Who cared about that when he could be kissing her? "I'd rather you teach my mouth some more instead."

Edouard shuddered and shut his eyes. "'Twouldn't be prudent right now."

Pippa leaned forward and rested her hand on Edouard's knee, her pulse racing again at touching him. "So?"

Crushing his script in his fist, Edouard jerked upright and glared at her. "We can't. 'Tis too dangerous. I'll see you at the group rehearsal this afternoon."

As Edouard bolted from the library, she frowned after him. What danger could a few more kisses possibly pose? Although another might take advantage and go too far, Edouard never would. He was the most steady and chivalrous gentleman she'd ever met.

She sighed and studied her script that had tumbled onto the floor when Edouard had pulled her into his lap. Hopefully, he'd be his usual calm self at the group rehearsal in a few hours.

Yet that afternoon at Childes House, Pippa almost winced when Edouard stormed into the ballroom and barely returned her bright smile. He was still upset, although he claimed 'twas due to Lady Blaine attempting to take part in Wren's play. But after Mel convinced Lady Blaine to leave, Edouard remained tense, so his stepmother hadn't caused his upset—she had.

As they left the ballroom following rehearsal, she swallowed and studied Edouard through her lashes. "Shall you visit tomorrow morning to rehearse together?"

Edouard stayed silent for several heartbeats. Then he sighed and inclined his head. "I think I'd better. I'll never memorize my lines otherwise."

She beamed as her heart quickened. And perhaps they could enjoy more kisses too. Surely, Edouard wouldn't protest if he wanted to spend time alone with her.

But when Edouard met her in the library the following morning, he sat in the chair in the corner, and as she began dragging another chair closer, he pointed at the floor before her. "No, stay there. We'll not rehearse anything if you sit too close."

Pippa sighed while she dropped into her chair so far from Edouard. Kisses would be impossible with half the library between them. "We'd rehearse more kisses."

Edouard tapped his script on his knee. "I know, that's the danger."

Her chest squeezed. Edouard was so determined to avoid her. Why? She licked her lips. "Was our kiss so disappointing that you don't want another?"

His pale-blue gaze darkening, Edouard eyed her lips like a starving manticore eyed a unicorn. "'Twas the opposite of disappointing. I burn for our next kiss, but we must be careful. Your father hasn't given his blessing for our courtship yet."

Pippa exhaled. Edouard was still worried about that? "Father shall as soon as you can distract him from his magical experiments long enough to ask him." And since Edouard attempted to speak with Father every time he visited, he should succeed before too long. She hummed. "I suppose you intend to wait until Father gives his blessing to kiss me again." 'Twould be painful.

Holding her gaze, Edouard leaned forward. "Oh no, I intend to kiss you today. We're just waiting until I'm about to leave. That shall make it easier to stop when we should."

She inhaled and blushed as tingling surged through her at kissing Edouard again before he left. If only they were kissing *now*.

Edouard quirked a wry smile. "Somehow I suspect we'll require frequent kisses to control our hunger for each other. Not that I'm opposed to that. We just must be particularly discreet to avoid causing talk that might reach your father." He straightened. "Shall we start practicing our lines?"

Pippa sighed but nodded, and they began rehearsing. Yet her mind kept returning to their upcoming kiss, and every time she'd blush and fumble her lines.

Thankfully, after an hour of that, Edouard closed his script. "I should go."

She leapt upright while Edouard strode across the library. Another kiss at last! Her pulse swift, she threw her arms about his neck and lifted her mouth as he pulled her against him.

Edouard groaned. "Your innocent ardor shall be the death of me."

Then he kissed her, even deeper than yesterday. When their lips met, heat flooded her, and she sighed. Tangling her fingers in his silky hair, she nestled closer to further deepen their kiss. So right.

When Edouard eventually began lifting his head, she gripped his hair to keep him close. They'd not kissed enough yet.

Edouard lifted his head despite her efforts then brushed a tender kiss against her brow. "I'll see you this afternoon."

Pippa huffed as Edouard released her and stepped back. Why must he always be so sensible and restrained? Her tender lips curved in a rueful smile while he hurried from the library. Yet if he wasn't, he'd not allure her the way he did.

THE FOLLOWING TWO DAYS, Pippa and Edouard rehearsed alone in her library every morning, and he waited until he was about to leave to kiss her. Yet he didn't kiss her in the library like usual after their fourth private rehearsal. Wren had canceled their group rehearsal that afternoon, so they didn't part after rehearsing alone together. Instead, they enjoyed luncheon together then headed to the fashionable shops near Broad Street to purchase the costume accessory they each needed for the fete play. Fortunately, as the king and queen, their accessory wasn't difficult to decide.

Yet Edouard sighed as they studied the selection of costume crowns at Bewitching Raiments. "These are all too ostentatious, don't you think?"

She giggled and squeezed his arm. Adorable man. "They're costume crowns. They're meant to be ostentatious to show we're 'royalty.'"

Sighing again, Edouard shook his head. "If real crowns look anything like these, no wonder King Devon never wears one."

Pippa smiled. Yes, her distant cousin possessed simple taste very like Edouard's. 'Twas doubtless why King Devon was mad for that mysterious mermaid he'd met at his summer masquerade rather than the beauteous Lady Annalise he'd courted for years or other flowery court ladies. Hopefully, he'd find his mermaid soon for the sake of the essential Night-mara-Calatini Treaty. The matriarchal nightmara were now refusing to negotiate with anyone but Calatini's future queen.

She selected the simplest pair of costume crowns, which were gold circlets studded with diamonds. There was even a tiara that matched for Elise to wear as the play's princess. "How about these? We can purchase the matching tiara for Elise."

As Edouard grimaced and took the larger crown to examine it, the elegant clerk swept across the room and said, "An excellent choice. Our lightest costume crown, but stunning once you activate its illusion." She pressed the center diamond, and light began to sparkle and swirl about the crown.

Pippa swallowed her laugh when Edouard winced and almost dropped the crown before pleading, "Could you deactivate that?"

Once the clerk pressed the center diamond again and the light faded, Pippa arched her brows at Edouard. "We needn't activate the illusion if you don't want."

Edouard shuddered. "I don't." He gave the clerk a tight smile. "We'll take these two crowns and the matching tiara. How much?" After paying the requested eleven gold, he escorted Pippa from the apparel witch shop then grinned at her. "Shall we have a sweetice before I take you home?" She beamed back. Edouard wasn't ready for their outing to end either. "Yes, please."

Edouard led her to Layne's Tea Room, and they sat at a table near the window. She ordered a peach sweetice, while he ordered shokolat raspberry. Halfway through, she tilted her head and asked, "Could I try a spoonful of yours?"

Edouard hummed while extending a spoonful. "If you like."

Pippa leaned forward and wrapped her lips about the spoon Edouard's had touched, tingling as she held his gaze. "Delicious."

Edouard swallowed. "Behave. We *are* in public."

She couldn't help a sigh. "Unfortunately." She nodded at her peach sweetice. "Care for a spoonful of mine?"

Edouard smiled and shook his head. "I'll taste it later in the carriage."

Pippa blushed. She could hardly wait. "Didn't you just tell *me* to behave?"

Grinning now, Edouard chuckled. "In public. My carriage isn't that."

She set her spoon beside her half-eaten sweetice. Thank the Goddess for his carriage. "I'm done. Shall we go?"

Their gazes meshed, Edouard rose and took her arm then escorted her outside and into his carriage. As it departed, he lowered the curtains then scooped her into his lap and captured her mouth.

Pippa sighed into Edouard's thorough kiss. He tasted of shokolat and his own masculine flavor. She could kiss him forever and never have enough. She fisted her hands in his hair and pressed against him as they kissed the entire ride home.

When the carriage halted, Edouard shuddered and yanked his head back. Panting, he lowered his arms. "Go inside before my chivalrous restraint shatters completely."

Heat flaring in her veins at that, she brushed a kiss against Edouard's lips. "Would that be so terrible?"

Edouard frowned at her. "Your father still doesn't even know we're courting, so yes. Now go inside. I'll see you tomorrow."

Pippa grinned and kissed his cheek before sliding from his lap. Her dear chivalrous Edouard. "Until tomorrow."

Over the days before the Duchess of Childes's fete, Pippa and Edouard continued their private morning rehearsals, and he continued to insist on waiting until just before they parted to kiss her. But he did kiss her every time with hungry passion, albeit not as much as in his carriage. And although she'd not have chosen to wait, somehow anticipating their kisses made them more exciting.

She smiled as Betty helped her into her gleaming amber ballgown for the duchess's fete. Tonight would be such fun. After performing their paired parts in the play, she and Edouard would dance and enjoy the rest of the fete together before he escorted her home and kissed her in his carriage again. Perhaps she could convince him to leave early to begin their kisses sooner.

After dressing, she bounced downstairs and met Edouard, who was returning from Father's workroom like usual, in the entrance hall with a bright grin. Her grin grew when he smiled back and handed her a thornless white rose. How romantic. She snapped off the stem and pinned it to her bodice with her pearl brooch. "Thanks, Edouard. It matches my ballgown perfectly."

Edouard chuckled while he escorted her outside. "'Tis why I brought a white rose. I knew 'twould match no matter what color you were wearing."

Pippa curled against Edouard as the carriage headed to Childes House. Romantic, yet still practical. "Clever."

Edouard wrapped his arm about her shoulders then caressed the rose pinned above her heart. "No, just determined you could wear my token tonight."

She rubbed her cheek against his chest, warmth filling her. "I'd have worn your token even if it clashed, you know."

Edouard kissed her hair, but before he could truly kiss her, the carriage halted, and he led her into the fete. When they entered the crowded ballroom, they headed to the cerulean curtain beneath the musicians' balcony where they'd perform the play.

While they waited for the other players, Pippa murmured to Edouard, "Did you get to speak with Father this evening?"

Edouard sighed. "No, he refused to answer my knock again."

She echoed Edouard's sigh. Father did that whenever he was particularly engrossed in his magical experiments, which was often. She usually entered Father's workroom without awaiting a reply, but Edouard couldn't risk that when seeking his blessing. Yet Father couldn't ignore Edouard forever, and once Father listened, he'd approve their courtship. Fingering Edouard's rose on her bodice, she smiled and squeezed his arm. "Father shall answer one day soon."

Edouard hummed and laid his hand over hers on his arm. "I hope so."

A moment later, Wren joined them, and Pippa nearly gasped. Dark green with gold wrens, the arachne silk Wren wore possessed all the magical allure Hawke had promised. He and his merchant partner would make a fortune. "Wren's ballgown is stunning."

Edouard laughed while they watched Wren and Hawke talk. "From the dazed expression on Hawke's face, I'd say he agrees with you."

Pippa tsked. "Be nice. You've worn that expression on occasion too." Like when they'd first met.

Laughing again, Edouard grinned. "Yes, but *I've* never claimed we're just friends to any who ask."

She blushed, but she'd not managed a reply when the Duke and Duchess of Childes thanked everyone for attending their fete and announced Wren's play. Pippa and the other players bowed then slipped behind the curtain and donned their accessories to begin the play.

The performance passed swiftly with few mistakes, and the ballroom erupted into applause once they'd finished. Pippa and Edouard traded grins as they took their bows together. Once the applause quieted, the duchess announced the first waltz, and Edouard led Pippa out onto the floor.

As they twirled, she beamed at Edouard. "The play went marvelously, don't you think?"

Edouard exhaled. "Yes, but I'm relieved 'tis over."

Pippa giggled and nodded at Wren, who was trembling as she and Hawke danced nearby. "Not as relieved as Wren." Although the shy lady's trembling mightn't be due to relief but dancing in Hawke's arms closer than was strictly proper.

Edouard followed Pippa's nod, and his brows flew upward.

"Hawke appears about to kiss Wren in the middle of the ball-room. That'll cause talk."

Pippa flashed a coy smile. "Yes, private kisses are much more sensible—and satisfying." As Edouard had proven over the past nine days and would prove again when he escorted her home.

After the first waltz, Pippa and Edouard strolled about the outskirts of the ballroom like they usually did during all but the first and last waltzes. She glanced at him beneath her lashes while they talked and sipped sparkling wine. How could she persuade him to leave early so they could kiss sooner?

She'd yet to decide when the second waltz ended, and Lord Ravenstone and Miss Winston, the nearest dancing couple, joined them. After congratulating them on the fete play, Lord Ravenstone suggested trading partners for the next dance, which she and Edouard did to avoid being rude.

As their waltz began, Lord Ravenstone smiled down at her. "Your courtship with Lord Blaine seems to be progressing well. I imagine you'll have a happy announcement soon."

Pippa beamed. Even acquaintances saw her and Edouard as a couple. And Father would too, once Edouard spoke with him. "Most likely."

Lord Ravenstone's amber eyes flickered. "Lord Blaine is fortunate that his regard is returned and supported by your families. Not everyone can say that."

She blinked. What a peculiar comment. So when Lord Ravenstone returned her to Edouard after their waltz, she stared after the rugged count for a moment.

Edouard leaned toward her. "Why are you almost frowning?"

Pippa described her conversation with Lord Ravenstone then said, "But enough about Lord Ravenstone. Shall we dance once more then leave?"

Edouard inhaled and gripped his flute of sparkling wine. "We shouldn't. People shall notice if we leave early."

She flashed a brilliant smile. "Then we'll tell them performing tired us." Not that it had.

Edouard chuckled. "A plausible excuse, I suppose." He led her onto the floor for the next waltz then began escorting her from the ballroom.

They'd almost escaped when Elise and Lord Farson joined them near the door. Elise asked, "Leaving already?"

As Edouard stiffly nodded, Pippa managed to smile at Elise. He'd been right about people noticing, but at least his twin wouldn't protest them leaving early together. "We're tired after performing in the play."

Elise's eyes gleamed. "Of course you are." She flicked her husband a flirtatious glance. "It tired me too. We should leave now as well."

Lord Farson smiled, his gaze heated. "And get you to bed."

Pippa and Edouard exchanged grins as the four of them slipped from the ballroom. Elise definitely wasn't protesting.

Once they were ensconced in his carriage, Edouard drew her into his lap. "I've been burning for this all evening."

Her heart pounding, she sighed and threaded her arms about Edouard's neck. "Me too. Why do you think I asked to leave early?"

Edouard began lowering his head. "Why do you think I agreed?"

Then Edouard kissed her, and they devoured each other's mouths as the carriage rumbled home, even more passionately than on their ride six days ago.

When the carriage stopped, Edouard groaned against her lips. "We need to stop."

Panting and trembling, Pippa tightened her arms about Edouard. "No, I never want to stop."

Edouard groaned again then lifted his head. "We really must since we're not married yet."

She inhaled as warmth swamped her. If they were married, she and Edouard could kiss and enjoy hours alone together whenever they wished. Sounded blissful. She could never get enough of either with him—she loved him, and every day his calm strength and steady devotion made her love him more.

Edouard cupped her face in his hands. "We've the rest of our lives for kisses."

Pippa beamed. Her serious and sensible Edouard wouldn't kiss her with such passion or promise forever unless he loved her the way she loved him. No doubt he'd propose to her as soon as Father gave his blessing, and they'd be married before Longnight. Perhaps the next wedding at court would be theirs. How perfect.

She extracted her arms from Edouard's neck. "Would you care to visit for a bit? I don't want tonight to end yet."

CHAPTER 11

$\mathcal{A}$ching from kissing Pippa for the past quarter hour, Edouard swallowed and stared at her. He really should refuse her invitation, but 'twas too tempting to resist since he didn't want tonight to end yet either. He pressed a kiss against her palm. "I'd love to visit for a bit."

Pippa beamed and grasped his hand then bounced from his carriage and tugged him past the rigid Hodges. "We can share a drink in the drawing room."

He grinned as he let Pippa sweep him upstairs. Goddess, she was adorable. Their time alone in recent days had only proven how he needed her beside him for the rest of their lives. Her exuberant joy, radiant vivacity, and sweet passion always cheered him, balanced his sober nature, and inspired him to risk uncertainty. No wonder he'd fallen in love with her and couldn't resist kissing her when they were alone. And from how she never tired of his company and eagerly returned his kisses, she surely felt the same. When he finally managed to speak with Sir Julian, he'd *have* to ask for her hand instead of permission to court her. Waiting would just be too painful. And knowing Pippa, she'd not want a long betrothal, so they'd probably marry before the new year began on Longnight in four months. As long as them being presumptuous enough to court without asking didn't provoke her father into withholding his blessing, which Pippa seemed certain it wouldn't.

Since they'd likely marry soon, Edouard didn't protest when Pippa nestled against him on the sofa after fetching him spiritwine and herself doublewine. She sipped her doublewine then murmured, "I could become accustomed to ending every evening like this."

His body hardening again at their embrace, Edouard chuckled and squeezed Pippa's shoulders. "So could I, as long as 'twas a prelude to kisses." And more than kisses once they were married.

Pippa set their barely touched glasses on the nearby table and threaded her arms about his neck. "What a marvelous idea." Then she kissed him.

Although feeding their mutual hunger when they were so alone wasn't prudent, he still crushed Pippa against him and deepened their kiss. He couldn't deny her or himself. Heat flared in his veins as their mouths fused, and he caressed her back above her ballgown. When she shivered and kissed him harder, he began loosening her laces to slide a hand beneath her shift. He needed—

"What in the Goddess's name is going on?!" a masculine shout ricocheted through the drawing room.

Edouard and Pippa both froze. Then he jerked his hands from her skin, and she whirled to face Sir Julian scowling in the doorway. Flashing a brilliant smile, she said, "Evening, Father."

Edouard stiffened further when Sir Julian's scowl darkened. Sir Julian discovering them torridly kissing was the worst way for him to learn of their courtship. The usually neglectful baronet was obviously furious. Edouard set his jaw. He would be too if Pippa was his daughter. Somehow he must explain and soften Sir Julian's fury. Perhaps asking for her hand tonight would help.

He couldn't let her furious father come between them by withholding his blessing.

Sir Julian surged into the drawing room. "When Hodges found me in my workroom to inform me you'd brought a gentleman inside alone at this hour, I couldn't believe you'd be so brazen, Philippa Grace Hawke. Then to find you two making love in the drawing room."

As Edouard winced, Pippa's face turned scarlet, but she replied, "We weren't making love, just kissing."

Sir Julian snorted and crossed his arms. "Not for long, you weren't." When Pippa began to protest again, he glared at her. "I believe 'tis time for you to retire for the evening."

When Pippa's eyes narrowed, Edouard drew her upright. Until he assured her father of his honorable intentions, Sir Julian would remain too upset to calmly address his daughter. "Go on, Pippa. Your father and I have matters to discuss."

Pippa pursed her lips. "Matters that concern me. I've every right to stay."

He held Pippa's gaze. And if Sir Julian wasn't so furious, he'd ask for her hand in front of her, but her father wouldn't react politely right now. "Yes, but I suspect Sir Julian would prefer you elsewhere."

Pippa sighed yet inclined her head. "Very well. I'll see you tomorrow when you escort me to the Duke and Duchess of Merrilea's ball." She frowned at Sir Julian. "Don't you dare rant at Edouard, Father."

Once Pippa swept from the drawing room, Edouard offered the older gentleman a tight smile. "I apologize for our brazen behavior tonight. We should have been more restrained. However, I would like your blessing to ask Pippa to marry me."

Sir Julian snorted as he poured himself a hefty snifter of spiritwine. "You're only asking that because I discovered you two kissing so wildly."

Tensing at Sir Julian's insult, Edouard straightened to his full height. His voice cold, he retorted, "Actually, I was kissing Pippa so wildly *because* I wish to marry her. I love her dearly, and I believe she loves me just as much."

Sir Julian snickered into his spiritwine. "My daughter is much too young to truly love anyone."

Edouard's chest tightened. Although he'd once worried about that, Pippa had proven over and over she wasn't. "You insult Pippa's loving heart, sir. Yes, she's only eighteen, but in the nearly four months we've been courting, her regard has never wavered."

His lips twisting, Sir Julian drained his snifter. "Believe me, four months of marriage shall cause whatever affection Pippa feels for you to wither."

Edouard stilled. From Sir Julian's bitterness, he must be referring to his deceased wife. Pippa *had* mentioned her parents had eloped at seventeen, but it mustn't have been the blissful marriage she believed. So how could he convince Sir Julian he and Pippa weren't repeating the past? In Sir Julian's current temper, whatever he said now would only infuriate the baronet further. He'd best wait until Sir Julian calmed and he'd decided on a plan for winning Pippa's father's blessing.

He inclined a respectful nod. "I should go. Good evening, Sir Julian."

As he rode home, he drummed his fingers on the carriage seat and considered how to sway Sir Julian. Clearly he must prove he was serious about Pippa and that their regard would last. Although he'd gladly marry her tomorrow and she'd likely prefer that, perhaps slowing their courtship would convince Sir Julian. They could continue attending events together, but he'd quit escorting her so that they'd not be alone. 'Twould only lead to kisses which were becoming harder and harder to control.

He frowned and drummed his fingers harder. Yet slowing their courtship wouldn't convince Pippa's father if he wasn't around to see it. And Sir Julian was obsessed with his magical experiments and rarely left his workroom. Maybe planning events he'd enjoy or spending time at his townhouse would inspire him to join them. Edouard hummed. Then to further prove their commitment, he could join Pippa's family in Childes once the season ended in a month and remain there through Longnight. Surely Sir Julian seeing their steady courtship flourish for several months would be enough. Pippa would love a romantic proposal during the Longnight season, and they could marry early in the new year before everyone returned to Ormas in spring.

So the following day, Edouard penned a note to Pippa stating he'd meet her at the Duke and Duchess of Merrilea's ball and that he'd explain everything then.

When Pippa arrived at Merrilea House with Dane and Xavier, she swirled straight toward him, leaving her brothers behind. "What did Father say to make you break our plans for tonight?"

He sighed and handed Pippa the flute of sparkling wine he'd fetched for her the moment he'd arrived. "He made it clear that he believed you much too young to marry."

Pippa glowered into her flute. "Father's always forgetting how old I am. I'm eighteen, not eight—plenty old enough to marry."

Edouard sighed again as they began strolling about the ballroom. Pippa was so prickly about her age. "I know, but you require your father's blessing to marry until you reach your majority, so we can't provoke him, unless you wish to wait over a year and a half to marry."

A laughing smile curved Pippa's lips. "We could always elope."

He frowned and eyed Pippa askance at her reckless suggestion. "We'll do no such thing. 'Twould be a scandal." He inhaled. "No, we must win your father's blessing." Then he described the plan he'd developed in his carriage, although he didn't confess his love or mention proposing during the Longnight season. His eager Pippa would never be able to wait if everything was settled between them.

Once he finished, Pippa exhaled and inclined her head. "I don't care for the idea of slowing our courtship, but I suppose we must. Although getting Father to join us shall probably be difficult. And when can we kiss if we're never alone?"

Edouard swallowed as heat flooded him at kissing Pippa. "We can't. Our kisses were becoming dangerous anyway."

Pippa grimaced. "Yes, I definitely don't care for slowing our courtship." She blew a sigh. "But I'll do it for you."

He grinned and handed their flutes of sparkling wine to a nearby servant as the opening strains of the first waltz began. "Good. Now shall we dance?"

Pippa beamed while accepting his hand. "At least slowing our courtship doesn't preclude us from dancing the first and last waltzes and enjoying entire events together."

His chest warming, Edouard led Pippa onto the floor. There was his ever-cheery Pippa finding the sunny aspects of any situation. He smiled at her as they began to twirl. "True, my sweet sun nymph."

Pippa blushed. "Careful with those poetic compliments, Lord Blaine." She licked her lips. "Or I might kiss you mid-dance."

He inhaled as his body tightened. Although kisses should remain private, he'd not protest too much if Pippa kissed him like that once they were married.

OVER THE FOLLOWING WEEK, Edouard and Pippa continued meeting at events and spending them together, although they never managed to get Sir Julian to join them, even when they attended an illusion demonstration they'd felt certain would interest him. Yet court didn't notice their slowed courtship. Everyone was gossiping about King Devon's still-missing mermaid and the foundering nightmara talks as well as Wren's scandalous pregnancy that Kit told everyone about the day after she'd discovered it. Although nothing changed for King Devon, Wren's pregnancy was soon resolved by invitations to her and Hawke's wedding ceremony, arranged barely a week after the gossip spread through court.

When Edouard strode into the Moon Chapel at the Great Temple for Hawke and Wren's wedding ceremony—alone since they'd not invited Kit after all her gossiping—he sat beside Pippa and her brothers rather than Elise and her family. He smiled and threaded his fingers through Pippa's. "Where's Sir Julian?" Although the baronet rarely attended social events, surely he'd attend a family wedding ceremony.

Pippa sighed as she caressed his palm with her thumb. "Father refused to leave his workroom."

Dane grimaced beside Pippa. "He's never cared much for wedding ceremonies."

Edouard nearly grimaced as well. Nor marriage, it seemed. Winning Sir Julian's blessing wouldn't be easy. Especially now that the baronet didn't trust him with Pippa.

Beside Dane, Xavier snorted. "And unlike for Aragon and Selena last year, Father didn't feel compelled to attend today since Hawke isn't the future duke."

Pippa stiffened. "You know Father couldn't possibly leave his magical experiments. They're at a critical stage."

As Dane and Xavier traded a sardonic glance, Edouard's mouth tightened. Pippa had said that to explain Sir Julian missing the king's summer masquerade. No doubt 'twas the baronet's typical excuse. How could Pippa's father always be so thoughtless? To distract her and her brothers, he asked, "Are you looking forward to seeing the bloodbinding ceremony today? I've never seen one."

Relaxing, Pippa sighed with a soft smile. "Me either, although I'm looking forward to it. I suspect the ceremony shall be quite romantic."

As her brothers shook their heads, Edouard swallowed and eyed Pippa, who'd made her love of romance clear since the moment they'd met. "Shall you seek a bloodbinding with your husband then?"

Pippa smiled and squeezed his hand. "No. Binding my soul to my husband's until death seems extreme and unnecessary. Genuine love between us is enough for me."

He exhaled. Thank the Goddess for that. Not only was the risk of no heirs too great since bloodbound couples could only have children together, but what if tragedy struck like it had with Mother? Bloodbound couples often died together, so their children would be left orphans if they died young. "I agree. Bloodbindings have always seemed too risky to me."

Pippa chuckled, her gaze gleaming with laughter. "Somehow that fails to surprise me." She squeezed his hand again. "But your dislike of them hardly matters. The lady you love would never need to magically bind herself to you to ensure your devotion."

Warmth heating his cheeks, Edouard said to deflect Pippa and her brothers, "Despite my dislike, Hawke and Wren wanting a bloodbinding ceremony wasn't unexpected."

Dane rumbled, "Bloodbindings *are* perfect for proving eternal commitment to the one you love."

Smoothing his mustache, Xavier smirked. "Which Hawke needs after being a rakehell for years rather than admitting his love for Wren."

Pippa tsked and frowned at Xavier. "I doubt Wren requires such proof now that they're a couple at last."

Edouard hummed. "Although she'll doubtless enjoy being irrevocably bound to Hawke." The shy lady had never been interested in anyone else.

Then he asked about the eerie veiled woman sitting across from them in the pews for Wren's guests, and they discussed the other guests until Mel strode to the altar to begin the wedding ceremony.

Midway through when Mel cut Hawke's and Wren's left palms to begin their bloodbinding, Edouard tensed at Pippa's sniff beside him then turned toward her. She was beaming, but tears shone on her lashes like diamonds. He swallowed and extracted his favorite pocketcloth from the pocket above his heart and handed it to her.

Smiling and squeezing his hand like earlier, Pippa dabbed her damp eyes and mumbled, "'Tis just so lovely."

He swallowed again. Yet Pippa hadn't cried at Aragon and Selena's wedding ceremony. Perhaps she secretly wanted a bloodbinding after all. So after Hawke and Wren left with Mel, Aragon, and Wren's orphanage friend Mistress Kiera to sign the matrimony certificate, he asked, "Did seeing a bloodbinding ceremony change your opinion of them?"

Pippa blinked. "Of course not. Although a bloodbinding was obviously perfect for Hawke and Wren. They were bursting with joy." Her eyes shimmered again. "I hope my husband and I look as radiant on our wedding day."

As Pippa wiped away her fresh tears, Edouard smiled at her with all of his unspoken love. "You're never anything less than radiant, my sun nymph."

Pippa blushed and glanced at Dane and Xavier, likely checking if they'd overheard. When her brothers continued their conversation without pause, she relaxed and grinned at him. "What did I tell you about those poetic compliments, Lord Blaine?"

Although his heart quickened, Edouard slanted Pippa a stern look. "Behave. We're in a holy chapel and not the couple who married today."

Pippa giggled, her coy gaze lowering to his favorite pocketcloth crumpled in her hand. She inhaled. "This is the embroidered pocketcloth I gave you for your natalday last year."

He shrugged as he helped Pippa rise so they could head to the Keyes's townhouse for the reception. "I always carry it. My valet Abbot washes it for me every evening."

Her blush darkening her cheeks once more, Pippa studied him through her lashes. "I should have embroidered more than one pocketcloth then. I'll make you more."

He chuckled and winked at Pippa. "Abbot would greatly appreciate that." Her brothers lingering several paces behind while he handed her into their carriage, he whispered near her ear, "And so would I." As she blushed more, he straightened and said louder, "I'll see you at the reception." Then he turned and strode to his carriage before he could sit beside her instead.

CHAPTER 12

$\mathcal{W}$aiting for Edouard to arrive, Pippa stood between Dane and Xavier near the door of the Keyes's drawing room and ignored her brothers' debate about the refreshments being served. What was taking Edouard so long? He should have left the Great Temple directly behind them.

Eventually, Edouard strode into the drawing room with Elise, Lord Farson, and the gangly Duke of Golddell beside him. As the young duke and her brothers headed to the refreshments table and Lord Farson joined Hawke's merchant partner, Edouard smiled at Pippa and nodded toward Elise beside him. "Sorry for the delay. Elise waylaid me at the Great Temple."

Elise grinned and winked at Pippa. "Well, I've hardly seen you since our mourning ended a month ago, my dear twin."

Pippa chuckled as Edouard snorted and replied, "What nonsense. We still meet for breakfast at least once a week and see each other most days."

Elise arched her brows, her pale-blue eyes gleaming. "But at court events, you're always busy when Pippa is near."

As a blush warmed Pippa's cheeks at that truth, Edouard shook his head and said, "Today is hardly a court event. Hawke and Wren managed to keep it to family and close friends, despite his mother's protests."

Elise laughed. "True." She turned to Pippa. "How did you enjoy the wedding ceremony and bloodbinding?"

Tears pricking her eyes again, Pippa smiled. "'Twas so lovely."

Edouard shook his head with a wry grin. "And long overdue. Hawke and Wren—" He quieted as the eerie veiled woman who'd sat in Wren's pews glided into the drawing room. "Elise, do you know who that veiled woman is? We didn't recognize her from court or the orphanage."

As the veiled woman joined Cassandra Weston, the elder granddaughter Lord and Lady Weston had discovered at the orphanage play several weeks ago, Elise leaned forward and murmured, "According to Selena, she's the witch who created the glamour spell that prevented Hawke from recognizing Wren. Apparently, she's rather powerful—a Rhiannon descendant, I believe."

Pippa inhaled sharply and traded a wide glance with Edouard. Descendants of early witches bloodbound to the founder of human magic, Rhiannon descendants were uncommon and the most powerful of all witches. Pippa swallowed and eyed the veiled witch. No wonder she possessed that eerie air. "I've never met a Rhiannon descendant before."

Edouard nodding too, Elise replied, "Me neither. I must make sure to consult with her before she leaves."

Pippa blinked, but before she could ask why, Hawke and Wren entered with Mel, Aragon, and Mistress Kiera, so everyone cheered to welcome the newlyweds.

Smiling at Hawke and Wren, Elise nodded her farewell. "I'd best find Seanian so we can congratulate the blissful couple."

Once Elise left to join Lord Farson, Pippa arched her brows at Edouard. "We should do the same." Then they'd be free to spend the rest of the reception together.

Edouard hummed. "Let's have some refreshments first. King Devon is congratulating them now."

She nodded, and they headed to the refreshments table, which was still full despite the young duke and her brothers already visiting it twice. Over their sparkling wine, shokolat tortes, and krab pastries, she asked Edouard, "Why does Elise want to consult with the veiled witch?"

Edouard sighed, his face tightening. "Probably about a fertility spell. The ones Elise's healer has attempted haven't succeeded so far."

Pippa frowned and tilted her head. Elise was already risking fertility spells? Those could have a high magical cost. "But Elise and Lord Farson have only been married for two years."

Edouard grimaced. "I know, but Elise assumed she'd become pregnant within a month, and when she didn't, she began to fret. I've attempted to convince her that she must be patient, but she's always wanted a large family, especially after Mother died."

Pippa's chest squeezed. How upsetting for Elise. "I'm certain she'll enjoy that one day."

Edouard sighed again. "I hope so." He glanced at the newly-weds. "King Devon has finished congratulating Hawke and Wren. Shall we?"

She agreed, so they joined Hawke and Wren, who were still glowing. She couldn't help her happy sigh at their joy. Once she and Edouard won Father's blessing, which shouldn't take much longer, they'd doubtless appear the same.

After congratulating Hawke and Wren, Pippa and Edouard drifted along the wall. Inspired by how he treasured her natalday gift from last year, she said, "Your and Elise's natalday is just two and a half weeks away. Any plans yet?"

Edouard shrugged as he sipped his sparkling wine. "Not really."

She smiled and tilted her head. "How about I host a family dinner for you both at our townhouse?" Since they weren't betrothed or married yet, she couldn't give Edouard anything expensive or a faegift, but hosting a family dinner wouldn't be improper. And successfully hosting such an event should prove to Father that she wasn't a child and was old enough to marry. Plus, since 'twould be at the townhouse, she could convince Father to attend so he'd see her and Edouard together.

Edouard grinned at her. "I'd enjoy that very much."

Pippa beamed back, warmth flooding her. "Anyone I should invite besides yourself, Elise and her family, my brothers, and Father? Our Hawke cousins, perhaps?"

Edouard shook his head. "Let's not. The Duchess of Childes would attend too, and I prefer a quiet natalday."

Pippa chuckled and glanced at the duchess laughing with Wren's mother Lady Keyes. The duchess did enjoy arranging elaborate events, and only someone as stubborn as Hawke could resist her. While Pippa was turning back to Edouard, her gaze caught on two other guests, and she stilled. King Devon was talking with Mistress Kiera, his stare as intense as at his summer masquerade with his mermaid. And although she'd not noticed until now, Mistress Kiera possessed the same dark-blonde curls as King Devon's mysterious lady.

Edouard leaned closer. "Pippa, what is it?"

She grinned as she nodded toward King Devon and Mistress Kiera. "I suspect King Devon has found his mermaid at last."

Edouard peered at the engrossed couple then chuckled. "I suspect he has too. Who would have guessed his mysterious mermaid was actually an orphanage matron?"

Pippa hummed and sipped her sparkling wine. "Well, it does explain why King Devon never found her at court." She sighed. "But him finding her at his cousin's wedding is so romantic."

Edouard slanted her a warm glance. "Yes, cousins' weddings seem the ideal event to meet your future spouse."

She giggled, her heart fluttering at Edouard referring to their first meeting. "I agree."

· · ·

THE FOLLOWING MORNING, Pippa wrote inviting Elise and her family to the natalday dinner. She also wrote to their cooks inquiring about their favorite dishes. Then she embroidered half a dozen pocketcloths with Edouard's initials in an ornate tenth-century style like she'd promised, which she'd hand to him beneath a table at Lady Morwynne's card party the following evening. People would gossip if they saw her giving him a gift.

After embroidering Edouard's pocketcloths, she visited the fashionable shops near Broad Street to find a small natalday gift for him because just hosting a family dinner didn't seem enough. At Rose's Ribbons, her favorite haberdashery in Ormas, the owner's grandmother, an expert on historical needlework, taught her how to embroider like they did in the tenth century with the traditional materials. Edouard would love such a piece even though 'twas a mere imitation.

Since Edouard's natalday embroidery was elaborate, she embroidered it whenever she could, including at her embroidery party four afternoons after Hawke and Wren's wedding, despite it being the first event she'd hosted for court. Thankfully, her event went well, and only Elise noticed her unusual embroidery. The other ladies who attended spent the entire afternoon gossiping about King Devon's mysterious mermaid being a foreign princess. Both Pippa and Elise exchanged puzzled frowns at that curious rumor since they'd guessed his mermaid was Mistress Kiera from his behavior at the reception. Yet neither said anything because they couldn't reveal the king's private affairs, although they did discuss it once the other ladies had left and agreed that King Devon would introduce Mistress Kiera as his future queen before the season ended on Harvestfete.

So when King Devon's invitation to a Harvestfete masquerade arrived a few days later, Pippa knew that must be when he'd introduce Mistress Kiera to court. Because of that, she attempted to persuade Father he should attend, but he vehemently refused to leave his magical experiments for such a frivolous event, and she couldn't risk the servants overhearing and starting gossip by revealing the truth, so she sighed and accepted his refusal. However, she and Edouard discussed the upcoming masquerade on a ride with her brothers and planned their costumes together like they had for the king's summer masquerade.

She collected her costume on Edouard's and Elise's natalday in the morning before finishing her preparations for their natalday dinner. Then she dressed in an ivory silk gown embroidered with gold suns in honor of Edouard's endearment for her and headed to Father's workroom.

As Father sprinkled faedust into vials without looking up, Pippa smiled and touched his shoulder. "Don't forget, dinner is within the hour."

Eyeing his vials, Father scribbled notes into his journal. "I'll just have a tray here. I can't leave my experiments since they're at a critical stage."

Her chest twisted. Of course they were. She inhaled then brightened her smile. "You can't skip dinner tonight, Father. We've company, remember? Edouard—Lord Blaine—along with his sister and her family, including the young Duke of Golddell."

Father snorted and scribbled harder. "I'm not socializing with that rakehell and his family."

Pippa stiffened. Until now, Father had said nothing when she'd mentioned Edouard, so she'd thought he'd forgotten the ardent kisses he'd seen. "Edouard isn't a rakehell. You'd see that if you got to know him. Please, Father. 'Tis important to me."

Father scowled as he grasped a bubbling vial. "No." He waved toward the door. "Run along. I've experiments to perform."

Her shoulders sagged. Father was too engrossed in his magical experiments to listen right now. But he would as soon as he truly got to know Edouard. Straightening, she headed to the drawing room.

When she joined them, Dane and Xavier traded frowns, then

Dane rumbled, "Father refused to attend, didn't he? Do you want us to drag him out?"

Pippa grimaced. That would only make Father more determined not to get to know Edouard. "No, but thanks for the offer."

Xavier smoothed his mustache. "The rest of us shall probably enjoy ourselves more if Father isn't here. He'd spend all evening quizzing Farson and Arvan about the nightmara's magical abilities and asking if they could acquire nightmara hair or some such for his magical experiments."

She almost sighed. That *did* sound like Father, and 'twouldn't be an enjoyable natalday for Edouard or Elise. Then Edouard strode into the drawing room, and she beamed. "Happy natalday."

As Dane and Xavier echoed her, Edouard inclined his head. "Thanks."

Pippa clung to her bright smile while she explained, "It shall be just us plus Elise and her family tonight. Unfortunately, Father is too busy with his magical experiments to attend."

Edouard's jaw tightened. "I see."

Xavier slapped his shoulder. "Don't take it as a personal affront. Father rarely joins us for any meal other than breakfast."

She winced when Edouard humphed before replying, "I don't, but I'd hoped to speak with Sir Julian tonight. I've only met him briefly a few times, and we need to become better acquainted."

Dane and Xavier exchanged knowing smiles, then Dane said, "Probably your best chance of becoming better acquainted with Father is asking to see his magical experiments. Just remember to appear sincere in your interest, or Father shall take offense."

Pippa blinked. She should have thought of that, except Father's magical experiments were so esoteric that she'd couldn't imagine anyone wanting to see them.

Edouard arched a brow. "Are his magical experiments practical?"

She and her brothers glanced at each other then shrugged in unison. She replied, "I'm not sure, but I doubt it from what he's mentioned."

Edouard shook his head and grimaced. "I probably shouldn't ask about them then. I doubt I could feign sincere interest, and I don't want to offend Sir Julian further."

Dane and Xavier both frowned, but before they could ask how Edouard had offended Father, Elise swept into the drawing room on Lord Farson's arm with the Duke of Golddell behind them. Elise grinned at them. "Evening, everyone."

Once she and the others wished Elise happy natalday, Pippa waved toward the door. "Now that we're all here, let's head to dinner." She smiled as Edouard escorted her to the family dining room. He and his twin were certain to enjoy the meal she'd arranged.

Then she beamed when Elise smiled as her husband served her the first course, giving her two crusty rolls rather than one. Elise said, "Rolls and butter—my favorite. And cream of mushroom soup with thyme—Edouard's favorite. How did you know?"

Pippa chuckled over her first spoonful of soup. "I consulted your cooks, of course. What kind of natalday dinner would it be if I didn't serve your favorite foods?" She chuckled again. "Although not all your favorites go together as well as these two. For twins, you two have disparate tastes."

Squeezing her hand beneath the table, Edouard grinned at her. "'Tis because Elise adores bread and other starchy foods, while as a sensible gentleman, I prefer more substantial foods like meat and dairy."

Pippa and the others laughed when Elise pursed her lips at Edouard's clearly usual jest then drawled, "Butter is dairy too, you know."

Edouard shrugged then squeezed Pippa's hand again while he began devouring his cream of mushroom soup. "Thanks for arranging such a wonderful dinner for us. 'Tis a perfect natalday gift."

Her cheeks warming, Pippa returned Edouard's squeeze. "I'm glad you like it." Then she turned to Elise and asked what else she'd done to celebrate her natalday.

The delicious natalday dinner she'd arranged passed swiftly amid lively conversation and laughter. Edouard and Elise enjoyed the later courses of pastry-wrapped beefsteak, butter-garlic noodles, sour-cream chicken, and savory crepes as much as they enjoyed the first. Then they all chuckled as Edouard toasted his younger—by five minutes—sister for her improved taste over their molasses-crumb pie, the one favorite food they shared.

Following dinner, Pippa and the others returned to the drawing room, the gentlemen not lingering about the table over their spiritwine. Then everyone played riddle games and dancing chairs until Elise decided she and her family had best return home.

After they'd gone, Edouard rose as well. "I should leave too. 'Tis late."

Pippa swallowed her sigh. If only Edouard could stay longer. Yet she smiled and took his arm. "I'll walk you out." She must give him his natalday gift in private. And perhaps a kiss or two. Their last kiss had been ages ago, and surely he couldn't refuse a natalday kiss. Once they were alone, she said, "Before you leave, I've something for you in the morning room."

Edouard eyed her. "We really shouldn't risk being alone in a room together."

Almost sighing again, she drew Edouard to a stop before the morning room. Given his unease, she'd better not attempt any kisses. Too bad. "Please? 'Tis a natalday gift."

His brow furrowing, Edouard blinked. "But you already hosted tonight's delicious dinner."

Pippa shrugged. "I felt dinner wasn't enough." She beamed to persuade Edouard then tugged him toward the morning room. "Come on."

CHAPTER 13

While Pippa drew him into the morning room, Edouard gulped a steadying breath to control the heat flaring in his veins at being truly alone with her for the first time in a month. Surely he could manage to accept a natalday gift in private without kissing her like a lusty satyr.

Still beaming, Pippa handed him a cheerful, neatly wrapped gift. "Here you are."

He opened his gift without tearing the vivid paper. Pippa had clearly taken time wrapping it, and he couldn't destroy her effort. Then he inhaled at the exquisite embroidery inside. Sewn in the ornate tenth-century style, the silk and goldwork embroidery was of a sun nymph twirling about a meadow at dawn.

Pippa leaned forward, her gaze bright. "I consulted an expert on historical needlework and used silk and gold thread on silk canvas like they preferred in the tenth century. And of course, I chose a magical, pastoral scene like they would have and used their ornate style. Do you like it?"

Edouard caressed the glowing sun nymph in the embroidery. Except for the hair, she embodied Pippa. "'Tis perfect. I'll hang it in my chambers where I can see it every morning. It might make mornings more bearable."

Pippa giggled and touched his arm. "I'm glad my gift shall cheer you."

He laid his hand on Pippa's, his heart quickening. "Not just your gift cheers me." Unable to resist, he brushed a tender kiss against her lips but withdrew before either of them could deepen it. "Everything about you does."

Her cheeks pink, Pippa cupped his face with her free hand. "Oh, Edouard."

Holding her gaze, he shifted to kiss her palm, and they both shivered and began leaning forward as their hunger thickened the air. Then a door down the hall thudded, and he jerked back, stumbling into the sofa behind him. He didn't dare kiss Pippa again. Neither of them could resist each other, and Sir Julian would never approve of their betrothal if he discovered them torridly kissing once more.

He gritted a tight smile. "I must go. Thanks for the wonderful natalday dinner and gift. I'll see you at the Harvestfete masquerade tomorrow."

Pippa sighed but nodded. "Until tomorrow."

Edouard strode from the morning room then hurried back to Blaine House and headed upstairs to his chambers to hang Pippa's embroidery like he'd promised. And the following morning, he smiled when he opened his eyes and saw it first thing. He must tell her when they met at tonight's masquerade.

To not be late like he'd been for the king's summer masquerade, he ate an early dinner then changed into his horned man costume and headed to the palace before even the fashionable Kit was ready. As one of the first guests to arrive, he sat beneath the musicians' balcony to wait for Pippa without attracting attention. Not long later, he stiffened when Kit arrived wearing gauzy Tsarkan veils and bedlah that hid little. *What* was his frivolous stepmother wearing? And why? Although always flattering, her attire had never been that revealing before.

He was about to speak with Kit when Pippa and her brothers arrived, so he fetched two flutes of sparkling wine and joined them instead. Speaking with Kit would likely accomplish nothing anyway since she never listened to him and would doubtless refuse to leave or change into a more appropriate costume. He smiled at Pippa. "You look lovely."

Glittering in her gold deer costume, Pippa beamed as she accepted her flute of sparkling wine. "Thanks. You look very manly."

Dressed as matching werebears, Dane tsked at Pippa's flirting, while Xavier simply chuckled. Then Xavier's eyes widened, and he asked, "Have you seen Lady Blaine's costume? She must be *desperate* to catch Lord Ravenstone to dress as a harem lady."

Edouard grimaced as Pippa and Dane turned to study Kit. Although she was only his stepmother, everyone staring at her and gossiping was still embarrassing. Thankfully, if King Devon introduced Mistress Kiera like they suspected he would, everyone would be gossiping about that tomorrow, not Kit.

Pippa tilted her head, her enchanted gold glitter from the previous masquerade sparkling in her rich chestnut hair. "Lady Blaine does look beautiful though. She certainly possesses the perfect figure for such a costume. I could never wear anything like that." She glanced at him beneath her lashes. "In public, at least."

He swallowed as his body tightened at Pippa wearing a similar costume in their chambers one day. Dear Goddess, he'd not resist ravishing her if she did.

Dane and Xavier exchanged a grimace, then Dane arched his brows at Edouard and asked, "Did Father happen to overhear brazen flirting like that? Was that how you offended him?"

His hunger doused, Edouard winced then admitted, "No, he discovered us kissing after the Duchess of Childes's fete."

Pippa pursed her lips. "Now Father has this ridiculous notion that Edouard is a rakehell and refuses to get to know him."

As Dane hummed and eyed Edouard, Xavier coughed a laugh then drawled, "Awkward."

Heat creeping up his neck, Edouard held their gazes.

Somehow he must reassure Pippa's brothers about his intentions without revealing them to her. Until they'd won Sir Julian's blessing, their courtship needed to remain restrained, and they barely managed that with matters unsettled between them.

Before he could devise a reply that Pippa could overhear, Elise and Farson glided over, dressed as a mara couple. Arvan wasn't with them tonight since he was much too young to attend a masquerade, even if 'twas to introduce their future queen. While Pippa and Elise complimented each other's costumes with Farson chuckling beside them, Edouard murmured to Dane and Xavier, "I intend to marry Pippa as soon as your father approves."

He began to relax when Dane smiled and replied, "We know. Your intentions were obvious from the start."

Xavier snickered. "As were Pippa's to accept you."

Dane frowned at his younger brother. "Which initially concerned us since Pippa appeared to be settling for the first eligible gentleman she met."

Edouard tensed again. *Settling*?

Xavier smoothed his mustache beneath his werebear mask. "But Pippa has met plenty of other eligible gentlemen since her come out, and her interest in you hasn't wavered."

No longer frowning, Dane nodded. "So Pippa was simply fortunate enough to meet the right gentleman first."

Edouard smiled at his future brothers-in-law. "I'm the fortunate one." He exhaled. "If I can ever meet with your father and win his blessing. Hopefully, he shan't be able to continue avoiding me once I join you at Hawke Manor after the season ends tonight."

She and Pippa having just fallen silent, Elise interjected, "Haven't you noticed the continued invitations? I doubt the season is ending on Harvestfete this year."

As Edouard stilled, Farson sighed and added, "The council at least can't adjourn until the Nightmara-Calatini Treaty is renewed."

Elise chuckled. "And you know the rest of court shan't leave Ormas until the most influential nobles do, so the season shall be extended indefinitely."

Edouard suppressed a grimace. Not only would he need to endure more court events, but Sir Julian could continue to easily avoid him. "How wonderful."

Pippa grinned at him. "I'll miss returning to the country too, but at least we'll still be together."

He was smiling back when Elise gasped as Kit swept past them. Elise muttered, "Why is Kit dressed as a Tsarkan concubine?" Her brow furrowing, she eyed Kit flirting with an unreceptive Lord Ravenstone. "She's not been herself since Hawke and Wren announced their betrothal. I always thought she flirted with Hawke to needle Wren, but perhaps she truly cared for him."

Edouard couldn't help snorting. Their fashionable stepmother only cared about her influence at court. "Or more likely, she's embarrassed her gossip was silenced by their inevitable marriage."

While Pippa eyed him, Elise pursed her lips and said, "Kit isn't as heartless as she likes to pretend. I'd better talk to her after King Devon opens the masquerade. Maybe she'll admit what's troubling her."

Before Edouard could reply, King Devon swept Mistress Kiera to the center of the palace's teeming ballroom, and silence echoed as the crowd gawked. Although the king hadn't proclaimed her his mysterious mermaid yet, everyone could recognize her from her arachne silk costume which resembled her costume from the previous masquerade. So the silent crowd continued to stare as King Devon and Mistress Kiera danced the first waltz alone.

When the second waltz began, Edouard and Pippa joined them, as did Elise and Farson along with their Hawke cousins, but the floor remained nearly empty. Despite the weight of everyone's stares, which were mostly fixed on King Devon and

Mistress Kiera, Edouard grinned at Pippa as they twirled. "I hung your embroidery in my chambers last night, so 'twas what I saw first this morning."

Pippa grinned back and squeezed his shoulder. "Did it cheer you as much as you'd hoped?"

He leaned closer, his heart warming. Only waking with Pippa beside him would have cheered him more—not that he could tell her that yet. So he simply replied, "I smiled when I woke for once, so yes."

Her grin turning radiant, Pippa eased closer until her gold skirt brushed his legs. "I'm glad."

Although his pulse surged, Edouard spun her in a complicated turn rather than pulling her against him. They were in public after all.

A blush darkening her cheeks as she returned to his arms, Pippa peeked at him through her lashes. "Sorry, in my delight that my gift cheered you, I forgot we were in public."

He couldn't help a laugh. "How could you forget when most of court is watching us?"

Pippa pursed her lips. "They're watching King Devon and Mistress Kiera, not us." Her voice softened, "Although even if they were, being with you often makes me forget everything else."

His pulse flaring again, Edouard pulled Pippa closer until her skirt brushed him like earlier. Surely he could risk that despite being in public. "I understand that."

Yet as they danced, he ached more and more to pull Pippa even closer and kiss her.

After he spun her in another complicated twirl to prevent that, Pippa glided back into his arms but didn't protest when he held her at the proper distance. Obviously attempting to distract them both, she grinned and said, "The palace's ballroom is even more stunning the second time. How many times have you visited the palace?"

He shrugged as he eyed her tempting lips. "A dozen times or

so. Since I'm not interested in politics, I rarely attend petitions at court, and King Devon only hosts one or two events a season. Although that may change once he marries."

Pippa's grin brightened. "I hope so. I'd love to study the palace's architecture more. 'Tis fascinating and so beautiful."

Edouard nodded and returned Pippa's grin. She'd definitely enjoy a tour of the palace as much as she had that of the Great Temple. Once King Devon was no longer busy introducing Mistress Kiera to court, he'd write to arrange a tour of the palace. Although the palace wasn't a public building like the Great Temple, the king wouldn't deny a tour for his cousin.

Even though they probably shouldn't, Edouard and Pippa continued dancing together during the next waltz when other couples filled the floor at last. Fortunately, King Devon halted the dancing after that and introduced Lady Kiera as his betrothed before announcing the Harvestfete pantomime. And watching the comedy about a witch who could see the ghosts of her ancestors with often hilarious consequences helped ease the hunger simmering between him and Pippa.

Since they'd be too tempted to dance a third time, which would cause talk, if they remained alone like they usually did, Edouard escorted Pippa to the nearest group after the Harvestfete pantomime, and they continued circulating throughout the masquerade.

King Devon and Lady Kiera joined them while they were talking with Lord Frederic Cassell—the only son of Lord Osteen, the councilor who represented Edouard's home duchy of Landcastle—and Lord Frederic's wife Madeleine, who'd been Selena's first bride witness and adored art like all of Selena's friends. Once everyone exchanged greetings, Lady Kiera asked Lady Frederic about her paintings, and they discussed that until the Cassells left to join Lord and Lady Osteen.

Pippa beamed at Lady Kiera. "How amazing you knew all about Lady Frederic Cassell's paintings."

Lady Kiera shrugged and flashed a wry smile. "Over the past

two weeks, the Duchess of Childes taught me about everyone at court, and she knew plenty about her daughter-in-law's friend."

His green eyes warm, King Devon grinned at Lady Kiera. "She's been impressing everyone tonight by greeting them with personal details as if she already knows them."

Edouard and Pippa blinked at each other, then Pippa said to Lady Kiera, "You remembered details about *everyone* at court? I could never do that. You'll make an amazing queen, Lady Kiera. King Devon was blessed to have found you at last."

Edouard nodded to echo Pippa. Despite her common birth, Lady Kiera naturally possessed a regal yet warm air, and she was both insightful and industrious—the perfect match for the dutiful King Devon. And the matriarchal nightmara who valued merit over rank would adore her, which was excellent for the renewal of the essential Nightmara-Calatini Treaty.

As King Devon beamed, Lady Kiera blushed and twisted the Vireni betrothal ring on her left hand. "Nonsense, I was the blessed one for Devon to find me and ask me to act as his queen."

To ease Lady Kiera's blushes, Edouard arched a brow and asked her, "Since the duchess helped you prepare for tonight, I assume her dinner tomorrow is in your honor?"

Lady Kiera nodded. "I hope you both can attend. I'll be relieved to see more friendly faces there."

King Devon squeezed Lady Kiera's arm. "They'll all be friendly as soon as they get to know you."

Edouard and Pippa traded smiles. The obvious love between their king and future queen boded well for Calatini's future. And was heartwarming as well. He replied, "Pippa and I shall both gladly attend the duchess's dinner."

Pippa tilted her head. "And since 'tis in your honor, Lady Kiera, Father shall doubtless attend too."

Edouard almost snorted. Meeting their future queen *should* be more important than performing magical experiments. Then he smiled. Sir Julian attending tomorrow meant he could finally begin proving to Pippa's father that he and Pippa belonged together.

Although King Devon's eyes narrowed, Lady Kiera merely nodded and said, "I'll look forward to meeting Sir Julian."

Then King Devon and Lady Kiera left to talk with other guests, so Edouard and Pippa headed to the refreshments table for more sparkling wine before circulating again. However, he stilled when they encountered Kit flirting with the suave Duke of Oakmoor. Unlike the genial Lord Ravenstone, the aging rake-hell couldn't be trusted not to seduce his scantily clad step-mother in public.

He muttered to Pippa, "We'd better rescue Kit before trouble befalls her." At her nod, they strode over to Kit and the Duke of Oakmoor. He managed a beseeching smile. "Stepmother, Pippa is tired. Could you escort her home with me?"

Her smoky gaze flickering, Kit sighed. "I suppose." She turned to the duke and fluttered her lashes. "Until later, your grace."

Once he and Pippa settled in his carriage across from Kit, he frowned at Kit draped across the forward seat. "Why did you choose to dress as a Tsarkan concubine tonight?"

Kit smirked back. "Elise asked me the same thing earlier. Twins."

His mouth tightening, Edouard sighed. How could Father have left this frivolous and brazen lady as his responsibility? "Why, Kit?"

Kit tossed her head. "My coterie expects bold and sultry attire from the fashionable Countess of Blaine. I couldn't *possibly* disap-point them."

He snorted. Kit's gauzy Tsarkan veils and bedlah were worse than bold and sultry.

Nestled against him, Pippa blinked at Kit. "How could you bear wearing such a revealing costume in public?"

Kit purred a laugh. "But I wasn't." She snapped her fingers, and her costume became a crimson ballgown. Her lips pinched, she drawled, "An illusion. Fitting, wouldn't you say?"

Edouard glowered at Kit. "Father wouldn't have called his wife appearing like a concubine *fitting*."

Kit straightened from her sultry sprawl. "No, he wouldn't have."

Pippa frowned and leaned forward. "Are you all right, Lady Blaine? Elise said you've not been yourself recently."

Warmth filling his chest, he smiled at Pippa and squeezed her shoulders. Her tender concern for his often sardonic stepmother was sweet. No wonder he couldn't help loving Pippa.

CHAPTER 14

*a*s Edouard squeezed her shoulders, Pippa eyed his fashionable stepmother with a frown. Lady Blaine pretending to flaunt her body with an illusion and calling that fitting wasn't right—Elise's concern had been well-founded. So although Lady Blaine probably wouldn't admit anything to her, she'd still needed to ask if Lady Blaine was all right.

Her smile blinding, Lady Blaine replied, "I'm fine." She arched a brow. "Although you calling me Lady Blaine makes me feel ancient. Call me Kit, Pippa. We share the same cousins after all." Kit studied them nestled together and smirked. "And one day, we'll be closer family than that."

Pippa blushed but couldn't help her smile. So they would, once she and Edouard could win Father's blessing. And now that Lady Kiera was at court, Father *had* to attend at least one event to meet their future queen, which meant he'd see her and Edouard together too. After he did, he'd soon realize they were in love and allow their marriage.

Before she or Edouard could reply, the carriage halted at her family's townhouse, and Edouard helped her alight then escorted her up the front steps. At the door, he pressed a tender kiss against her palm. "I'll see you tomorrow."

Tingling flooding her, she sighed and caressed Edouard's face. If only they could exchange a true kiss, but he was clearly determined to wait until Father approved. "Until tomorrow."

Pippa drifted inside and up to her chambers. She'd find Father directly after breakfast tomorrow to tell him about the Duchess of Childes's dinner in honor of Lady Kiera. He'd grumble for a bit but would concede to the inevitable before luncheon.

So the following morning, Pippa bounced into Father's workroom with a grin. "How are your magical experiments going?"

Hunched over his journal, Father vaguely smiled toward her. "Well enough, except I ran out of faedust this morning." He sighed. "I must visit Over the Walle for more."

She suppressed her laugh. Father made visiting the witch shop for magical creatures sound like an onerous quest to defeat an army of bloodthirsty orcs. "You could send a footman to purchase more faedust and continue your magical experiments while he's shopping."

Father grunted. "No point. Besides, I'm the only one who can test if the faedust is pure enough."

As Father rose, Pippa touched his arm to draw his attention. "Before you leave, I've some important news from court. King Devon introduced his betrothed Lady Kiera at his Harvestfete masquerade yesterday. The Duchess of Childes is hosting a dinner tonight in her honor. You should attend to meet her."

Father patted her hand. "Not tonight. Since I must waste the morning purchasing more faedust, I shan't have time for dinner. Another evening perhaps." He grabbed his satchel then hurried from the workroom.

She frowned after Father, her chest tight. Surely meeting Calatini's future queen was more important than his magical experiments. She'd ask him again once he returned from Over the Walle.

And she did when Father returned several hours later, yet he still refused to attend. So she asked him a third time before dressing for dinner, and he repeated his earlier refusals, almost shouting this time. After that, she withdrew, her chest tighter than ever.

When she entered the duchess's drawing room with just Dane and Xavier flanking her, Edouard frowned and took her arm. "You couldn't convince Sir Julian to attend tonight?"

Pippa managed a wry smile as her chest twisted again. "Unfortunately not. I just hope King Devon and Lady Kiera don't notice Father's absence after I promised he'd attend."

His lips tight, Edouard rubbed her palm with his thumb. "'Tisn't your fault that Sir Julian wouldn't listen." He grinned at her. "So what food do you think the duchess shall serve in honor of King Devon's mysterious mermaid?"

Edouard's attempt to cheer her banishing the ache in her chest, she chuckled and returned his grin. "Seafood, obviously."

Her quip was proven correct. Every course except dessert featured several seafood dishes, from whitekrab soup to seared scallops to honey-glazed salmon. Amid all the delicious food and toasts to Lady Kiera, Pippa was soon beaming, and everyone else was enjoying themselves too—other than perhaps Kit, who appeared unusually subdued.

Over her spiced apple tart with vahnila sweetice molded into seashells, Pippa nodded at Kit then murmured to Edouard, "Kit still doesn't seem herself. Did she say why after we parted last night?"

Edouard shrugged. "No, but Kit and I aren't in the habit of exchanging confidences. I'm simply relieved she's wearing a less revealing gown tonight."

Pippa tilted her head. Maybe Kit was regretting how she flaunted herself at the Harvestfete masquerade. "I hope she's more cheerful before long."

Edouard quirked a wry grin as he finished his apple tart. "I expect she shall be since she mentioned she'll be hosting another court event in a few weeks. That always cheers her."

After dinner, everyone returned to the drawing room, and

once they'd fetched sparkling wine, Pippa and Edouard joined Elise and Lord Farson, who were alone again tonight at the young Duke of Golddell's request. Despite the excellent food, the teenage boy hadn't wanted to endure a lengthy court dinner, and he'd already met Lady Kiera at Hawke and Wren's wedding ceremony.

Edouard arched a brow at Lord Farson. "How did Lady Kiera's meeting with the nightmara queen-heir go this morning?"

Lord Farson grinned. "Well. Lady Moonbud was impressed that Calatini's future queen isn't the usual court lady."

Pippa studied King Devon and Lady Kiera circulating about the drawing room. Although not the usual court lady, Lady Kiera was charming everyone at court tonight like she had yesterday at the Harvestfete masquerade. Definitely an amazing future queen.

Lord Farson continued, "Although Lady Moonbud did request time to become acquainted with Lady Kiera before negotiating the treaty."

Edouard sipped his sparkling wine and shrugged. "Taking time is always prudent."

Elise slanted a pointed look at Pippa. "Somehow I'm not surprised you agree."

While Edouard stiffened at his twin's unfair reproach, Pippa pursed her lips. Yes, he'd taken their courtship slowly at first because of her age, but he'd have proposed by now if Father wasn't proving difficult. Yet she couldn't say that, so instead she asked Elise, "Did Kit share what was troubling her yesterday?"

Elise sighed as they eyed Kit sipping spiced cider alone with her gaze averted from Hawke, Wren, and Mel beside the refreshments table. "No, but I'm certain it involves Hawke and Wren, considering how she's been avoiding them tonight." Elise frowned. "I should try talking with her again while she's alone. Come along, Seanian."

Once Elise and Lord Farson left to join Kit, Edouard smiled at Pippa. "Thanks for distracting Elise."

She smiled back, her heart soft with love. "Of course."

They were drifting toward the refreshments table when King Devon and Lady Kiera joined them. Lady Kiera smiled at her and said, "You must introduce me to your father, Pippa. I'm curious about those magical experiments of his."

She gripped her near-empty flute of sparkling wine, heat scorching her neck. "Sadly, Father was unable to attend tonight."

His eyes narrow, King Devon hummed. "He couldn't leave his magical experiments at a critical stage, I suppose."

As Edouard squeezed her arm, Pippa blushed harder. Although a distant cousin, even King Devon knew Father's frequent excuse. "Yes."

Lady Kiera leaned toward her with a gentle smile. "It must be difficult for Sir Julian to get away, but I'll be glad to meet him whenever he does." She chuckled. "And his absence means we can discuss topics that would bore him. I've been wanting to ask, as another lady who's new to court, what's been your favorite part of the season?"

Her embarrassment about Father fading at Lady Kiera's kindness, Pippa smiled and glanced at Edouard beneath her lashes. "Spending time with people I'd not see otherwise."

Despite their royal audience, Edouard returned her warm glance. "'Tis my favorite part as well."

King Devon and Lady Kiera exchanged grins, then Lady Kiera said, "I must remember that when frayed by court gossips."

They talked for a few more moments, then King Devon and Lady Kiera excused themselves to continue circulating.

Returning their empty flutes to a nearby servant, Edouard smiled at Pippa. "Shall we find Kit and have her chaperone us home again?"

She nodded but murmured as they threaded through the crowd, "I'd prefer if you escorted me home alone."

Edouard sighed. "So would I, but you know we can't risk that until we win your father's blessing, so Kit joining us is the closest we can get to alone."

Pippa echoed Edouard's sigh. True, if they asked her brothers or Elise and Lord Farson, 'twould be two people rather than one. But needing a chaperone at all was irritating. She *had* to get Father to attend some court events soon.

THE FOLLOWING MORNING, Pippa found Father in his workroom like she had before. Keeping her voice light, she said, "You missed an excellent dinner last night. Lady Kiera asked to meet you too. She's curious about your magical experiments."

Father lifted his tousled head, his blue eyes bright. "Is our future queen a witch then?"

She smiled. She'd known Lady Kiera's interest would please Father. Surely he'd agree to attend a court event now. "The only gossip I've heard about Lady Kiera is that she's a lost princess who grew up in an orphanage. Nothing about her possessing magic, so I doubt she's a witch."

Father sagged and turned back to his journal. "She was probably just feigning interest to be polite."

Pippa beamed at Father to hearten him. "Perhaps, but Lady Kiera did ask, so you should meet her and find out."

Father humphed as he began measuring out faedust. "No point. If she's not a witch, she'd not comprehend anything about my experiments. Just like you and your brothers."

Her throat tightening, she touched Father's shoulder. She'd not realized her disinterest in his magical experiments was so obvious. "Father—"

He pulled away and waved her toward the door. "Go on, Pippa. I've a busy morning ahead of me."

She sighed and left Father's workroom. She'd attempt to convince Father again later.

Over the next three weeks, she kept asking Father to attend court events to meet Lady Kiera, but he kept refusing. She practically begged him to attend Elise's rout party, saying him attending an event hosted by Edouard's twin was important to her. Yet Father still flatly refused to leave his magical experiments. So by the evening of Kit's fire ball, she didn't even bother asking him to attend.

Since that morning had been the first hard frost of the season, Pippa dressed in her warmest gown of goldenrod wool before joining Dane and Xavier in the carriage heated by wrapped fire stones at their feet.

Xavier quirked his brows at her as the carriage headed to Jade Garden for the fire ball. "I see Father refused to join us again."

She sighed and smoothed her heavy cloak. "I didn't ask him this time. He's clearly not going to attend any court events. Edouard and I shall have to figure out another way for Father to get to know him." If only she knew what.

Dane frowned. "Yes, Father has been even more resistant than normal about this. He wouldn't listen at all when I attempted to talk to him about Edouard."

Pippa smiled at her oldest brother. "Thanks for trying, Dane." She pursed her lips. "But Father is convinced that Edouard is a rakehell thanks to a few kisses." If she wasn't in love with Edouard, she'd bring home a *true* rakehell like the Duke of Oakmoor to prove to Father how wrong he was.

Dane and Xavier traded a glance, then Dane replied, "I'm not certain that Father is objecting to Edouard specifically. He keeps muttering that you're too young."

She blinked. But Mother and Father had both been a year younger when they'd married. She sighed. Father had probably forgotten how old she was again. "What nonsense. I'm sure once Father sees me and Edouard together at events, he'll realize I'm no longer a child."

Xavier smirked at her. "Especially if he discovers you two kissing again."

Pippa almost winced as the carriage slowed. "Considering Father's fury before, *that* wouldn't be wise." Then she leapt from the carriage and swirled to Kit, who was her sultry, fashionable self again. After their brief greetings, Pippa asked, "Where's Edouard?"

Kit waved toward Edouard striding over from the near wall. "There. He's been hovering nearby like a griffin awaiting his lost mate."

As Edouard captured her arm and swept her into the crowd, leaving her brothers behind, she gazed about the sprawling garden. The many open braziers lighting the velvety night and the wild music of the fire dancers made the air thrum with excitement and romance—like a masquerade or the Summerday festivities they'd seen here, but more so. "Kit plans the most spectacular events."

Edouard hummed while handing her a mug of spiced cider. "So she does." He grimaced. "They're *almost* worth the fortune they cost."

Pippa giggled at Edouard's usual irritation over his young stepmother's frivolous extravagance. She smiled at him over her steaming mug. "A few lively dances amid the braziers shall make you forget all about the expense."

Edouard slanted her a heated glance. "We must test that once we finish our spiced cider."

Tingling warmth surging through her, she set aside her mug untasted. "I'm finished now. Shall we?"

Edouard grinned as he set his full mug beside hers and drew her into his arms. Staring into each other's eyes and moving as one, they whirled to the fire dancer's wild music. With every step, they drew closer and closer, making her pulse pound faster and breath grow ragged. As their song ended, they were nearly pressed together with their lips a mere handbreadth apart.

Heat flared through Pippa when Edouard shuddered and

hustled her into the alcove along the far wall where they'd watched the Summerday bonfires. Unlike then, he was going to kiss her, almost in public despite his distaste for public kisses. She purred and wrapped her arms about his neck as his mouth seized hers once the alcove's shadows concealed them.

CHAPTER 15

As Pippa returned his desperate kiss, heat flared in Edouard's veins, and his body hardened until it ached. Goddess, she tasted sweet and so right. How had he managed not to truly kiss her since after the duchess's fete two months ago? Gripping her hips, he pressed her against the alcove wall and kissed her fiercer. When she purred again and fisted her hands in his hair, he shuddered and slid a hand up to cup her bodice then groaned. He needed more.

He was about to loosen her laces to caress her skin beneath her shift when nearby giggling pierced the alcove.

Both he and Pippa froze. Then he jerked back and staggered a few steps away. Although concealed in the alcove's darkest corner, how could he have been making love to Pippa in a public garden? 'Twas stupid and reckless and *mad*. If someone had seen them and gossip reached her father, Sir Julian would be even more convinced that he was a rakehell and never let them marry. Yet not being alone or kissing had made their kisses impossible to control once they'd finally succumbed.

Burning to yank Pippa back into his arms, Edouard eyed her and rasped, "We can't continue courting like this. We *need* your father's blessing."

Pippa licked her swollen lips, making him shudder with hunger anew. "I know, but Father flatly refuses to attend any court or family events to get to know you. We must figure out another way."

He clenched his hands to avoid pacing. Movement might attract attention to their shadowy alcove. "But what? He's refused to come meet our future queen or join a family dinner in his own home or attend magical demonstrations that should interest him."

Her usual radiance dimming, Pippa sagged against the ivy-covered wall. "I wish I knew. Nothing I've attempted has had any success. Even Lady Kiera asking about his magical experiments failed once he knew she wasn't a witch."

Edouard almost growled. Damn Pippa's neglectful father for hurting her by always refusing to listen. *What* would get the obsessed baronet's attention? He inhaled. Perhaps... "Do you think me bringing a witch to see his magical experiments would succeed?"

Pippa blinked at him then brightened. "It might. Father doesn't have anyone to talk to about his magical experiments who would comprehend them."

He exhaled. Pippa appeared her cheery self again. Thank the Goddess. He smiled at her. "I'll ask Hawke and Wren for directions to the veiled witch's shop. A Rhiannon descendant visiting to see his magical experiments should impress your father."

Pippa beamed and straightened. "Definitely. Just let me know when she can visit, and I'll arrange a meal to encourage Father to socialize too."

Edouard grinned back. He and Pippa made such a wonderful team. "Since we've a plan about your father, shall we return to the fire ball?"

Pippa sighed. "I suppose we should."

Unable to risk touching her again, he waved Pippa toward the alcove's entrance. They rejoined the other guests, who were all engrossed with the exotic fire dancers or their own partners, so no one seemed to note their absence or slightly rumpled appearance upon returning.

Once they'd fetched fresh mugs of spiced cider, he glanced at Pippa, and tingling warmth filled him again at the radiant smile curving her still swollen lips. How he adored her. Please let their plan for Sir Julian succeed. He couldn't wait much longer to confess his love and ask her to marry him.

Pippa turned to him, her smile somehow even brighter. "Shall we dance after we finish our spiced cider?"

Edouard swallowed. If only they could, but their control would vanish like earlier if they did. They needed each other too much. "I think we'd better not risk it tonight. We need time to calm before we touch again. And I probably shouldn't escort you home either—even with chaperones."

Pippa's sigh scattered the steam wafting from her mug. "No doubt you're right. After we finish our spiced cider, we should find Dane and Xavier to escort me home."

He nodded, and they turned to watch the fire dancers and other guests while they silently drank their spiced cider. Then they found Pippa's brothers, and she left after giving him a final warm smile.

Edouard stared after Pippa, his heart squeezing. One day soon, please Goddess, they'd be married, and they'd not need to part or control their kisses.

As soon as he rose the following morning, Edouard devoured a hasty breakfast then rode to Hawke and Wren's townhouse. However, his cousins were already at Waterstreet Orphanage, so he had to ride across Ormas to find them. He located Hawke in the orphanage's dining hall teaching the older children proper fighting and asked for directions to the veiled witch's shop. Flashing a crooked grin, Hawke told him, and Edouard continued to Rhiannon's Veils, which was only a few streets away.

He strode through the tiny witch shop's weathered red door into a dim, mostly empty chamber redolent of incense. 'Twas both eerie and magical—exactly like the veiled witch, which was doubtless the idea.

As if thinking about her had called her, the veiled witch sashayed through the door of glass beads at the back. The tinkling of the glass beads echoing through the witch shop, she performed a fluid bow then sank into the chair behind the wooden table. "How may I serve you today, my lord?"

Edouard sat across from the veiled witch, scrutinizing the black veils that concealed her hair and all of her face except her exotically lined eyes. Yes, a visit from such a witch would impress Sir Julian. He leaned forward. "I want to hire you to come see some magical experiments."

Her dark eyes narrowing, the veiled witch tilted her head. "Whose exactly? You're no witch, so they can't be yours."

He flashed a wry smile. Of course a powerful Rhiannon descendant could somehow sense that he wasn't a witch too. "They belong to the father of the lady I'm courting."

A chuckle undulated the witch's veils. "An attempt to impress your future father-in-law, I see."

Edouard held the veiled witch's amused gaze. Her seeing *that* wasn't surprising, even if she'd no magical powers at all. "Indeed. Shall you visit?"

The veiled witch flicked her fingers, jingling bracelets and tiny bells. "Yes, although I shan't lie about your future father-in-law's magical experiments to further your cause."

He stiffened and almost glared at the veiled witch. "I don't want you to. I doubt Sir Julian would appreciate lies." He tossed a bag of gold coins on the table. "Is this enough for an evening of your time?"

The veiled witch quirked her dark brows as she took the bag. "'Tis plenty. When should I visit?"

Edouard hummed. A week would give Pippa enough time to arrange their dinner, and the main court event that day was the

Duchess of Wildewall's autumn garden party, which was a midday event. He made himself smile at the veiled witch. "How about for dinner a week from today? I'll send a carriage an hour before sunset."

The veiled witch nodded. "Very well." Then she drawled, "Although perhaps you should introduce yourself before you do. I'd hate to take the wrong carriage."

He inclined his head. 'Twould appear odd if he brought someone to visit who didn't know him. "I'm the Count of Blaine, and we'll be visiting Sir Julian Hawke's townhouse. His daughter Pippa—Philippa—shall be there too, and probably so shall his sons, Dane and Xavier."

As they rose, the veiled witch chuckled. "Hawke, hmm? No doubt the bubbly young lady you were with at Lord and Lady Beza Hawke's wedding ceremony. I should have guessed." She swept a curtsy. "I'll see you in a week, my lord."

Edouard nodded in return then hurried from the tiny witch shop. He'd visit Pippa on his way home to update her. Please let their plan to soften her father succeed.

WHILE THEY STROLLED about the Duchess of Wildewall's vibrant garden a week later, Edouard sipped his spiced cider and smiled at Pippa. "Everything prepared for tonight?"

Pippa beamed. "Yes, I chose all of Father's favorite foods for dinner and convinced his valet to insist he dress for the evening. Although we'll need to bring the veiled witch to his workroom to persuade Father to join us for dinner."

Edouard grinned into his mug. Pippa was almost as excellent at arranging events as Kit. "I wondered how we'd manage that. But it sounds like you've got everything in hand."

That evening, he escorted the veiled witch to Pippa's family's townhouse where Pippa greeted them in the entrance hall with one of her glowing smiles. "Thank you for visiting, madam witch. Father's in his workroom; follow me."

Pippa led them to the large room in the back of the townhouse filled with tables cluttered by magical accoutrements, spell ingredients, and vials containing substances in every color imaginable. At the table near the window, Sir Julian was hunched over a journal scribbling notes. Slipping between the tables, Pippa smiled and touched her father's shoulder. "Edouard has brought someone to see your magical experiments, Father."

Sir Julian grunted without looking up from his journal. "I haven't time to waste on whoever that magicless rakehell brought to flatter me."

Edouard suppressed a wince. Not a promising start to the evening. He was clearly far from winning Sir Julian's blessing. Please let the baronet's scorn not have insulted the veiled witch.

Thankfully, the veiled witch appeared almost amused as she glided forward to peer at the vials beside Sir Julian and drawled, "Are you attempting to determine the nature of faedust by testing it with all these substances?"

His head jerking up, Sir Julian gaped at the veiled witch. "Yes! Your magical sight must be keen if you can see that." He grinned and leaned toward her. "Determining the nature of faedust shall decipher the nature of magic itself since fae create it to enhance spells and its concentrated power produces clearer results. I've already determined..."

As Sir Julian began to explain his magical experiments to the veiled witch in thorough, *thorough* detail, Edouard and Pippa traded wide glances. Her father's magical experiments were esoteric indeed. No wonder he never explained them to people who weren't witches.

However, the veiled witch had no trouble following Sir Julian and even injected several comments that had Sir Julian beaming and scribbling more notes in his journal. His glowing smile was so like his daughter's that Edouard couldn't help but smile too.

Once Sir Julian quieted at last, Pippa grinned and asked, "Shall we proceed to dinner now? All your talk must have made you ravenous, Father."

Energy surged through Edouard when Sir Julian smiled at him and Pippa then nodded. 'Twas the first that her father hadn't eyed him with suspicion. Sir Julian's acceptance continued throughout their dinner of his favorite foods, so Edouard escorted the veiled witch back to her witch shop afterward with a broad smile.

When he returned late the following morning to join Pippa and her brothers on a ride, Hodges said once he entered, "Sir Julian requested you visit him in his workroom, my lord."

Edouard nodded at the butler, his stomach tightening. In all his months attempting to speak with Sir Julian about Pippa, her father had never requested to see him. Hopefully the baronet didn't intend to scold like he had after discovering them kissing.

Edouard strode to Sir Julian's workroom then coughed to gain the baronet's attention because he remained engrossed in his magical experiments like always.

Sir Julian blinked then glanced toward him and muttered, "Lord Blaine, there you are. Thank you for bringing the veiled witch yesterday. Her insight was most helpful."

Edouard managed a polite smile. From Sir Julian's distant manner, his acceptance had waned. Not encouraging. "I'm glad you enjoyed her visit. I'll give you her witch shop's address so you can consult her again."

Sir Julian's eyes narrowed. "How very accommodating."

Edouard clung to his smile as he held Sir Julian's narrow gaze. "Pleasing you pleases Pippa."

Sir Julian grunted. "You were sincere about marrying my daughter, weren't you?"

Still holding Sir Julian's gaze, Edouard inclined his head. "Very much so. I adore Pippa—she's the sunshine in my life."

His face softening, Sir Julian nodded too. "Pippa is like that, isn't she?" He turned back to his vials. "You'd best find her before she worries that you forgot your ride."

When Edouard told Pippa during their ride about his conversation with Sir Julian, Pippa beamed as she urged her mare to a trot. "A promising start to winning Father's blessing. Now he just needs to see us together more. How about you join us for meals whenever possible? I'm certain I can convince Father to dine with us more since he's no longer so set against you."

He grinned back and matched Pippa's pace. Eating together often would be a taste of what their married life would be like. "I'd enjoy that."

So over the following two weeks, Edouard ate most of his luncheons and dinners with Pippa and her family. Sir Julian only joined them around half the time, but Pippa said that was encouraging since 'twas more than usual. Plus, Sir Julian no longer called him a rakehell and even smiled at him on occasion. *And* Sir Julian said his understanding of magic was excellent for someone without magical powers after he'd said that the magically disruptive ore responsible for the recent deadly explosion in Magehaven would only be neutralized by something with greater magic, like a potion of faedust, unicorn water, and opposing ores. Surely an excellent sign from a gentleman who ranked his magical experiments about understanding the nature of magic above all else.

During dinner before the Duchess of Childes's art gala, Pippa smiled at Sir Julian sitting at the head of the table. "You should join us at Childes House tonight, Father. You'd finally get to meet Lady Kiera, and the art is certain to be superb. Edouard even lent the duchess some pieces from his renowned art collection, including a tenth-century dancing music box, one of the first enchanted in Calatini."

As Dane and Xavier exchanged knowing glances, Sir Julian arched his brows at Edouard over his beefsteak with parsnip mash. "Such a piece must be rare."

Edouard nodded. That and its special meaning to his family were why he'd chosen it for the duchess's gala. "'Tis my favorite piece. Father purchased it for Mother for their tenth anniversary, and they often danced to its melody until she became ill."

Pippa beamed and laid her hand on his. "*Fantasia Dance*'s

delicate yet haunting melody is impossible not to dance to—so romantic."

Tingling warmth flooding him, he returned her glowing smile. Yes, their dance in the art room had been wonderful. He couldn't wait to repeat it every day once they were married.

Sir Julian hummed. "I take it you two danced to it then."

Edouard made himself face Pippa's father. "When Pippa visited to see my art collection almost six months ago."

Dane rumbled from across the table, "They danced as a tribute to Edouard's parents."

Smoothing his mustache, Xavier chuckled beside Dane. "A tribute that would have led to kisses if we hadn't interrupted them."

Sir Julian's mouth twisted. "Somehow I'm not surprised." Before Edouard and Pippa could do more than tense, he smiled at them. "I'd enjoy seeing that dancing music box one day. But not tonight. The Duchess of Childes's events are too crowded, and I must return to my experiments."

Edouard relaxed. They *must* be close to winning Sir Julian's blessing. Finally. "We'll arrange a family dinner soon, so you can see my entire art collection." And he should arrange the tour of the palace for Pippa not long after. King Devon was no longer busy introducing Lady Kiera, and Pippa's father wouldn't object to them visiting the palace together since his blessing was almost won.

Pippa beamed as she began her creamy mushroom chicken. "You'll love it. Edouard's collection is exquisite, and he knows the most interesting tales about all the pieces."

Sir Julian inclined his head. "Just name the evening."

Edouard and Pippa grinned at each other. Quite a change from her father's earlier refusals. Edouard murmured, "Pippa and I shall arrange an evening later this month."

He smiled throughout the rest of the congenial dinner with Pippa and her family. If her father's visit went like tonight, he could ask for her hand shortly afterward then propose during the Longnight season like he'd planned.

Once they finished eating, he, Pippa, and her brothers headed to Childes House. They greeted the duke and duchess, who said his pieces were set up in an anteroom on the back wall.

As her brothers visited the refreshments table, Pippa beamed at him and asked, "Shall we visit your pieces first?"

Edouard swallowed as his pulse quickened. They really shouldn't. The anteroom was probably empty, and being alone together was too dangerous until they were safely betrothed. Their kisses at Kit's fire ball had proved that.

Pippa squeezed his arm. "I'd enjoy seeing your dancing music-box sculpture again."

He exhaled. So would he. And he'd enjoy dancing with Pippa to its melody even more. Hunger flaring in his veins, he nodded and led her into the quiet and empty anteroom. He clapped then said, "Sonareh," to activate the enchanted sculpture. He inhaled and offered his hand. "Dance with me?"

Pippa flew into his arms with a radiant smile. "I'd love to."

While they twirled about the anteroom, Edouard drew Pippa closer until their bodies pressed together and they moved as one. Dancing with her was as incredible as ever. Once the lyrical melody faded, they stilled but remained entwined. Her sweet peach scent surrounding him and his pulse surging, he lowered his head and captured her lips.

Pippa hummed as she threaded her fingers through his hair and deepened their kiss.

When he burned to go further than kisses, he wrenched their mouths apart. They had to stop. All of court was in the other room. His heart fluttered as he gazed into Pippa's warm-brown eyes turned black with passion, and he breathed, "Goddess, how I love you."

Then he froze. He'd meant to wait until he proposed to confess that. And he couldn't propose without her father's blessing. But their romantic dance and hungry kisses had loosened his tongue. Yet now that he'd confessed his love, how could he convince his eager Pippa to wait?

CHAPTER 16

At Edouard's breathed confession, Pippa beamed as tingling surged from her chest through her entire body. "Oh, Edouard, I love you too." She tightened her fingers in his silky hair and pulled his head down for another kiss.

Edouard shuddered a sigh when their lips met. But before their kiss could deepen, he wrenched his head back like he had earlier. "We have to stop, Pippa. All of court is in the other room."

She chuckled and extracted her hands from his hair to cup his face. Her darling, protective Edouard. "Given our courtship over the past few months, no one would be surprised to find us kissing."

Edouard frowned at her. "Have you forgotten that we've yet to win your father's blessing? Talk about us kissing torridly at a court event shall destroy any chance of that."

Pippa hummed and caressed Edouard's clenched jaw. His kisses and confession of love *had* made her forget Father, but still... "I doubt Father shall hear such talk. He doesn't leave his workroom enough."

Edouard pulled himself free then strode across the anteroom. "Talk about us kissing shall probably be the one bit of court gossip he *does* hear, and we can't risk that. We're so close to winning his blessing. I never should have brought you to this empty anteroom."

She stilled. Visiting his pieces first had been her idea, although Edouard had swiftly agreed. "Why did you then?"

Edouard exhaled and rubbed his brow. "I couldn't resist dancing with you again to the melody of my dancing music-box sculpture."

Warmth suffusing her, Pippa bounded to Edouard and flung her arms about him. Her prudent Edouard had behaved recklessly for her—like after the duchess's fete and at Kit's fire ball. "Because you love me."

Edouard echoed his earlier sigh as he rested his forehead against hers. "Yes."

She drew back to eye Edouard, her ribs tightening. "Why don't you sound happy about that?"

Edouard grimaced and extracted himself from her embrace. "Because we're not free to act on our love until your father approves, and our kisses are becoming impossible to control."

Pippa tilted her head. But their ardent kisses were wonderful. Yet to hearten Edouard, she said, "Considering Father finally accepted your invitation to a family dinner, your plan to convince him is beginning to succeed. We'll win his blessing before long."

Still frowning, Edouard shook his head. "Not fast enough."

She smiled. Edouard truly loved her to be so impatient. "Then we'll redouble our efforts to convince Father, starting with your family dinner. How soon can we have it?"

Edouard rubbed his jaw. "Five days from now, perhaps? The court events that evening are minor."

Pippa swallowed a sigh. And unfortunately, the evening events before then were hosted by councilors or other influential members of court. They couldn't skip those events, especially after already accepting the invitations. "Very well. I'll send you a list of Father's favorite foods to provide to your cook."

Edouard nodded. "Send yours as well. I must prove to your father that I intend to take care of you, not just flatter him."

She beamed at Edouard. He proved his steadfast devotion for her with everything he did, but extra proof wouldn't go amiss. "Of course."

His gaze fixed on her lips, Edouard swallowed and stepped closer. Then he stiffened and shook his head before waving toward the door. "We should rejoin everyone."

Pippa sighed but nodded, and Edouard escorted her back to the drawing room without touching her. She smiled. Probably because he'd kiss her again if he did. Or she would. Prudent man.

No one in the drawing room noticed their quiet return because everyone was staring at Lord Ravenstone and his mother talking with King Devon, Lady Kiera, Aragon, Selena, *and* Lady Annalise Greysnowe. Conversations between the feuding Greysnowes and Ravenstones were always explosive. Except the beauteous Lady Annalise was coolly polite like always, and the genial Ravenstones were just as polite. Yet their truce was shattered when Lord and Lady Greysnowe stormed over and yanked their daughter away despite the king and future queen's presence.

Pippa smiled at Edouard while he handed her a flute of sparkling wine. "Thank the Goddess Father has never yanked me away like that. Poor Lady Annalise must be burning with embarrassment."

Edouard shuddered and sipped his sparkling wine. "I imagine so. That Greysnowe-Ravenstone feud is truly ridiculous. And it inspires both families to act like indiscreet children."

Elise and Lord Farson joined them, and Lord Farson said, "I don't envy the Duchess of Wildewall for having those two families in her duchy. Maintaining relations with the sovereign, matriarchal nightmara inside my duchy is nothing compared to handling the Greysnowes and Ravenstones—even when the nightmara queen-heir is delaying renewing their essential treaty with Calatini."

Pippa and Edouard exchanged a glance, then Edouard murmured, "I thought the meetings between Lady Moonbud and Lady Kiera were going well. Elise mentioned Lady Moonbud was teaching Lady Kiera to ride, and nightmara queens or queen-heirs never let anyone ride them."

Lord Farson rubbed his beard. "Their meetings *are* going well. Lady Moonbud likes Lady Kiera a great deal and is impressed by her insightful strength and warm dedication. However, they've been meeting for over a month, and even the first time, negotiating the Nightmara-Calatini Treaty didn't take so long."

Sipping her sparkling wine, Pippa smiled at Lord Farson. Surely he was worrying over nothing. "No doubt Lady Moonbud has excellent reasons for delaying."

Elise grinned. "That's what I keep telling Seanian, but he continues to fret."

Lord Farson arched a brow. "Can you blame me? The Night-mara-Calatini Treaty is vital to our southern defense against the vast and rapacious Tsarkan Empire."

As Edouard soberly nodded, Elise slanted her husband a pointed look and replied, "I can when your fretting makes you restless at night." Then she turned to Pippa and Edouard. "So where did the two of you disappear to when you first arrived? You were alone for ages."

While Pippa smiled at their time alone, Edouard stilled then murmured, "We visited the anteroom containing the pieces of my collection that I lent to the duchess for tonight."

Elise and Lord Farson traded knowing grins, then Elise quirked her brows at Edouard and asked, "Don't you see your pieces enough at home?"

When Edouard began to blush at his twin's teasing, Pippa said to defend him, "But I don't. I was most eager to see his dancing music-box sculpture again."

Elise sighed with a tender smile. "That piece is lovely, isn't it?

Mother and Father used to dance to its melody whenever they visited the art room."

Pippa beamed at Edouard and squeezed his arm. "I know."

Elise and her husband traded knowing grins once again. Elise drawled, "Told Pippa about that, did you, Edouard? Do you intend on continuing Mother and Father's tradition?"

Obviously blushing now, Edouard sipped his sparkling wine but held Elise's gaze. "If Pippa agrees, yes."

Pippa repeated her earlier squeeze, her heart fluttering. "I definitely do. 'Tis such a romantic tradition." She smiled at Edouard. "And not the least bit impractical."

His pale-blue eyes soft, Edouard smiled back and laid his hand atop hers. "I'm glad you agree."

As they smiled into each other's eyes, Elise chuckled and said, "Perhaps you two should return to that anteroom—else you may titillate court by kissing in public."

A blush heated Pippa's cheeks as Edouard jerked back. Despite their love, he was much too private for public kisses. Not that she'd mind them.

Edouard cleared his throat. "Pippa and I also visited that anteroom so we could privately discuss the family dinner I'm hosting for her family in five days." He turned to Elise. "Are you, Farson, and Arvan free to attend?"

Elise hummed and arched her brows at Lord Farson, who nodded. Then she replied, "Of course."

Before Elise could tease Edouard about hosting another dinner for her family, Pippa turned to him and asked, "Shall we view the rest of the art?"

Edouard inclined his head, and without touching, the two of them strolled about the drawing room, pausing to study each piece. As the duchess had promised, they were all stunning and evinced Selena's love of art. Pippa and Edouard were midway through when King Devon and Lady Kiera left, causing gossip to flare through the guests. Tonight was the first court event the royal couple had attended since Lady Morwynne's ball three days ago, and they'd spent much of it exchanging heated glances before leaving early.

Pippa sighed into her sparkling wine. If only she and Edouard could do the same.

As they turned back to the moving painting they'd been studying, Edouard flashed a wry grin. "Despite tonight being an art gala and the confrontation between the Greysnowes and Ravenstones earlier, I doubt court shall discuss anything other than King Devon and Lady Kiera for the rest of the evening."

Pippa smiled. "True. Yet the obvious love between them is beautiful to behold. And so romantic." She pursed her lips. "Although enduring court's constant attention must be hard. Just imagine the talk if they'd disappeared into an anteroom like we did."

Edouard shuddered. "I'm often glad I'm a mere count who's boring enough to not attract such constant attention."

She threaded her arm through Edouard's, her chest warm. "You're not boring. You're steady with a quiet strength. 'Tis why I couldn't help falling in love with you."

Edouard swallowed and squeezed her arm against his side. "Your radiant joy and sweet passion are why I couldn't help falling in love with you, my sun nymph."

Pippa blushed as happy tears pricked her eyes. Near poetry again. She beamed and breathed, "Oh, Edouard."

Edouard cleared his throat then faced the moving painting from before. "Shall we finish viewing the rest of the art?"

Still beaming, she let Edouard distract them. Confessions of love were better done in private where kisses could accompany them.

YET OVER THE days before his family dinner, Pippa and Edouard were never in private even though he escorted her to court events every day. And he never hinted at his love for her either. No doubt because he believed them being alone or discussing their love was too dangerous since they weren't free to act on it without Father's blessing. But with Father so close to giving that, no doubt they could relax their restraint. She'd get Edouard alone after his family dinner to persuade him of that.

As soon as she rose on the morning of the family dinner, she reminded Father's valet to prepare his evening clothes tonight then visited Father's workroom. She touched his arm with a smile. "You remember about the dinner at Blaine House this evening?"

Father lifted his head from his journal and blinked at her. "That's tonight?"

Pippa smiled brighter, her chest tightening. Please let Father not renege now. "Yes, and you promised to attend." When Father frowned, she added, "Please, Father, 'tis very important to me that you attend tonight."

Father sighed and patted her hand. "Very well, I'll attend. Now go on so I can finish today's experiments before we leave."

She exhaled then hurried from Father's workroom. Hopefully he'd remember his promise tonight, and his magical experiments wouldn't run long. Otherwise, he still might fail to attend.

However, Father's day must have gone smoothly because he joined her and her brothers in the entrance hall just a few minutes late—which was on time for him. And he was almost smiling. He waved toward the door and asked, "Shall we go?"

On the carriage ride to Blaine House, Pippa managed to feign interest while Dane asked Father about his magical experiments. But her mind was fixed on the upcoming dinner. Surely 'twould impress Father and win his blessing.

Once they arrived, Edouard welcomed them inside his entrance hall with a warm smile. "I thought we could head straight to the art room to see my collection, Sir Julian." He took her arm and turned to Dane and Xavier. "You're welcome to join us, or you could join Elise, Farson, and Arvan in the drawing room. Kit is at Reid House this evening."

Dane and Xavier glanced at each other, then Dane rumbled,

"We'll go to the drawing room. We must arrange our next ride with Arvan anyway."

She grinned at Father as Edouard escorted them down the hall. "You'll find the magical art in Edouard's collection fascinating, Father, especially his exquisite dancing music-box sculpture."

Father hummed and inclined his head.

Then Edouard ushered them into the art room. "My collection of tenth-century masters. The dancing music-box sculpture is in the middle of the room."

Father halted just inside the threshold and gaped at the enchanted sculpture. "Pippa was right. 'Tis exquisite."

CHAPTER 17

$\mathcal{A}$s Sir Julian strode toward *Fantasia Dance,* Edouard traded a grin with Pippa. Her father was as interested as they'd hoped. Please let that interest inspire him to finally approve their betrothal and marriage. While Sir Julian flicked his fingers and muttered a probing spell, Edouard and Pippa joined him beside the dancing music-box sculpture, then Edouard described its romantic tale, ending with, "Lascelle had his bard witch cousin, Carteret, enchant *Fantasia Dance* as a dancing music box to capture more of the dancers' mesmerizing performance."

Sir Julian hummed while he peered at the enchanted sculpture. "Carteret was among the best bard witches in Ormas during the tenth century. Not surprising he created one of Calatini's first dancing music boxes. Could you activate it?"

Edouard nodded then clapped and said, "Sonareh." As the delicate melody filled the art room, he and Pippa drifted closer together, almost swaying with their gazes locked. If only they could dance like before, but her father was with them.

Sir Julian's sudden laugh made them stiffen and turn toward him. His tousled head cocked like an inquisitive moonowl, Sir Julian was beaming at the dancing marble couple on the pedestal. He muttered, "Amazing! Absolutely amazing. The intricate spell woven into the sculpture appears as pure and strong as if 'twas just cast. Who do you bring in to renew it?"

Edouard shrugged. Not surprising Sir Julian cared about that, rather than *Fantasia Dance*'s beauty or meaning. "Witches from The Arte of Spells. They visit every spring to renew all the magical art in my collection, although this piece is by far the most complicated."

Sir Julian rubbed his chin. "They do an excellent job."

Pippa chuckled. "Of course they do. Edouard wouldn't hire anyone who didn't."

Edouard shrugged again. "Taking proper care of everything is important." Especially those you loved or who depended on you. Yet stating that would sound too obvious, so he remained silent. Although Pippa understood his unspoken words given her glowing smile as she squeezed his arm.

Sir Julian slanted them a considering glance. "I see." He turned back to the dancing music-box sculpture. "I'm going to cast a deeper probing spell to better study this impressive spell."

As her father cast his spell, Pippa grinned at Edouard. "How about you show me the pieces I didn't get to see last time? I've been longing to see them these past six months."

He inclined his head and returned Pippa's earlier squeeze while they began toward the paintings they'd skipped to see *Fantasia Dance* on her first visit. "I should have arranged another family dinner sooner. Why didn't you remind me?"

A coy smile curving her lips, Pippa studied him beneath her lashes. "I knew you'd arrange one eventually, and I was more interested in pursuing... other things."

Tingling heat flooded him. Other things like kisses. And if her father wasn't with them, he'd happily provide more of those right now. Wrenching his gaze from Pippa's tempting lips, he faced the moving painting before them of a young girl on a headland high above the sea, her lavender ribbons and white dress fluttering in the breeze while fluffy clouds raced behind her. "This is *Lost Lavender*..."

Edouard showed Pippa the rest of his collection, sharing the tales behind each of the pieces as well as how Father had acquired them and any associated family anecdotes. Pippa grinned throughout and kept her arm threaded through his while she asked interested questions.

When he finished, Pippa tilted her head. "I notice you didn't acquire any of the pieces in your collection. Why not?"

He hummed as his throat thickened. How he still missed Father. "When Father was alive, 'twas really his collection. He purchased all the pieces in it, although since my first season, we did visit places together looking for new pieces. Occasionally, I even found some alone that I showed him, but he still purchased them."

Pippa nodded. "Understandable. But I'm surprised you've not purchased pieces in the past fifteen months."

Edouard lifted his free shoulder. "I *was* in mourning the first year, and going without Father since then just hasn't felt right." To distract himself from that, he caressed Pippa's wrist with his thumb and said, "Besides, I've been courting a certain young lady. Escorting her everywhere and arranging outings like tours of the palace has engrossed me."

Her eyes glowing, Pippa straightened like an eager faebird. "We're touring the palace? When?"

He smiled at Pippa's delight and caressed her wrist again. "Tomorrow morning. Elise has agreed to chaperone us."

Pippa squeezed his arm. "How wonderful." Then she peeked at him through her lashes and drawled, "Your young lady must be a demanding creature for you to have no time to purchase new pieces. Perhaps you should court a more accommodating lady."

After glancing at Sir Julian, who was still absorbed by *Fantusia Dance*, Edouard leaned toward Pippa until their lips almost met. His pulse quickened while he held her gaze. "You're plenty accommodating, my sun nymph." Then he withdrew to the proper distance before he kissed her.

Pippa sighed and licked her parted lips. "If Father wasn't here, I'd show you just how accommodating." When he swallowed as hunger flared in his veins, she shook herself then flashed a brilliant smile. "We should visit places together looking for new pieces for your collection. It sounds diverting."

He forced his pulse to settle then returned Pippa's smile. "I'd like that—if your brothers or Elise accompany us." Being alone together was definitely too dangerous.

Pippa sighed again. "Right." She turned and studied her father for a moment. "We should rouse Father and head to dinner. Everyone is probably starving."

Edouard suppressed a chuckle. "True. I'm surprised Arvan hasn't fetched us already."

Pippa grinned while they began across the art room. "No doubt Elise ordered him not to, and my brothers are distracting him." She touched Sir Julian's arm. "Come along, Father. 'Tis time for dinner."

Sir Julian started then waved them away, mumbling, "But I'm not finished studying this spell yet."

Pippa patted her father's shoulder. "I'm sure Edouard shall let you study it more another day."

Edouard nodded. His future father-in-law would always be welcome, even when not wanted. "Yes, return whenever you like."

Sir Julian grumbled but allowed them to herd him from the art room and join the others in the drawing room.

As expected, Arvan brightened when they arrived, but before the young duke could comment, Edouard smiled at everyone and asked, "Shall we proceed to dinner now?"

They did, and a lively discussion began as they ate. Yet Sir Julian remained silent until the creamy parsnip soup was replaced with braised venison. He arched his brows at Pippa beside him. "Another of my favorites. I sense your touch in this, Pippa."

Edouard warmed as Pippa took his hand beneath the table and replied with a radiant smile, "Of course. Edouard and I planned tonight together."

He squeezed Pippa's hand and grinned at her and her father. "Yes, Pippa and I make a wonderful team."

Across the table between Farson and Arvan, Elise chuckled as she spread butter on another roll. "Just like a pair of matched mara ponies."

Edouard quirked a brow at his twin's teasing. The mara had bred the sturdy mara ponies as draft animals—not exactly flattering. He sipped his red wine. "What a romantic comparison."

Pippa beamed at him over her braised venison. "But a good one." She giggled. "As long as you don't expect us to pull a caravan together. The best we could manage is a dog cart."

He returned Pippa's smile. "I'll let my horses pull my carriages." He toasted her. "Our combined talents are better used elsewhere."

Dane and Xavier traded smirks, then Xavier smoothed his mustache and drawled, "*Where* exactly?"

His neck heating at the suggestive question, Edouard shifted in his seat. Pippa's father wouldn't like such innuendos about his daughter. Indeed, Sir Julian was frowning at him and Pippa.

But before he could reply, Pippa narrowed her eyes at her brothers and said, "Don't twist Edouard's meaning." She turned to Elise. "When's your musical evening again?"

Her gaze bright with laughter, Elise smiled back. "'Tis Arvan's musical evening, but in eleven days."

While everyone discussed that, Edouard feigned interest, but Sir Julian scrutinizing him and Pippa kept distracting him. Was her father watching with approval or censure? His blank expression was impossible to read. Yet he smiled when their gazes met over their apple tarts.

Edouard exhaled. Approval, probably. Thank the Goddess for that.

Yet they'd barely settled in the drawing room after dinner when Sir Julian said, "We should be returning home."

As Dane and Xavier grimaced, Edouard and Pippa glanced at each other on the sofa across from her family. Her father wanting to leave so early was rude, especially considering their serious courtship. Not encouraging.

Pippa turned back to Sir Julian and laced her fingers in her lap with a tight smile, clearly upset and longing to stay. "So soon? I thought we could remain to talk a while longer."

Edouard inhaled to not take Pippa's hand to hearten her, which might nettle Sir Julian. Instead, he arched his brows at the baronet and suggested, "Or you could return to the art room to finish studying *Fantasia Dance*."

Sir Julian shook his head. "Another time. I want to bring some faedust before I study that intricate spell again. Besides, I keep country hours, so I'm not accustomed to late evenings."

Edouard and Pippa frowned at each other while her brothers sighed beside Sir Julian. At least her father's desire to leave early wasn't due to their courtship, yet him asking to leave was insensitive considering Pippa's obvious desire to stay. Why must Sir Julian always be so blind to his daughter's needs? But forcing him to remain wouldn't help sway him to approve their marriage.

After a moment, Pippa sagged but inclined her head. "As you wish, Father."

From the sofa on the back wall with Farson, Elise leaned forward and said, "We've room in our carriage for one more, and we'd be glad to take Pippa home when we leave, Sir Julian. Then you can return now while she remains a while longer."

Sir Julian hummed. "Very well."

As Pippa straightened and smiled once more, Edouard relaxed. Perhaps her father wasn't so blind after all; he just disliked being away from home and his magical experiments.

And they must be close to winning his blessing if he was willing to leave Pippa alone here. Edouard and Pippa traded smiles then rose as one, and he nodded at Sir Julian and her brothers. "We'll walk you out."

After they said farewell to her family in the entrance hall, Pippa squeezed his arm with a beseeching grin. "Could we talk alone for a moment before returning to the drawing room? We must discuss tonight and our plans."

He sighed. They shouldn't risk being alone while not betrothed, but Pippa was right that they must talk. Since the art room with his dancing music-box sculpture would be too tempting, he escorted her to his study where he could keep a desk between them. Yet her frown as he moved to sit behind his desk had him returning to the chair beside her. So much for keeping a desk between them. He sighed again as he waved for her to talk.

Pippa beamed at him. "Even though Father left early, which really isn't unusual for him, tonight went well. You should speak to him about marrying me—perhaps after we return from our tour of the palace. I'm sure he'll give his blessing now."

Edouard drummed his fingers on his knee. Sir Julian's behavior tonight *had* been encouraging for the most part. And with the Longnight season under a month away, he needed Pippa's father's approval soon so he could start planning the perfect romantic proposal. He nodded. "Meeting with your father tomorrow afternoon sounds good."

Pippa beamed brighter and bounced in her seat. "Wonderful." She leapt into his lap and twined her arms about his neck. "And with Father's blessing so close to won, we can relax our restraint at last."

His body tightening, he attempted to return Pippa to her seat. "Close isn't the same as won. We can't count our faebirds before they hatch."

Pippa clung to him. "Nonsense." Then she captured his mouth in a deep kiss.

Edouard shuddered. Goddess, he needed her. He dropped

back into his chair and yanked Pippa closer. When she purred and caressed his chest, he shuddered again and hardened further. He undid her laces and splayed a hand beneath her shift. So good.

"Time to go, I think," Elise's voice cut through their desperate kisses.

A blush burned his skin as he and Pippa wrenched apart then turned to face his twin. Their control had vanished again. He never should have agreed to talk alone with her. His fingers trembling, he retied her laces.

Elise tsked and shook her head. "'Tis fortunate I discovered you two rather than any of Pippa's family."

Blushing too, Pippa rose from his lap. "We were just kissing."

His skin burned hotter when Elise's brows flew upward as she murmured, "*Just* kissing?" She took Pippa's arm. "Good night, Edouard. We'll talk before our tour of the palace tomorrow." Then she swept Pippa from his study.

Edouard sagged in his chair and gulped air to help settle his aching body. Although he should thank Elise for interrupting them, talking with her tomorrow wouldn't be enjoyable, and not just because of the early hour.

He'd only taken his first bracing sip of kahve when Elise strode into the breakfast room the following morning. She was earlier than expected. Marvelous. Thankfully, she spoke with Kit about Kit's evening at Reid House last night while he devoured his breakfast. Once he finished, he and Elise said farewell to Kit then headed out to his carriage.

As the carriage rumbled to Pippa's family's townhouse, Elise eyed him with a faint frown. Time for their talk. How thrilling.

Elise tsked. "Why haven't you proposed to Pippa yet? You've been courting since her come out over six months ago, the love between you has been obvious for ages, and you don't have a young ward to consider like Seanian and I did. So why are you still delaying? 'Tis becoming ridiculous."

Edouard shifted in his seat across from Elise. "At first, I wanted to make sure Pippa knew her own mind, and I had to speak with her father about courting her. She *is* just eighteen and new to court."

Elise snorted. "Considering how I found you two last night, Pippa knows her own mind, believe me. And so do you. I'm guessing you've not spoken with Sir Julian for some reason."

He almost winced. "No, I have. But he proved remarkably elusive, so only after he discovered us torridly kissing nearly three months ago. He was furious when I told him I wanted to marry Pippa and refused to consider it. So we've been attempting to win his blessing since then."

Elise hummed and slowly nodded. "I see. Well, Sir Julian didn't appear disapproving at dinner yesterday."

Edouard grimaced. "At long last. I'm visiting him this after-noon to ask for Pippa's hand again." Please let it go well this time.

Elise began to grin. "Good. I expect to be your first groom witness, remember."

He grinned back. Just like he'd been her first bride witness during her wedding ceremony two and a half years ago. "Of course." He arched a brow. "So where are Farson and Arvan riding this morning?"

Elise tilted her head as the carriage slowed at Pippa's family's townhouse. "I'm not certain. We were intending to ride to Blacke Woods, but Seanian said they'd wait until I could join them. Probably somewhere in or around Ormas."

Edouard leapt from the carriage and grinned when Pippa met him in the entrance hall. So eager. He swept her into his carriage, and they settled in the seat across from Elise. Then they all spent the ride to the palace discussing the latest news about Lady Kiera's negotiations with the nightmara.

As he'd arranged with King Devon, the regal palace butler met them at the door then escorted them about the palace, starting with the more public rooms, like the throne room and ballroom, but continuing on to lesser visited rooms, like the royal portrait gallery, palace chapel, and council room. The only area they didn't visit was the royal wing itself.

While the butler described the history of the palace, Pippa bounced beside him and pelted him with insightful questions, like about when the massive and ornate ceiling rose above the council room table had been added to symbolize the councilors' freedom to speak openly to Calatini's kings and queens without repercussion.

Edouard and Elise exchanged smiles as they trailed behind Pippa and the regal palace butler, who both beamed as they discussed the palace. Pippa was definitely enjoying herself.

After the butler regretfully said farewell, the head palace gardener took them on a tour of the gardens closest to the palace, although the palace grounds were too extensive to see more than a few of its many gardens.

On the return ride to her family's townhouse late that afternoon, Pippa grinned and threaded her fingers through Edouard's. "Thanks so much for arranging the tour of the palace. I loved it."

Tingling warmth surged through him. And he loved Pippa. Goddess, if only he could pull her against him and kiss the radiant joy on her lips. But Elise was sitting across from them. Probably fortunate since their kisses would be impossible to control like yesterday, and they must wait until her father agreed to their marriage. He swallowed then rasped, "I'm glad you loved it."

Pippa beamed then turned to Elise. "What did you think of the tour?"

Elise chuckled. "'Twas interesting, although I preferred the gardens rather than the palace itself. Unlike you."

Pippa playfully gasped, then they all spent the rest of the ride discussing their favorite parts of the palace tour.

When they reached Pippa's family's townhouse, Elise smiled

at him and Pippa. "I'll wait in the carriage while you visit Sir Julian."

Edouard inhaled but nodded then escorted Pippa inside, his stomach tensing. At the door, he said to Hodges, "I'd like to see Sir Julian."

Once the butler disappeared from the entrance hall, Pippa squeezed Edouard's hand. "I'll remain here while you talk with Father. Unless you want me to join you?"

He shook his head. Although he'd like to approach her father together, 'twas traditionally the gentleman's duty, and they couldn't risk nettling Sir Julian. "I'd best talk with your father alone."

Pippa nodded and squeezed his hand again. "Your talk shall go well. I know it."

Edouard returned Pippa's squeeze. Hopefully so.

Then Hodges returned with an apologetic smile. "I'm sorry, my lord, but Sir Julian isn't at home to visitors today. He said his magical experiments are at a critical stage."

As Pippa frowned, Edouard stiffened. Not at home to visitors or him specifically? But why would Sir Julian refuse to see him? Had his approval yesterday not been genuine? Or was he truly too busy?

Pippa sighed and released his hand. "Unfortunate that Father is too busy this afternoon. But you can try again tomorrow. Perhaps the morning would be better."

Edouard made himself smile and nod. "I'll visit straight after breakfast tomorrow."

And he did, with the same result. Then he returned every day over the following nine days, attempting different times each visit, but Sir Julian kept refusing to see him and quit joining everyone for meals. Pippa's father was clearly avoiding him. The baronet's apparent approval at the family dinner must have been false.

As Edouard left to attend the musical evening at Golddell House, he frowned into the night. Matters couldn't continue on like this. He and Pippa would be old and gray before they could marry. They must decide how to handle her father, and since tonight was hosted by family, they could easily slip away to talk. They'd just need to remain apart to avoid impossible-to-control kisses.

CHAPTER 18

$\mathcal{A}$s soon as Pippa and her brothers arrived at Golddell House, Edouard grasped her arm and murmured, "We must talk alone, Pippa."

Her pulse quickening, she nodded. Perhaps some of their talk might be kisses. "Of course. Now?"

Edouard shook his head. "Once the first song starts. Let's take seats in the back row so we can slip away unnoticed."

She nodded again, and they sat in the end of the back row closest to the wall. Soon a string quartet along with a soprano and a baritone entered and began to perform an intricate serenade made popular by sirenic plays. The voices of the human singers didn't possess the exquisite and enthralling clarity of sirens, although their performance was still excellent.

When the baritone gripped the soprano's hand and sang into her eyes, Edouard took Pippa's arm and ushered her into the nearby anteroom. She sighed as he settled her on the sofa by the door then sank into a chair along the opposite wall. Clearly he was determined to avoid kisses. Too bad.

She eyed Edouard's faint frown and laced her hands in her lap. "What is it? You appear troubled."

Edouard exhaled. "Your father. We must get him to quit avoiding me. Otherwise, we'll never be able to marry."

Her chest twisted. In the days since the family dinner at Blaine House, Father had been avoiding *everyone*, not just Edouard. Father had always been engrossed in his magical experiments, but he'd never been completely inaccessible before. She swallowed. Why now when Edouard needed to speak with him? It couldn't be because Father didn't approve of Edouard. His approval had been evident at the family dinner. Her chest easing, she pursed her lips. Perhaps he'd made headway in his magical experiments after studying Edouard's dancing music-box sculpture. That would explain Father avoiding everyone.

She hummed. "How about I arrange a meeting between you two?"

Edouard arched a brow. "Do you think you can? You didn't have success persuading him to attend court events."

Pippa grimaced at those ineffective weeks of begging. "True, but Father hates court events, and he doesn't dislike you. He's just busy with his magical experiments."

Edouard ran a hand through his blond hair. "I *hope* that's all this is. I don't think I can wait until you turn twenty to marry."

She giggled as warmth suffused her at Edouard's obvious love. "So impatient."

Edouard held her gaze. "Very." He leaned forward. "Do you think you can arrange a meeting before the Longnight season?"

Pippa blinked. How oddly specific. "I'm sure I can. The beginning of the Longnight season is more than two weeks from now. But why?"

Edouard's gaze skittered away. "I've plans for the Longnight season that shall be ruined if I can't speak with your father."

Her heart surging, she bounced in her seat. Longnight celebrated new beginnings, hope, and love, so a marriage proposal during the Longnight season would be wonderfully romantic. "Plans?"

Edouard coughed. "Yes."

Pippa leapt upright and flew across the anteroom. Her serious Edouard had planned the perfect romantic proposal for her. Because he loved her above everything, just like she loved him. She dropped into his lap and threaded her arms about his neck. "Then I'll definitely arrange a meeting before the Long-night season."

His body hardening beneath hers, Edouard stilled. "Pippa, 'tis dangerous for us to be close like this."

She smiled and nuzzled Edouard to encourage him to kiss her. "I don't care."

With a groan, Edouard crushed her against him then kissed her as if they'd not kissed in years. She purred and returned his kiss with equal hunger. Goddess, how she needed him. And soon they'd be married and could kiss like this—and more—every day.

After a timeless moment, Edouard wrenched their mouths apart. Panting, he rasped, "Enough. We must return to the others before someone notices we're missing. We can't risk causing such talk now."

Pippa tilted her head. Even though Father likely wouldn't hear it, Edouard was right. Nothing must prevent his romantic proposal. She rose and smoothed her teal skirt. "Very well."

Edouard waved her toward the door, and they returned to the drawing room without touching. Yet once they settled in their seats to enjoy more romantic duets, she threaded her fingers through his. Surely they could risk that. She smiled when he caressed her palm with his thumb. Obviously he agreed.

The musical evening passed swiftly, and she sighed when Edouard helped her rise. If only they could remain together longer.

As he escorted her back to Dane and Xavier, Edouard murmured, "I almost forgot. There's an estate sale tomorrow afternoon that should have some tenth-century art. Did you want to attend with me?"

Pippa beamed at him. He was finally looking for new pieces

for his collection, so he must be recovering from his grief over his father. Good. "Yes, please."

Edouard returned her smile. "Once you leave, I'll ask Elise if she can accompany us. We'll collect you shortly after luncheon."

She nodded. And she should have spoken with Father by then, so she could tell Edouard when their meeting was. "I'm looking forward to it."

AFTER BREAKFAST THE FOLLOWING MORNING, Pippa headed straight to Father's workroom, yet the door was locked when she attempted to open it. She frowned. Peculiar. Father never locked his workroom. He simply refused to answer whenever engrossed in his magical experiments, which was most days. Yet she couldn't blatantly disregard Father's desire for privacy by having his door unlocked. 'Twould be disrespectful as well as upset Father.

She knocked firmly then called Father several times, but he didn't answer like usual. Her chest tightening, she left and returned just before luncheon. However, those attempts met with the same silence. Eventually, she sighed and lowered her hand. She couldn't tell Edouard about his meeting with Father when she saw him today. She inhaled and straightened her shoulders. Well, she'd try again after the estate sale.

When Edouard collected her for the estate sale, she curled beside him in the carriage, and he draped his arm about her, even though Elise was in the forward seat. Not that Elise commented on their embrace. She simply smiled and said to Pippa, "Edouard tells me you've never attended an estate sale before."

Pippa grinned back. "No, but it sounds diverting." Mostly because Edouard was excited to find new pieces for his art collection.

Elise chuckled. "I've not been to an estate sale since before I married Seanian. But then, I was never enamored by tenth-century art like Father and Edouard."

Edouard shook his head. "As I recall, you used to become bored and wander away when we'd inspect the art."

Elise chuckled again. "Only because you two would inspect it for *hours*. Your discussions about every tiny detail of each piece were painful. And most of the time, you wouldn't even purchase the pieces you discussed."

At Edouard's wry shrug, Pippa laughed and said, "They could only purchase the best for their renowned art collection of tenth-century masters."

They soon arrived at the shabbily elegant townhouse just outside of the fashionable area of Ormas that belonged to a merchant family who'd lost their fortune at sea. Like all the contents inside, the townhouse was for sale too. They first toured the townhouse to scan everything available before returning to the room containing most of the art.

Pippa beamed as Edouard inspected each piece from the tenth century and told her about them in thorough detail—exactly like Elise had described. But his delight was wonderful to see and made her ache to kiss him, so unlike Elise, she didn't become bored and wander away. They left the estate sale several hours later without purchasing anything. Although Edouard enjoyed inspecting the nice pieces, none were stunning enough for his collection.

Afterward, they visited Layne's Tea Room to thank Elise for accompanying them. While Edouard left to order their desserts, Elise grinned at Pippa and said, "I'm so happy Edouard met you. You bring him such joy."

Her cheeks warming, Pippa smiled at Edouard across the tea room. "He brings me the same." Her voice softened, "I know I can depend on him to always be there and keep his promises."

Elise grinned brighter and squeezed her hand on the table. "Exactly. Once you're betrothed, let me know if you require any help with the wedding ceremony. As Edouard's first groom witness, I'll be involved anyway, and planning a wedding cere-mony can be difficult when you have no mother to help. I know —I at least had Kit, who's skilled at planning events, but 'twasn't the same."

Although touched by her future sister-in-law's offer, Pippa blinked and stared at her. "I've not really thought about the wedding ceremony, not even who I want as my bride witness. I've always been more concerned about the marriage instead. That's the important part."

Elise laughed. "Oh, Pippa, you're an ideal match for Edouard. He said the same while I was planning my wedding ceremony. I'll be glad when I can call you sister."

Pippa blushed again. "Me too." *Please let Father agree to meet with Edouard soon.*

Then Edouard returned with a pot of tea and three different slices of cake. He handed Pippa the pale cake packed with apples. "Apple-lymon cake for you." He handed Elise the white cake with kokonut frosting. "Kokonut cake for you." He kept the dark cake with cream frosting for himself. "And shokolat-cherry cake for me."

While Elise poured the tea, Pippa eyed Edouard's cake. If they were alone, she'd ask for a bite like when they'd had sweetice here three months ago. But she couldn't behave so brazen in front of his sister when they weren't even betrothed yet. Perhaps once they were married.

After they began their desserts, Edouard asked, "What did you two discuss without me?"

Elise chuckled. "You, obviously."

Edouard arched a brow over his teacup. "All good things, I trust."

Pippa swallowed a laugh when Elise winked at her then drawled, "Maybe..."

As Edouard grimaced at his twin, Pippa toasted him with her teacup. "Don't fret; if Elise had said anything too terrible, I'd have thrown a napkin at her."

Edouard grinned, his gaze warm. "I can always count on you to defend me."

She beamed back. She loved him too much not to. "Of course."

As Pippa and Edouard beamed at each other, Elise laughed and said, "You two are adorable. I hope you can marry before long." She turned to Pippa. "Are you looking forward to the Duchess of Wildewall's ball tonight? Her events are always exciting since both the Greysnowes and Ravenstones attend."

Pippa lifted a shoulder. "I'm looking forward to dancing the first and last dances with Edouard. I don't care about the rest of it."

Elise laughed again. "Yes, you and Edouard are definitely a match. I'm wearing arachne silk tonight. What are you wearing?"

They continued discussing tonight's ball while they finished their tea and delectable slices of cake. Then Edouard escorted them back to his carriage.

WHEN SHE RETURNED to the townhouse, Pippa headed straight to Father's workroom and attempted to speak with him again. But her efforts remained ineffective. Her chest aching, she frowned and left to change for dinner and tonight's ball. *Why* was Father so determined to hide right now?

Over the following two weeks, she continued attempting to speak with Father, but he avoided her just like he'd avoided Edouard since the family dinner at Blaine House. With every failed attempt, she became more and more upset. Father's inexplicable determination to hide from everyone was going to ruin the perfect romantic proposal Edouard had planned for her.

The morning before the Longnight season began, her patience had evaporated. She'd not allow Father to ruin Edouard's romantic proposal. Today was her final opportunity to arrange their meeting prior to the Longnight season. So even though 'twas disrespectful, she ordered Hodges to unlock

Father's workroom when she found it locked after breakfast yet again.

After sending the butler away, Pippa swept into Father's workroom with a doggedly brilliant smile. "Good morning, Father. How are your magical experiments going?"

Father hunched his shoulders over his journal. "Fine. How did you get in? I locked the door."

She tsked, still clinging to her brilliant smile. "I know. You've been locking it the past month. Not very safe. What if one of your magical experiments explodes again and you need to escape quickly?"

Father humphed. "There's little chance of that. Now, run along and let me return to my experiments. Lock the door behind you."

Her ribs constricting, Pippa narrowed her eyes at Father. "Not until we talk first."

Father hunched further as he scribbled more notes in his journal. "About what?"

She exhaled to loosen her tight chest. Why must Father always be engrossed in his magical experiments? "About Edouard. He's been attempting to meet with you for the past month."

Father shifted on his stool. "I've been too busy. My experiments have been at a critical stage."

She inhaled. They always were. But she must get Father to listen for once. She gritted another radiant grin. "I know, but this is important. Edouard and I are in love, and he needs to ask you for my hand."

Father grunted. "There's ample time for that." He shot her a narrow glance. "Unless he's seduced you and got you with child like Hawke did with the erstwhile Miss Keyes."

Her radiant grin transforming into a glare, Pippa fisted her hands on her hips. "Edouard isn't Hawke. He'd never do that."

Father turned back to his journal. "Well, then. Like I said, ample time."

To avoid shouting, she gulped a calming breath. Except Edouard's romantic proposal would be ruined if he didn't meet with Father *today*. "But why should we wait? We're in love, and neither of us are children."

Father grumbled, "That's debatable."

Pippa clenched her hips as heat flared through her. Why must Father always forget how old she was? "I'm eighteen, not eight, Father. You and Mother were a year younger when you married."

Father stiffened and began measuring out faedust into the vial before him. "So?"

She inhaled then leaned forward. "So I'm plenty old enough to marry." When Father continued measuring out faedust without answering, she snapped, "Must I destroy your magical experiments to get you to *listen*?"

Father whirled to face her. "You wouldn't."

Pippa glared back. For Edouard she would. "Don't force me to. Agree to meet with Edouard this afternoon."

Father gaped at her for a lengthy moment. Then he sagged on his stool. "Very well."

She relaxed. Father had agreed at last. A pang darted through her. Yet why had she needed to threaten Father to force his agreement? She made herself smile. "Thank you, Father. I'll leave you to your magical experiments now and send Edouard to you as soon as he arrives."

Pippa penned a note to Edouard informing him about his meeting with Father then gave it to Hodges to have delivered. She also ordered the butler to make sure Father ate, to tell her if Father left his workroom, and to unlock his workroom door if he locked it again. Nothing must prevent Edouard from meeting with Father.

CHAPTER 19

When Edouard strode past Hodges into her family's townhouse, Pippa stepped forward and took his hands with a brilliant yet tight smile. She was clearly as tense about his meeting with her father as he was. She said, "Father's waiting for you in the study."

Edouard blinked. Sir Julian wasn't in his workroom like usual? "Is that good or bad?"

Pippa blew a sigh, her smile fading. "I'm not sure. Father's probably annoyed by how I forced him into meeting with you."

Edouard stilled and eyed Pippa. She appeared upset at doing that. And Sir Julian being annoyed wouldn't help sway him to give his blessing. "Forced how?"

Pippa sighed again. "I threatened to destroy Father's magical experiments to get him to listen." As Edouard stared at her, she winced and worried her lip. "I know I shouldn't have, but I was so upset. He refused to listen to anything I said. Plus, he insulted you."

Edouard's stomach tightened. Such a bitter quarrel with her father must have distressed his loving Pippa. He squeezed her hands to hearten her. "Your father must know you wouldn't actually destroy his magical experiments." Hopefully.

A hint of her usual radiant smile reappearing, Pippa straightened. "I'm sure you're right."

He squeezed Pippa's hands again before releasing her. Thank the Goddess he'd cheered her enough to smile. "I'll head to the study now."

Pippa nodded, her eyes bright once more. "I'll wait for you here to find out how everything went."

He smiled at Pippa then hurried down the hall to the study. After inhaling a bracing breath, he knocked and entered. "Good afternoon, Sir Julian. Thank you for agreeing to meet with me."

Sir Julian snorted with a scowl. "Pippa gave me little choice."

Edouard winced as he sat before the desk. Pippa's father had taken her threat seriously. Wonderful. "Pippa isn't proud about how she forced this meeting, but we were becoming desperate."

His gaze narrowing, Sir Julian tensed. "Why are you both so desperate? Pippa said she wasn't pregnant."

Edouard blushed and shifted in his seat. Pippa had discussed *that* with her father? No wonder she'd been so upset. "She's not."

Sir Julian arched a brow. "Considering how I found you two nearly four months ago, I'm almost surprised to hear you both say that."

Edouard blushed harder. He'd probably feel the same if Pippa was his daughter. "I swear that the furthest we've gone has been torrid kisses. Although that restraint has been painful to maintain, and I'm not sure how much longer we can manage it."

Sir Julian glowered and drummed his fingers on the desk. "Are you threatening to seduce my daughter?"

Edouard stiffened. Damnation, his meeting with Sir Julian was going all wrong. "No, of course not. But given how desperately we love each other, 'twould be best if we marry soon, so we can begin our lives together."

Sir Julian humphed. "Pippa is too young to marry."

Still tense, Edouard leaned forward to show his sincerity. What would make Sir Julian see that Pippa wasn't a child any longer? "Plenty of ladies marry at eighteen—many of them happily."

Sir Julian shook his head. "But what about those who aren't? When the healer first placed Pippa in my arms while her mother breathed her last, I swore that I'd never allow her to repeat our mistakes. Her mother and I married much too young. We let passion overwhelm us then had to elope when she fell pregnant, not realizing how unsuited we were until after we were married."

Edouard inhaled. Well, *that* explained why Sir Julian kept harping on Pippa being pregnant. If Pippa ever learned the truth about her parents' "romantic" elopement, she'd be devastated.

Sir Julian glared at him. "Pippa has always been so bubbly and full of joy. I can't let her exuberance be destroyed by an early marriage, like her mother's was."

Edouard straightened and held Sir Julian's angry gaze. Had his and Pippa's attempts to prove their love and commitment done nothing? "You've seen me and Pippa together over the past few months. Do we seem unsuited to you?"

Sir Julian sighed. "No, you seem to balance each other well, and the love you share is apparent."

Edouard couldn't help his frown. "Then why are you so resistant to our marriage?"

Sir Julian grimaced with a shrug. "Because Goddess knows if your love shall last, especially under the pressures of marriage and children."

Edouard stared at Pippa's father. Didn't Sir Julian know his daughter at all? His jaw tightened. Probably not, thanks to years of neglecting everything but his magical experiments. Why couldn't the baronet take care of his family like a father should? Pippa deserved so much more. But at least his sweet sun nymph now had him to love and care for her like she deserved.

Edouard leaned forward again. "It shall. Neither of us waver once we know our own minds." When Pippa's father continued to grimace, he added, "I admit our love shall change during our lives together, but it shan't ever wither. No matter what happens."

Sir Julian snorted. "You seem confident of that." He drummed his fingers on the desk like before. "Very well, I'll approve your marriage—on several conditions."

His chest easing, Edouard began to smile. At last Pippa's father was seeing and addressing her needs. Whatever conditions the baronet demanded, he and Pippa could handle them. "Name your conditions."

Sir Julian humphed and leaned back in his chair. "You shan't like them, given your impatience to marry, but my conditions shall prove to me that your love shall last."

Edouard stilled as his stomach tensed. That didn't sound promising.

Sir Julian continued, "First, you must wait until after Pippa's natalday in spring to propose. Then you must remain betrothed for a year. That way, you'll have been together for two years before you commit yourselves forever."

Edouard gaped at his future father-in-law. Those conditions meant he and Pippa must wait until she was *twenty* to marry. They wouldn't even require Sir Julian's permission then. How could either of them wait so long?

Sir Julian flashed a sharp smile. "I told you that you wouldn't like my conditions."

Edouard snapped his mouth shut. "I don't. And neither shall Pippa."

He eyed Sir Julian. Somehow Pippa's father had consented without addressing his daughter's needs at all, simply his own. And from Sir Julian's set jaw, he'd not change his conditions either. Edouard stiffened. The baronet might even do something draconian like sequester Pippa at Sutton Manor and ban him from the estate until she turned twenty if he didn't agree to delay. And that would be much worse than waiting. He swallowed his heavy sigh. Perhaps once their betrothal was safely announced, he and Pippa could persuade Sir Julian to agree to a shorter betrothal. Although that would be in four and a half months, rather than during the Longnight season like he'd planned.

He reluctantly inclined his head. "Very well, I'll accept your conditions, Sir Julian. Although they're not necessary."

Sir Julian straightened. "I think they are. Good afternoon, Lord Blaine."

Nodding again but unable to manage a polite smile, Edouard rose. "Good afternoon, Sir Julian." Then he left.

As soon as he joined her in the entrance hall, Pippa bounced toward him with a glowing grin and asked, "Well, how did everything go?"

He hummed. How could he explain Sir Julian's conditions without upsetting Pippa? Delaying their betrothal and marriage would frustrate her, which would further strain her relationship with her father. And although the baronet was a neglectful excuse of a father, she deserved to enjoy the best relationship with him she could while he still lived. Plus, explaining Sir Julian wanted them to wait because of her parents' unhappy marriage would distress her. He'd better not tell Pippa anything until he knew what to say.

He grasped her hands and made himself smile. "It went." He pressed a kiss against her palms, his heart squeezing. "I must go. I'll see you at the Duchess of Childes's Longnight ball tomorrow."

Pippa blinked as he released her. "Edouard, what—"

Before Pippa could finish, Edouard interjected, "Save me the first and last reels." With Pippa silently gaping after him, he strode from her family's townhouse. He'd some serious thinking to do before he saw her again.

THAT EVENING and the following day, Edouard spent much of his time in the art room, listening to the melody of his dancing music-box sculpture while pondering what to tell Pippa. He certainly couldn't propose during the Longnight season like he'd planned. Goddess knew *what* Sir Julian would do if he discovered an early proposal.

Edouard sighed while activating the dancing music-box sculpture yet again. Why had he insinuated his romantic plans to Pippa before he'd spoken with her father? 'Twould be much easier to delay if he hadn't. And he couldn't explain his delay without hurting her and her relationship with her father either. Perhaps remaining silent would be best.

He grimaced as the haunting melody faded. If he arranged for Pippa and her family to join him and Elise for Longnight, she might believe that had been the plans he meant earlier. Hiding the truth from Pippa was distasteful, but he couldn't bear to hurt her, and this way she'd remain content at least. With a firm nod, he hurried from the art room to change for the duchess's Longnight ball.

Since Kit was waiting for the rakehell Duke of Oakmoor to escort her as he had for the past month, Edouard headed to Childes House alone. After greeting the Duke and Duchess of Childes, he glanced about the ballroom. Pippa and her brothers hadn't arrived yet, but Elise and Farson were near a garden balcony with Arvan. He fetched two flutes of sparkling wine then joined them.

Once they exchanged greetings, Edouard smiled at Elise. "I've been considering our Longnight plans. I assumed I'd celebrate with you at Golddell House, but could we invite Pippa and her family to join us?"

Her arm entwined with Farson's, Elise chuckled and replied, "I presumed we would. I thought we could have Pippa act as our first-foot this year instead of you."

Edouard sipped one of the flutes of sparkling wine he'd fetched. Having Pippa be their first-foot, the first Longnight visitor who arrived around midmorning with traditional gifts to bring good fortune for the year, would make their first Longnight together more special. That would make it more believable that those had been the plans he'd meant earlier. He arched his brows at Elise. "Do you mind if I invite Pippa myself?"

Elise and Farson traded an amused glance, then Elise drawled, "As you like."

Arvan suddenly gestured to the back with his mug of spiced cider. "The Hawkes are here."

His heart quickening, Edouard grinned as he and the others turned to face Pippa and her brothers sweeping toward them. Now that he knew what to say, seeing her was wonderful. And she was so radiantly lovely in her gold ballgown with intricate suns shimmering across the fabric, arachne silk from its magical luster. When she reached them and threaded her arm through his, he handed her the untasted flute of sparkling wine. "You look radiant."

Pippa beamed and squeezed his arm as she sipped her sparkling wine. "As radiant as a sun nymph? I thought that and wearing my arachne silk for the first time appropriate for tonight."

He swallowed. Pippa was definitely expecting a proposal before they left. Please let asking her to join them for Longnight satisfy her. "You're always as radiant as a sun nymph."

Farson smiling beside her, Elise giggled while Pippa's brothers tsked and Arvan grimaced. Elise said, "I never expected to hear such flowery flirting from *you*, Edouard."

A blush heating his neck, he shrugged with a wry grin. "Pippa inspires me, I suppose."

Then the beginning strains of the first Longnight reel permeated the ballroom, so Edouard led Pippa out to the floor, forming a set with Elise and Farson.

While Edouard and Pippa bounced through the vigorous reel full of hops, sprightly steps, and elbow spins, they grinned at each other, and energy flared in his veins. When the reel brought them close, he nearly crushed her against him and kissed her. Goddess, dancing reels with Pippa was incredible, even more so than ordinary dances. Her cheerful vivacity made her irresistible. If only he could propose to her tonight like she expected.

Thankfully, before his control could vanish, the Longnight reel changed, and Edouard danced with Elise while Pippa danced with Farson. Dancing with his sister settled him enough that he could restrain himself when the reel changed again and he danced with Pippa for the rest of it.

After the first Longnight reel, he and Pippa spent the evening talking and laughing with Elise and her family along with Pippa's brothers. Although Pippa kept hinting they should take a turn about the ballroom alone, he ensured they remained with their families to delay disappointing her for as long as possible.

However, after they romped through the final Longnight reel of the evening with Elise and Farson, Edouard inhaled to quiet his racing pulse then murmured, "We must talk alone before Dane and Xavier escort you home. Now that I've met with your father, we must discuss my plans for Longnight."

CHAPTER 20

$\mathcal{H}$er heart surging, Pippa beamed at Edouard. He was going to propose at last. But a slowly emptying ballroom was no place for a romantic proposal, especially since she meant to kiss him after she said yes. She leaned closer and squeezed his arm. "Shall we head to an anteroom?"

Edouard swallowed. "No need. We'll just take a turn about the ballroom."

She almost sighed. Edouard still mustn't trust them to be alone, even for a proposal of marriage. So much for kissing him after accepting his proposal. But at least they'd finally be betrothed. She squeezed his arm again. "Very well."

His faint smile tight, Edouard glanced at her. "Would you and your family like to celebrate Longnight at Golddell House with me and my family? Elise thought you could act as first-foot."

Pippa stared at Edouard as her breath stilled. *That* was the extent of his plans? To celebrate Longnight together? Why had he needed to meet with Father first? She inhaled. Unless he was planning a proposal on Longnight day. What a gift that would make.

She smiled up at Edouard. "We'll gladly celebrate Longnight with you, and I'd be honored to act as first-foot. What kind of

Longnight sweet biscuits should I bring?" The three other first-foot gifts were simple.

Edouard lifted a shoulder. "Whatever kind you like best. And as for Longnight gifts, we typically only exchange small ones, so nothing too elaborate."

She hummed. Small gifts for everyone should be easy enough, even though she must purchase the ones Father gave like usual. "I'd prefer to get you something special. Could we exchange our gifts privately?" 'Twould be the perfect opportunity for Edouard to propose too.

Edouard swallowed again but nodded. "As long as we get another gift to exchange with everyone else. Otherwise, our families shall notice and tease us."

Pippa couldn't help a chuckle. They'd endure enough teasing about finally becoming betrothed to need more. "Getting you another gift shall be no problem."

Edouard sighed. "Now that our plans are settled, I should escort you back to your brothers." Once he did, he released her with a warm smile. "I'll see you at the Nolans' Longnight charity auction tomorrow evening."

On the carriage ride home, Pippa told Dane and Xavier about Edouard's invitation for Longnight.

Sprawled beside Dane in the backward seat, Xavier smoothed his mustache and drawled, "You accepted for us without asking us first?"

Before she could more than blink in response, Dane shook his head at Xavier then said, "Ignore his teasing, Pippa. Given your courtship, we expected we'd be celebrating Longnight with Edouard and his family, and we're fine with that."

As she grinned at her brothers, Xavier chuckled and added, "Of course we are. Hopefully, Father is too since he'll need to abandon his magical experiments all day instead of an hour or two."

Pippa suppressed a frown. Even on festival days, Father *did* usually slip away to his workroom when they weren't participating in festivities. But surely he could forego that to celebrate with his future son-in-law, although he'd doubtless grumble about it at first. "I'm certain Father shan't mind just this once."

The following morning, she headed to Father's workroom to tell him about their Longnight plans. Unlike before he'd met with Edouard, it was no longer locked. Promising. She smiled and touched Father's arm. "Good morning, Father. I see you quit locking your door."

Father grunted as he added faedust to a vial containing an amber liquid. "'Twould be futile. You'd just have Hodges unlock it again."

Her lips quirked. Probably true. Letting Father hide hadn't helped, and Longnight was less than two weeks away. So she brightened her smile and told him about celebrating Longnight at Golddell House.

Father nodded and scribbled a note in his journal. "Not surprising. I'll be prepared to leave my experiments for the day."

Pippa beamed at Father's acceptance without a single grumble. Edouard had definitely won his blessing during their meeting. She squeezed Father's arm. "Thanks, Father. I'll leave you to your magical experiments."

She bounced from Father's workroom then took the carriage to the fashionable shops near Broad Street to begin her Longnight shopping. Since she was purchasing gifts for everyone, she just took her maid Betty rather than having her brothers or Edouard escort her. Before she returned that afternoon, she found small gifts for Elise, Dane, and Xavier as well as spotted possibilities for most of the others. Not that her partial success concerned her because she'd plenty of time to finish her Longnight shopping.

During the fierce yet cheerful bidding at the Nolans' Longnight charity auction that evening, Pippa told Edouard about her family's acceptance of their Longnight plans and her day spent shopping for Longnight gifts.

Edouard smiled while he bid on a set of ornate tenth-century candelabra donated by the Duke of Oakmoor. "I began my Longnight shopping as well. Although I only managed to find a gift for myself—a new piece for my art collection. Would you care to see it tomorrow morning before resuming your Longnight shopping?"

She grinned. His new piece must be truly stunning, considering how he'd rejected all the pieces at the estate sale the other day. "Yes, please. I wish I'd been there when you finally found a piece worthy of your collection. What is it?"

Edouard chuckled and caressed her palm with his thumb as he bid again on the candelabras. "You'll see it tomorrow. Oh, could you ask your brothers to join us? Elise already has plans."

Pippa swallowed a sigh at Edouard's continued prudence. Thankfully, 'twouldn't be necessary soon. "I suppose, although they'll be bored." Then she smiled when Edouard was declared the winner of the candelabras. "Congratulations, another tenth-century find for you today. How fortuitous."

AT BREAKFAST THE FOLLOWING MORNING, Pippa asked her brothers about joining her and Edouard. They both sighed over their eggs and tubers, but Dane agreed to come along rather than visiting Aherne's with Xavier like he'd planned.

She smiled when Edouard arrived just after breakfast—early for him, so he must be eager to show her his new piece. Talking about the many upcoming Longnight-themed events at court, they and Dane took Edouard's carriage back to Blaine House, then Edouard led them straight to the art room and halted before a covered painting.

Edouard grinned at her. "It reminded me of you as soon as I saw it at The Arte of Spells, so I had to purchase it." Then he pulled off the white silk covering.

Pippa inhaled at the tenth-century circular painting in a gold sunburst frame. Seated on a bank of fluffy clouds with the sun's glow radiating behind her, a sun nymph with wavy golden hair and amber eyes glanced over her shoulder at the viewer with a bright yet wise smile. Unlike many moving paintings, its enchantment was subtle. The only movement was the sun's glow shimmering in the background and the sun nymph's hair shifting in a gentle breeze.

Edouard murmured, "'Tis called *The Waking of the Sun*. Stornaway modeled the sun nymph after his sun witch wife then had her enchant the painting and create the frame with her magic. Their granddaughter is one of the founders of The Arte of Spells. She has no descendants to leave the painting to, but she only agreed to sell it to me when I told her about you, although my renowned art collection surely influenced her as well."

Aching to touch the sun nymph's radiant face, Pippa breathed, "'Tis beautiful—a very worthy addition to your collection."

Dane frowned and tilted his head. "But why did it remind you of Pippa? She doesn't resemble the sun nymph at all."

A faint blush coloring his cheeks, Edouard shrugged. "Physically, no. But they share the same air of sweet and radiant joy."

Warmth suffusing her at Edouard admitting that poetic sentiment to her brother, she nestled against him. She'd kiss him if Dane wasn't with them. Maybe she could persuade her brother to leave for a bit.

Dane chuckled as he studied them. "Well, that explains your flowery flirting at the Duchess of Childes's Longnight ball."

Pippa narrowed her eyes at Dane's gentle teasing. 'Twas fortunate Xavier wasn't here too. His teasing would be worse. "Don't you require air after seeing such a stunning painting?"

Dane chuckled again. "I suppose for a moment or two."

Once Dane strode out, she turned and cupped Edouard's face in her hands, her palms tingling at his freshly shaven jaw. "I adore your romantic tribute, although not as much as I adore you."

His gaze soft and warm, Edouard wrapped his arms about

her. "Oh, Pippa. I adore you too. So much." Then he lowered his head and kissed her.

She sighed and slid her arms about Edouard's neck then returned his tender kiss.

But before their kiss could deepen, a knock and a cough echoed through the art room. Dane said, "It's been a moment."

Pippa sighed again as she and Edouard separated. A moment wasn't near long enough.

Edouard smiled while he ushered her and Dane from the art room. "We should return to your townhouse so Pippa can continue her Longnight shopping." He nodded at Dane. "Thanks for agreeing to chaperone us today."

Dane grinned and nodded back. "You two clearly need it. Hopefully, you can marry soon so your ever-patient siblings can resume their own lives."

Pippa beamed. Yes, please. Then she stilled when she glanced at Edouard, whose smile had tightened. Why did her brother mentioning them marrying soon appear to trouble him? He wanted that too. Perhaps he was nervous about his proposal on Longnight.

OVER THE DAYS BEFORE LONGNIGHT, Edouard escorted Pippa to the many Longnight-themed court events, although he ensured they remained with their families, and Pippa let him since she was looking forward to his proposal on Longnight and didn't wish to ruin it. The festive court events were merry and a delight to attend, even when politics intruded. First, young Lord Morwynne had assumed his mother's position on the council after magically confining her to their country estate because she'd gone mad. Then a few days later, Lady Kiera and Lady Moonbud would be finally renewing the Nightmara-Calatini Treaty soon, which inspired Elise to host a ladies' luncheon celebrating that.

At Golddell House, Pippa lingered in the entrance hall as the other guests arrived for Elise's luncheon. Although Edouard had no reason to attend a ladies' event, he'd said he'd be visiting to keep his brother-in-law and the young duke company, and she couldn't miss seeing him. She beamed, her heart quickening, as he entered with Kit. When he dropped his stepmother's arm and strode over, Pippa beamed brighter and grasped his extended hands.

Once Kit sashayed from the entrance hall, Pippa smiled into Edouard's eyes. "What are your plans with Lord Farson and the Duke of Golddell?"

Edouard caressed her palms with his thumbs. "A ride, I think."

Tingling flooding her at Edouard's caress, she hummed. She needed more time with him, and he'd not protest since they'd be with family. "A ride is a much more appropriate way to celebrate the upcoming nightmara negotiations than a ladies' luncheon. Mind if I join you?"

Edouard frowned. "Elise and the others shall notice your absence, and you're not dressed for riding."

Pippa squeezed his hands. Her prudent Edouard. "I'll send Elise a note, and the skirt of this dress is wide enough for riding."

Edouard sighed but ushered her toward the study. "Very well."

When they arrived, Edouard told Lord Farson and the young duke that she meant to join them while she wrote her note to Elise.

As a maid collected her note, Lord Farson flashed an amused smile, and the gangly Duke of Golddell grinned at her and said, "Dane and Xavier would approve of your choice, Miss Hawke."

She grinned back at Arvan and Farson. "Pippa, please." They'd be family soon enough. "Except my brothers wouldn't approve of us skipping luncheon."

Arvan chortled. "Oh, we're not skipping luncheon, Pippa—

I'd starve. Farson promised we're eating at a tavern near the eastern gate."

She straightened and gripped Edouard's arm. As a sheltered young lady, she'd never done *that* before. "How exciting."

His smile warm, Edouard laid his hand on hers. "Just promise you'll stay close."

She glanced at Edouard beneath her lashes. "To you? Of course."

While Farson and Arvan chuckled at their flirting, the maid returned and said, "Lady Farson said to have fun and that you should borrow one of her riding habits and her mare."

Pippa headed upstairs and changed into Elise's riding habit, which didn't fit too badly. Then she and the others rode through the crowded streets of Ormas. Her gait smooth yet energetic, Elise's rose-gray mare was a delight to ride, even better than her own mare Honey. Not surprising since riding was vital in the Golddell duchy because of the nightmara and mara.

The hearty luncheon of ham stew and dark bread at the tavern was delicious too, and it kept them fueled during their lengthy gallop along the eastern road. Farson and Arvan were serious about their riding. Again, not surprising. Most of the non-mara humans from Golddell were just as horse mad as the mara.

When they returned to Golddell House, Elise greeted them with a bright grin. "How was your ride?"

Pippa returned Elise's grin. "Strenuous. Thanks for the riding habit."

Elise winked. "What else is a soon-to-be sister-in-law for?"

As Edouard stilled beside her, Pippa almost frowned. He was troubled again at someone mentioning them marrying soon. Definitely nervous. Yet he shouldn't be since he knew she'd say yes. She arched her brows at Elise. "How was the ladies' luncheon?"

Elise flicked a shrug. "Gossipy, but a success. No one quarreled, not even Lady Greysnowe and Lady Ravenstone. And only Kit seemed to notice your absence." She took Pippa's arm and escorted her upstairs to change. "I hope you'll join us in Arvan's box at tomorrow's Longnight play."

Pippa smiled, touched by Elise's invitation. "I'd love to."

During the final few days before Longnight, she and Edouard continued attending festive court events together. The merriment at the events burgeoned when word spread that Lady Kiera had negotiated the best treaty with the nightmara that Calatini had ever had. A perfect gift for the Longnight season. King Devon and the kingdom were undeniably blessed that he'd met Lady Kiera at his summer masquerade.

On Longnight morning, Pippa donned a white wool gown with gold thread and trim. She must look her best for Edouard's romantic proposal. Too bad she couldn't wear her arachne silk ballgown again, but 'twasn't suitable for a family event.

Then she collected her bag of Longnight and first-foot gifts before finding her brothers in the gamesroom and Father in his workroom. As they took the carriage to Golddell House, she smoothed her skirt with a dreamy smile. In just a few hours, Edouard would propose, and they'd be betrothed at last.

CHAPTER 21

When Edouard arrived alone on Longnight morning, Elise frowned at him after everyone exchanged Longnight greetings and asked, "Where's Kit?"

He shrugged while placing all his gifts except Pippa's special one on the winter palace, an enchanted ice sculpture that held Longnight gifts. "Kit sent me a note this morning stating that she must leave to tend some unexpected business."

Elise traded a frown with Farson then tilted her head. "Unexpected business?"

Edouard shrugged again as he sat on an empty sofa so Pippa could sit beside him once she arrived. "I wondered if Kit might have fallen pregnant." 'Twould be fitting given how she'd told all of court about Hawke and Wren's scandalous pregnancy. "After all, she's been courting the rakehell Duke of Oakmoor for the past month and a half."

Elise pursed her lips. "I doubt it, considering how Kit never fell pregnant during five years of marriage to Father. She probably is suffering one of her vicious megrims and doesn't want anyone to see her."

He hummed and nodded. Kit *did* hide when she had her

megrims. But before he could agree aloud, Pippa bounced into the drawing room with her father and brothers.

Pippa beamed at them. "Happy Longnight, everyone!" Once they all returned her Longnight greeting, she began removing first-foot gifts from her bag. She gave Edouard the bag of coal, Elise the jar of salt, Farson the flask of spiritwine, and Arvan the tin of Longnight sweet biscuits. "May these bring you all good fortune in the coming year."

As Pippa placed her other gifts on the winter palace while her brothers did likewise, Arvan opened the tin of Longnight sweet biscuits and said, "Ooo, apricot pinwheels. I've not had these for ages."

Edouard smiled when Pippa sat beside him and replied, "They're my favorite Longnight sweet biscuits." Good, she'd done as he asked. Despite her father's gaze on them, he threaded his fingers through hers and squeezed her hand.

Arvan grinned. "Let's eat them now before we open Long-night gifts."

Everyone chuckled at Arvan's perpetual hunger, but they devoured the pinwheel sweet biscuits with nutmeg-spiced dough wrapped around apricot preserves and nut filling.

Then they swiftly exchanged their small Longnight gifts amid animated talk and laughter. 'Twas obvious from his mild surprise when giving them that Sir Julian hadn't purchased the gifts he gave. Doubtless Pippa had done so.

Edouard smoothed the embroidered pocketcloth Pippa had given him as her public gift. 'Twas very Pippa to quietly take care of her father like that. Perhaps that was one of the reasons Sir Julian didn't wish her to marry yet. In addition to his fear of them repeating his own unhappy past, of course.

Edouard sighed as he managed to cram his new pocketcloth into the pocket above his heart, despite it already containing Pippa's special Longnight gift and one of the pocketcloths she'd given him over three months ago.

After the gifts were exchanged, everyone headed to the

family dining room for the traditional Longnight feast of venison, wild boar, roasted root vegetables, fresh orenges, and Longnight cake. Their merry talk and laughter continued throughout the delectable meal, and he risked flirting with Pippa even though her father narrowly eyed them most of the time.

While Farson teased Arvan for eating a second slice of the rich Longnight cake, Pippa leaned toward Edouard and said, "I could use a walk after all that food. Shall we?"

His heart surging, Edouard nodded. They must exchange their special Longnight gifts before returning to the drawing room for Longnight games, and a walk to settle their digestion was a suitable excuse. He took Pippa's arm and made their excuses then began escorting her from the family dining room.

As they passed Sir Julian, the baronet gripped Edouard's arm until he halted and bent down. Sir Julian muttered in his ear, "Remember, you can't propose until after Pippa's nataldday."

Not letting himself glare at that unnecessary reminder, Edouard straightened. "I remember."

Once they were alone in the hall, Pippa glanced at him. "What was that about?"

He swallowed. He couldn't truly explain without hurting Pippa. So he merely said, "Your father was just reminding me about what we discussed during our meeting."

He almost winced when Pippa began to glow even brighter than usual. She was clearly still expecting a proposal. Hopefully, exchanging their special Longnight gifts would satisfy her. His jaw tightened. Oh, why had Sir Julian been blind to Pippa's needs and demanded they wait? He hated continually disappointing her. Yet he couldn't devastate her with the truth behind her father's demands.

Pippa drew him into the morning room then extracted a small white box from her pocket and thrust it into his hands. "Your true Longnight gift. Open it."

Edouard couldn't help a chuckle. Pippa was so adorable. He tugged her slim box wrapped in shimmering gold paper from his overfull pocket and gave it to her. "Only if you open yours at the same time."

Pippa giggled. "Gladly."

While Pippa tore the gold paper from her gift, he deftly unwrapped his, and they opened their boxes together. He inhaled at the gleaming bronze inkwell with asymmetrical swirls and sunbursts adorning it. What a beautiful accessory from the tenth century, and so suited to his nickname for her. 'Twould look perfect on his desk and always remind him of her. Not that he needed a reminder to think of her.

Pippa sighed as she fingered his gift, a delicate gold bracelet with three sun charms carved from yellow butterscotch amber. "'Tis exquisite, Edouard. Put it on me, please."

He smiled and set aside his inkwell then freed Pippa's bracelet from its box. She adored his gift as much as he adored hers. To tease her, he said while he fastened it about her left wrist, "You know you can't wear it when we rejoin everyone. They'll notice its sudden appearance and realize we exchanged secret gifts."

Pippa sighed as she admired the sparkling bracelet on her wrist. "I know, but I can wear it here. And I'll definitely be wearing it tomorrow and every day after that."

Warmth suffusing his chest, Edouard pulled Pippa into his arms. He *had* to hold her—just for a moment—before they rejoined the others. He smiled down at her. "I adore the inkwell you gave me. I'll think of you whenever I see it on my desk."

Pippa beamed back while she nestled against him and threaded her arms about his neck. "I'm glad."

His body tightening at Pippa's soft curves and sweet peach scent, he shuddered but didn't release her like he should. Goddess, how was he ever to resist her for the next year and four months until they were married?

The silence humming about them, he and Pippa stared into each other's eyes, and his pounding heart quickened further.

Unable to not, he brushed a kiss against her upturned lips. "I love you so, my sweet sun nymph."

The bracelet he'd given her warm and hard against his neck, Pippa pulled his head down for another kiss. "I love you too, Edouard."

He let himself kiss Pippa again until his body ached. Then he wrenched their mouths apart. "We'd better rejoin everyone before they begin looking for us."

Pippa blinked up at him, her warm-brown eyes dark and hazy. "What?"

He forced himself to release Pippa at last then unfastened the bracelet about her wrist and poured it into her palm. "Your father especially shan't approve us being alone so long."

Pippa licked her lips while she slid her bracelet into her pocket. "Don't you have a question to ask me first?"

His chest twisting, Edouard gritted a smile. If only he could. "Another time. We must rejoin the others now."

Pippa exhaled and swallowed before slowly nodding, and they returned to the drawing room without touching. He'd whisk her back in the morning room and beg her to marry him if he did. But defying her father's conditions would be disastrous if Sir Julian discovered it, and he doubtless would. Vital secrets were always discovered by those who shouldn't learn them.

When they entered the drawing room and settled on the empty sofa, everyone paused their Longnight riddle game to glance at them. Then after Arvan triumphantly answered the riddle, Dane arched a brow and rumbled, "Quite a lengthy walk to settle your digestion."

Xavier smirked and smoothed his mustache. "Delayed by kisses, perhaps?"

Pippa blushing beside him, Edouard tensed and glanced at her father, who was studying them with a twisted smile. Sir Julian obviously accepted that kisses between them were inevitable but didn't entirely approve. Please let him not decide to forbid their courtship and banish Pippa to Sutton Manor until she turned twenty.

On the sofa across the drawing room with Farson, Elise tsked and said, "Kisses aren't the only reason to be gone for ages." She grinned and leaned toward them. "Perhaps you two have a happy announcement to share?"

As Pippa drooped and Sir Julian glared, Edouard swallowed and nearly clenched his hands. They must quit discussing kisses and proposals between him and Pippa before her father exploded. He muttered, "Not yet."

While Elise and Pippa's brothers stared at him and Pippa, Farson coughed then asked, "Shall we play a round of blind seer's chase to energize us before we attempt snap-drake?"

Edouard smiled at his brother-in-law and nodded. Normally he'd protest playing a risky game like snap-drake, but vigorous Longnight games were just the thing to distract everyone from his and Pippa's courtship.

Arvan grinned and leapt upright. "I'll be the seer."

While Farson rang and requested servants prepare snap-drake, the gangly young duke donned a blindfold to play blind seer's chase. Then Dane and Xavier twirled him several times before everyone except Sir Julian, who declared he was too old for such amusements, scattered about the drawing room. Arvan prowled about the room while they all attempted to evade him. Eventually, Elise stumbled on a chair, and Arvan managed to catch her, guessing her identity within moments.

Once everyone's mirth quieted, Farson dimmed the witch-lights and lit the spiritwine in the shallow bowl to play snap-drake. Starting with Arvan and ending with Sir Julian, they each took turns snatching raisins and nuts from the bowl without getting burned by the blue flames flickering across it. Then amid cheers and laughter, they extinguished their fiery treat by eating them. They continued snatching treats until the burning spir-itwine was empty. Fortunately, no one caught themselves on fire like sometimes happened when playing snap-drake.

Edouard and the others spent the rest of the afternoon playing Longnight games and singing carols full of festive cheer until they headed to the Great Temple for Longnight Vespers.

The always stunning Great Temple was resplendent for the crowded festive service. Witchlights were ablaze throughout the main temple, casting a warm glow on its white limestone with green and gold ornamentation as well as the gold-veined white marble altar and matching statue of the Goddess. In addition to the usual priests, many from court were in attendance. Although only the devout attended the daily services, people often attended Vespers on Longnight since 'twas the first day of the year, and those from court who attended usually chose to attend at the Great Temple because 'twas the most prestigious.

As Edouard and the others found seats in the nave, Mel strode over to join them, his priest robes flapping. "Happy Longnight. Mind if I sit with you?"

Edouard smiled and waved for their cousin to sit on the end beside him. "Of course not."

On his other side, Pippa beamed at Mel. "Where are your parents and the rest of the family?"

Mel hummed as he sat. "Celebrating at the local temple near Waterstreet Orphanage with the orphans. I had to return to the Great Temple instead."

Farson smoothed his beard. "I imagine King Devon and Lady Kiera are there too."

When Mel nodded, Elise chuckled and said, "'Tis fortunate that court didn't realize they'd attend there—otherwise, that poor local temple would be overrun."

Then Longnight Vespers began with an opening prayer, so Edouard and the others quieted and turned toward the altar. During the first carol, he glanced at Pippa, who was grinning as they sang. So sweet and full of joy. His heart warming, he threaded his fingers through hers. He and Pippa held hands throughout the festive service full of prayers, readings, and carols celebrating new beginnings and the gifts of hope and love.

After Longnight Vespers, Mel invited them to join him at the Great Temple's dining hall for dinner. Since Mel clearly missed celebrating with his immediate family, Edouard and the others accepted despite still being full from their Longnight feast at midday. Dinner at the temple was jolly and delicious, although they were the only ones there who weren't priests.

Following dinner, Edouard escorted Pippa to her family's carriage. He smiled as he handed her inside. "I'll see you tomorrow at the Duke of Oakmoor's charity luncheon." Since they were courting, Kit had planned the charity luncheon for the duke, and the family refuge they'd chosen to support was a very worthy charity too.

Pippa leaned toward him. "You can't accompany us home for a drink?"

He swallowed and clung to his smile. If he did, Pippa would surely expect a proposal. "'Tis been a long day. Happy Long-night, Pippa."

Then he turned and hurried to Farson's carriage before he did something mad like kiss her on the steps of the Great Temple in front of their families or blurt out the proposal she was expecting. Thanks to her blind and begrudging father, that must wait until her natalday in spring.

CHAPTER 22

$\mathcal{A}$s soon as Pippa and her family returned to the townhouse, she said good night and retreated to her chambers. She slipped her sun-charm bracelet from Edouard beneath her pillow then let Betty help her into her nightgown before wishing her maid a happy day off tomorrow. Since the day after Longnight was about charity, servants never worked that day and stayed home with their families.

Once alone, Pippa retrieved her bracelet and refastened it about her left wrist. She blew a sigh as she caressed the delicate gold chain and yellow butterscotch amber suns. The bracelet was truly exquisite and showed Edouard's love for her. The perfect Longnight gift—almost. The proposal she'd been expecting would have been better.

She began to pace about her chambers. *Why* hadn't Edouard proposed today in the morning room? It had been the perfect opportunity. Had he been too nervous about delivering a romantic proposal on Longnight day itself? Or had he waited to propose some place special to them, like his art room? She frowned. *Or* had whatever Father reminded him about in the family dining room discouraged him? But why would it when Father had clearly approved of him since their meeting?

Still stroking her sun-charm bracelet, Pippa hummed while she paced. 'Twasn't as if Edouard didn't want to propose. He'd confessed his love on multiple occasions and admitted being impatient to marry her. And he habitually demonstrated his steadfast devotion—he'd chosen that perfect Longnight gift, kissed her as if desperate whenever they were alone, and held her hand throughout Longnight Vespers with their families.

She exhaled. She'd been so certain Edouard would propose on Longnight. Beginning their lives together at the start of the year was just the sort of deliberate plan he'd make. *What* could be delaying his proposal? She nibbled her lip. She'd not been the only one expecting his proposal today. From their stares after Edouard had muttered they weren't betrothed yet, their siblings had all assumed that had been why she and Edouard had slipped away. Doubtless the others had too, although their reactions hadn't been as obvious.

Pippa firmed her mouth and forced herself to quit pacing. Although Edouard hadn't proposed today, he'd never break his promise to propose during the Longnight season. He just needed to overcome whatever was making him delay proposing. Surely continuing to show him her love and encouraging his proposal would manage that. Then she'd happily say yes, and they'd be betrothed at last. They could arrange their wedding ceremony within a month or two and would be blissfully married before her natalday in spring. Or perhaps even before the new season officially began on Plantfete. She smiled. Attending court events as a married couple would be so much better. Then they could dance every dance together like they both wanted, rather than just the first and last ones.

So the following morning at the Duke of Oakmoor's charity luncheon, she headed straight for Edouard once she paid three gold to receive her initial luncheon task. She beamed at him as she slid her arm through his. "Kit's idea for us to pay for luncheon tasks was brilliant. Not only does it address the lack of servants today, but it also gets everyone to donate to Goddess's

Refuge." Goddess's Refuge was one of the family refuges that priests ran to help people escaping abuse—Kit had chosen a worthy yet unexpected charity. "I should compliment her. Where is she?"

Edouard grimaced. "I'm not certain, but not here. She wrote again last night that Longnight had inspired her to reflect on her life, so she'd be away for a while, but that Mel could contact her if needed."

Pippa blinked at Edouard. Odd that his fashionable step-mother had abandoned her life at court. But since he likely couldn't explain why, she simply asked, "Wrote again?"

Edouard hummed with a shrug. "Yes, Kit wrote yesterday morning that she must leave to tend some unexpected business. 'Twas why she didn't celebrate Longnight at Golddell House with us."

Pippa echoed Edouard's hum. Definitely odd. "I just assumed she was celebrating with the Duke of Oakmoor. They're courting, after all." She glanced across the drawing room at the suave duke, who was smiling as he talked with King Devon and Lady Kiera. "How's the duke handling Kit's unexpected absence since she planned his charity luncheon?"

Edouard shrugged again. "Well enough. Kit apparently sent the Duke of Oakmoor a note providing him with detailed instructions about how to handle everything."

Pippa nodded. Given Kit's always spectacular court events, 'twasn't surprising she'd thought of that. She'd not want an event she'd planned to fail in her absence because 'twould damage her reputation. Pippa squeezed Edouard's arm. "Well, enough about Kit. What luncheon task did you get? We should trade until we've the same ones."

Edouard glanced at his slip of paper. "Serving the first course."

She frowned at her slip of paper. Darn. "I got performing Longnight carols. Which would you rather do?"

Edouard chuckled and arched a brow. "In front of all these

people? Serving the first course. I don't want a repeat of the fete play."

Pippa giggled. How Edouard had hated that. "Performing together in the fete play wasn't so terrible." She studied him beneath her lashes and fingered her sun-charm bracelet. "Plus, our private rehearsals were exciting." She licked her lips to remind him why.

Edouard swallowed and looked away. His voice rough, he said, "Shall we find someone who has serving the first course for you to trade with?"

She inclined her head, and they bustled about the drawing room, asking everyone about their luncheon tasks. They succeeded when they talked with the Westons. Lady Weston had serving the first course as hers and was eager to trade for performing Longnight carols. To be expected considering the musical evenings that the older couple frequently hosted. So Pippa and Lady Weston each donated three more gold to trade their luncheon tasks.

That settled, Edouard fetched them both mugs of spiced cider.

As they began strolling about the drawing room, Pippa sighed and eyed the elegant furnishings. They suited the wealthy and influential Duke of Oakmoor, but they were dull compared to the townhouse's true jewel—the ballroom's stained-glass ceiling created by his duchy's fantastic artisans and made unbreakable by magic. When Edouard glanced at her, she sipped her spiced cider and answered his silent question, "I wish today's luncheon was in the ballroom. I've only seen its stained-glass ceiling at night, during the Duke of Oakmoor's soiree a month and a half ago. I'm sure the ceiling is even more magnificent with the daylight shining through it."

Edouard swallowed. "Probably." His eyes flickering, he said, "Perhaps we could slip away for a moment to see it."

She beamed and squeezed Edouard's arm. And they could manage a kiss or two while in the ballroom. "Yes, please."

But before they could slip away, the Duke of Oakmoor called for luncheon to begin. She sighed. They'd missed their chance. Yet the duke's luncheon, which was splendid and merry despite the inexpert service, soon had her grinning and laughing again.

After luncheon, everyone split into groups based on their luncheon task to play Longnight games, so Pippa was even more thankful that she'd traded with Lady Weston because she and Edouard could remain together. The Longnight games were boisterous, and wagers about them flew, enhancing the excitement. Although neither of them were typically frivolous with their money, they wagered too since everything won was donated to Goddess's Refuge like the payments for the luncheon tasks.

Despite not seeing Oakmoor House's ballroom ceiling, she was still grinning and laughing when Edouard escorted her home along with Dane and Xavier. Warmth flooded her as she nestled against him and he wrapped his arm about her then kissed her hair. For her private Edouard to hold her like that in front of her older brothers was tantamount to a proposal. But she'd get a real one before they parted.

So when the carriage halted at their family's townhouse, she flashed a brilliant smile at her brothers. "I'll be along in a moment."

Dane and Xavier exchanged knowing glances, but they left without protest.

As Edouard tensed around her, Pippa turned and smoothed his cravat then beamed to encourage him. "Now would be a wonderful time for your plans for the Longnight season."

Edouard swallowed, his pale-blue gaze dark. "We already celebrated Longnight together and exchanged special Longnight gifts."

She tsked. "So we did, but there's a question you neglected to ask me." Her heart pounding, she leaned forward and brushed a kiss against Edouard's lips then withdrew. "I'll say yes, you know."

Edouard shuddered and shut his eyes. "Oh, my sun nymph, how am I ever to resist you?"

Pippa caressed Edouard's rough jaw, and her pulse quickened. "I don't want you to."

Edouard groaned and jerked her against him for a desperate kiss. She fisted her hands in his silky hair and returned his kiss. So perfect. Then she purred when he undid her laces and touched her bare back beneath her shift, his hand hot and possessive. Oh, Goddess, she needed him to touch her like that *everywhere.* And she needed to touch him too. She yanked at his cravat.

When it unraveled and she began on his waistcoat, Edouard stiffened and thrust her away from him. "Enough. I never should have escorted you home."

Breathless and aching, she eyed him and licked her tender lips. "Why did you?"

Edouard sighed. "Because I was too excited from the Longnight games to remember sense. Now, head inside before we go too far."

Her blood still racing, Pippa swayed toward Edouard. "There is no too far for us."

Edouard's jaw clenched. "Yes, there is. Inside *now*, Pippa."

She shuddered a sigh then turned her back to Edouard. "You must retie my laces first." She shivered with hunger as he silently did so. If only they hadn't stopped. But he was determined to remain prudent like usual.

Once Edouard finished, she murmured good night and slipped from the carriage. He'd not propose in his current temper. But they still had thirteen more days left in the Longnight season.

YET OVER THE FOLLOWING DAYS, Pippa and Edouard were never alone even though they continued attending Longnight-themed court events together every day. And although she kept showing him her love and encouraging his proposal, he refused her many hints about slipping away to talk in private and never proposed.

She worried her lip while she prepared for the Greysnowes' ball on the last day of the Longnight season. Edouard *had* to propose tonight. He was too reliable to ever break a promise. Surely he'd escort her home and propose then. Like on the first day of the Longnight season, she wore her arachne silk ballgown to look her best, but this time she used a drop of blood to turn it the same sunny yellow as the charms on the bracelet he'd given her.

When she joined Edouard in Greysnowe House's ballroom—which was resplendent with scenes of magical creatures, fitting for a family from Wildewall—Edouard smiled at her, his gaze warm and intent. "You resemble sunshine itself tonight, my sun nymph."

She returned Edouard's smile as her chest eased. Yes, he'd definitely propose tonight. Perhaps she could even encourage him to leave early to do so.

Her arm threaded through Farson's, Elise giggled while her husband, Arvan, and Pippa's brothers traded amused glances. She said, "More flowery flirting, Edouard?" She winked at Pippa. "You've changed my serious twin beyond recognition."

As both she and Edouard blushed, Pippa shook her head. "Nonsense." To distract Elise, she asked, "Who do you think the Greysnowes shall announce as their new son-in-law?"

Pippa and the others glanced across the boisterous ballroom at Lord and Lady Greysnowe, who were grinning as they greeted their still arriving guests while their son Lord Alexander laughed with Lord Morwynne nearby. Their daughter Lady Annalise and her mysterious new husband were nowhere to be seen. The Greysnowes' ballroom could barely contain all the guests thanks to the gossip they'd circulated about their daughter's sudden marriage without disclosing her husband's identity.

Elise chuckled and replied, "I've no inkling, but all of court is agog to discover whom the beauteous Lady Snow considered suitable to marry."

Farson drawled, "Whoever he is, the Greysnowes appear more smug than when Lord Alexander nearly killed Lord Ravenstone at their duel last Summerday, so he must be influential enough for them to consider it a triumph over the Ravenstones."

Edouard quirked a wry grin. "Since King Devon is taken, he must be one of Calatini's unwed dukes." He arched a brow at Arvan. "Perhaps even Arvan."

Pippa swallowed her laugh as the gangly duke blushed and said, "N-not me. Lady Annalise is nine years older than I am. And much too beautiful."

Before they could tease Arvan further, the Greysnowes swept to the front of the ballroom and thanked everyone for attending. Then with Lord Alexander almost snickering beside them, Lord and Lady Greysnowe gestured for their daughter, her chosen husband, and her new mother-in-law to enter.

Everyone gasped as the erstwhile Lady Annalise glided into the ballroom on Lord Ravenstone's arm followed by his grinning mother. Pippa gaped at them. Lady Annalise had married her family's ancestral enemy! What a way to end the centuries-long feud. No wonder the Greysnowes had appeared smug. Their daughter's marriage would be the talk of court for months.

Once Lady Greysnowe and the Dowager Lady Ravenstone embraced, chatter erupted, and nearly everyone surged toward the Greysnowes and the Ravenstones like they were rare rainbow unicorns in a menagerie. However, Pippa, Edouard, and their families remained near the musicians' balcony and eyed the rambunctious crowd.

Pippa chuckled when Elise drawled, "Well, I certainly wasn't expecting *Lord Ravenstone* to be Lady Annalise's mysterious husband."

Farson smoothed his beard. "Given their dedication to the feud, I'm surprised the Greysnowes approved of their marriage."

His smile twisted, Edouard rasped, "They didn't have to. Lord Ravenstone and the new Lady Ravenstone are both over the age of majority, so they could easily elope. And considering the centuries-long feud, court would probably consider their elopement romantic rather than scandalous and reckless like most elopements."

Pippa studied Edouard, her chest tightening. He appeared troubled again. Why? Because they still required Father's approval? But they had that. She squeezed Edouard's arm with a brilliant grin. "The Greysnowes wouldn't have hosted a ball to celebrate their marriage if they didn't approve."

Edouard exhaled. "True."

Pippa and the others stayed across the ballroom and talked while they waited for the crowd to clear about the Greysnowes and the Ravenstones before heading up to offer their congratulations. Eventually, Dane, Xavier, and Arvan left to fetch refreshments, and Mel joined her and the others.

After they greeted Mel, Edouard eyed the still unruly crowd across the ballroom. "Goddess, 'tis madness. I don't think I want a ball celebrating my betrothal or marriage."

Her heart softening, Pippa smiled. Her private Edouard would despise such melodramatic fuss. Not that she wanted it either.

Elise giggled and winked at her. "You're not the only one with a say in that, Edouard."

Pippa squeezed Edouard's arm again to reassure him. "I wouldn't mind having a ball, but I agree nothing like this one."

Warmth suffused her as she and Edouard beamed at each other. When could they leave so he could propose at last? While Elise and the gentlemen discussed the missing Kit, Pippa remained silent. Somehow she must get Edouard to risk the crowd so they could congratulate the Ravenstones and leave.

After Mel left and her brothers and Arvan returned, Pippa smiled at Edouard and said, "I'm beginning to tire. We should congratulate the Ravenstones, then you can escort me home."

Edouard stilled. "Why don't you and your brothers congratulate them while I fetch your carriage? That way you can leave sooner." Before she could protest, he strode away.

Her head whirling, Pippa congratulated the Ravenstones with Dane and Xavier. Why had Edouard fled like that? He'd not proposed yet, and 'twas the end of the Longnight season. Perhaps he would in the carriage once they reached her family's townhouse and her brothers headed inside. His proposal couldn't go too far then. But when she and her brothers went out to their carriage, he was nowhere to be found. Her chest clenched as the carriage jerked forward sans Edouard. He'd disappeared without ever proposing.

Back in her chambers half an hour later, she paced and twisted her sun-charm bracelet about her wrist. Edouard hadn't proposed, even though he'd promised he would during the Longnight season. *Why* had he broken his promise? He was too steadfast for that without a compelling reason. Her body numb and stomach hard, she set her jaw as she slid into bed. She must ask him tomorrow.

After a restless night, Pippa made herself wait until midmorning to head to Blaine House. Considering how Edouard disliked mornings, talking to him earlier would be futile.

Unable to manage her usual smile, she burst into his study as soon as she arrived. Her ribs tight, she said, "Good morning, Edouard."

Edouard stared at her as he leapt upright. "Pippa, what are you doing here?"

She swallowed then sat before Edouard's desk and folded her hands in her lap. She held his gaze and calmly replied despite her tension, "We must talk."

Edouard winced while dropping back into his seat. "About what?"

Pippa fisted her hands until they ached as fiercely as her heart. How could Edouard have behaved like Father did whenever engrossed in his magical experiments? She gave Edouard a flat glance. "About why you broke your promise and didn't propose during the Longnight season."

CHAPTER 23

*E*douard swallowed at Pippa's reproach, his stomach tight. How could he explain without hurting her further with the truth behind his delay? "I didn't promise to propose during the Longnight season."

Her usual radiant smile absent, Pippa stared at him across the desk. "Perhaps not explicitly, but you certainly implied it."

He inhaled as his chest clenched. So he had, and Pippa had taken that as a promise. He should have realized she would. *Why* hadn't he waited until after he'd spoken with her father? His impatience for everything to be settled between them had made him imprudent. Now they were reaping the consequences of that. He leaned forward and held her gaze. "I'm sorry for misleading you."

Pippa's lips compressed. "Why did you?"

Edouard almost winced and lowered his gaze to the gleaming inkwell Pippa had given him on Longnight. She'd been so full of joy then—unlike now, all because of his impatience. He straightened and made himself look at her again. "I didn't mean to."

Pippa blew a sigh. "Then why?" Her eyes darkened. "Did you forget your promise?"

He stiffened. Exactly like Pippa's neglectful father often did. Aching to pull her into his arms, he gripped his knees and leaned forward again instead. He'd kiss her if he held her, and she was too upset for that. "I didn't forget. My plans simply changed." Thanks to Sir Julian's senseless conditions.

A frown furrowing her brow, Pippa scrutinized him. "Why did they?"

Edouard swallowed to ease his constricted throat then forced himself to lace his fingers together on his desk. If only he could truly explain. But sharing that Sir Julian had insisted they wait and why would shatter Pippa's already strained relationship with her father. And although flawed, that relationship was too precious for her to lose before her father died. Since Father's death, he knew how painful 'twas not to have such a relationship, so he must protect it for her.

He drew a shuddering breath. "'Twasn't time yet for us to become betrothed." Damn her father.

Pippa gaped at him. "*'Twasn't time yet?* But we've been courting for over eight months. Plenty of couples are betrothed by then." Her mouth snapped shut. "Or did you decide I was *too young* again?"

He nearly grimaced. 'Twas certainly what her idiot father thought. "Of course not."

Her jaw hard, Pippa leaned forward and grasped the front of his desk. "Then why wasn't it *time yet*?"

Edouard tightened his mouth to avoid blurting why. Goddess, Pippa was so upset. But he still couldn't hurt her with the truth. Unable to find any words, he silently shook his head.

Paling whiter than a grieving banshee, Pippa sagged back in her chair. "Unless you decided we can't marry because you don't truly love me, after all."

He jerked up in his seat, his heart freezing. "What? No!"

Pippa leapt to her feet and began toward the door. "What other explanation is there?"

Edouard surged upright and seized Pippa's wrist to halt her

flight. How could she possibly think he didn't truly love her? By refusing to explain, he'd *hurt* her and made her doubt his love. He had to tell her everything, even though 'twould shatter her relationship with her father.

Her sun-charm bracelet biting his palm, he drew her toward him. "Pippa, wait—"

Pippa whirled around. "No!" Then she fiercely punched his stomach. As he wheezed and bent over, she wrenched her wrist free and bolted from his study.

Once he could breathe again, he hurtled after Pippa, but her carriage was already gone. He swore as he snatched the coat his butler Rooke offered before racing to the stables. He ordered a groom to saddle his gelding and yanked on his coat while he impatiently waited. Then he galloped to her family's townhouse despite the sidelong glances he received during his frantic yet freezing ride.

Yet when he pounded on the door and demanded to see Pippa, Hodges stiffened and replied, "Miss Hawke isn't at home, my lord—to anyone."

Edouard winced, his chest as cold as the air outside. Anyone meant him especially from the butler's austerity. Pippa was clearly furious with him. But if he could just explain. He gritted a beseeching smile. "I must apologize to Pippa for our quarrel."

Hodges didn't budge. "I'm sorry, my lord, but I can't let you enter."

Edouard swallowed a curse and ran a hand through his hair. He *must* speak to Pippa at once. Perhaps he could shove the butler aside and find her. No doubt her brothers were out, and her father would be too engrossed in his workroom to notice.

Yet before he could, Sir Julian grumbled from behind the butler, "What's going on here? First Pippa slams inside so hard that I dropped faedust into the wrong vial, and now Lord Blaine is growling at my door. I can't concentrate at all."

As Sir Julian replaced Hodges in the doorway, Edouard gripped his hands behind his back. Of course Sir Julian would notice *today*. He gritted another smile and nodded at the baronet. "Pippa and I quarreled, and I must apologize, but she's not at home to anyone."

Sir Julian hummed and quirked a sardonic brow. "Then you'd better leave and return when Pippa is at home." When Edouard began to protest, Pippa's father narrowed his eyes. "Unless you want me to retract my approval."

His pulse flaring, Edouard clenched his hands tighter. If not for Sir Julian's unnecessary and bitter conditions, he and Pippa wouldn't have quarreled. And obviously smug about their quarrel, the baronet was threatening him. Why had he bothered to protect Pippa's relationship with her father? Sir Julian continually neglected her, broke his promises, and remained selfishly blind to her needs. Although the baronet was her father, Sir Julian was *nothing* like Father. If he was, he would have celebrated that his daughter had found love, not attempted to obstruct it. The flawed relationship Pippa suffered with Sir Julian wasn't worth saving. He'd been as idiotic and blind as the baronet to rank that above their love.

He inhaled then made himself nod at Sir Julian. Forcing himself inside would infuriate the baronet, who would then likely forbid his and Pippa's marriage. He'd best retreat for now. "Very well. Good day, Sir Julian."

Edouard pivoted and returned to his gelding. He'd speak with Pippa at the St. Claires' ball tonight. Even if it caused talk, he'd whisk her to an anteroom so he could apologize and explain. Although they still couldn't become betrothed yet and risk her father withdrawing his begrudging approval, at least she'd forgive him if he explained. Please, Goddess.

YET PIPPA never appeared at St. Claire House that evening, nor at any of the other court events Edouard attended over the following week. She also continued to not be at home when he visited her family's townhouse every morning. He even asked

Dane and Xavier to get Pippa to see him, but they apologized the next day and said that Pippa had utterly refused.

Although he rarely drank, he began tossing back several snifters of spiritwine alone in his study every evening after unsuccessfully hunting for Pippa at court events. She was definitely still furious and avoiding him, so he'd *deeply* hurt her. But he could resolve that if she just let him apologize and explain.

Thankfully, a note from the Duchess of Childes arrived the week after his quarrel with Pippa, inviting him to a family luncheon in a couple days. If the duchess had invited him, surely she'd invited Pippa as well. And no matter her fury with him, Pippa couldn't skip an event hosted by the duchess, so he'd finally be able to see her. Thank the Goddess.

Edouard arrived early at Childes House and asked Perkins if Pippa had appeared yet. Once the august butler replied she hadn't, he lingered in the entrance hall to wait for her. 'Twas nearly time for luncheon and everyone else had arrived, including King Devon and Lady Kiera, when Pippa finally entered flanked by Dane and Xavier.

His chest tight, he strode toward Pippa with a warm smile. "At last. You're almost late. I'd begun to think you weren't attending."

Pippa tensed, her drawn face blank as an empty communication mirror. She flatly replied, "I couldn't skip the duchess's luncheon." She glanced at her brothers. "We should get to the drawing room and not delay luncheon."

Edouard stepped in front of them, his smile fading as his heart twisted. Shorn of her cheerful vivacity, his sweet Pippa no longer resembled the sun nymph he'd named her. He'd been a damned fool for hurting her so and stealing her joy. He murmured, "Unless you want everyone pestering us about our quarrel, you'd better let me escort you. The duchess, especially, shall attempt to meddle."

Pippa winced then swallowed. "Very well."

Edouard exhaled as he took Xavier's place beside Pippa. He'd convince her to talk to him during luncheon, then they could slip away to talk alone. None of their family would even remark about that.

Yet when he served Pippa oyster soup at luncheon, she only acknowledged him with a rigid nod. Convincing her to talk to him might take the entire meal.

He was just about to ask Pippa if she liked the soup when the duchess began explaining why she arranged luncheon, concluding, "Hawke and Wren are having *twins*."

As congratulations swept about the table, Edouard tensed and glanced at Elise, who'd paled slightly. Given her desperate longing for children, hearing about Hawke and Wren's good fortune would doubtless upset her. However, when their gazes met across the table, Elise managed a tremulous smile, which she clung to during the remaining courses.

After only managing to wring a few words from Pippa during luncheon, he almost scowled once he and the other gentlemen joined the ladies in the drawing room. Pippa had taken the chair between the duchess and Selena, rather than a sofa with space for him like she would have before their quarrel. She was clearly ensuring he couldn't approach her.

While everyone toasted Hawke and Wren as well as Aragon and Selena for their upcoming offspring, Edouard sipped his sparkling wine and eyed Pippa. Perhaps once the toasts quieted, he could ask her to join him for a turn about the room. She couldn't refuse him without the duchess and Selena wondering why.

But before he could, Elise slipped from the drawing room, and he tensed. His twin was undeniably upset to leave like that instead of congratulating their cousins. As the elderly lady who was Mel's new assistant bustled after Elise, he turned to Farson beside him. However, Farson was arguing with Arvan about the young duke's sparkling wine, so Edouard followed Elise and Mel's assistant Kay himself.

He knocked on the partially open door then inhaled and

stepped into the morning room. Elise was sobbing on a sofa while the elderly lady held her hands. His throat thickened at his twin's distress. "Elise?"

As Elise turned her tear-ravaged face away, Kay narrowed her eyes at him and ordered, "Go fetch Lord Farson."

He jerked a nod then fled. Back in the drawing room, he hurried to Farson, who was watching a sulky Arvan sip lymonade. Edouard murmured in Farson's ear, "Elise is crying in the morning room."

Farson paled then rushed from the drawing room.

After glancing at Pippa, who was still ensconced between the duchess and Selena, Edouard followed his brother-in-law. He could talk to Pippa once he'd checked on Elise.

He'd just returned to the morning room when Kay slipped into the hall. The elderly lady smiled at him and patted his arm. "Elise just needs time alone with her husband."

His chest tense, he frowned as they began down the hall. "Do you think so? I've never seen Elise so miserable before, not even when Mother died."

Kay nodded. "Yes, but if you want to help Elise, you could bring her some fresh bread and butter in a quarter of an hour."

Edouard smiled as his tension eased. "Devouring that does always cheer Elise. Thanks."

He strode to the kitchen, fetched Elise's treat, then returned to the morning room. Fortunately, his twin's tears had slowed when he arrived, although she was still in Farson's arms. They'd been kissing from the flush on her cheeks, so Edouard quickly left the bread and butter before departing.

He exhaled after he rejoined the others in the drawing room. The duchess and the duke were talking with Mel and Kay, so the seat beside Pippa was empty at last. His pulse surged as he dropped into the empty seat and leaned toward her. "We must talk."

Pippa stared at him, her face stiff. "We've nothing left to talk about."

Edouard clenched the arms on his chair until his fingers cramped. Oh, Goddess, for Pippa to still treat him with such icy reserve meant she was *more* than hurt by him delaying his proposal then refusing to explain. A chill pierced his stomach. Perhaps she even hated him now. Pippa was too sweet to maintain such fury for anything less. Would his apology and explanation be enough to inspire her to forgive him?

He swallowed but held Pippa's gaze. "You know that we do. Take a turn with me about the drawing room."

CHAPTER 24

Clinging to her cool mask as tears pricked her eyes yet again, Pippa stared at Edouard and gripped her hands in her lap. She'd spent much of the ten days since their quarrel crying bitter tears whenever alone, which wasn't like her. If she cried at all, 'twere typically tears of joy, and when she cried out of sorrow or pain, she soon quit because she could see the positive aspects. But not this time. Edouard not truly loving her after having promised forever had shattered her, and nothing had eased that.

She swallowed. And seeing Edouard again knowing he didn't love her enough to marry when she still adored him was excruciating—like spirits poured on an open wound. Letting him escort her to luncheon and him sitting beside her had just worsened that. Somehow she'd buried her tears beneath a cool mask so far, but she couldn't manage that much longer. She must leave before she began to sob in front of their families. They'd attempt to comfort her and ask why, and she couldn't bear to discuss her and Edouard's dead courtship with anyone.

Pippa inhaled a steadying breath then answered Edouard's request to take a turn about the drawing room, "No, I should be returning home. Excuse me, Lord Blaine."

Before Edouard could protest, she leapt upright and fled to her brothers, who were consoling Arvan about having to drink lymonade instead of sparkling wine during the toasts. She gritted a brilliant grin. "Could you escort me home?"

Dane and Xavier traded frowns, then Dane rumbled, "Perhaps you should let Edouard do so."

Xavier hummed as he glanced past her. "From how he's striding after you, he's eager for the chance."

Pain pierced her chest. Oh, Goddess, she couldn't handle being alone with Edouard. She'd sob and beg and kiss him, even though 'twas futile and would only embarrass her. After he'd made his decision, he'd not waver. And even though he'd once said they'd the rest of their lives for kisses, in the end he'd decided he didn't love her enough to ask her to become his wife. She glared at Dane and Xavier. "No. Take me home. Now."

Dane and Xavier sighed then ushered her from the drawing room. Thankfully, Elise's return with Farson prevented Edouard from following.

As soon as they returned to their family's townhouse, Pippa bolted to her chambers and resumed her sunflower embroidery with trembling hands. 'Twas her sixteenth piece since her quarrel with Edouard. In addition to crying whenever alone, she'd embroidered feverishly to distract herself. The enjoyable pastime hadn't stemmed her tears, yet she kept embroidering. Perhaps it would eventually. But not today. Scalding tears cascaded down her face as she finished that piece and began another of yellow daisies.

She choked down the chicken stew and rolls Betty brought for dinner then crawled into bed early rather than attending an evening court event to reassure her brothers. Since they'd gone to a family event today, she needn't bother with a court event she'd no interest in attending anyway. Without Edouard, balls and parties didn't appeal, and she'd purposely chosen small events that he'd never attend to avoid seeing him.

After another restless night suffused with dreams of

Edouard, Pippa woke late the following morning to a pounding at her door. She yanked on a dressing gown then staggered across her chambers and wrenched her door open. Dane and Xavier stood outside, dressed in riding clothes and looking much too cheerful. She scowled at them. "What?"

As Dane narrowed his eyes at her, Xavier quirked a brow and replied, "We're going riding to the royal bay. Get dressed."

She lifted her chin. A vigorous ride with her brothers, who'd surely want to discuss Edouard, sounded painful. "Did you get permission for that?"

Dane exhaled. "We asked King Devon at the family luncheon yesterday. We thought a ride to the royal bay would cheer you."

When she grimaced, Xavier leaned forward and said, "Don't bother to protest. We're taking you riding if we have to toss you on your mare in your nightgown."

Dane added dryly, "Although we'd prefer if you ate and dressed first." He smiled. "And here's Betty now with your breakfast. Meet us downstairs once you're ready."

Pippa sighed and stepped from the door for her maid to enter. She'd better eat and dress. Her brothers were clearly determined for her to ride with them. "Very well."

Once she forced herself to eat the eggs, toast, and tea Betty had brought, she let her maid help her into a muddy-brown riding habit that suited her mood. Then she donned her heavy cloak and headed downstairs and met her brothers in the entrance hall with a tight smile. "I'm ready."

Both Dane and Xavier scrutinized her for a long moment, then Dane nodded and said, "Let's go. 'Tis almost midmorning already."

Xavier slanted her a sidelong glance as they strode out to the stables. "Late enough for Edouard even. We could stop by Blaine House to invite him to join us. He'd eagerly accept."

Her heart twisting, she glowered at Xavier. Must he keep shoving her at Edouard, who didn't want her? "No."

Dane and Xavier glanced at one another then sighed. Dane replied, "As you like, Pippa. Do you need help mounting?"

She shook her head and climbed atop Honey without her interfering brothers' help. Then they rode through the crowded streets of Ormas and out the northern gate. Not wanting to talk, she urged Honey to a canter once outside the city and kept to that until the royal bay.

When they halted at the cliffs above the royal bay, she sighed while weight compressed her chest. The view was as stunning as ever, and unlike when she'd first ridden here with Edouard over seven months ago, the sun was shining in a cloudless sky, the breeze was still, and no storm threatened despite the bracing cold. Yet without Edouard, neither the stunning view nor the glorious winter morning delighted her.

She said little as she and her brothers rode down the winding path to the beach and then across the sand just beyond the icy surf. Last time, she'd ridden beside Edouard, flirting like a hungry venus to encourage their first kiss. She blinked back the tears suddenly blurring her vision. How full of hope she'd been then. And already in love with Edouard, although she'd not recognized that until later. But why else had she been so determined to kiss him? Not that he'd obliged her here in front of his family. She shuddered another aching sigh. Their entire courtship, she'd pushed Edouard for more than he wanted to give.

As they turned around at the far end of the royal bay, Dane slanted her a narrow glance. "The royal bay doesn't appear to be cheering you."

Pippa shrugged while she steered Honey around a pile of driftwood. Nothing but Edouard truly loving her would cheer her right now. "Riding here reminds me of my first visit with E— Lord Blaine."

Dane and Xavier glanced at each other, then Xavier asked, "You rode to the royal bay with Edouard?"

She swallowed a wry laugh. Edouard had been right about

her brothers finding out about that, although 'twas months too late to matter. "On that ride here with Elise. I didn't mention he was joining us because I wanted to see him without enduring your frowns."

As Xavier snorted and raised his eyes skyward, Dane shook his head then said, "Somehow your determination to court Edouard fails to surprise me." Dane eyed her. "What happened between you two, anyway?"

Pippa stiffened and clenched Honey's reins. She'd *known* they'd want to discuss Edouard. "I told you, we quarreled."

While Dane arched his brows, Xavier leaned toward her and asked, "Yes, but about what? You and Edouard have been mad about each other since the moment you met. What could have come between you?"

She lifted her chin as her throat constricted and tears pricked her eyes once more. Edouard hadn't been mad about her. If he had, he would have proposed like he'd promised. She eked a brilliant smile. "Nothing that concerns either of you."

Dane tsked while he steered his brown gelding back toward the cliffs. "You two shall never resolve anything if you don't talk."

Xavier nodded and smoothed his mustache. "Which Edouard definitely wants. He always asks after you whenever he sees us. You should talk with him."

Pippa shuddered. Except seeing Edouard, let alone talking with him, hurt too much. Perhaps she could manage it once she ceased crying whenever she was alone. "I can't." When her brothers began to object, she snapped, "I don't wish to discuss this any longer."

Then she urged Honey to a gallop to prevent further discussion. She kept up a brisk pace until they returned to the townhouse, where she immediately retreated to her chambers and found a note waiting for her from Elise. She stiffened but opened it. 'Twas an invitation to luncheon in a couple weeks. She crumpled the invitation and shoved it in a drawer. Attending a luncheon hosted by Edouard's twin was impossible now. She sank into a chair and resumed her embroidery, letting free the tears she'd suppressed earlier.

OVER THE FOLLOWING DAYS, Pippa continued remaining alone in her chambers and avoiding Edouard. And she began attending fewer of the small court events with her brothers to prevent them from lecturing her about him. But she kept joining everyone for dinner to reassure them. When Father ate with them, Dane and Xavier never mentioned Edouard, and when Father didn't, she could often deflect them by talking about the food they were eating or the latest family news, like Aragon and Selena's daughter Isabel being born on Aragon's natalday.

Yet at dinner three weeks after her quarrel with Edouard, Dane cleared his throat once he served her haddock soup. "Edouard found me and Xavier at Aherne's this morning. He begged us to get you to meet him at the Landcastles' soiree tonight, Pippa."

Not glancing toward Father at the head of the table, she froze with her spoon halfway to her mouth. Why was Dane discussing Edouard with Father listening?

Xavier frowned. "Yes, and Edouard looked as wretched as you have since your quarrel. You should end his misery and agree to meet him."

Her throat clenching, Pippa lowered her spoon before she splattered soup across her chest. Edouard doubtless only looked wretched because he felt guilty for distressing her, not because he grieved for their dead courtship. She swallowed. "I can't."

Father smiled while he devoured his haddock soup. "Still quarreling with Lord Blaine? I knew your love wouldn't last. You're much too young."

As Dane and Xavier gaped at Father, fire flared through her, and she glared at him. How dare Father be so smug? And blame her age yet again? Why could he *never* see who she actually was?

Fisting her hands in her lap, she leaned toward Father. "My love has lasted just fine."

Father snorted and arched a brow. "Has it? Then why are you no longer pursuing Lord Blaine? Even before you could crawl, you've always gone after what you wanted—usually with a sunny smile that almost disguised your determination."

Her anger crumbling to ash, Pippa sagged back in her chair. True, but she'd been too shattered to continue pursuing Edouard. And she'd yet to recover. She made herself straighten and pick up her spoon. "Regardless, I love Edouard as much as ever."

Dane laid his hand on hers. "Then you must stop hiding and talk to him about your quarrel."

Xavier leaned toward her. "You'll never recover if you don't. And we want our bubbly sister back."

Warmed by her brothers' loving advice, Pippa blinked to contain the tears pricking her eyes. Perhaps she should heed them, even though she still felt like a communication mirror shattered on the rocks. Yet she couldn't pursue Edouard like before. She ached too much for sunny smiles, and she mustn't push him for more than he wanted to give. But she could stop avoiding him and let him approach her, no matter how much it hurt to see him knowing he didn't truly love her.

She attempted a brilliant smile, although it trembled rather than shone. "I'll consider it. But not tonight." She must look her best when she saw Edouard again, which meant more rest and hours getting ready beforehand.

As Father humphed, Dane and Xavier sighed and traded grimaces. Then Dane said, "As you like."

After dinner, Pippa returned to her chambers and requested a tonic to help her sleep. She gulped down the tonic Betty brought then slid into bed. Thankfully, the tonic worked, so she fell asleep swiftly and wasn't tormented by dreams of Edouard. She woke refreshed when the morning light shone across her face.

She spent the day in her chambers preparing to see Edouard. After a lengthy bath, she basked before the fire and had Betty brush her hair until it glowed. Then she donned a gold silk gown and her sun-charm bracelet from Edouard for the first time since their quarrel before joining everyone for dinner.

Xavier whistled when she entered the drawing room. "Imitating a sun nymph again?"

Dane chuckled. "Edouard shall certainly think so." He arched his brows. "I assume you intend to meet him at Lady Ducharme's rout party tonight."

A blush heating her cheeks, Pippa nodded and caressed the sun-charm bracelet. She'd missed its comforting weight about her wrist the past few weeks. Almost as much as she missed Edouard. Please let her not cry and kiss him as soon as she saw him. He'd not want that since he'd decided he didn't truly love her.

She and her brothers ate dinner, without Father tonight, before heading to Ducharme House. Once they greeted Lady Ducharme and her husband, Pippa scoured the tasteful drawing room furnished with ocean art and wave carvings for Edouard. Her ribs tightened when she didn't find him.

She managed to smile at Dane and Xavier. "Shall we greet Elise, Farson, and Arvan?" Edouard would surely join his twin and her family the moment he arrived.

Her brothers nodded, and they strode across the drawing room.

After they'd exchanged greetings, Elise eyed her while the gentleman began discussing today's horse auctions at Aherne's. Elise murmured, "I've hardly seen you since Longnight. Everything all right?"

Pippa swallowed then smiled to reassure Elise. "I've not felt well lately, but I'm better now." Hopefully.

Elise pursed her lips. "I suppose 'tis also why you refused to let Edouard visit you. He's been desperate to see you the past few weeks."

Her heart quickening, Pippa twisted the sun-charm bracelet Edouard had given her. "Has he?"

Elise's brows flew upward. "Can you doubt it?" When Pippa's gaze fell, Elise hummed. "Are you attending my luncheon in a few days? You never replied to my invitation."

Pippa almost winced. No, she hadn't. Although attending had felt impossible, she'd been unable to decline Edouard's twin, who she'd believed would become her sister-in-law one day. She made herself lift her gaze. "If Edouard asks me, I shall."

Elise hummed again. "I see."

To distract Elise from her and Edouard, Pippa asked Elise about the latest gossip regarding the royal wedding ceremony and Lady Kiera's coronation on Plantfete in two months. Yet she kept scouring the guests for Edouard the rest of the evening. However, he never arrived, so she left Ducharme House with slumped shoulders.

Over the days before Elise's luncheon, Pippa continued attending court events that Edouard should also attend, but he never appeared. And he never contacted her about his twin's luncheon or attempted to visit her. Plus, Dane and Xavier said Edouard quit approaching them about her.

So when she should have been dressing for luncheon at Golddell House, she retreated to her chambers and began embroidering again with tears burning her eyes. Edouard clearly no longer wanted her, not even to talk. She'd have to live the rest of her days with a shattered heart.

Her scalding tears bursting free, Pippa dropped her embroidery and twisted Edouard's sun-charm bracelet on her wrist. Why, oh why, couldn't he love her the way she loved him?

CHAPTER 25

Edouard groaned when his valet Abbot shook him awake late on the morning of Elise's luncheon. After Pippa had refused to meet him at the Landcastles' ball, he'd given up attending court events to see her because 'twas futile. If she still wouldn't even attend the same court event three weeks after their quarrel, she was determined never to forgive him. Instead, he'd spent his evenings alone in his art room or study, nursing a spiritwine or three to help him forget her unrelenting fury. But those evenings made his sleep disturbed and mornings even more wretched than usual.

His head throbbing, he forced himself to accept the steaming cup of kahve Abbot thrust at him. He gulped the bitter brew and winced as it scalded his mouth and throat. Yet that pain was nothing compared to the burning ache hollowing his chest since he'd realized that Pippa couldn't forgive him. Goddess, he'd ruined everything by delaying his proposal then refusing to explain.

Abbot coughed. "You'd better hurry and dress, my lord, or you'll be late for Lady Farson's luncheon."

Edouard blew a sigh. He wasn't looking forward to choking down a meal without revealing his misery to his twin, who knew him better than anyone other than Pippa. Elise had noticed things weren't right in the weeks since he and Pippa had quarreled and kept asking him about Pippa. But he couldn't admit his embarrassing foolishness to Elise, so he'd remained silent. Yet the other day, she'd ordered him to ask Pippa to today's luncheon. Not that he had. Pippa would only have refused, and another icy refusal from her would have destroyed him.

He let Abbot help him dress then forced himself to head to Golddell House. When he shuffled into the drawing room, Elise was speaking to Mel and his elderly assistant Kay, while Farson and Arvan were talking on the sofa nearby.

Elise turned from Mel and Kay to frown at him. "Where's Pippa?"

Edouard stiffened and headed to the spiritwine decanter. He really couldn't discuss Pippa in front of everyone. He muttered, "She refused to attend." Or as good as.

Elise tsked. "*What* happened between you two?"

His neck prickling at everyone's stares, he forced a shrug and poured himself a spiritwine then downed it in one gulp. He had to get Elise to stop discussing Pippa. He frowned and turned to face the others again. "Nothing that you can help with, so quit asking."

As Elise began to protest, Farson grasped her arm. "We should eat luncheon before Arvan expires from hunger. Growing boys, you know."

Elise sighed but allowed her husband to escort her from the drawing room. Thank the Goddess.

However, Edouard tensed when Kay shooed Mel toward Arvan and said, "You join the Duke of Golddell. Lord Blaine shall escort me." Did the elderly lady intend to continue Elise's probing? He required another drink to endure that.

While Mel and Arvan strode out, Edouard poured himself a second snifter of spiritwine. He grimaced as Kay murmured, "Drinking yourself into a stupor shan't solve whatever happened between you and Miss Hawke." Yes, more probing.

He made himself turn around then snorted and tossed back his spiritwine. "No, but it allows me to forget for a time." And he desperately needed that.

When he reached for the spiritwine decanter again, Kay blocked him with a fierce frown. "Such thinking leads to becoming a drunkard. Not a pleasant sight. I'd know—my father is one. He's lost everything to drink. And he's cruel with it too."

Edouard blinked at the elderly lady. Her father must be *ancient*. Unless all that spiritwine had made him misunderstand. "Your father is still alive?"

Kay stilled. Then she asked, "What happened between you and Miss Hawke?"

His stomach clenching, he glared at Kay. Must she be so persistent? 'Twas none of her concern. "What's it matter to you?"

Kay held his gaze. "I want to help, and you clearly need to talk."

He sagged and quit glaring. Helping him doubtless *was* Kay's concern, given her profession. "That's right; you're Mel's assistant. You probably want to help everyone like him. But nothing you can do shall help."

Kay tsked. "Perhaps not, but talking shall make you feel better."

Edouard couldn't help but snort. How could talking with Kay help? She'd barely met Pippa.

Kay sternly eyed him. "Sometimes you need an outside perspective."

He humphed. Maybe he did. He'd certainly been unable to resolve matters himself. He studied Kay. "I suppose you're practically a priestess, so I can trust you not to gossip." And Mel's elderly assistant would be both wise and caring. Hopefully that was enough, despite her not knowing Pippa.

When Kay nodded, he exhaled and dropped on the nearby sofa. "After the Longnight season, Pippa and I quarreled, and she's been furious with me since then. She stopped accepting my escort and began avoiding me at court events. She quit attending family events too—except for the duchess's luncheon. No matter how furious, Pippa couldn't skip *that*."

Kay hummed as she sat beside him. "What did you and Miss Hawke quarrel about?"

Edouard stared at his hands, his throat constricting. "That I hadn't proposed during the Longnight season when I'd implied I would." His voice broke. "Pippa accused me of not truly loving her."

Kay frowned. "'Tis obvious to everyone you adore Miss Hawke, although I can see why she might doubt it if you implied you'd propose and didn't. Why didn't you?"

Edouard grimaced and clenched his hands. "When I asked for Sir Julian's blessing just before the Longnight season, he said I must wait until Pippa's natalday in spring to propose. *And* that we must have a year-long betrothal to ensure our feelings are genuine." As Kay pursed her lips then shook her head, he ran his hand through his hair and continued, "But unfortunately, I'd already implied that I'd propose before I spoke to Pippa's father, so she was upset when I didn't."

Kay inhaled. "You didn't explain why you delayed, did you?"

He shifted in his seat. "I couldn't further strain Pippa's relationship with her father, and I didn't realize telling her 'twasn't time yet would hurt her so." Goddess, he'd been such a damned fool.

Kay snorted and raised her eyes skyward. "Why are gentlemen such idiots?" She poked his arm. "Of *course* 'twould hurt Miss Hawke."

Edouard winced. Yes, definitely a dammed fool. "I know that now. But afterward, Pippa wouldn't let me apologize and explain."

Kay leaned toward him. "You must do something dramatic —something not like your prudent self—to convince Miss Hawke to listen. Then you must tell her Sir Julian insisted you delay."

He swallowed and stared at Kay. Something dramatic? He

didn't excel at that. But he could try. "You think that shall inspire Pippa to forgive me?"

Kay nodded. "If you're dramatic enough and grovel sufficiently." She poked him again. "Don't squander the deep love you and Miss Hawke share. Not everyone is fortunate to enjoy a love like that."

Edouard smiled as the warm rapport, vibrant joy, and irresistible kisses between him and Pippa before their quarrel echoed through him. True, so he must fight to regain that, even if it seemed futile. He leapt upright. "I'll go visit Pippa now and beg for her forgiveness."

Kay rose and grasped his arm. "Perhaps you should wait until after luncheon. You just drank two snifters of spiritwine without eating."

He blinked. So he had. "Sir Julian wouldn't approve if I arrived to see his daughter tipsy, would he?" And Pippa's father was begrudging enough already.

Kay's mouth quirked. "No, he wouldn't. Let's join the others in the family dining room."

Edouard nodded, and as they strode to the family dining room, he beamed and squeezed Kay's arm. She'd been right about an outside perspective helping. "Thank you for your invaluable advice, Miss Kay."

Kay blushed but shrugged. "Of course. Although Elise would have said the same. Why didn't you talk to her?"

Heat warming his neck, he coughed and lowered his gaze. "I was too embarrassed to admit what I'd done." Then he chuckled when Kay smiled and shook her head. Yes, he'd been ridiculous.

When they entered the family dining room, he couldn't help grinning as Farson told Arvan, who was mournfully eyeing his empty plate, "Don't fret; you shan't starve before they join us."

While he escorted Kay to her seat beside Mel, Edouard said to tease the perpetually hungry Arvan, "Even though it may feel like it."

Elise beamed at him and gestured for the servants to bring

the first course. "Finally. You appear more cheerful than you have in weeks."

Still grinning, Edouard began his creamy rhubarb soup. Because he finally knew what to attempt to win back Pippa, although he'd yet to decide his precise plan. But he would after luncheon. "Miss Kay helped me see how to inspire Pippa to forgive me."

Her gaze probing, Elise leaned toward him. "Why must Pippa forgive you?"

Edouard grimaced and shifted in his seat. He couldn't discuss his foolishness in front of everyone. "I'll tell you later. Now, I must concentrate on eating so I can get to Pippa."

Elise pursed her lips. "Very well." Then she turned to Mel and Kay, asking them about life at the Great Temple.

Edouard remained silent and attended to his meal while Mel and Kay discussed visiting local temples and community programs with Elise and Farson. But his mind kept drifting to the dramatic gesture he must plan to inspire Pippa's forgiveness.

So when the servants brought the shokolat hazelnut mousse for dessert, he leapt upright. He'd waited long enough. He must get to planning and preparing to see Pippa. "I need to go. I'll see you later."

Before Elise and the others could protest, Edouard rushed out and returned to Blaine House. Once there, he headed straight to his study then sat and drummed his fingers on his desk. What was not like his prudent self?

He frowned. Something that risked causing talk and earning her father's disapproval if 'twas ever discovered. Pippa would adore if 'twas also romantic. And it must be private as well. They'd a lot to discuss, and he burned to kiss her again. Pippa surely did too.

His body hardening at kissing Pippa, Edouard gulped a steadying breath as his gaze fell to his parents' wedding tokens on their gold chain in the clear bowl beside the bronze inkwell from Pippa. He must focus in order to figure out how to inspire her forgiveness so that they could enjoy a happy marriage like Father and Mother had. What was the best way to approach her?

He drummed his fingers faster. How about visiting Pippa in her chambers while everyone slept? *That* was certainly scandalous and private, although not making love to her would be painful. Perhaps he could remain across the room most of the time. But how to make his visit romantic?

After an hour thinking through everything, Edouard had decided his plan. He wrapped his parents' wedding tokens with their necklace in one of his embroidered pocketcloths from Pippa and slipped it into the pocket above his heart then took a carriage to Rhiannon's Veils. Once the veiled witch sashayed into the empty witch shop, they sat at the wooden table, and he said, "I require two enchanted items, madam witch. Peach blossoms, which aren't in season for a month or two. And a charm to reach Miss Hawke's chambers without being noticed."

The veiled witch hummed. "Your first request is simple enough. My garden in the back has both melissae and peach trees."

He almost gasped. The veiled witch had a garden with the huge bee-like melissae? They were wary of humans, and their stings were deadly, although their ambrosia could cure any ill. Yet since flowers pollinated by melissae were hardier and in season longer than normal, Pippa's favorite flowers would be available already.

Her black veils fluttering, the veiled witch tilted her head. "The second request would be easier if you've Miss Hawke's hair or blood to set the charm." When he grimaced and shook his head, she sighed. "But I suppose I could set it with her full name, although 'tis harder."

Edouard nodded and handed the veiled witch a bag full of gold coins. That should be enough for his requests. "Philippa Grace Hawke."

The veiled witch accepted his money then rose and gathered a glass bowl, some herbs, three vials, and a length of rope from the cabinets behind her. She dropped the herbs into the bowl and poured the three vials on top then waved her hand over the bowl and began crooning a singsong chant. The potion in the bowl started shining like the sun at noon until the veiled witch placed the rope into the bowl. The potion wicked into the rope, which shone briefly before fading to a constantly shifting shimmer.

The veiled witch handed him the shimmering rope. "To activate the charm, picture Miss Hawke and say her full name. But wait until you're near her window because the rope must be long enough to reach it. The charm shall end at dawn, so make sure you leave before then." Once he thanked her, the veiled witch rose and beckoned him to follow. "Come along for your peach blossoms."

He followed the veiled witch through the door of glass beads at the back of the witch shop. Then he gasped when he entered her magical garden. Despite it being winter still, 'twas like summer in the veiled witch's garden. The balmy air was sweet and heady with the scent of flowers, while butterflies, faebirds, and melissae buzzed about the many verdant plants. A secret paradise concealed in a poorer part of Ormas. Amazing. If only Pippa was with him to see it.

The veiled witch glided to the peach tree, which bore fragrant flowers on one side and ripe fruit on the other—just like the rest of the fruit trees in the magical garden. She plucked several blossoming twigs and tied them together with a gold thread then handed them to him. "Here you are. If you put them in water with honey and vinegar, the peach blossoms should last four weeks or so."

Edouard cradled the sweet-smelling bouquet against his chest and swept a bow. "My deepest thanks, madam witch."

Her exotically lined eyes crinkling, the veiled witch waved him from her magical garden. "Of course, Lord Blaine. Miss Hawke shall love your romantic apology."

A chill prickling his skin, he stared at the veiled witch. How did she know he was apologizing to Pippa? Maybe 'twas best not to know since he didn't possess the slightest powers. So he simply bowed again and left.

He returned home then spent most of the evening in his art room and listened to the haunting melody of his dancing music-box sculpture while planning what he'd say to Pippa. He devoured a hearty dinner, drinking tea rather than wine or spiritwine since he required a clear head when he saw her later. Then he forced himself to wait until midnight to don his heavy black cloak and walk to her family's townhouse.

Edouard halted beneath the red brick building and unfurled the shimmering rope. Then he pictured Pippa and whispered her full name. The rope glided upward and attached itself to the middle window. He inhaled and began to climb. Goddess, please let his plan succeed.

CHAPTER 26

*P*ippa jerked awake when a thump rattled her window, her pulse pounding. What in the Goddess's name was *that*? She peered at her window and almost fell from bed at Edouard's face staring back. The ever-prudent Edouard was outside her upper-story window well after midnight? Was he mad?

She darted across her chambers, yanked open her window, and hissed, "*What* are you doing here?"

His jaw set, Edouard leaned closer, and tingling swept through her. She could kiss him if she just bent her head. As she forced herself to remain still, he said, "Visiting you. And I'm not leaving until we talk. May I come inside? My arms shall go numb if I hang onto this rope for hours."

Concealing her hunger for Edouard behind a sigh, she twisted his sun-charm bracelet about her wrist and stepped back. "Very well. 'Twould be a scandal if you were discovered unconscious beneath my window."

While she slipped into a dressing gown, Edouard heaved himself inside then hauled the shimmering rope he'd used to climb up the townhouse wall in after him before latching the window. He turned to face her with a wry smile. "The charm on the rope is supposed to let me reach your chambers without being noticed, but I'd rather not risk anyone seeing the rope. Besides, the night air is freezing this time of year."

Pippa frowned at Edouard as she tightly tied her dressing gown. Why was he discussing trivialities in her chambers during the middle of the night? She crossed her arms. "Are you really here to talk about charms and the weather?"

Edouard winced. "No, I'm here to apologize and explain why I delayed my proposal then beg your forgiveness."

Her heart quickening, she lowered her arms. Edouard must be desperate to risk invading her chambers like this. Perhaps she'd been wrong about him not truly loving her. She perched on the edge of her bed. "Go on then."

Edouard swallowed, removed his heavy cloak, and began to sit on the chair near the window until the bundle tied to his back rustled. He leapt upright and removed the bundle then strode toward her while unwrapping it. He thrust a large bouquet of peach blossoms at her. "First, these are for you. I hope I didn't crush them too badly on the climb."

Pippa cradled the bouquet of her favorite flowers and inhaled its sweet fragrance as she caressed a few of the delicate pink and white blossoms, which weren't in season for another month or two. Yet somehow Edouard had found them for her. She smiled up at him. "They're not crushed at all. They're lovely, Edouard, thank you. How did you manage to find them so early?"

Edouard shrugged as he returned to his seat. "I purchased them from the veiled witch, along with the charm to reach you. They're pollinated by melissae. The veiled witch has the most amazing magical garden behind her witch shop. You should visit it sometime."

Warmth suffusing her chest, she buried her face in the melissa peach blossoms. Such a romantic faegift. And since gentlemen only purchased magical gifts for family, wives, or ladies they were courting, she *must* have been wrong about Edouard not loving her the way she loved him. She lifted her head and beamed at him. "Melissa peach blossoms? No wonder they're in season already and not crushed. Let me put them in water. 'Twould be a shame if they wilted."

While she leapt up and arranged her lovely flowers in the pitcher of water on her bedside table, Edouard murmured, "The veiled witch said they'll last four weeks if you add honey and vinegar to their water."

Pippa nodded. Not surprising that cut melissa peach blossoms would last over twice as long as ordinary ones. "I'll do that in the morning." She settled back on her bed, laced her fingers in her lap, and studied Edouard. "Now about that apology, explanation, and begging you mentioned?"

Edouard inhaled and gripped the arms of his chair. "Right." Holding her gaze, he leaned forward. "I'm sorry for not proposing when I promised I would then refusing to explain why. I was a damned fool to hurt you so and make you doubt my love. You're the most important person in the world to me, Pippa."

Tears pricked her eyes, although not sad ones for the first time since their quarrel. She blinked them back without breaking her locked stare with Edouard. "You more than hurt me. Believing you didn't truly love me shattered me, and I was unable to recover because I couldn't stop loving you. Why else would I have avoided you so fiercely?"

Edouard shuddered and shut his eyes. His voice breaking, he whispered, "Oh, Pippa. I'm so, so sorry. Please forgive me."

She clenched her laced hands to keep herself from bounding across her chambers, wrapping him in her arms, and kissing him to comfort him. They'd more to discuss first. She hummed then replied, "I might, if you ever explain why you delayed proposing."

Edouard opened his eyes and blew a sigh. "Because when I

met with your father, he refused to allow our betrothal until you turned nineteen."

Her mouth falling open, Pippa stared at Edouard. "He *what*? Why didn't you just *tell* me?" She'd not have been shattered by Edouard's delay then.

Edouard shifted in his chair. "I was attempting to protect your already strained relationship with your father as well as your belief about your parents' marriage."

She blinked at Edouard. What did Mother and Father's happy yet tragically short marriage have to do with her and Edouard?

Before she could ask, Edouard sighed again and continued, "Your father was so vehement about you waiting to marry because he didn't want you to repeat their mistakes. They were forced to elope when your mother fell pregnant and were unhappy together because they weren't suited. But you believed their youthful elopement proof of their deep love, so I knew the truth would devastate you."

Pippa inhaled, her throat tightening. Mother and Father hadn't truly loved one another and only eloped out of necessity? Then Father's refusal to mention Mother wasn't because he missed her too much, but because of their unhappiness together. A pang darted through her. Poor Mother and Father. She stiffened. Mother and Father's unhappy past certainly explained Father's blind prejudice toward Edouard and their love. Yet how could Father not *see* that she and Edouard weren't her parents? They loved each other and were ideally suited, so their marriage would be a happy one. Her chest twisted. The only things Father saw clearly were his magical experiments. Probably because he actually paid attention to *them*.

Shoving that aside, she swallowed and leaned toward Edouard. "Knowing my parents' unhappy past could never devastate me as much as believing you didn't truly love me did. And although I appreciate you wanting to protect me, I'm not a child. I can handle knowing the truth."

Edouard winced. "I know you're not a child. I never should have kept secrets from you, even to protect you. I promise I shan't do so again—unless I'm planning a surprise for you."

The ache in her chest vanishing, Pippa almost laughed. Trust her thorough Edouard to clarify that. She bounded across her chambers and dropped into his lap. "And I promise the same." She cupped his face in her palms, and tingling swept through her like earlier at his heat and rough jaw. She'd never thought she'd enjoy that again. She brushed a kiss against his lips. "Secrets involving surprises are acceptable. I adored the surprise you planned tonight."

His pale-blue eyes bright, Edouard wrapped his arms about her. "Oh, my darling sun nymph, I love you so." Then he captured her mouth in an ardent kiss.

She purred and kissed Edouard back with matching hunger as heat flooded her. How she needed him. Like a firebird needed flames. Between kisses, she panted, "I love you too." He groaned and kissed her harder.

Eventually, Edouard wrenched their mouths apart. "We must stop, or you'll never receive the rest of your surprise."

She smiled and combed her fingers through Edouard's silky blond hair to encourage further kisses. "There's more?"

Edouard lowered his arms. "Yes, now go sit across your chambers so you can receive it. I can't concentrate with you in my lap."

Pippa giggled. "I think you concentrate very well—on kisses." She brushed another kiss against Edouard's lips then returned to her bed like he'd asked and grinned at him. "Please proceed."

Edouard inhaled and extracted one of her embroidered pocketcloths from the pocket above his heart. "We can't risk becoming betrothed before your natalday. Goddess knows what your father would do if he discovered that." He strode toward her then opened the pocketcloth. "But I'd like you to wear my parents' wedding tokens as a promise that we'll marry one day."

Her heart fluttering, she caressed the pair of gold, tenth-century garden rings gleaming in the pocketcloth along with a gold necklace. The heads of the asymmetrical rings were diamonds set in a floral spray, with the larger ring possessing a much smaller spray, and the bands were delicate floral and leaf scrolls. Exquisite.

Edouard continued, "Father wore them beneath his clothes after Mother died. To keep her close to his heart, he said. You could do the same until we're officially betrothed on your natalday."

Pippa gazed up at him, tears pricking her eyes again as light filled her chest. "Oh, Edouard, how romantic." Just like the tradition of dancing to the dancing music-box sculpture. And Edouard wanted to do both. He was definitely his steadfast yet romantic father's son, and he truly loved her as deeply as she loved him. She beamed. "I'd love to wear your parents' wedding tokens."

Edouard grinned and fastened the gold chain about her neck. She warmed as the two garden rings nestled between her breasts. She and Edouard may not be officially betrothed, but they were as committed as any married couple. To express the joy bubbling in her veins, she leapt upright, flung her arms about his neck, and kissed him.

Devouring her mouth, Edouard rumbled and tumbled her onto the bed. She sighed as his weight pressed her into the mattress and his desperate hands caressed her everywhere, leaving fire in their wake. Oh, Goddess, more please. She yanked open his cravat and waistcoat.

When her hand slid beneath his shirt, Edouard cursed and lurched backward. "Enough. We may be almost betrothed, but we can't make love yet."

Her body throbbing and empty, Pippa propped herself on her elbows then arched her brows. "Why not?"

Edouard ran a hand through his hair and staggered back to his chair across her chambers. "'Tis too risky. You might fall pregnant."

She blinked while she sat upright and inhaled to settle herself. "Aren't you wearing a contraceptive charm?" 'Twasn't like Edouard not to take precautions.

Edouard grimaced as he repaired his disheveled clothes. "Of course I am. Father gave contraceptive charms to me and Elise during our first season. But they're not always effective—just look at Hawke and Wren. He invariably wore one, yet somehow she still fell pregnant." Edouard leaned toward her. "And what if I died before we could marry? You'd have to explain to your future husband why you weren't a virgin. Imagine how distressing that would be."

Pippa buried the last of her unfulfilled desire then smiled and shook her head. Her careful Edouard. Neither event was likely, yet he didn't want to risk distressing her. She tsked. "*If* I ever found a future husband, I'd not mind explaining that we consummated our love, but we can wait if you like. As long as we can resist each other."

His grimace turning wry, Edouard sighed. "We *really* must avoid being alone like this until we're married. Your father insisted we have a year-long betrothal too."

She stared at Edouard. Although year-long betrothals weren't uncommon, waiting that long would be painful as well as completely unnecessary. "We'll never be able to resist each other until we're married."

Edouard swallowed. "We *have* to." He managed a tight smile. "But I'm hoping we can persuade your father to let us marry sooner once we're safely betrothed." As she nodded at that sensible plan, he rose and donned his heavy cloak. "I'll see you at the Dracwyns' ball tonight."

Aching to kiss Edouard again, which wouldn't be at all wise given he didn't want to make love yet, Pippa smiled at him instead. "Until then, my love." Once he climbed out her window on his shimmering rope, she mimed a kiss then shut her window before curling back in bed. Yet for most of the night, she fingered his parents' wedding tokens rather than slept.

. . .

DESPITE HER LACK OF SLEEP, Pippa bounced from bed when Betty slipped in to refresh the fire. After letting Betty help her into a light-yellow dress, she headed downstairs for breakfast.

Both Dane and Xavier stared at her when she swept into the breakfast room with a cheery greeting. They exchanged a glance, then Dane murmured, "You're looking well this morning."

Xavier smoothed his mustache. "Better than you have since your quarrel with Edouard."

Pippa sipped her tea to avoid fingering Edouard's sun-charm bracelet about her wrist or his parents' wedding tokens beneath her dress. "Because we've talked and resolved our quarrel." And more. Yet she couldn't tell her brothers about her and Edouard's secret understanding here. Although Father wasn't with them, the servants might overhear, and he could discover it. But she should tell them soon, and Edouard should tell Elise.

So at Dracwyn House that evening, she murmured to Edouard during the first waltz, "We must tell our siblings our happy news, but somewhere we can't be overheard."

Edouard hummed as he spun her in a complicated turn. "How about a picnic at the royal bay later this week? I'll handle arranging it."

She grinned at Edouard, shifting closer than was strictly proper. "Sounds perfect." And while he was arranging that, she must purchase a faegift for him to show her love and thank him for his dangerously romantic gesture this morning. Now that they were almost betrothed, she could give him an extravagant gift.

She'd decided Edouard's faegift by the following morning and asked Betty to acquire a lock of his hair for it from his valet then wrote to Wren requesting directions to the veiled witch's shop. Then after luncheon the next day, she and her maid headed to Rhiannon's Veils for Edouard's faegift, although she instructed Betty to wait in the carriage during her shopping to keep it secret.

On the way, Pippa visited Healer Althea and requested the witch healer enchant the sun-charm bracelet as a contraceptive charm. Although cautious about their complete efficacy, Edouard would appreciate them both possessing contraceptive charms when they succumbed to temptation. And since she never took off the bracelet he'd given her, she'd always be protected. Plus, having his gift enchanted into such a prudent charm seemed fitting. After Healer Althea enchanted the sun-charm bracelet, Pippa listened to all of the healer's instructions about it before thanking her.

Then she continued to Rhiannon's Veils, a tiny witch shop with an unremarkable door yet an eerie air inside—the perfect setting for the mysterious veiled witch. She requested a pair of matching lockets for her and Edouard with moving portraits of each other inside, and the veiled witch created the faegifts in an impressive display of magic. Afterward, Pippa asked to visit the magical garden Edouard had mentioned and gasped when the veiled witch ushered her into the summer-like garden. Full of verdant, fragrant plants and alive with melissae, faebirds, and butterflies, 'twas as amazing as he'd said and an even more perfect setting for the veiled witch.

Pippa thanked the veiled witch and left, her head whirling. The veiled witch was definitely the most powerful Rhiannon-descendant witch she'd ever met, or even heard of. Why was she working in a tiny witch shop in a poorer area of Ormas? At the Westons' musical evening that night, she told Edouard about her visit, although she didn't mention purchasing his faegift, and he said perhaps the veiled witch didn't care for renown but wanted to be available to help King Devon and Lady Kiera. Apparently, the veiled witch was a seer and had provided the prophecy that had led to the dangerous Magehaven ore finally being neutralized today. The veiled witch being a Rhiannon-descendant seer certainly explained her knowing so much about everything, including Father's esoteric experiments.

Before Pippa and her brothers left, Edouard invited them to the picnic at the royal bay in a few days. When Dane and Xavier eagerly accepted, she and Edouard grinned at each other. Their plan was progressing well. She brushed his parents' wedding tokens beneath her gown. And the picnic would be the ideal time to give Edouard his faegift. She could hardly wait.

CHAPTER 27

The morning of their picnic to the royal bay, Edouard leapt from bed with none of his usual reluctance. He and Pippa were finally going to tell their siblings about their secret understanding. 'Twould be a relief even though they couldn't tell anyone else until after her natalday. He glanced out the window as he dressed. The sun was shining amid a cloudless sky—a promising auspice.

Around midmorning, he met Pippa and her brothers at their family's townhouse with two baskets full of food tied behind him. From there, they rode to Golddell House to meet Elise, Farson, and Arvan. Amid cheer and laughter, everyone rode out the northern gate and trotted to the royal bay.

At the royal bay, while Farson and Arvan settled the horses, Edouard and Dane spread the blanket on the golden sand, then Pippa and Elise unpacked their picnic, and Xavier distributed flasks of tea. Once everyone sat, Edouard eyed Pippa beside him before tucking her heavy cloak closer about her. Although sunny, the royal bay was cold, and the occasional breeze freezing. "Are you warm enough?"

Pippa slid closer until their bodies nearly touched, and his pulse surged. She smiled at him beneath her lashes. "Yes, but if I become chilled, I'll simply nestle against you."

Xavier groaned between Dane and Arvan. "Must you two flirt like that? It shall put the rest of us off our food."

Beside Edouard, Elise accepted a full plate from Farson that was half rolls. "Not me. I think Edouard and Pippa are adorable together." She smiled at them. "I'm glad you resolved your quarrel."

Light suffusing his chest, Edouard squeezed Pippa's free hand as he handed her a plate of food. "So am I."

Pippa beamed back. "Me too." When Xavier gave another teasing groan, she narrowed her eyes at him. "Would you stop that?" Then she flashed a glowing grin at the others. "Edouard and I arranged today's picnic so that we could tell you how we resolved our quarrel."

Everyone grinning back over their plates, Elise blurted, "You're betrothed."

Edouard and Pippa traded wry yet warm smiles, then he said, "Not quite. Sir Julian shan't allow that until Pippa turns nineteen. But we've promised we'll marry one day."

Dane arched his brows. "And that's different from being betrothed *how*?"

Pippa sighed while nibbling a miniature peach preserve tart. "'Tisn't official, and we daren't let Father discover it."

To hearten her, Edouard took her free hand again. "We consider it being almost betrothed."

The others glanced at one another, then Farson smiled and toasted them with his flask of tea. "Congratulations."

Edouard and Pippa grinned as the others heartily echoed him, even young Arvan. The opposite of Sir Julian's begrudging approval, thank the Goddess.

Once the congratulations quieted, Xavier waved to the empty royal bay around them. "I suppose you told us here where no one can overhear so Father doesn't discover your *almost* betrothal." He snorted. "Not that he likely would, considering how rarely he leaves his workroom."

Edouard grimaced. Sir Julian discovering their secret understanding was more likely since 'twas vital he didn't. Edouard shook his head while finishing his cold beefsteak. "But Sir Julian might, and we can't risk that."

Dane frowned and nodded. "'Twould be bad if Father did. He'd doubtless forbid you two from ever marrying, and you'd be forced to elope."

As Pippa sighed, Edouard suppressed a shudder. Although he hungered to marry her, eloping would be too scandalous. He said, "Neither Pippa nor I want the talk an elopement would cause."

Elise chuckled while sipping her tea. "That doesn't surprise me. Yet if you're forced to resort to eloping, no doubt the Duchess of Childes could manage the gossip, like she did for Aragon, Hawke, and King Devon." She grinned at Pippa. "So tell us how Edouard proposed."

Before Pippa could, Edouard frowned at his twin and interjected, "Almost proposed." Why did everyone keep forgetting the almost?

As Elise raised her eyes skyward, Pippa giggled and replied with a radiant smile, "He brought me a bouquet of melissa peach blossoms and confessed his love again." She fingered Father's gold necklace. "Then he gave me your parents' wedding tokens as a promise we'll marry one day."

Her eyes soft, Elise sighed. "Oh, how sweet."

Between Farson and Xavier, Arvan muttered, "Sounds mawkish to me." He glanced at Farson. "Do all ladies really want that?"

Farson chuckled. "Most ladies enjoy romance on occasion." He smiled at Elise beside him. "Although what they consider romantic depends on the lady, and performing it isn't onerous if you love them."

As Xavier and Dane began teasing Arvan about a mara girl he'd mentioned before, Edouard and Pippa smiled at each other. Telling their siblings their happy news had gone well. Soon, Farson turned the conversation from Arvan to the preparations for the royal ceremonies on Plantfete, and the rest of luncheon passed swiftly with lively talk and loving laughter.

Once everyone finished their molasses-crumb pie, Pippa tugged on Edouard's arm. "Shall we walk along the surf before we ride back to Ormas?"

His pulse quickening, he helped Pippa rise, and they excused themselves then strolled on the damp sand by the ocean. "You *are* aware we can't kiss here. Our families could see us, and there's nowhere to hide."

Pippa laughed, smiling up at him. "I know. I just wanted to talk alone for a bit. And give you something to thank you for your romantic apology and almost proposal. 'Twas so wonderful —sweet and sincere, yet dangerously romantic."

A blush heated his neck. "Miss Kay advised me to do something dramatic and not like my prudent self to inspire your forgiveness."

Pippa halted and turned him until his back faced their families. "I'm glad she did." She caressed his jaw. "Although you were still your prudent self when you followed her advice. You reduced the risks of anyone discovering your visit and restrained our passion to avoid potential consequences. But I adore you for that, my love." She beamed. "Impractically romantic gestures like public kisses on Summerday are nothing compared to sincere and practical love that shall last a lifetime."

Tingling warmth surging through him, Edouard held her glowing gaze and kissed her palm. "Are you attempting to get me to kiss you in front of our families, my sun nymph?"

Pippa chuckled but flashed a coy smile. "No, although I'd not protest if you did." When he shuddered and swayed closer, she lowered her hand and pressed it against his chest. "How about I give you my gift before kisses distract us?" She extracted a small gold locket and handed it to him. "I had the veiled witch enchant a pair of matching lockets for us during my visit the other day."

He studied the tenth-century scrolling that adorned his locket. 'Twas exquisite. "Enchant how?"

Pippa grinned. "The veiled witch created them from unfashioned gold using a spell, and there are moving portraits inside. Yours with my portrait, and mine with yours. That way, we can both see each other when we're apart."

Edouard flipped open his faegift then inhaled at Pippa's portrait grinning up at him exactly like her real face was. Extraordinary. "The veiled witch enchanted the moving portraits to mirror our *actual* movements."

Pippa tilted her head, her portrait echoing her. "Incredible what the veiled witch can do with a lock of hair and her magic, isn't it?"

He snapped shut his locket and slipped it into the pocket above his heart beside one of Pippa's embroidered pocketcloths. "Very. I'll treasure this extraordinary faegift forever."

Pippa touched her riding habit between her breasts. "Me too. I'm wearing my locket on the necklace with your parents' wedding tokens."

Unable to resist, Edouard pulled Pippa against him for a brief yet thorough kiss. Their families couldn't see much since his back was to them, anyway. But he forced himself to raise his head when she began lifting her arms to embrace him. "Shall we return to the others?"

Pippa hummed. "I suppose we'd better. Neither of us can restrain our kisses much longer."

He inhaled to settle his aching body and quirked a wry smile. So true. Then he took Pippa's arm and escorted her back to their families.

· · ·

OVER THE TWO and a half months before Pippa's natalday, Edouard and Pippa attended court events together nearly every day as well as spent many afternoons going riding, visiting impressive architecture about Ormas, or attending estate sales for tenth-century art. Although they avoided being completely alone together, they did risk slipping into anterooms at various court events for kisses several times a week. Kisses were easier to control there since all of court was in the other room.

During their almost betrothal, a lot changed in their families. Aragon and Selena's four-week-old daughter Isabel was introduced to the family at an intimate luncheon at Childes House. In grand and moving ceremonies on Plantfete, King Devon and Lady Kiera were wed, and she was crowned queen. A couple weeks later, Kit told the family she was actually Mel's elderly assistant Kay thanks to an illusion from the Goddess. Then she revealed her identity to court a few days later at the Duke of Oakmoor's soiree to help save Wren, who was nearly dying in childbirth. Thankfully, Hawke sent notes the following morning that Wren and their twins were healthy. The day after at a family luncheon, Mel and a no longer elderly Kit shared their betrothal, and Kit explained how she'd broken the Goddess's illusion and disclosed her mother, believed dead for years, was still alive. The Duchess of Childes immediately began planning a betrothal fete in a month to celebrate.

A week after the family luncheon at Childes House, Edouard rose early with a grin. 'Twas *finally* Pippa's natalday. To reach her sooner, he didn't bother with breakfast, only gulping a bracing cup of kahve before hurrying to her family's townhouse. Thank the Goddess he could officially propose at last.

When he strode into the breakfast room, Pippa had clearly just joined her brothers since her plate was empty and she was pouring herself tea. She stilled and stared at him. "Edouard, why are you here so early? What's wrong?"

His heart fluttering, he handed Pippa a large bouquet of peach blossoms, ordinary ones this time. He'd vowed to bring her some today when she'd nearly cried at her melissa peach blossoms dying four weeks to the day after his almost proposal. Fortunately, peach blossoms were still in season—barely. He grinned at Pippa. "Nothing. I was simply eager to see you today. Happy natalday, Pippa."

Pippa flashed a radiant smile as she caressed the peach blossoms against her cheek. "Thanks." She chuckled. "You must be eager, considering how you dislike mornings." She set down her bouquet and waved at the platters of food. "Have you eaten yet? Join us for breakfast."

Still grinning, Edouard took Pippa's hand and pulled her upright. He wasn't delaying his proposal a moment longer. "Later. Could we talk alone first?"

Her warm-brown eyes brightening, Pippa slid her arm through his. "Of course." She tossed her brothers a smile. "We'll be in the morning room."

Dane and Xavier traded amused grins, and Dane murmured, "Don't be too long. Cold eggs make an unpalatable breakfast."

Xavier snickered. "And perhaps lock the door so Father doesn't discover you kissing again."

As Pippa blushed but grimaced at her brothers, Edouard couldn't help his smile. Kissing his betrothed would be entirely proper, although not as torridly as Sir Julian had discovered them last summer. He swept Pippa into the morning room, and after locking the door like Xavier suggested, they settled on the nearest sofa.

His pulse pounding, he captured Pippa's face in his palms. "Will you marry me, my sweet sun nymph? I adore you like a griffin adores his mate, and you're the sunshine in my life. I can't bear to live without you."

Pippa laid her hand on his heart, and tingling surged through him as her charmed locket in his pocket pressed his chest. She beamed. "I adore you too and need you beside me just as much, so yes." Still beaming, she hummed. "Although I wasn't expecting your proposal until tonight after the dinner you're hosting for my natalday, perhaps while dancing to the melody of your dancing music-box sculpture."

Edouard rumbled a laugh and pulled Pippa fully against him. Finally. "I thought about it, but I couldn't wait that long."

Pippa threaded her arms about his neck and breathed, "Oh, my love."

He seized Pippa's mouth in a desperate kiss. So sweet. When she hungrily returned his kiss, heat flooded him until he ached. He groaned and kissed her harder while caressing her breast through her dress. If only he could remove it and make love to her.

He was about to tumble her beneath him when their empty stomachs rumbled in unison. Both chuckling, they pulled apart. He murmured, "Perhaps we should eat that breakfast you offered earlier."

Pippa grinned and wobbled upright then smoothed her rumpled dress. "Although I suspect the eggs are cold by now."

Edouard took Pippa's arm then escorted her from the morning room before he kissed her again. "Settling our betrothal was worth the cold eggs."

When they returned to the breakfast room, Dane arched his brows at them. "Officially betrothed now?"

Edouard and Pippa grinned at each other and nodded as they began serving themselves breakfast.

Xavier smirked and smoothed his mustache. "I'm surprised you two emerged until after luncheon then."

Edouard began devouring his eggs and bacon, which thankfully weren't the least cold. "We needed sustenance for the surprise outing I've planned for Pippa today."

Pippa turned toward him and grinned at him over her toast. "What surprise outing?"

He tsked as he playfully shook his head. "If I explained, 'twouldn't be a surprise. But it involves the natalday gift I got you."

Pippa blinked then glanced at her bouquet on the table. "It involves peach blossoms?"

Edouard chuckled. She was adorable. "No, your bouquet isn't your natalday gift. And neither was my proposal."

As Pippa grinned at him again, her brothers laughed, then Dane said, "You're spoiling Pippa, Edouard."

Xavier waggled his brows. "Don't forget, you'll need to keep that up for the rest of your lives."

Edouard shrugged. He didn't mind. And Pippa deserved some spoiling after how her idiot father had neglected her. He warmed when her grin brightened at his silent reply. Plus, his solicitude always made her happy. After they finished breakfast, they said farewell to her brothers, and he escorted her to his carriage.

Pippa nestled against him. "I'm surprised you didn't ask my brothers to join us. We're completely alone."

His body tightening at Pippa's soft curves, Edouard wrapped his arm about her. "Not for long. We're meeting Kit at the Great Temple to visit various prayer houses." He passed Pippa the voucher he'd won at the final auction of the Great Temple's court event shortly after Plantfete. "So you know where you want to spend your three-night retreat."

Pippa nestled closer as she accepted the voucher. "You said you'd won that for Elise, you liar."

He grinned then kissed Pippa's rich chestnut hair, inhaling her sweet peach scent. "You told me secrets involving surprises were acceptable."

Pippa caressed his jaw. "They are. Thank you for the marvelous natalday gift, my love." She chuckled. "Father shan't approve though. 'Tis too extravagant between anyone other than married couples or immediate family."

Edouard shrugged and kissed her palm. "I know, but I couldn't resist when you wistfully said you'd never visited one. I simply hope he never discovers your true natalday gift."

Pippa smiled. "I'll ensure he doesn't."

His heart quickening, Edouard bent his head and truly kissed Pippa. Fortunately, before their kisses became too heated, the carriage halted at the Great Temple.

A serene air about her and wearing novice priest robes over her simple dress, Kit met them in the nave with a warm smile. Except for her sultry beauty, she hardly resembled his grasping and frivolous stepmother. Kit had truly changed in the months since she'd disappeared on Longnight. Instead of a burden he needed to endure for Father, she'd become a lady he could respect and admire—tender, devoted, and insightful. Although perhaps she'd been that all along like Mel had always said, considering how she'd secretly donated most of her allowance to charities since she'd married Father. And he was forever grateful for the invaluable advice she'd given him as Kay to inspire Pippa's forgiveness. Kit would make a wonderful priestess one day as well as the perfect wife for Mel.

Kit hummed as she studied them. "You two appear cheerful."

Edouard squeezed Pippa's arm, and she beamed up at him. Light filling him, he replied, "Pippa officially accepted my proposal."

Kit grinned. "I suspected as much. Congratulations." She beckoned them. "We'll begin your tour with Peaceful Minds. 'Tis the largest prayer house in Ormas and the closest to the Great Temple. My friend Sarah serves there and is excited to meet you both."

He and Pippa spent the rest of the morning and afternoon with Kit visiting prayer houses across Ormas. By the end, Pippa decided to spend her retreat at Peaceful Minds, mostly because she and the affable Sarah had liked each other at once. Then he and Pippa headed to Blaine House for her natalday dinner, although they forced themselves to wait for everyone in the drawing room rather than dancing in the art room.

Soon their guests—from their immediate families to their cousins, including King Devon and Queen Kiera, as well as Wren's parents and Kit's newly discovered family—arrived.

Edouard and Pippa preceded everyone to the family dining room, which could barely hold all the guests. Once everyone had a flute of sparkling wine, or lymonade for Arvan and Kit's young siblings, Edouard raised his flute to Pippa beside him. "Happy natalday, my sun nymph. And thank you for agreeing to marry me this morning."

CHAPTER 28

*H*er heart fluttering at Edouard's toast, Pippa raised her flute to him as well. "Your proposal was the perfect natalday gift, my love." Despite him not calling it one.

As congratulations swept about the table, Father frowned at Edouard and rasped, "You asked Pippa to marry you already? But you agreed to wait until *after* her natalday."

While the others blinked at Father, she and Edouard exchanged a lengthy glance. Father was truly grumbling about one day? He was being unreasonable again—no wonder he and Mother had been unhappy together. She pursed her lips. "'Twas merely a day early."

The Duchess of Childes smiled at them. "And about time too. You two have been courting and in love for ages. If either of you were my children, I'd have ensured your betrothal before the end of last summer."

Pippa almost laughed when Aragon, Mel, and Hawke traded wry looks. Her and Edouard's cousins knew *all* about their mother's matchmaking.

Father sighed into his redkrab soup. "Oh, very well. But we should wait to make a public announcement until after Melchior and Lady Blaine's betrothal fete to avoid trumping them."

Pippa swallowed another laugh when Mel blurted without consulting Kit, "We'd not mind sharing our betrothal fete." Clearly, the modest priest wasn't anticipating all the fuss.

As Kit agreed to Mel's offer with a smiling nod, Edouard gripped his spoon and glanced at Pippa then said, "Whatever Pippa wants."

Pippa smiled at Edouard and squeezed his knee beneath the table. He'd despise the fuss even more than Mel—he'd even said as much at the Greysnowes' ball for their daughter's marriage— yet he'd endure it for her. She shook her head. "I'd prefer a simpler event."

Father narrowly eyed her. "Then 'tis only proper that it wait."

While the others stared at Father's insistence, except her brothers who sighed, Pippa and Edouard exchanged another lengthy glance. Father was determined to be difficult. Yet since he'd done so in front of their extended family, perhaps she could secure a shorter betrothal. The duchess would surely agree with her, and Father would have to relent. Pippa flashed a brilliant smile. "I suppose our public announcement can wait, as long as we begin planning the wedding ceremony now. If we're to wed before the end of the season, we've less than five months."

As Edouard inhaled and Father's jaw tightened, the duchess smiled then said, "True, but 'tis possible, and you two have waited long enough to wed. If you require any assistance, please let me know."

Her chest lightening when Father sagged in clear acquiescence, Pippa nodded and beamed at Edouard, who smiled back. Her strategy had succeeded.

Elise grinned and buttered another roll. "Join me for luncheon at Golddell House tomorrow, Pippa, and we'll begin planning your wedding ceremony as well as the rout party I'll host to announce your betrothal." She tilted her head. "On the day after Mel and Kit's betrothal fete, I think."

Xavier's smile echoing his, Dane raised his flute of sparkling wine and rumbled, "To Pippa and Edouard's happy marriage. I can't imagine a better match for our little sister."

Xavier chuckled. "Mostly because she was determined to have him from the day they met, and he was only slightly less besotted."

While everyone toasted them, even Father slowly raised his flute, Pippa blushed but traded a warm smile with Edouard. How well her brothers knew them.

The rest of dinner passed swiftly with lively conversation and frequent toasts, then everyone returned to the drawing room without the gentlemen bothering to remain behind for spiritwine.

After several riddle games, Father approached her and Edouard on the sofa along the back wall. He muttered, "Shall we leave? 'Tis getting late."

Pippa frowned at Father. Midnight was hours away. Why must Father always want to leave early? Especially when 'twas rude. She murmured so the other guests couldn't overhear, "Considering everyone is here to celebrate my natalday and betrothal, 'twould be impolite to leave until all the guests have departed."

Father humphed. "Do you mind if *I* leave now? I must rise early. My experiments are at a critical stage. I'll send the carriage back for you and your brothers."

Her chest twisted. Like always, Father was more devoted to his magical experiments than he was to anything else. Then she relaxed when Edouard caressed her palm with his thumb, no doubt to comfort her. With him by her side, Father leaving hardly mattered. He was never truly there anyway. She smiled and shook her head. "I'll see you later, Father."

Once Father left, everyone else continued playing rousing games for another couple hours, although the evening ended earlier than court events often did because King Devon and Queen Kiera as well as Mel and Kit had pressing duties early the following morning.

After they said farewell to Elise and her family, who were the last to leave other than Pippa and her brothers, Edouard arched his brows at Pippa while Dane and Xavier stepped outside to give them privacy. He said, "Quite a risk you took earlier, demanding a shorter betrothal."

She threaded her arms about Edouard's neck, tingling warmth flooding her. "A strategic one that succeeded. I knew that everyone's approval, particularly the duchess's, would compel Father to agree. And now that he's agreed in front of everyone, he can't force us to wait until after my next natalday to marry."

Edouard chuckled. "My clever sun nymph." Then he kissed her before releasing her with a sigh. "We'd better part before we get too heated. I'll see you tomorrow."

Pippa echoed Edouard's sigh then smiled at him. Thank the Goddess they'd only five months instead of a year before they married. "Until tomorrow, my love."

In the weeks before Mel and Kit's betrothal fete, Pippa and Edouard continued seeing each other every day like they had during their almost betrothal. Yet pretending they were simply courting was annoying since they were still restricted to two dances during an evening and occasionally had to partner others.

At Mel and Kit's betrothal after greeting the duke and duchess, Edouard handed Pippa a flute of sparkling wine and muttered, "Thank the Goddess tonight is the last evening we need to conceal our betrothal."

Her pulse quickening, she fluttered her lashes at Edouard over her flute. "So impatient. Where has my cautious love gone?"

Edouard sipped his sparkling wine. "There's nothing left to be cautious about between us." He sighed. "And restraining ourselves is becoming tortuous."

She smiled. How sweet for Edouard to say that. "*Becoming* tortuous? I've found it that for months."

Edouard grimaced and inclined his head. "True." Eyeing the front, he shuddered as more and more guests filled the already crowded ballroom. "This fete promises to be even more mad than the Greysnowes' ball for Lord and Lady Ravenstone."

Pippa chuckled. Because the duchess had insisted that Kit breaking the Goddess's illusion and becoming a novice priestess remain family secrets until the fete. "All of court is agog to see the elderly-looking Countess of Blaine, especially since she's marrying the last unwed son of the Duke and Duchess of Childes."

Edouard's lips twisted as he finished his sparkling wine. "I know. But I'm relieved you decided not to share the fete with Mel and Kit."

She studied the crowd, who were almost rowdy. A quiet rout party would be much better. "Me too."

When the stream of guests finally slowed, the duke and duchess announced Mel and Kit. Everyone stared when they glided from an anteroom, and whispers rippled across the ballroom. All of court was shocked at Kit's youthful appearance and novice priest robes—exactly like the duchess had planned.

Then the first waltz began, so Pippa and Edouard joined Mel and Kit on the floor, along with the other couples in their families and many more. As she and Edouard silently twirled, they stared into each other's eyes and drifted closer until her cream skirt brushed his legs. When the music faded, they sighed and pulled apart. If only they didn't have to.

She made herself grin as she turned to Mel and Kit beside them. "So what charity-themed entertainment have you arranged, Kit?"

Mel beaming at her, Kit grinned back and replied, "Auctions for services, charms, and art from the Great Temple. The proceeds shall be split equally between Lady's Way Almskitchen and Goddess's Refuge."

Pippa and Edouard both nodded. Not surprising Mel and Kit

had chosen to support the almskitchen Mel had served at and the family refuge Kit had secretly donated to for years.

The Duke of Oakmoor strolled over with a suave smile. "You've always favored supporting that family refuge, haven't you? You chose it as the cause for my Longnight charity luncheon." He studied Mel and Kit. "Congratulations on your betrothal. You two make a splendid couple." He grinned. "Would you favor me with the next waltz, Lady Blaine?"

Pippa and Edouard traded a glance. Kit's former suitor was requesting a dance at her betrothal fete?

Her gaze glowing, Kit smiled at Mel, who grinned back. She murmured, "I'm afraid Mel has claimed all my dances tonight, except for those with family. Excuse us."

As Mel and Kit glided back to the center of the ballroom, the Duke of Oakmoor quirked a wry smile. Then he turned to Pippa, his smile warming. "Shall you oblige me instead, Miss Hawke?"

Edouard grasping her arm, she almost grimaced. Dancing with the rakehell duke and enduring his habitual flirting wouldn't be enjoyable, but she mustn't be impolite to the influential and wealthy councilor. So she inclined her head. "Very well, your grace."

Edouard's gaze warm on her skin, she allowed the duke to sweep her onto the floor, but she ensured they remained a bit farther than the proper distance to avoid encouraging him.

The Duke of Oakmoor chuckled as they twirled past the Duchess of Childes, who was beaming at Mel and Kit. "The Duchess of Childes looks more smug than a sphinx with an unanswerable riddle."

Pippa smiled, her lips twitching. How true. "The duchess is pleased to see all her sons so happily settled."

The duke chuckled again and arched a brow. "Doubtless she'll soon turn her formidable attention to her unwed relatives, like you or Lord Blaine."

Unable to help a radiant grin, Pippa lowered her gaze to hide her eyes. Except the duchess didn't need to settle her or

Edouard, which all of court would discover tomorrow. "I suppose."

The Duke of Oakmoor hummed. "Your father shall probably be grateful for the Duchess of Childes's assistance, considering how rarely he attends court events. Is he here tonight?"

She suppressed a snort. Given his begrudging approval of her and Edouard's betrothal, Father would have been the opposite of grateful for the duchess helping settle her. "Father is too busy with his magical experiments to attend most court events."

The duke blinked at her. "Magical experiments? What kind?"

Pippa pursed her lips. How had Father described his esoteric experiments to the veiled witch? "Attempting to determine the nature of faedust and thereby magic itself."

The Duke of Oakmoor whistled. "Impressive."

She shrugged as their waltz thankfully ended. At least the duke hadn't flirted as much as she'd feared. "Could you escort me back to Lord Blaine? I believe he's fetched a flute of sparkling wine for me."

The duke nodded and returned her to Edouard. Before releasing her, the duke bowed and kissed her hand. His voice caressing, he said, "I greatly enjoyed our waltz, Miss Hawke. Until later."

As Pippa resisted the urge to wipe her hand on her skirt, Edouard glowered after the Duke of Oakmoor and gritted, "What was *that* about?"

She grimaced. "No inkling. I certainly didn't encourage him."

Edouard snorted and handed her a flute of sparkling wine. "I know. The duke must have found you too tempting to resist. Damned rakehell."

Pippa slipped her arm through Edouard's and smiled at him. "Not that I'll need to worry about him after tomorrow."

Edouard relaxed and warmly returned her smile. "True."

She and Edouard spent the rest of the betrothal fete together, only separating for a few dances with family, and they danced the last waltz together like usual.

Once they said farewell to Mel and Kit, Kit embraced Pippa and said, "I'm sorry Mel and I can't attend Elise's rout party for you and Edouard tomorrow. Our duties at the Great Temple don't allow us to attend court events two evenings in a row."

Mel smiled at Pippa and Edouard. "But you've our heartiest well-wishes."

Edouard smiled back and inclined his head. "Thanks. Good luck with your duties tomorrow."

Pippa grinned at Mel and Kit. "Elise and I shall visit you soon to discuss performing the wedding ceremony. We've most of the other details arranged." Too bad she and Edouard couldn't marry before the end of the season, but Father would be furious if they did.

Mel and Kit nodded, then Mel replied, "Of course."

Edouard escorted Pippa back to her family's townhouse with her brothers. When Dane and Xavier headed inside, he pulled her against him for a thorough kiss. He released her and said, "Until tomorrow, my sun nymph. I can't wait for everyone to know we're betrothed."

Her heart light, she caressed Edouard's rough jaw. "Me too, my love." Then she alighted and followed her brothers inside.

Several hours later, Pippa jerked awake at the thump rattling her window. Had Edouard risked visiting her chambers again? How desperately romantic. She darted to her window and flung it open then froze. 'Twasn't Edouard.

Her pulse racing, she began slamming shut her window, but the Duke of Oakmoor shoved his way inside, and she stumbled backward.

The duke flashed his suave smile. "Good evening, or morning rather, Miss Hawke."

Pippa swallowed but straightened and glared at the duke despite her tight chest. "W-what are you doing here?"

The Duke of Oakmoor grimaced. "Kidnapping you, I'm afraid."

She gasped. "No!" Then she fiercely punched the duke's stomach like her brothers had taught her. She must escape at once.

The duke wheezed and bent over but gripped her wrist, pressing Edouard's sun-charm bracelet into her skin. "None of that, my darling." He crooned a singsong chant and flicked the fingers of his free hand at her.

Pippa yanked on her captured wrist and swayed as the duke's spell engulfed her. Oh, Goddess! Then her vision dimmed, and impenetrable blackness swallowed her.

She roused Goddess-knew how many hours later, but from her rumbling stomach, she'd likely missed breakfast and possibly luncheon as well. She shivered then swallowed to wet her dry throat before lurching upright to eye her surroundings. She was in a massive bedchamber brimming with every luxury—doubtless in Oakmoor House from the stained glass above the main windows.

Pippa burst from the soft bed then hurtled across the room and twisted the doorknob, but it was locked. So she flew to the windows and attempted to wrench them open, yet they were locked too. She hurled a heavy candelabra at the clear glass panes to break them, but it bounced off without cracking them. They must be enchanted against breaking like the ballroom's stained-glass ceiling. Damnation!

She wrapped herself in the modish dressing gown draped across the bed then sank into a plush chair by the ornate dressing table. She'd best conserve her energy until she'd a chance to escape. As soon as she did, she'd head to Edouard at Blaine House. He'd protect her from the Duke of Oakmoor, who surely must be mad to kidnap her like this. She gripped Edouard's sun-charm bracelet on her wrist and his parents' wedding tokens with her charmed locket about her neck. Did he know she was missing yet? If so, he must be frantic.

An hour or so later, the locked door glided open, and the Duke of Oakmoor strode inside, bearing a tray laden with food, tea, and a deep-red rose. "Good evening, my darling. I cooked you some dinner."

Pippa stared at the smiling duke as she stood while gripping shut her dressing gown. Him cooking and serving her dinner was like a dominant nightmara mare carrying anyone. She swallowed a wild giggle. The reverse of her thought when first discussing riding nightmara with Farson and Elise at Aragon and Selena's wedding. She lifted her chin. "*You* cooked me dinner?"

The duke nodded. "I sent away all my servants, so I had to." He set the laden tray on the tea table with a warm grin. "And I'll even share it with you, so you know 'tisn't drugged."

She clenched her jaw. If only she could refuse to dine with the duke, but starving herself would make her too weak to escape. She settled at the tea table and poured tea while the duke filled their plates. As they began eating, she murmured, "Why have you kidnapped me, your grace?"

The Duke of Oakmoor studied her and hummed. "To marry you. I require a lady like you to fall in love with me and agree to marry me in order to break the curse about to befall me."

Her eyes widening, Pippa blinked at the duke. He was suffering a curse? No doubt due to his rakehell past. She gritted a brilliant smile. "I'm afraid you'll need to find another lady to break your curse. I'm already in love and betrothed to Edouard."

The duke arched his brows. "There's been no announcement about your betrothal to Lord Blaine."

She sighed and held the duke's gaze. "Father insisted we wait until after Mel and Kit's betrothal fete." Darn him for being so unreasonable about her and Edouard. "We're announcing our betrothal at Elise's rout party tonight."

The Duke of Oakmoor scrutinized her for a lengthy moment. Then he groaned, his face twisting as he briefly transformed into a beast with a lion's mane and claws, a goat's horns, and a snake's face, although his hazel eyes remained unchanged.

Pippa gasped and jerked backward as her pulse spiked and ice flooded her veins. Dear Goddess! The duke's curse was to transform into a hideous chimera-like beast? Chimeras, especially when crazed with rage, always left disaster behind them. And the cursed duke clearly would too. After all, in a futile attempt to break his terrible curse, he'd stolen her from Edouard, the gentleman she adored and wanted to marry, in order to force her to fall in love and marry *him*. An impossibility.

Once his appearance was human again, the duke lurched upright even though he'd only eaten a few bites. He smiled at her. "Despite your unannounced betrothal to Lord Blaine, regrettably I can't let you go, Miss Hawke. You match the veiled witch's prophecy about breaking my curse, and I'm certain you'll learn to love me and agree to marry in time. Now, please excuse me. Since 'tis finally six hours to midnight, I must begin setting the wards the veiled witch provided me to prevent anyone from entering or leaving Oakmoor House until my curse is broken."

As the duke left, she bolted after him. She must escape before he finished setting those wards because she'd *never* marry him, so they'd be trapped in Oakmoor House forever. Yet when she reached the door, 'twas already locked. She shivered as she sank to the floor. Goddess, what was she to *do*? Tears scorching her cheeks, she forced herself to rise and stagger to the tea table. She required sustenance to remain strong enough to get out of this quagmire.

CHAPTER 29

The evening of Elise's rout party, Edouard couldn't contain his grin as he took his carriage to Golddell House for dinner beforehand. Soon, all of court would know he and Pippa were betrothed. Then they could quit restricting themselves to just the first and last dances, and he could openly keep flirtatious gentlemen like the Duke of Oakmoor away from her.

When he strode into the drawing room, he sighed because only Elise, Farson, and Arvan were there. He sat on an empty sofa so Pippa could sit beside him once she joined them. "How long until Pippa and her family arrive?"

On the sofa across from him with Farson, Elise arched her brows. "Not for half an hour at least. You're early." Her eyes gleaming, she chuckled. "I've never seen you so eager for a court event."

Before Edouard could reply to his twin's teasing, Farson laughed and drawled, "Even the most reclusive gentleman would be eager to announce his betrothal to the lady he loves."

Edouard quirked a wry smile. Desperate better described it. "Especially after waiting for nine months like I have."

Arvan grimaced from his seat near the door. "Well, I hope the Hawkes arrive sooner than half an hour. I'm hungry."

Edouard, Elise, and Farson were chuckling at the young duke's usual complaint when Sir Julian burst into the drawing room with a frowning Dane and Xavier close behind. Edouard eyed Pippa's family then began frowning too. Why wasn't Pippa with them?

Sir Julian growled, "Where is my daughter, you deceitful rakehell?"

Edouard stiffened at the baronet's vitriol. "What?"

Sir Julian sneered back and snorted. "Don't act like you don't know. Pippa's been missing since before her maid went to wake her this morning."

Ice freezing his chest, Edouard leapt upright. "*What*?! Why didn't you contact me then?" When Sir Julian simply glared, Edouard frowned at Dane and Xavier. "Tell me!"

Dane sighed, his eyes dark with worry. "We didn't know until just before we left."

His expression echoing Dane's, Xavier nodded. "Betty assumed you'd whisked Pippa away for a romantic outing. To shield you from Father, she didn't tell anyone until Pippa failed to return tonight."

The ice in his chest spreading, Edouard shook his head. "I've not seen Pippa since I escorted her home with you both yesterday." Dear Goddess, where was she?

Sir Julian fisted his hands and rushed toward him. "Liar! You stole her away."

Edouard glared and flung a hand at the drawing room not containing Pippa. Why was her father making idiotic accusations instead of focusing on *finding* her? "If I had, she'd be here, wouldn't she?"

Sir Julian sneered again. "Not if you tied Pippa to your bed to keep her from me. You've always lusted after my daughter."

Edouard inhaled to prevent himself from punching Pippa's

father. Yes, he desired Pippa, but because he loved her, and he'd never seek to hurt her by keeping her from her family. And why would he steal her away when their betrothal was being announced tonight? Goddess, the baronet was always so damned *blind*. He narrowed his eyes at Sir Julian. "You, sir, are a neglectful idiot who knows *nothing* about your daughter, let alone me."

As Sir Julian turned white then red, Edouard faced Dane and Xavier, who were talking sense—unlike their idiot father. "Did Pippa's maid notice anything odd this morning?"

Xavier grimacing beside him, Dane rumbled, "Other than Pippa being missing? No."

Edouard swore and ran a hand through his hair then began to pace. With no clues and Pippa being missing for hours, she'd be impossible to find by ordinary means. And a tracing spell would require her hair or blood. He halted, his hand covering the pocket above his heart. The charmed locket she'd given him! Pippa had said the veiled witch had created the moving portraits with a lock of hair.

He inhaled. "I must go. A tracing spell from the veiled witch should find Pippa." Hopefully before 'twas too late.

While Sir Julian scowled and Pippa's brothers nodded, Farson replied, "I'll saddle my stallion for you. He's the fastest in the stables and can maintain a grueling pace for hours."

Arvan added, "And I'll fetch dinner you can eat in the saddle."

As her husband and ward dashed from the drawing room, Elise gripped Edouard's arm. "I'll make your excuses at the rout party. Contact us as soon as you find Pippa."

Edouard squeezed Elise's hand to reassure her. "Of course."

When he surged toward the door, Dane called after him, "Xavier and I shall join you."

Edouard paused and turned to face Pippa's brothers. Although more people looking for her might be nice, they couldn't risk causing talk about her disappearance. "All three of us racing about Ormas shall attract too much notice. I'd better go alone."

Dane and Xavier sighed then traded a glance before slowly nodding.

Xavier narrowed his eyes at Edouard. "Just make sure you find our sister."

Dane crossed his arms over his brawny chest. "Or you shan't like what we do to you when we find *you*."

Edouard set his jaw. "I'll find her."

His blood coursing through his veins, he turned and hurtled down to the stables. He vaulted atop the brown-dun stallion Farson was holding and accepted the rolls stuffed with meat and cheese from Arvan. As they wished him luck, he nodded his thanks then spurred the stallion to a gallop.

He raced across Ormas, devouring Arvan's stuffed rolls. Please, please let the veiled witch's tracing spell work quickly. Pippa had already been missing for far too long. *Anything* could have happened to her by now. Not that whatever happened would make him love her any less. But, Goddess, her suffering... He urged the stallion faster.

At Rhiannon's Veils, Edouard jumped from the saddle and shoved on the witch shop's door, but it refused to budge. He swore and pounded on the weathered red door, yet the veiled witch didn't appear. Where was she? Shouldn't a Rhiannon-descendant seer know when she was desperately needed?

Swearing once more, he leapt on Farson's stallion again and galloped back the way he'd come. He'd obtain a tracing spell from Lady Juliet instead. Although finding Pippa wasn't a kingdom matter and he'd not requested permission to approach the royal witch, surely King Devon and Queen Kiera wouldn't mind. They were compassionate, and Pippa was a distant cousin, after all. Plus, Lady Juliet should be at Elise's rout party. The royal witch always attended events hosted by councilors or other influential members of court.

When Edouard returned to Golddell House, he gritted a faint smile and forced himself to walk rather than run. Talk would start if court noticed his desperation. He scoured the crowd for Lady Juliet, shaking his head at his and Pippa's families as they began to approach. They'd never keep Pippa's disappearance secret if they discussed it here, and he'd no news anyway. Finally, he located Lady Juliet talking with the Orandian ambassador and the ambassador's husband near the refreshments table, and he headed toward the trio.

Still smiling, he nodded at the royal witch. "Good evening, Lady Juliet. Could we talk for a moment?"

Her brows rising to her fashionable coiffure, Lady Juliet returned his nod. "Of course, Lord Blaine." She smiled at the mature couple with reddish hair wearing tunics and long over-coats. "Until later, Siobhan, Lorcan."

Edouard took the royal witch's arm and began escorting her toward the door. They must leave for her to cast her magic.

After a moment, Lady Juliet slanted him a sidelong glance. "I'm surprised that Miss Hawke isn't with you."

His jaw tightened, but he clung to his faint smile. "'Tis why I wished to talk with you." He checked that no one could overhear then murmured, "Pippa went missing this morning, and I need a tracing spell to find her."

Lady Juliet inhaled, her eyes widening. "I see."

Edouard touched the pocket above his heart. The royal witch *had* to help him. "I've Pippa's hair in a charmed locket to cast the spell."

Lady Juliet pursed her lips. "Since 'tis already enchanted, I may not be able to use it for another spell. Could I see the locket?"

He glanced at the other guests again, his skin prickling. Were any of them watching and wondering at his discussion with the royal witch? He nodded at her. "Of course, but not here."

Lady Juliet scanned the crowd too. Then she flicked her fingers while whispering a singsong chant. "No one shall notice our departure now, Lord Blaine, unless they already know of Miss Hawke's disappearance."

Edouard exhaled as he swept Lady Juliet from the drawing room. "Thank you." While they continued to the entrance hall, he handed her the charmed locket.

Lady Juliet scrutinized it then stiffened, and her mouth tightened. "This is the veiled witch's work. Why didn't you ask *her* for a tracing spell?"

He glowered at Lady Juliet. She'd better not refuse to help because of her obvious jealousy toward the other witch. "I would have, but her witch shop's door was locked."

Lady Juliet frowned. "Peculiar." She sighed and returned the charmed locket when they reached the entrance hall. "Very well, I'll see if I can create your tracing spell, but we must head to my workroom at the palace."

His chest almost easing at the royal witch agreeing to help, Edouard nodded as they strode outside. "I assumed as much."

He climbed atop Farson's stallion and pulled Lady Juliet behind him before urging the stallion to a gallop again. Fortunately, Farson hadn't lied about his stallion's endurance.

Soon, they reached the palace and hurried to the royal witch's wing upstairs. When they entered the immaculate workroom filled with magical accoutrements, the little maid in starched livery, who was stacking ingredients on the orderly shelves, whirled around to face them. She asked, "Lady Juliet, why are you back so early?"

The royal witch smiled at her maid as she donned a canvas apron over her modish gown. "Lord Blaine requested a small spell for Miss Hawke." She waved toward the door. "Go retire for the evening. You can finish stacking in the morning. Thank you, Lara." Once the little maid bobbed a curtsy and left, Lady Juliet turned to Edouard. "Give me the veiled witch's charmed locket then sit on the sofa by the door while I create your tracing spell."

He handed her the locket then made himself sit. Pacing

would likely distract the royal witch. Yet he couldn't help drumming his fingers on his knee.

After setting the charmed locket on her worktable, Lady Juliet whisked to the cabinet in the corner then crooned and weaved a pattern of light before it. The door creaked open, and she extracted a silver hand mirror adorned with purple flowers from inside. She weaved another pattern of light before the cabinet, which locked with a click, before placing the mirror beside the charmed locket. From the shelves behind her table, she gathered a massive silver bowl, shimmering water, several herbs, and a silver potion.

The royal witch poured the shimmering water into her massive bowl and added the other ingredients, and the water began to steam. Then she flipped open the charmed locket.

He inhaled and leapt to his feet then strode to the worktable. Why hadn't he checked Pippa's moving portrait sooner? 'Twould mirror her current expression. He relaxed at her unsmiling yet calm face with no evidence of tears. Whatever had happened, Pippa didn't appear to be suffering. Thank the Goddess.

Lady Juliet frowned at him. "What are you doing, Lord Blaine? I've not even begun casting your tracing spell."

Edouard managed an apologetic smile. "Sorry for distracting you. The veiled witch enchanted the moving portrait to mirror Pippa's actual movements, so I wanted to see if she was well."

The royal witch blinked and eyed the charmed locket. "Actual movements? Impressive. Too bad that removing the hair shall destroy the enchantment."

He straightened, his mouth firming. He'd figured it would. "I don't care as long as we find Pippa."

Lady Juliet smiled at him and patted his arm. "We shall. Now, please sit so I can concentrate."

Once he returned to the sofa, Lady Juliet extracted Pippa's chestnut hair from the locket, and the moving portrait flickered then faded. She scrutinized it, her brows rising. "Even more impressive—the veiled witch managed to set her enchantment to not consume the hair's magical link to Miss Hawke like most similar charms would. Creating a tracing spell with it shan't be a problem."

Edouard exhaled. Fortunate.

The royal witch dropped Pippa's hair into her silver bowl then stirred, and the rising steam thickened. She swirled her hand over the bowl while chanting in the melodic witch's tongue. Then she leaned over and peered into the massive bowl, her eyes wide and blank.

He gripped his knees as the royal witch remained still for several dozen heartbeats. Did tracing spells always take so long?

Eventually, Lady Juliet shuddered and straightened. "Miss Hawke is at Oakmoor House, locked in a bedchamber with a trap spell. Let me scry her surroundings before we leave to rescue her."

His heart surging, Edouard forced himself to remain seated as the royal witch bent into the steam again. The Duke of Oakmoor had kidnapped Pippa? Why? The decades older gentleman had never appeared seriously interested in Pippa, despite his irritating flirting at Mel and Kit's betrothal fete yesterday.

Lady Juliet hummed and murmured, "The townhouse appears empty except for Miss Hawke in that bespelled bedchamber. The duke is outside along the left wall." Then she gasped. "Is Oakmoor setting *wards*?" Her face pinched. "Since when does *he* have magical powers?"

Edouard leapt upright. Set wards might make rescuing Pippa impossible. "How long until the Duke of Oakmoor finishes setting his wards?"

Lady Juliet humphed. "Several hours at least. His wards appear intricate and incredibly powerful." She leaned closer to her massive bowl. "Not that he created the wards himself—the veiled witch did."

Edouard strode toward the royal witch and clenched the

edge of her worktable. They must go. "Have you scried enough yet?"

Lady Juliet straightened and tossed him the magicless gold locket. "For now. Let me transfer the tracing spell to my scrying mirror."

He frowned as he slid the locket back into the pocket above his heart. Why was transferring the tracing spell necessary? They already knew where Pippa was. But asking that would only delay them, so he nodded for her to proceed.

Lady Juliet held her silver hand mirror face down over her massive bowl then swirled her other hand over both of them. The steam sucked into the mirror with a swoosh until all the magical mixture in the bowl had evaporated. She snatched the satchel hanging on the wall and swept the contents of her orderly shelves into it. The now bulging satchel must be enchanted because it all fit inside. Then she used her magic to unlock her cabinet again and added several tomes, a gold dagger, a silver chalice, a copper pendant, and a slim walnut box before relocking her cabinet and stuffing her massive silver bowl inside her satchel. Yes, definitely enchanted.

Panting, Lady Juliet slung the satchel over her shoulder and grasped her scrying mirror in her free hand. She glanced at him. "Shall we go?"

As they rushed from the royal witch's wing, Edouard asked her, "Why did you pack all those magical accoutrements?"

Lady Juliet grimaced. "I wanted to ensure I'd have anything I needed. Considering Oakmoor's inexplicable magic and the veiled witch's involvement, matters could be complicated."

The bells tolling two hours to midnight, Edouard leapt back onto Farson's stallion and pulled the royal witch behind him. She wasn't any heavier than before, despite everything in her bulging satchel. They galloped through the emptying streets of Ormas to Oakmoor House. As they did, he clenched his jaw. Dear Goddess, he'd almost lost Pippa, and without Lady Juliet's help, he would have. Once they rescued Pippa, he *must* prevent that from ever happening again. No more delays—no matter what her idiot father had demanded or the scandalous talk 'twould cause at court.

While he tied the stallion to a railing, Lady Juliet peered into her scrying mirror. Then she murmured, "Everything looks the same as before. Come along."

He and the royal witch slipped inside through the servants' entrance then crept upstairs. At each creak, his pulse flared, and body tensed, but they kept going.

When they reached the third bedchamber door, Lady Juliet halted him with a raised hand. She whispered, "This is it. Now be quiet while I weave an opening in the trap spell."

Edouard nodded as the royal witch set her satchel on the floor. He fisted his hands to remain still while she cast her spell.

Lady Juliet slid her scrying mirror into the satchel then extracted a skein of glittering electrum thread. Humming another singsong spell, she tossed the skein, and it hovered at the center of the door. Still humming, she waved her hand, and the skein slowly unraveled in an ever-widening spiral. When it covered the entire door, she spread her hands, and the electrum thread formed a massive ring framing the door.

The royal witch smiled and nodded at her spell. "It should be safe to enter now."

Energy bursting through him, he surged forward and flung open the heavy oak door. At last!

CHAPTER 30

When the bedchamber door flew open, Pippa leapt upright, her pulse pounding. Then she relaxed and beamed as Edouard burst inside. Somehow he'd found her. Thank the Goddess! She darted across the bedchamber to fling herself against him.

His arms tight about her, Edouard captured her lips in a fierce kiss.

She sighed, fisted her hands in his blond hair, and pressed closer as she kissed him back. If he'd not found her before the duke set his wards, she'd have never kissed Edouard again. The wards... She gasped and wrenched their mouths apart. "Edouard, we must escape at once. If the Duke of Oakmoor finishes setting his wards, we shan't be able to leave until I fall in love with him and agree to marry him to break the curse transforming him into a chimera-like beast. And since that shall never happen, we'll be trapped here forever."

Edouard scowled. "The duke kidnapped you to force you to *marry* him to break some curse?" He took her hand and tugged her toward the door where Lady Juliet was beckoning a massive ring of electrum thread through the surrounding wall. The royal witch must have helped him find her. Strange that he'd contacted Lady Juliet rather than the veiled witch. He smiled and squeezed Pippa's hand. "Let's go."

Lady Juliet turned and cleared her throat. "Not so fast, Lord Blaine. If Miss Hawke leaves now, the trap spell shall alert Oakmoor, and he'll thwart your escape." The royal witch smiled at them. "But if I shift the focus of the trap spell to myself, you can escape with him none the wiser."

Pippa inhaled. Then *Lady Juliet* would be trapped here with the rakehell duke transformed into a hideous beast. "You'd do that? But you'll be unable to leave until you break his terrible beast curse by falling in love with the duke and agreeing to marry him."

Lady Juliet sniffed then extracted a silver hand mirror adorned with purple flowers and a massive silver bowl from inside the bulging satchel at her feet. "I'm sure I can break Oakmoor's curse without resorting to falling in love and marrying him." Her longstanding dislike of the duke, which was mutual according to court gossip, dripped from her drawl.

As Pippa and Edouard exchanged wide glances, the royal witch snapped her fingers over her silver hand mirror. Steam poured from the mirror into the massive bowl, condensing into shimmering water. Then she pulled a gold dagger from her satchel and approached Pippa. "Before I shift the focus of the trap spell, I'll assume your appearance, and we'll trade garments. Give me your hand."

Edouard gripping her other arm, Pippa swallowed but extended her hand to the royal witch. Lady Juliet pricked her finger and shook three drops of blood onto the face of the silver hand mirror. Then Lady Juliet waved her hand over the mirror while chanting a singsong spell, and the face of the mirror began to glow like the sun. The glow flared and engulfed the royal witch. When it vanished, another Pippa stood in her place.

Pippa stared. How eerie to see herself a few steps away without the aid of a cheval mirror.

The disguised Lady Juliet twirled her hand at Edouard. "Turn around, Lord Blaine, so Miss Hawke and I can trade garments."

Pippa swallowed again. 'Twas even *more* eerie to hear her voice coming from someone else. Once Edouard released her and whirled away, she doffed her dressing gown and night-gown, although she didn't remove his sun-charm bracelet or his parents' wedding tokens with her charmed locket. Then she donned Lady Juliet's modish silver gown, which didn't fit too badly even though the royal witch was curvier and half a hand taller.

Lady Juliet murmured, "You can turn back around now, Lord Blaine." She smiled at Pippa. "Your hand again, please, Miss Hawke."

While Edouard took her arm once more, Pippa offered her other hand to the royal witch. Lady Juliet pricked her finger again and shook four drops of blood onto the face of the silver hand mirror, which bore no traces of the blood from the illusion spell. Then she pricked her own finger and added four drops of her blood to Pippa's. She waved her hand over the mirror with another melodic chant while walking along the bedchamber walls.

Once she finished, Lady Juliet smiled at Pippa and Edouard. "I've shifted the focus of the trap spell. Hurry and leave—I suspect Oakmoor shall finish setting his wards at midnight in half an hour."

Grateful tears pricking her eyes, Pippa tightly embraced the royal witch then swept a curtsy. "My deepest thanks for helping rescue me and taking my place, Lady Juliet."

Edouard bowed as well and flashed a warm smile. "Mine too."

Lady Juliet waved them toward the door. "Of course. Now go." She inhaled. "Could you inform King Devon and Queen Kiera where I am? I may be unable to once Oakmoor sets his wards."

Pippa and Edouard both nodded, then they hurried from the

bedchamber and slipped downstairs. As they crept through the dark and empty halls, her skin prickled at every noise, but they soon escaped through the servants' entrance without the duke catching them.

Untying the stallion tethered to the railing, Edouard mounted and pulled her behind him. Tingling suffusing her, she nestled against him, wrapping her arms about his waist and laying her head on his back while inhaling his scent. Goddess, how she loved him. And she might have been parted from him forever.

She only roused when Edouard halted the stallion some time later. She lifted her head and blinked. They weren't at her family's townhouse or even Blaine House. "Why are we at Rhiannon's Veils?"

Edouard swung from the saddle then slid her to the ground, their bodies pressed together. As her pulse flared and heat swamped her, he rasped, "You need a nausea-healing charm to elope."

Pippa gaped, her breath stilling. He'd planned out them eloping to the Sisters of the Heart's abbey on Hazeen Isle? Only the Sisters of the Heart would perform underage elopements in Calatini, and their abbey on Hazeen Isle was the closest to Ormas, just two days by ship. But her prudent Edouard had resisted such a scandal before. 'Twas why they'd spent months winning Father's blessing. "*You* want to elope?"

Edouard smiled as he captured her face in his hands and brushed a featherlight kiss against her lips. "Very much. But a poor street after midnight is no place to discuss it." He grasped her hand and pulled her toward the weathered red door. "I only hope the veiled witch has returned."

Pippa blinked. The veiled witch had been gone? That explained why Edouard had contacted Lady Juliet. Yet despite his muttered comment, the door swung open at his touch.

When they entered the dim witch shop, the veiled witch nodded at them from behind her wooden table. "Lord Blaine, Miss Hawke, at last." She waved to the gold pendant beside some paper and two pens. "I've the nausea-healing charm you need ready."

Pippa and Edouard glanced at each other then stepped forward. Her neck prickled as they sat across from the veiled witch. Although not surprising, the Rhiannon-descendant seer already knowing their needs was eerie.

The veiled witch scrutinized them. "I've booked you passage to Hazeen Isle on The Silver Mermaid, one of Mr. Buford's ships, and I had your trunks sent to your cabin." Her bracelets and tiny bells jingling, she extended her hand to Edouard. "I'll repair your charmed locket while you write your notes to your families."

A pang darted through Pippa as she donned the nausea-healing charm. Edouard must have used the hair in the locket she'd given him to find her. Yet without destroying her faegift, he might never have found her before 'twas too late.

Edouard handed the veiled witch the locket and murmured, "How kind of you to handle all our travel arrangements. You even chose a ship belonging to our cousin's merchant partner like we would have."

The veiled witch chuckled, her black veils fluttering. "I had to —'twas my fault Miss Hawke was kidnapped, after all." When Pippa and Edouard both gasped, she chuckled again. "I knew the Duke of Oakmoor would misunderstand my prophecy, but if I'd been plainer, neither he nor Lady Juliet would have accepted that she was meant to break his beast curse. I *am* sorry for the distress my ploy caused you both though."

Pippa gave a glowing grin. "Your ploy also inspired us to marry now rather than waiting another four months, so I think we can forgive you."

His eyes narrowing, Edouard slowly nodded but remained silent. Clearly, he didn't feel quite as forgiving, although he was doubtless grateful too.

The veiled witch's dark brows quirked. "Write your notes. Don't bother writing to King Devon and Queen Kiera for Lady Juliet. I'll speak to them myself."

While Pippa wrote to her brothers and Edouard wrote to Elise, the veiled witch collected a fresh lock of hair from Pippa, added it to the destroyed locket, then waved her hand over the locket while murmuring a singsong chant. The locket flared before dimming, and the moving painting inside once again mirrored Pippa's face.

The veiled witch returned the charmed locket to Edouard then gathered their notes. "I'll take these to your families on my way to the palace. You two should head to the ship. It leaves at dawn. One of Mr. Buford's cabin boys can return Lord Farson's stallion. Good luck to you."

After thanking the veiled witch, Pippa and Edouard followed her instructions then settled in their tiny, windowless cabin, where Pippa immediately changed into one of her own dresses while Edouard faced the wall. Once changed, she slipped beneath his arm and eyed the bright witchlight he was studying. She asked him, "So what made you decide to elope now?"

Edouard pivoted and turned her to face him. "Almost losing you." He shuddered. "I couldn't risk that happening again, regardless of the scandal."

Warmth filled her as she cupped Edouard's face. "Oh, my love, how sweet."

Edouard quirked a wry smile and kissed her palm with the wrist bearing his sun-charm bracelet. "Besides, if I returned you to your father, I suspect we'd need to elope anyway. He accused me of kidnapping you and refused to listen when I said I hadn't."

Pippa sighed, her heart twisting. Why could Father never see how wonderful Edouard was and how much they adored each other? "Of course he did. I'm sorry." To distract them both from Father, she twined her arms about Edouard's neck and beamed into his eyes. "'Tis well after midnight, and I'm exhausted. Shall we go to bed?"

Edouard exhaled and rested his forehead against hers. "Me too. But if we get in bed together, I doubt we'll sleep."

Her breath quickened as tingling flooded her. "Is that a problem? We'll arrive at Hazeen Isle in two days and wed shortly after. Surely we can anticipate our marriage vows by that much. And the risk of pregnancy is minimal. I had your sun-charm bracelet enchanted into a contraceptive charm months ago, so we're both protected."

Edouard groaned before withdrawing and grabbing half the bedclothes, which he tossed on the floor. "We can't, my tempting sun nymph. You deserve better than making love for the first time in a cramped, stuffy cabin. No, we must wait until we're properly wed."

Pippa sighed as she curled on the bed and Edouard did likewise on the cold, hard floor. Well, at least they needn't wait much longer.

Two afternoons later after a calm voyage where she suffered no nausea thanks to the charm from the veiled witch, Pippa and Edouard disembarked at Hazeen Isle and headed straight to the Sisters of the Heart's abbey, a circular complex of buildings at the center of the island built from the dark-gray basalt found there. The priestesses promptly escorted them outside to the vegetable garden the elder priestess was tending to speak with her. Although the Sisters of the Heart would perform underage elopements because of their founding priestess's unhappy history, Pippa and Edouard must prove that they should be permitted to marry, and not every couple was. Mother and Father probably wouldn't have been if she'd not been pregnant when they eloped.

While Pippa curtsied and Edouard bowed, the elder priestess eyed them and wiped her hands on a towel. Then she smiled and beckoned them. "Give me your hands so I can cast a spell to read your auras while you tell your tale."

Pippa and Edouard traded a narrow glance. Aura spells were said to be difficult to cast and only possible for Rhiannon-descendant witches. Yet they gave the elder priestess their hands. Pippa suppressed a shiver when the elder priestess murmured her spell—she could almost sense it on her skin.

Once they finished describing their courtship, the elder priestess smiled again and nodded. "I agree you two should marry. We can perform the wedding ceremony after dinner, then you can remain in our guest quarters until you're ready to return to Ormas." She chuckled. "Some guests have remained for months."

Light danced in Pippa's veins as she and Edouard grinned at each other. They could *finally* begin their lives together. After thanking the elder priestess, they retreated to the guest quarters until dinner. Yet they didn't touch to avoid becoming engrossed in their hunger to make love.

Following a delicious dinner with the priestesses, the elder priestess escorted them to the chapel, along with two priestesses to act as witnesses. Pippa and Edouard beamed as the elder priestess read the sacred words from the Goddess about love and marriage then crowned them with daffodyl garlands and led them through their vows. Yet they froze when the elder priestess prompted them to exchange wedding tokens.

Edouard muttered, "I'm afraid we don't have any. We forgot about wedding tokens in our haste to elope."

The elder priestess smiled. "Many eloping couples do. Well, we can finish the ceremony without them."

Before the elder priestess could continue, Pippa inhaled as her heart surged. "Wait, we can use your parents' wedding tokens, Edouard. I'm still wearing them about my neck."

Edouard blinked at her. "I suppose we could, if Mother's fits you."

She grinned while extracting his parents' wedding tokens from beneath her amber gown. She'd tried on the smaller garden ring when debating their wedding tokens last month with Elise. Although she and Edouard had eventually settled on sun necklaces, his parents' rings were even better. "It does."

Edouard grinned back as he accepted the smaller garden ring. "And Father's should fit me since I inherited his build."

Pippa beamed brighter, caressing the other garden ring. "I know; 'tis perfect."

The elder priestess coughed. "Shall I continue the ceremony now?"

A blush warmed Pippa's cheeks as she and Edouard turned toward the elder priestess again. After he nodded for the elder priestess to proceed, she requested they exchange wedding tokens, then Pippa and Edouard slid the gold garden rings on each other's middle finger. The elder priestess said a prayer before announcing them to the two witnessing priestesses, and Edouard pulled Pippa close for a thorough kiss.

Panting, they pulled apart. Then they signed their matrimony certificate before saying their excuses and hurrying back to their guest quarters.

Once their door was safely locked, Pippa flung herself against Edouard, her entire body tingling. "We needn't restrain ourselves any longer."

Edouard wrapped his arms tight about her. "Thank the Goddess for that."

She couldn't help her joyful laughter as Edouard swept her across the room and tossed her on the bed. Then her breath stuttered and her tingling burgeoned into a fierce ache when he fell on top of her and devoured her mouth while unlacing her gown. Oh, yes. Returning his ardent kisses, she yanked open his cravat and waistcoat then buried her hand beneath his shirt.

Edouard shuddered and kissed her harder as he flung their clothes to the floor. Their hands desperate and kisses wild, they came together at long last, soon shattering in release.

Aglow and almost purring, Pippa rubbed her cheek against Edouard's chest as they cuddled afterward, his rough hair making her tingle anew. "That was *amazing*. When can we make love again?"

Edouard chuckled and pressed a tender kiss against her brow. "Unfortunately, not until tomorrow. You must be sore."

She kissed his chest. Her dear, protective Edouard. More joyful laughter bubbling in her throat, she sat up and straddled Edouard then grinned down at him. "Only a little, and not enough to stop me from enjoying my husband's lovemaking again."

Edouard flipped her beneath him and kissed her. He murmured against her lips, "You know I can't resist you, my sun-nymph bride."

Pippa giggled then replied to tease him, "Now that we're safely married."

Edouard rumbled a growl before kissing her deeper, and she forgot everything else as they made love like starving venuses. 'Twas even more amazing the second time.

AFTER A BLISSFUL MONTH on Hazeen Isle spent alone with Edouard except for meals with the priestesses, Pippa awoke suddenly craving to return to Ormas. Edouard obviously felt the same because after they made love that morning, he suggested they return. So they packed, said farewell to the priestesses, then boarded the ship back to Ormas that afternoon. They arrived in Ormas close to midnight the day before Summerday and fell into bed.

While they devoured breakfast the following morning, she glanced at Edouard with a faint frown. "For some reason, I feel compelled to celebrate Summerday at the Great Temple's Sun Chapel."

Edouard hummed and sipped his kahve. "Oddly enough, so do I."

When they arrived at the Great Temple, Farson was helping Elise alight while Arvan talked with Dane and Xavier. Elise gasped and darted over to embrace them both. She said, "You're back! I'd begun to think you never intended to return to Ormas and face court."

Pippa and Edouard exchanged a heated glance, then Edouard murmured, "No, just enjoying time alone being married."

As Elise laughed, Dane and Xavier briefly grimaced at each other. Then Dane and Xavier embraced Pippa and shook Edouard's hand. Dane said, "Welcome to the family, Edouard."

Xavier chuckled. "But refrain from alluding to making love to our little sister when we can hear you."

Edouard's lips twitched. "I'll try."

Pippa flashed a brilliant smile at her brothers. "But *I* make no such promises about Edouard."

Once her brothers' groans quieted, Farson waved toward the massive doors of the Great Temple. "Shall we head inside?"

Pippa and the others nodded, then they walked through the main temple to reach the Sun Chapel behind the sanctuary. They all gasped when they entered. An impossibly beautiful lady of middle years with lush curves, golden skin, and wavy hair stood before Mel and Kit at the front. Was that the *Goddess*?

Pippa gripped Edouard's hand as she genuflected with their immediate families then slid into the pew behind five priests, the rest of Mel's and Kit's families, and the Ravenstones. Then the Goddess wed Mel and Kit before vanishing with a poof. Everyone congratulated the grinning newlyweds with exuberant embraces and hearty well-wishes.

Once Mel and Kit left, the Duke and Duchess of Childes glided over to Pippa and Edouard. The duchess beamed at them and said, "Good to see you back. I'll begin planning a fete for next month to celebrate your marriage. Can't have court thinking we disapprove."

The duke quirked a crooked grin. "No doubt by the time of your fete, Caro will have convinced court that you simply married quietly rather than eloped."

Edouard smiled. "We'd be grateful to no longer be scandalous. Thank you."

Pippa almost chuckled. To repair their reputations, Edouard was willing to endure the fuss of a fete hosted by the duchess. She'd have to cheer him beforehand—with kisses and more. She smiled at that then arched her brows at the duchess, who knew everything that happened at court. "Any news about the Duke of Oakmoor and Lady Juliet?"

The Duchess of Childes shook her head. "Oakmoor House is still warded, and not even scrying or communication mirrors can penetrate them. However, Devon and Kiera have mitigated much of the gossip about the Duke of Oakmoor and Lady Juliet by claiming the pair are handling royal matters."

Pippa and Edouard glanced at each other. Hopefully, the royal witch would break the Duke of Oakmoor's beast curse soon.

Then everyone drifted from the Great Temple. Outside, Dane invited Pippa, Edouard, and the Farsons back to the rented townhouse until Summerday festivities this evening. Pippa and Edouard traded a glance, then Pippa accepted. She must face Father now that they'd returned.

Over luncheon, which Father unsurprisingly didn't bother to attend, Dane toasted her and Edouard. "We're glad that you're back. Ormas wasn't the same without our little sister."

Pippa grinned at Dane and Xavier. She drawled to tease them, "If you two miss a lady's presence so much, you should find yourselves brides." When her brothers groaned like expected, she turned to Elise. "How have you been the past month?"

Elise beamed while buttering her roll. "Wonderful." She slanted Farson a loving glance. "After King Devon and Queen Kiera told the council that she was carrying Calatini's next heir yesterday, Seanian *finally* agreed to attempt the advice the veiled witch gave me months ago about conceiving children. We'll leave for Orandia after the duchess's fete celebrating your marriage."

Pippa beamed back. Soon Elise would have the family she'd always wanted. "How exciting!"

Edouard frowned. "I hope whatever advice the veiled witch gave you isn't too risky."

Farson leaned forward. "We'd not attempt it if it was, and I'll protect Elise no matter what happens."

Edouard nodded and smiled at his brother-in-law. "I know."

Pippa squeezed Edouard's hand beneath the table. "Besides, the veiled witch is both clever and kind. Look how she managed that quagmire with us and the Duke of Oakmoor's curse."

After their delectable luncheon, Pippa smiled at the others while they left the family dining room. Time to face Father. "I'll join you in the drawing room after I speak with Father."

His pale-blue eyes darkening, Edouard gripped her arm as the others nodded and continued down the hall. "Do you want me to accompany you?"

She caressed Edouard's jaw, warmth suffusing her at his concern. "No, you being there shall make my talk with Father even more fraught. Thanks though, my love."

Edouard sighed and released her, then she headed to Father's workroom. She swept inside with a gritted grin. "Hello, Father."

Father stiffened over his journal without glancing at her. "You're back, are you?"

Pippa nearly winced at Father's stiff grumble but clung to her smile. "As a happily married lady."

Father snorted. "Not for long."

Heat flaring through her, she darted before Father. She must get him to *see*. "Edouard and I aren't you and Mother, Father. *We* married for the right reasons. We love each other and want to build a life together. He's always there for me like I am for him, and our love shall last a lifetime."

Father hunched further over his journal. "We'll see." He jerked some faedust into a vial. "Not that my approval matters any longer. You're already married, and the rest of the family approves."

Pippa swallowed, her ribs clenching. "But Edouard and I would like your approval, just the same."

Father turned red as he kept measuring out faedust. "That disrespectful rakehell cares *nothing* for *my* opinions. He wouldn't have stolen you away to elope if he did. Or called me an idiot."

She winced. She'd known Father would resent that insult when Edouard had described how he'd found her. "'Twas the Duke of Oakmoor who kidnapped me, Father. Surely Dane and Xavier told you that."

Father snorted again. "A likely story."

She fisted her hands on her hips. Must Father be so obstinately blind? "'Tis the *truth*."

Father whirled to face her. "The truth? The truth is that Blaine wanted you, so he seduced you and ensured all of court knew it. Then he eloped with you simply to shame me because I insisted he wait. But his lust shall soon cool, and you'll be trapped with him forever."

Fire flared through Pippa. How *dare* Father insult Edouard so? He was the most decent gentleman she'd ever met and would do anything to protect her. She glared at Father. "Why do you never *listen* or see the truth obvious to everyone else? Perhaps if you spent time outside this workroom, you would. Edouard was right to call you a neglectful idiot."

Father inhaled and gaped at her, but before he could retort, Edouard cleared his throat and said from the doorway, "Everything all right? I could hear your shouting from the hall."

She exhaled then smiled at Edouard. Even though she'd dismissed him, he'd followed in case she needed help. She would have done the same for him. Because they loved each other. She swept over to Edouard. "Yes, I was just explaining matters to Father."

As Edouard hummed and wrapped his arm about her, Father

scowled at him then rasped, "You turned my daughter against me, you deceitful rakehell."

Edouard arched a brow. "No, you did that yourself by not loving and taking care of Pippa like a father should." Edouard squeezed her shoulders and smiled at her. "Shall we return to the others?"

Pippa beamed back and nestled closer. "Yes." She glanced at Father, and a pang darted through her. He'd never change. He'd always bury himself in his magical experiments and refuse to believe anything that didn't suit him. Thank the Goddess she had Edouard now. "Goodbye, Father."

She and Edouard glided from Father's workroom. Once they were alone in the hall, Edouard brushed a kiss against her brow and asked, "Are you truly all right?"

She smiled and laid a hand over Edouard's heart. So steady and strong and loving. "I shall be. I've you beside me."

Edouard placed his free hand over hers. "Until my last breath."

After rejoining the others in the drawing room, Pippa and Edouard spent an enjoyable afternoon talking, laughing, and playing lively games with their families, rather than attending the Summerday crowning and pageants like they had last year. Along with Edouard, their loving and encouraging families compensated for Father's habitual neglect and blind obstinacy.

Following the traditional Summerday honey feast, Elise grinned and asked, "Shall we head to Jade Garden for the Summerday bonfires?"

When Edouard sighed but nodded with the others, Pippa shook her head at her sister-in-law. She and Edouard needed time alone. They'd not been around others so much since they'd eloped. "You all go. 'Tis been an eventful day, and I'm still tired from our voyage back to Ormas."

On the carriage ride to Blaine House, Edouard pulled her into his lap. "I'm surprised you didn't want to dance around the Summerday bonfires now that we're married. 'Tis romantic."

She threaded her arms about Edouard's neck, smiling at him beneath her lashes. "But public, and I know how you feel about kisses in public." When he chuckled, she leaned forward and kissed him, murmuring against his lips, "Plus, I'm eager for an even *more* romantic dance—in the art room."

Edouard crushed her against him with a devouring kiss. "Yes, please. Goddess, you're perfect for me."

After kissing for the rest of the ride, she and Edouard tumbled to the ground when the carriage halted and dashed inside to the art room. Her heart fluttered as he activated the dancing music-box sculpture then drew her into his arms.

While they twirled to the enchanted sculpture's lyrical melody with their bodies pressed together—like they could never do in public—Edouard kissed her until she was breathless. He raised his head and smiled into her eyes. "I adore you so, my sweet sun nymph. I'm elated we can spend the rest of our lives together."

Pippa beamed back, tingling heat flaring in her chest. "I adore you too, my love, and I always will." Then she pulled Edouard's head down for another passionate kiss.

WANT MORE?

Sign up for my newsletter for a bonus epilogue about Pippa and Edouard's happy afternoon with their two children in his art room as well as other exclusive stories and book extras, new book announcements, giveaways, and more.

And order the next book The Beast Curse about Juliet and Oakmoor today! Keep reading to learn more about the next book in the Calatini Tales.

LIKE THE SUN-NYMPH BRIDE?

Please consider writing a review. Reviews truly help spread the word about the titles you love.

THE BEAST CURSE

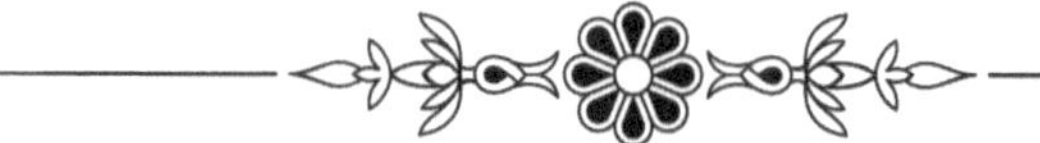

*I*n the Regency-inspired kingdom of Calatini, enemies can become lovers, and beauty can save the beast with her love... and powerful magic.

All of court knows about the fierce enmity between Lady

Juliet, the powerful royal witch, and the rakehell Duke of Oakmoor. What they don't know is that the two were once lovers —a mistake neither can forget. One Juliet vows never to repeat, no matter how her body longs for it, yet one Oakmoor would gladly repeat, if only to silence her sharp tongue.

But even Juliet doesn't know that in Oakmoor's youth, a jilted lover cursed him to transform into a hideous beast one day, and now that vindictive curse is finally about to manifest. Perhaps the royal witch could help him, but to ask Juliet would reveal—and risk—far too much. So Oakmoor consults a seer instead and discovers his curse can only be broken by true love.

Desperate, the cursed duke kidnaps an innocent young lady he believes can love him and break the evil spell. But that lady already loves another, so Juliet secretly takes her place. Trapped alone together until his curse is broken, Juliet and Oakmoor soon begin to feel more than enmity and unwanted desire. But getting to happily-ever-after isn't always as easy as breaking a curse...

In *The Beast Curse*, **Beauty and the Beast are reimagined as the warring Beatrice and Benedick for the perfect low-spice enemies-to-lovers fantasy romance. Dive into this tale—or the other books in the Calatini Tales series—for cozy, heart-warming HEAs.**

*Want more? Order **The Beast Curse** today!*

CALATINI TALES

The enchanting Calatini Tales includes...

The Spellbinding Courtship (Book 0.5)
The Enchanted Bird (Book 1)
The Nightmara Affair (Book 2)
The Secret Soulbond (Book 3)
The Goddess's Illusion (Book 4)
The Sun-Nymph Bride (Book 5)
The Beast Curse (Book 6)
The Lethe Elixir (Book 7)

ABOUT KATHERINE

A lifelong creator of her own bedtime stories, **Katherine Dotterer** writes cozy tales of fantasy romance inspired by Regency England. Born and raised in Maryland, she still lives there in an almost cottage surrounded by trees. When not writing, she enjoys reading anything she can find, singing in local choruses, hiking in nearby parks, watching the wildlife outside her windows, and cuddling with her cats. Visit her at Katherine-Dotterer.com to learn about her book releases, read her many book extras, and sign up for her newsletter.